AFRICAN CHESS

By Frank Graves

AFRICAN CHESS

Kindly Edited by Allan Gauci

AFRICAN CHESS

Written by Frank Graves

Copyright 1990

CHAPTER ONE

'African Chess starts the dawn, killing reveals a crimson pawn'

Pretoria - South Africa

He awoke to the sound of his own desperate screaming! Michael wasn't sure; he couldn't believe that his own voice had the power to waken him, even if it were caused by a bizarre dream. It had been the strangest yet, so real and lifelike that for a moment he wasn't quite certain whether it was real or not. Earth, wind and fire had fused together in one solitary moment, to create inexplicable contrasting colours and sonic noises. The stillness of morning devastated by this vision. One moment silence, the next a bright flash of colour, coupled with a thunderous roar that left his ears still ringing.

He had been tossed aside like a little rag doll with the intensity of the combined force. His dream was unlike any other nightmare before.

His eyes flickered open and shut again. The sheer relief of being able to control his thoughts was in itself a pleasant relief.

"Why do we have to have such vivid nightmares, yet on the other hand such gentle dreams?" he asked silently of himself. He lay there unmoving whilst pondering this unanswerable question, becoming blissfully happy to drift between exhaustive memories of a while ago and the reality of being unable to provide a suitable reply to his own question.

A gentle trickle of sweat beads strung themselves together across his forehead like an imaginary liquid crown. He now understood the unhappy discomfort suffered by Jesus of Nazareth on that day so many years ago. He gazed into the hazy purple blue sky and noted a small speck high above him. Lazily floating on the air currents, it carved ascending circles but was too distant for him to identify. It could be a large piece of paper caught in a swirling up draught, or a dancing swallow enticing the rain to relieve the sweltering heat, maybe even an eagle seeking some unsuspecting new prey to swoop down upon.

The possibilities were limitless, nothing moved, except for that circulating black predatory dot above. His thoughts were still caught in a hazy mist only starting to clear with a befuddled reasoning.

"The calm before the storm, it will probably thunder and rain down at sunset."

"That's extraordinary!"

His head seemed to be strangely locked in its present forward position as if someone had bolted an invisible strip across his body, stretching from his toes to his forehead. Being tall and athletic he carried no excess weight but had often woken during the small hours to find that he was unable to move a particular part of his body. Usually it was

4

because he had been lying in an awkward position. This time was different somehow; he had no painful numbness, or pins and needles.

"What the hell is going on?"

The realisation springing to his mind that this time heralded something different, he suddenly became agitated. The sun burnt down, the blue sky above, the deafening silence; the heat quickly disappeared, to be replaced by a cold sweat.

"Where the hell am I?" he questioned.

His normally fast thinking brain tried to understand. Somewhere someone to his left was groaning. His body heaved from the cold shock transmitted by instant understanding.

"Dammit! Shit!"

He uttered it quietly under his breath, refusing to let his true feelings show. This had always been his biggest failing. He didn't want anybody, not the groaning voice or even the cruising object above to hear, or feel, his immediate distress.

That precise moment, the incoming world about him suddenly seemed to spring alive around his prostrate figure. The groan raised itself to a high-pitched scream and the once majestic blue sky was magically transformed into a dull mud coloured haze. He couldn't believe his eyes or ears, it all seemed to be happening in slow motion, that serene silence was quickly becoming shouting, wailing and screeching; fast gaining momentum, changing everything about him. He couldn't see the lazy circling bird or whatever it could have been anymore. It was gone from sight, simply vanished into a thick haze of swirling dust. He knew then, with instant acute awareness, that his nightmare was fast becoming reality. All creation around him was steadily mounting into a deluge of compelling horror. A curious echoing sound of breaking glass sounded like a distant bell chiming for death. He tried gathering his sanity and thoughts.

"What happened to me?" he questioned urgently, "An explosion, where's the pain? There should be mountains of pain. But I can't feel anything!"

It hadn't merely been a bad dream. There had been a lot of people around. So where was everybody?

He could hear moaning and even screaming, there had been many bystanders around a few seconds before his blackout.

"Where are they now?" Michael squeezed his eyes tightly trying to persuade himself that this was simply another nightmare and perhaps it would go away.

"There should be pain!" he again thought.

A lonely shadow entered his line of vision; Michael thought for a moment that it was the black spot passing in front of the sun. He quickly realised that he was mistaken. A tall lean man was standing over him, wearing the most ridiculous outfit that Michael had ever seen, his clothes were simply remnants. They were tattered and torn as if punctured by thousands of knife cuts while pink pierced and bloody flabs of skin and fat were attempting to escape through the holes in the clothes. More peculiarly, the man had a strangely twisted left arm, as if it had been moulded into two separate pieces, one placed above the other. On the same side of his body the hair and skin were blackened.

"Quick!" this forlorn soul shouted in a highly distressed voice.

"Over here!" He looked like an overfed vulture waiting for some imaginary leftover to appear. Michael couldn't help smiling to himself, watching closely with morbid fascination, as small bright rose-shaped patterns gently formed from nowhere on the remnants of this man's trousers.

"You are going to be all right, hey!"

Michael looked directly into the broken mans eyes trying to search his soul. Then spat out venomously.

"Don't lie to me; tell me what you can really see!"

This one would never be a good poker player because his look betrayed all.

"Look man! It's probably looking worse than it is, really! Don't worry hey! They will get us to hospital soon." Michael tried to move, to have a look for himself but, his helper not being able to bend down, gingerly put his foot on his forehead, to try to stop him.

"No! You mustn't move, not until the ambulance arrives... OK!" Michael tensed irritably. He, the man who had never relied on anyone in his entire life; he, the self-made man was now in the hands of a funny thin stranger; he wasn't enjoying what was happening to him right now.

He instinctively knew he had to get away because his life must be in danger, the person responsible for this atrocity was still in the area and Mike recognised this. Lying helplessly on the ground, he knew that he stood no chance of recovery from a lurking killer. Another face then appeared in his line of vision; he noticed that her eyes were penetrating his inner being. They were the type that could send men to eternity, with their deeply catlike quality; her blonde hair was wafting on the wind and spraying it like golden tinsel against the hazy background. The sun shielded behind her head, it created a ghostly halo effect.

"An angel?" he thought to himself.

She was wearing a light blue uniform, carefully ironed and crisp. It seemed to him that this fresh flower was out of kilter with the immediate surrounding carnage.

"All I need is to hear the horn of Gabriel or see St Peter at his gate," he muttered. His despairing voice sounded loud to him but there was no reaction on the young woman's face.

He wondered again about the pain of death, certain this was still to come. Or was death simply that matter of passing over to the other side?

Kneeling low over him, she spoke hurriedly.

"Listen, I'm a nurse. There's been an explosion, you're badly wounded and so are many others. The ambulances are on their way, it won't be long, and I want you to lie still and try to be quiet."

Her voice carried complete command and authority behind it. Michael could hear the wailing of sirens a long way off, they sounded like the horns of Gabriel calling to him. The young woman was bending close over him.

"What's your name?" She hurriedly worked to free his trapped arm and body. He became aware of a large piece of concrete and other smaller bits of debris.

"Michael Roberts and yours?" he answered. He was reassured by her professionalism, knowing that her question was simply to try to keep him talking.

That old saying that your life passes by in a split second, when you're dying made him feel more comfortable with life. He hadn't experienced this vision. So this must mean he was a long way from meeting his maker. Again, a commonplace thought... *'While there is life'* comforted him.

"June Jillions but call me Jay," she said.

"Don't leave me alone Jay. The bomber is still around," he implored. She simply nodded her head, dismissing his thoughts as those of a man in deep shock.

During the summer Jay always left her home early, especially when on night shift ward duty; she would visit the zoo, the reptile park, the open museum. Coming from Cape Town, on secondment training to Pretoria for a year, she could not stand being cooped up in her small apartment, especially in the afternoons when it became so unbearably hot. Today she had decided to visit the Art Museum in Schoeman Street. She had walked from her home in its general direction, knowing her route would take her down across Meintjies Kop, on top of which stands the imposing Union Buildings, the heart of central government. Strolling slowly, she walked past the old copper sandstone building's west entrance with its domed clock tower. Curving around the main body of the building lay the beautifully manicured gardens, which fell away down the hill in even terraces until meeting a huge expanse of green lawn that was dissected by several stone paths. In the distance the continuous hum of the traffic reinforced the peaceful tranquility of these idyllic surroundings. Suddenly all hell broke loose destroying the calm, Jay knew immediately that it was a bomb when she saw the bright flash, instantly followed by the frightening thunderous roar.

Jay had heard that sound many times before near the Angolan border and without even thinking, reacted on instinct, she ran towards the front of the building. There were broken bodies on the ground whilst others were twisted around the strangely shattered columns. Some of the pillars were hanging precariously from the tiled roofing structure, like gigantic stalactites reaching down towards the waiting ground.

Like a vivid token of death, a long black scar smeared the inside wall of the building where the bomb had obviously been detonated. On the open veranda lay several more bodies, shattered, broken and torn apart. There was nothing she could do for them.

A black figure on the forecourt rolled over and got up, he looked towards her. Dazed, he slowly searched about the carnage around him and suddenly started screaming to her. She headed off quickly in his direction, carefully stepping over debris with pieces of human remains entangled amongst it. "God what a mess"

At first she thought that the screaming person was a black man; but he was white, just so badly burnt on the one side of his body. With professional calmness, she immediately assessed the situation. She looked down at Michael and knew that if she didn't stop the bleeding quickly he wouldn't make it. She got to work.

Squinting up at her he could see the uncanny resemblance to his cousin Sharon, his first and only real love.

"Sharon! Where are you now that I need you?" his brain screamed silently.It had all started on a similarly hot day an eternity ago.

Nestled in the parched grass with them, was his constant companion and best friend, Robert Molefe. Robbie, his tall black Zulu brother who since birth had grown up with him and shared life to the full among Natal's Drakensburg Mountains. They had been out hiking for the day, but Sharon was fast becoming a source of irritation to the two young men, constantly complaining about wanting to return to the hotel.

Sharon was a city dweller on holiday and unaware that the Champagne Hotel set amongst tall pine trees, was only about a hundred and fifty metres above the outcrop where they were now seated.

Mike's thoughts drifted back to that gold and dark green grass, overshadowed by the towering granite headstone of the mountain. Beyond those trees the sheer-faced escarpment of the south face of the mountain flattened high above the three young people like a tabletop.

The nurse was busily working on his leg and asked him whether he wanted something to drink.

"Yes, please," he murmured. His mouth contained the vile trace of blood. "Make it as cold as possible."

She disappeared and the comical stature of the rose-infected man re-materialised; he was wobbling to and fro like a drunk on a street corner.

"I was also caught in the blast," he said almost apologetically, "Look at my new clothes they're torn to ribbons. I would like to get my hands on the bastard, he wouldn't know what hit him."

Mike could clearly see rage and pain welling up inside this sorrowful onlooker, with a deformed appendage hanging limply by his side.

"If you knew that I've helped support those who did this horrific deed, I don't think you'd be so helpful towards me, lying here so helplessly at your feet," thought Michael. "Where are you from?" asked Michael curiously.

"I live here in Pretoria and you, where do you live and what's your name?"

Mike could see that the man was visibly weakening and wouldn't be able to remain standing for much longer; his remaining white skin had become distinctly sallow.

"Mike Roberts, I'm here on holiday from England. But this wasn't part of my itinerary," he tried to joke, attempting to humour his sorry looking companion.

Jay reappeared carrying two plastic cups.

"Fresh orange OK?" she asked and without awaiting any reply, handed one to the standing man and told him to sit down. She slipped her hand under Michael's head and very gently lifted it slightly, so that he could take a sip of the sweetened juice. The coldness, soothing as it was, did not fully quench his burning thirst. He could detect several different smells over the liquid; burning flesh and cordite from the explosion mingled with dust and the heat. He could also smell the panic hanging in the air and tried desperately to peer over the rim of the cup that was being held against his lips, partially blocking his view of the carnage. He tried raising his chin to indicate that she should remove the white and yellow cup; but she knew better. Rather than have him become overwrought by what he might see, she laid his head back on the ground.

"Why won't you let me look? I'm going to see sooner or later!"

"Don't worry about that now there will be plenty of time later on. You must try to remain still and leave the worrying to me. Just don't panic!" she replied.

"I'll stay with you, try to think of something relaxing, you are going to need your strength."

He closed his eyes in submission, realising again how closely she resembled Sharon, the same pleasant voice of authority, the same golden hair, penetrating eyes and even profile. With all these similar attributes, he wondered whether, under the calm and exterior angelic surface, she had his cousin's same fiery nature.

CHAPTER TWO
'A hungry lioness isn't mean, taking all because she's queen'

<u>Drakensburg Resort - South Africa</u>

"Best thing to do is stay where we are."

"Why?"

"In the hope that someone from the hotel will notice we're not back yet and organise a search party from the surrounding farms before it gets too dark," the two boys smiled.

"There are lots of wild beasts on the mountainside, such as leopards, baboons, venomous snakes and even an occasional pack of wild dogs," said Mike.

But unlike previous teenagers they had encountered, Sharon was definitely not the hysterical type and this was spoiling the boy's fun. They'd tried every trick they knew but Sharon had stuck to her guns, telling them if they were not prepared to get up off their backsides now, she was going on by herself.

"Seeing as how you two fools have gone and got us lost, I'm taking over," she said standing up.

"You don't know this area at all, we could be walking for days," suggested Mike.

"Well I'm prepared to take my chances rather than sit on my butt all day."

"I'm sure that the hotel is up that way, I have been here before," conceded Robbie, more as a way of not losing face than actually telling her that he knew exactly where they were. Sure enough Sharon soon saw the thatched roofs of the hotel's rondavels, or thatched roundhouse cottages, encircling the main building.

Although Mike would never have admitted it to anybody, it was that day that he first realised that he had met a girl that could be looked up to. She, on the other hand, suspected the boys had known their whereabouts all along but never admitted it. As usual, the two boys sat on the hotel veranda in their favourite spot discussing the day's exploits as they watched the setting sun drop behind their mountain. The hotel nestled on a small plateau directly below Champagne Castle; one of the highest peaks in the Drakensburg with massive grey rock walls rising to a tabletop over three and a half thousand metres above them. It received its name when two British soldiers tried reaching its summit, taking a bottle of champagne to celebrate their achievement. They'd taken turns carrying the haversack during the climb and at the point of giving up they found the bottle was only half full. Neither climber admitted to sneaking a drink so they decided to blame the mountain.

To the north could be seen a weirdly shaped ridge of spines and pinnacles known as the Dragon's Back, the ridge projected from the main wall to a strange-looking peak known to the Zulus as 'Ntunja' or, the eye.

Michael's father Ian and Sharon's father Peter pooled their funds in 1945 and bought a large tract of treed land from the Forestry Department, situated high above the Drakensburg

15

National Park.

They had built up the hotel midway between the goldfields and the coast promoting many activities such as horse riding, swimming, hiking and canoeing as they could. Popularity as an all year round holiday venue grew very quickly, mainly through word of mouth.

In 1955, the brothers split up the business after selling off a large portion of their land, making an enormous profit on their investment. Searching for something more lucrative to invest their profit into, the brothers acquired diamond-mining rights in Angola. The mining business was run from Johannesburg and soon afterwards Sharon's father moved there to concentrate on the diamond venture; leaving Michael's father in soul charge of the hotel.

Although Mike and Robbie had grown up together, Robbie remained living with his mother in a picturesque cottage next to the main house. His tall lean coffee coloured frame was unlike most other Zulu boys in the area and his features were distinctly refined to complement his uncharacteristic good looks. When they were barely in their teens they were instructing and guiding visitors around the mountainside, in the peaceful environment that was Champagne Castle. They would rest the horses at quaintly named sites, such as Angels Falls, where the exhausted and saddle-sore city dwellers would thankfully bathe in the cool pools of cascading mountain water. Tourists would stretch out on the black granite rocks under the boiling sun to dry themselves, to relax and survey the striking scenery. Both had seen at first hand how quickly this serene looking environment could destroy fools not aware of its inherent dangers. They had gained a grounding for later life by taking control of people, bending the will of others to accept their young knowledge and getting their own way every time.

Every night after dinner, while at home on holiday from his final year at school, Mike would collect his favourite gadget, a large telescope and head away from the hotel. Leaving behind the noise and glaring lights, he climbed up a small embankment into the darkness. It was here that he learnt to understand himself, in amongst all those towering peaks settled below a fantastically wide covering blanket of white glistening cosmic stars.

One evening however, someone lightly ran towards him across the Kikuyu grass that was now becoming damp in the warm night air.

"Mike, where are you going?"

He turned abruptly and said. "To study on my own," Sharon noted the slight acidity in his voice but chose to dismiss it.

As she moved towards him she heard a sound that made her blood run cold, stopping her dead in her tracks because somewhere between them, was the distinct sound of a hissing snake. She wasn't sure how near or how far it was from her.

"Don't move!" Mike shouted.

Quickly his eyes searched for something to defend themselves with, with his foot he located a couple of medium sized rocks, which would have to suffice. He laid the telescope down and picked them up. The lights from the hotel outlined Sharon as he moved slowly towards her. His eyes searched the ground between them for any slight movement that would betray the snake's whereabouts. About ten feet from his cousin, he heard again the nasty hiss. Mike stopped moving, trying to identify the sound, it sounded like the hiss that was given as a warning by a deadly king cobra; but what puzzled Mike was that it hadn't, as normal, reared itself and shown its spread hood to them.

He looked at his cousin expecting to see fear on her face, instead of which he saw excitement. This scared him more than the hidden snake, which he at least understood.

He gently placed one foot outward ahead of him and the warning hiss was repeated again, this time slightly to his left.

The partial light outlined the white rings on the reptile, which was about six feet from where Sharon was standing and well within striking distance.

"Sharon! Try and move very slowly that way," he said pointing to his right and trying to get her out of harms way by acting as a decoy.

As she moved the hissing broke out again and she stopped. He could only see the white rings on its back as it moved in a strange rotating movement.

"Keep going! Make your way in a large circle around it towards me."

He moved his foot to and fro to hold the snake's attention, all the time ready to intervene with the rocks, one in each hand, if it were to move an inch in the direction of his slowly moving cousin. He could sense her more than see her moving inch by inch around the snake's position until she had almost reached him.

"Kill it!" she hissed.

"Don't be silly, it's not a poisonous type and I wouldn't try something that stupid in this light, now move backwards carefully."

The two moved slowly out of range of the snake then Mike took her arm as they walked back to his telescope. She was shaking more from excitement than fear.

For Sharon this experience and the way in which Mike had handled it had been strangely exhilarating. She had been watching him carefully all day. He was extremely tall and muscular for a boy approaching adulthood. More like a twenty year old than sixteen, his darkly tanned athletic body and blond hair had attracted her immediately. Looking at him now she could see why she found herself fancying him. When they reached the top of the embankment, Sharon could make out the outline of a shed that had a large curved bulb on top. They entered the building and Mike flicked on the light, the small room had no windows and was painted black throughout, except for one wall containing a bookshelf.

In the centre of the room hung a large metal tube projecting through the domed roof, Sharon immediately recognised it as a more sophisticated and larger telescope then the one Michael carried.

"Why did you bring that one?" she said, pointing at the one he had carried with him.

"Sometimes I sit outside and watch the sky, other times, when there is something I especially want to see, I use this one because it can be coupled to a camera for any necessary readings: It all depends," he gestured with a casual smile. Mike carefully set down the telescope on the ground and in one cat like movement collected up the two chairs, taking them outside.

"Fancy a cola?" he asked.

For two hours he showed her the magnificence of the universe. Occasionally he leaned over or would gently coax her head towards his to show or explain something he had seen in the skies. When they packed up and he guided her back to the hotel along the same route where they had encountered the snake.

At the hotel, they bumped into Mike's father.

"Been showing Sharon your observatory?" he asked.

It was a habit that always annoyed Mike intensely. His father always made a statement out of a question. Little did he know that he had acquired the same trait?

"Yes! And I'm off to bed by myself now," he retorted sarcastically. "See you in the morning."

His father grunted something under his breath and continued his late night check of the buildings, a longstanding ritual. Michael had a shower and went to bed but could not sleep as his mind was filled with thoughts of his cousin. He was not at ease with himself; there had been something so electric between them this evening. He tossed and turned all night, disturbed by his inner thoughts.

The following morning Mike and Robbie were to lead a horseback party to the Cavern, a large cluster of underground caves some distance away across a long valley about eight miles from the hotel. Sharon arrived looking gorgeous in her khaki jumpsuit. She complained about having had a sleepless night but still wanted to go with them.

On the winding path down towards the valley floor both boys noticed that she was an accomplished horsewoman. Mike had chosen to let her ride one of the better horses, not one of the hacks normally used by the holidaymakers but one reserved for some of the hotel staff with good riding experience.

At the bottom of the valley was a wide, yet not very deep mountain stream flowing like a silver thread through the brown background. It had taken nearly an hour to reach this point and as they watered the horses Mike rode up alongside Robert.

"Can you look after this party alone?" he asked. "That man behind you has done this ride several times in the past; you can call on him for any help as I want to go upstream to check something".

They knew each other's every thought without having to say anything and Robbie had quietly noticed Mike's fidgety movements all morning since setting out from the hotel.

He knew that he wanted to break away to be alone with Sharon. This was the first time that his white brother had ever preferred the company of another person.

"What's so important up there?" he asked cheekily.

"Never you mind," came Michael's ambiguous reply and full-toothed smile.

Robert laughed because he hadn't missed the point "OK ride well and be careful not to have an accident," he replied. His manner was mocking yet knowing Mike would detect the double-edged meaning in his reply.

After offering necessary excuses and making arrangements with the group, Mike and Sharon headed off up the deep valley and rode for about an hour. The terrain made their trek hard going and at almost eleven o'clock they reached Devil's Drop where the river plunged and thundered into a bottomless clear pool that gently spread out from the base like an opening flower. Mike suggested dismounting for a lunch break of sandwiches and soft drinks that he had brought along in a small haversack still slung across his back. He watered the heavily sweating horses before tethering them to nearby bushes whilst Sharon admired the spectacular view of the valley and the surrounding area.

It was December and almost the end of the school holiday, she had completed her secondary education and would be leaving for university in England the following month. At this time of the morning the sun was already high in a cloudless sky; it was very hot and still, the brown grass stood erect without movement, the temperature already well into the thirties so to cool off she decided to have a quick swim in the cold mountain stream. When Mike finished tethering the horses he turned only to see her disappear below the water then reappear again.

"God, this is lovely!" she shouted.

He could hardly hear her above the thundering noise of the falls.

"Come on in! It's not cold."

He strolled to the edge of this clear pool then realised that she was naked, this taking him completely by surprise. Quickly the young blood stirred as he felt sudden excitement mounting from within. He turned his back on the watching water nymph and stripped to his underpants.

"Michael! Don't tell me you're bashful, take them off as well, I'm not swimming nude alone."

He was not prudish but now felt an embarrassing erection developing, which was not for show or study. Hesitatingly he sat down to remove the offending briefs and then slid smartly into the pool with crab-like sideways movement to protect him from her gaze.

Letting the cold mountain stream cool his heated ardor, he couldn't decide whether to swim in an arc around her or directly towards the torrent of plunging water. He could sit on a ledge behind the falls or simply swim towards her pretending that this was an everyday occurrence. He quickly opted for the former solution and struck out towards the falls.

She watched his initial awkwardness with slight amusement and as he started swimming and she realized that his movements were taking him towards the edge of the cascading falls. She swam strongly towards him and for a while both treaded water as if sizing up the opposition in a cat and mouse game; finally Mike decided that he had been outsmarted.

African Chess

The roaring falls blocked out his voice, he repeated himself several times before she understood his message.

"There's a cave around the back, be careful and follow me, I'll show you!"

They moved around to the side of the falls, being very careful not to be caught under the thundering cauldron below the high falling water. A massive overhanging ceiling that also formed a natural stairway towards the cave protected the ageless erosion of black rock.

Mike pointed up, shouting to be heard above the noise.

"Cavemen used to live here, they were safe from wild animals, you can get through at the back but it's very difficult to find the entrance from the other side!"

"Show me the cave," she returned. Sharon knew full well that this would force him to leave the safety of the water. She had outsmarted him and like a boxer conceding the inevitable count, he resolutely took her hand and carefully led her upwards towards the dark interior. There was nothing much to be seen as they looked towards the back of the cave, not even the sunlight from the far entrance that Mike had mentioned earlier. Sharon could just make out some faded rock paintings on the walls. The cascading water outside seemed to reflect light inwards into the opening, rather than shield it. The cave wasn't as dark as she had expected it to be.

Trying to act as nonchalantly as he could, Mike ran through a potted background history of the cave dwellers of years before. He could not restrain his wandering eyes from sneaking glances towards her body. She was fully aware of what was happening, milking the moment for all its worth by accentuating her every movement, in the full knowledge of what affect it was having on him.

Michael tried to continue his running commentary without much success, her petite round breasts pointing upwards towards the long forgotten hunting scenes painted high on the cave walls. They were unlike the breasts of the elderly Zulu women that he had seen bathing in the river. Theirs were generally large bulbous affairs, swinging freely around their midriffs. Her wet body glistened against the silver-mirrored light, giving a sparkling prism effect through the sunlit falling water. She let him finish his story before taking his hand to lead him to the centre of the cave like a little child. Moss covered the floor of the cave like green baize almost as if it had been especially laid out for his sacrificial initiation ritual. Still holding his hand Sharon sat down letting the light dance upon her naked body. The soft glow played strange reflective patterns on her body and her damp golden hair.

He awkwardly knelt forward over her to kiss her upturned lips. A charge of electricity immediately passing between them as their lips fused together for the first time. He had thought about this moment many times. His unsteady hand knew instinctively what to do as it moved straight to her young breast.

She gently pulled him down on top of her and as their two bodies made contact for the first time, an uncontrollable desire for each other instantly surfaced in this ancient animistic place. Michael wasn't quite certain about his next move, he knew the mechanics of what had to be done but theory and practice were two entirely different things at that moment. Sharon desperately wanted him inside her as she moved her body against his to assist his awaited entry.

"God he's a still a virgin!" She placed her hand between his legs, took hold of his proud member and swiftly placed it inside her. She smiled inwardly at the knowledge that she was taking his well-kept innocence from him in this fleeting moment. Then they began to move in harmony and became lost in each other for the briefest of moments, when he groaned loudly without warning.

"Jesus, not so quickly!" he cried out.

Not knowing what to do next, he lay quite still against her soft body crushing it against the cave floor and wondering whether or not to try again.

"Sorry," he whispered apologetically.

To avoid any embarrassment to her young lover she held him tightly then rolled onto her side. Still facing him and locked together, she gently placed his hand on her breast like a pacifying mother.

"Shush! There's nothing to be sorry about, believe me when I tell you that the next time will be much better."

She held him tightly against her until she felt that the embarrassing moment had abated.

"Let's have a swim and lunch," she said.

They left the cave and lazily swam under the midday sun.

Michael wasn't sure how to react towards her at first. The mood became more relaxed when she playfully tried to push his head under the water. Instantly the tension evaporated as the two frolicked again and allowed their hasty experience to be forgotten for the moment.

From then on, Sharon led him through an unknown fantasyland with expert knowledge; he became a willing student being allowed to travel through an awakening land of unrivalled pleasures. Before their summer holiday was over Mike had discovered untapped resources within himself as an accomplished lover entering the new world of adulthood. But try as he might, he never captured the sensation or experience of that very first day when they had completed their swim in the clear mountain teardrop and the coldness of the water eventually forced the two back to the smooth black rock. Before leaving the water they splashed it to cool its heated surface, then got out and sunned themselves dry while eating their packed lunch. Then hand in hand they lay on their backs, eyes closed to the harsh sunlight, on the silky stone surface that was cool and smooth to the touch.

CHAPTER THREE

'Joy beholds an opening eye, on silent air that whistles

<u>Pretoria - South Africa</u>

"Things always happen in threes, three is just a number isn't it?" he thought to himself; but the number three had steadily become an omen in his mind. He had lost his virginity in the same place he had shot his first leopard almost six years earlier; it all now seemed an eternity away. A rogue cat had been using the cave as its den when it had attacked a hiking party, badly mauling one of the women. The next day, with his father, he and Robbie had spent all morning tracking its spoor, which had eventually led them to a lair below the waterfall. Mike's father Ian knew that the cave had two exits and placed the two boys behind a bush outside the back entrance. After checking that both rifles were fully loaded and that the safety catches were off, he stealthily and cautiously made his way in a large arc around to the waterfall entrance; always remaining in full view of the boys as he moved. When he reached a position directly in front of the cave entrance, he settled down behind a small bush making sure that he was not in the boy's direct line of fire. Ian fired three shots from his Smith and Wesson revolver straight into the cave, hoping that this would help flush the leopard out of the back entrance into the waiting trap, for a while nothing happened. Suddenly Robbie pointed to a spot in the long grass behind Ian; Michael was horrified to see the large cat stalking his unsuspecting father.

The two boys quickly readjusted their sights for the longer shooting range. They couldn't shout a warning, as it wouldn't be heard over the sound of the crashing waterfall. How his friend had seen it Mike would never know, but lucky for them he did. Against the brown scrub the animal had become almost invisible, it was hunched and motionless looking neither left nor right but straight at Ian's back, as it prepared to attack him from behind. They raised their rifles into the new posture as the huge cat shifted into a final springing position; both boys knew that they were only going to be given one shot each at the beast and that it would have to count. Like a coiled spring being released the animal suddenly rocketed forward towards its unknowing prey.

Michael held his breath and squeezed the trigger gently, feeling the recoil as the rifle bucked against his shoulder, simultaneously hearing a loud crack from Robbie's rifle next to him. The animal looked as if an invisible hammer had hit it as it flipped up and died instantly while in full flight. The beast came to rest about three feet away from its intended victim.

Later, whilst examining the leopard, Ian found that two bullets had entered the animal, one to the head the other in its back. Like King Solomon he delivered his verdict that the spoils were to be shared by both boys; but Michael still maintained that his bullet was the one to the head, Robbie didn't agree. It was a proud moment for them as Ian carried out the hunter's traditional ceremony of removing the beast's testicles and giving one to each of them. The beautiful hide was presented to Robbie's mother.

Michael's second event took place three years later when Robbie was bitten by a puff adder, a sluggish short brown-coloured snake that has the dubious honour of being responsible for more deaths than any other more poisonous snakes in South Africa. After a swim, his friend had stepped off this same rock and the waiting snake had bitten him in the leg.

Michael killed it and then quickly cut two parallel lines into Robbie's leg to try to suck out the venom after tying a tourniquet around the leg. Fortunately the boys were leading a group from the hotel and they helped to carry Robbie down the mountain. Back at the hotel the resident nurse injected snakebite serum into the boy before Ian rushed him to hospital. For several hours his life had hung in the balance; the doctor had said that without their rapid action he would most certainly have died. This mystically ancient place of hot rocks, cool water, deep shade and bright light held the fantastic and most exciting adventures of his young life. Lying on the huge rock he was content with life in among those glorious mountainous surroundings, he loved this whole area.

He was so lost in his thoughts and enjoying the moment when, without warning, Sharon suddenly took hold of his now soft member in her small hand and gently started coaxing him. His proud muscle was smooth and shiny without any aging texture and surrounded at the edges by the sparsely darkening fluff of a teenager. She noted that his testicles were hardly visible, probably still suffering the effects of the cold water; with her free hand she gently began to scratch his tightened bag making him groan in absolute surprise and gratification.

Michael gasped in stunned pleasure as he felt the two

hands working in unison around his deepening delight, her continuous onslaught and momentum was placing his mind beyond the realms of control as the sensation of his body and soul descended down to this one delicate area.

Many years later he would still be able to recall with absolute clarity what happened next as he suddenly felt her warm breath and succulent lips descend upon him, taking his engorged member into her mouth. Sharon leaned forward, taking him deep into her throat, without halting her careful manipulation of his rocking actions. The change in pace, when it arrived, was abrupt for Mike; now it was more like meeting an approaching train in a tunnel. Nothing short of a miracle would stop a collision as Sharon relentlessly teased his taut nerve ends with strength beyond belief. The violence within him grew like a bedevilled monster, shattering everything in its path. He had become a rag doll being torn apart at the seams as he felt himself hurled into a boiling cauldron grappling for breath, he started drowning in his own sanity. Michael felt as if he was losing his mind to the tremendous power being generated; everything screamed for him to submit, as he fought the oncoming tidal rush, with his every being trying to break the stranglehold. He found that he could not fight the hastening whirlpool much longer as he was thrust downwards into a sea of oblivion. Sharon felt the rush developing and attacked the throbbing statue with greater vigour, like a thief in the night she was not going to be deprived of his creative juices for herself. She was determined to rob him of his wholesome bounty, as she ardently unlocked his treasure trove and raided everything from him with great pleasure and command. There was no way out, he needed air and there was none to be had, opening his mouth wide, allowing his sacred lifeblood to rush away while screaming defiance at the ever watchful mountain. For both of them it was a bombarding release, orchestrated by a massive throbbing explosion that was followed by whimpering tremors and an unnatural peaceful afterglow.

He surfaced again, half expecting to see Sharon's smiling face looking down at him, instead there was total pandemonium surrounding him and a sea of gloomy unrecognisable faces staring down on him.

"I'm back in the bloody nightmare," he thought.

His angel had not deserted him as she knelt forward.

"You must stop thrashing about and try to lie still until we can get you to hospital, do you understand?"

He simply smiled his acceptance, thinking only of his dream he tried to gauge how long he had been in that far off world. His wandering mind disappearing long enough for a crowd of onlookers to arrive and enjoy his misfortune, they had gathered like vultures waiting to pick at his ravaged bones.

Through the pain, that had now forcibly arrived with some vengeance, he asked her what had happened to the ragged fat man.

"He's in shock and badly burnt, but most of his wounds are only superficial, he'll be home in no time at all. That's more than I can say for you," she answered honestly.

When the doctor arrived he complimented her on her efficiency, quickly moving on to take over medical duties at the bombsight. She had helped with four of the surviving wounded that hadn't been killed outright; two ambulance men carefully lifted Michael onto a stretcher as the miserable crowd watched with interest. There was no way he was going to die here in front of these vultures, he didn't intend giving them that satisfaction. Michael lurched into panic mode for a moment as a recognisable face suddenly stood out like a shining beacon from the rest in the gruesome crowd of faces. His instant recollecting thought was that he must have been hallucinating once again.

The doctor had given him an injection; he felt them start moving the stretcher towards the waiting vehicle as he tried in vain to keep track of the face, it seemed to have melted away in among the gathering horde. He was fading fast; becoming very groggy and slipping into oblivion for the third time that day. Then he found the face he was searching for in among the swirling crowd, all he could manage was a half-hearted smile, now in the full knowledge that he had someone to rely on. The watching crowd reluctantly moved back to let them through, two sets of eyes watched with concern; one pair friendly and sorrowful, the other hatefully calculating Michael's possible chances of survival. These same eyes had witnessed the entire spectacle from the start, the wicked mind thought back to earlier events that had triggered such devastation.

"What a nice day you've picked to die!"

This lone supplication winged its way into blue skies as an index finger pushed down hard onto a small red button, while his calculating mind knew that this singular action was about to change the course of history for many ordinary people in several countries. Like some dispassionate camera lens recording a staggering world spectacle for posterity, his evil eye mirrored unfolding events before it without any sense of remorse from his distant vantage point. His gaze carefully documented unfurling events step by step in seemingly slow motion action as the bright mercurial flash started either side of massive doors springing outward and upward from their positions to herald the onset of genocide. The weighty blast hurled itself away from its initial birthplace behind a leading vortex of sharp flame carving a destructive path through the morning stillness. Following immediately in its wake the scorching firestorm carried a second errand of death, combusting and incinerating everything in its tentacle path. A reverberating crescendo rose across the open space into morning air like a messenger of doom and destruction, informing everybody of its terrorising handiwork. Soft dismembered bodies rocketed away in all directions propelled by a thunderous onslaught of the injurious detonation. Concrete, glass and brickwork debris split and shattered as it hurled deadly shrapnel thunderbolts in a widespread arc and for an instant after the intensity of the blast, nothing moved as wind and sound scurried away from its source into the distance. As clouds of brown dust lifted, the recording eye watched on and waited for the final tally.

CHAPTER FOUR

'The eagle doesn't bother with the fly, it's too small'

Kwazulu Natal - South Africa

Nicole Roberts was attending to the daily routine of the hotel by checking staff and generally making sure that all was flowing well. In the laundry rooms, working within its close confines, were five Zulu women harmonising traditional songs relating to childbirth. The beautifully lilted sounds in perfect barbershop harmony drifted up the long passageway drawing Nicole to the laundry; Mabel Molefe was seated like a goddess in her high backed wicker chair, she looked up at Nicole and smiled. She had always controlled this engine room of the hotel with the same iron fist with which she also controlled the black employees, male and female alike and was as much a part of the hotel machinery as was Nicole. Mabel was very different from the other women, who wore bright traditional clothes, red headdresses and enormously large earrings that were fitted into their earlobes at birth. She dressed plainly in comparison, wearing a simple shroud over her shoulders, no earrings and had unusually striking hair. Unlike the others, it hung down the side of her head in two finely stringed plaits held in place with a thick intricate beaded crown. Its stark whiteness contrasted sharply against her dark hair, the only marking on the crown was a red diamond shape woven into its front. It tilted forward, so that the blood red mark rested neatly upon the centre point of her eyebrows.

Red had traditionally symbolised Igazi, or blood, meaning tears or longing when discreetly sewn into women's beadwork as a subtle message. Mabel was also the local Ngoma, or diviner and Nicole had often seen her throw the bones onto her little mat to interpret messages from the spirit world. No black person ever questioned Mabel, with her leopard skin poncho lined with bone necklaces and feathered headdress, she held court in a little thatched hut built at the far end of the grounds of the hotel. Her orders became law among the blacks and even Nicole sometimes thought she often treated them too harshly. But she would never dare say so to her face because Mabel was part of the hotel's furniture and had worked for her husband, as his personal servant, long before he had come to Durban to collect the new white mistress. When Nicole had first arrived, instant animosity had sprung up between the pair and some form of pecking order had to first be determined between the two tough women. Then, slowly, as each created their own responsibilities within the hotel framework, a mutual trust and respect began to form; later becoming much more than just a bond between them. Later, Nicole was invited to become an honorary member of Mabel's tribe; she at once learnt their language and dialect fluently. This, in turn, led to her also understanding certain Zulu rituals; however, she did not really know then the important meaning of this singular gift that had been bestowed upon her.

Nicole Cranston-Smythe was an only child, had been brought up in the presence of high society, attended the best schools, belonged to the elite clubs and always had a string of young men attempting to marry her. As a child she had been a fat ugly duckling, yet as a teenager she had blossomed into a beautiful young lady bearing fine features outlined by honey blonde hair.

Her father Charles had inherited his family's vast sugar plantations and sugar mill in Natal and had expanded the business further by entering into shipping and manufacturing. He tended to be a bit of an extrovert, full of confidence and had always pushed his daughter to the extreme limit; consequently she had rebelled and became introverted and shy.

She met Ian Roberts at Greyville Racecourse in Durban during the July Handicap, her father having entered his favourite horse in this South African premier race. The Roberts brothers also had a race entry and even though Ian Roberts was ten years older than her, she saw in him a quiet inner strength; although he didn't talk much during their first meeting. She decided after their meeting that this was the man she wanted and who she was going to marry.

With the early morning chill of May in the air, the grass around the hotel lay gossamer white from early morning frost and a grey mist hung in the deep valleys below. Nicole enjoyed being in the laundry with its steaming irons and rumbling old washing machines; it was the best room to be in on a cold morning but could be sheer hell at the height of summer.

Both Nicole and Mabel were then heavy with child, while staff members had set up a book and were taking feverish bets on the first birth and the sex of each child. This was the quiet time of the year at the hotel so both women could relax from their normally tortuous duties, they both enjoyed being busy because it helped to pass their time.

After evening meals had been served and then cleared away, Nicole drove her little BMW down to the main farmhouse situated some eight hundred metres from the hotel. Nicole loved returning to her haven each night, this place remained her dream of happiness because she had been designer, builder and all the other trades combined after having insisted upon having her own house to return to, away from the place of work. As she edged her car towards the house she looked at it lovingly with self-satisfied pride as she so often did when taking in the beauty of her home. This house was her private space, built on the edge of the deep ravine with a magnificent panoramic view across the entire valley floor. In the opposite direction the view was equally spectacular, looking down the length of the eastern buttresses of the mountain stretching away from the hotel and into distant mists. A thick forested tree line stopped at the rear of the stone built house, which was almost hidden from sight of the hotel. Its large timber and glass French windows ran full length along the front of the house for maximum panoramic viewing.

Travelling with her in the vehicle, as usual, was her black friend and constant companion Mabel; who lived in a large cottage adjoining the main house. The rest of the staff lived in single house rondavels at the other end of the hotel complex.

After their first meeting, Nicole had tried everything to get Ian Roberts to give up the Champagne Castle Hotel and move to Durban so that he could be with her. He had obstinately refused; but then, with the sudden death of her father who had fallen from a polo pony, she had visited the hotel to recuperate and fallen in love with place.

She organised her father's managers to run the empire for her; while she still retained overall power of the company. Unbeknown to the Roberts brothers, she had acquired a large piece of adjoining property through one of her trustee companies and came to live at Champagne Castle. At first the couple had stayed in the large cottage while the main house was built to her specifications. She had always insisted that she wanted her own house to escape to when not busy with hotel business. When the house was finished, the cottage was given over to Mabel it, like the main house, was built from local stone. Downstairs was used as living accommodation and upstairs had two bedrooms and a bathroom. The understanding between them was that Mabel served her tribal duties from seven to ten o'clock each day and then worked at the hotel in the afternoon and evening.

The management of all large hotels felt honour bound to keep a fully qualified nurse on the premises at all times, because there were always climbing and horseback accidents. The nurse arrived as Ian walked towards the car park, the two got into his Land Rover and quickly drove towards the farmhouse. Both were totally unprepared for what met them. The women were calmly preparing large piles of cotton wool in the upstairs spare room and they had also set up two beds as a maternity ward. When they had then gone into labour simultaneously, nature had decided the subsequent course of events. The nurse delivered Michael into the world as Ian helped to deliver Robert at exactly the same time and a black and white pairing life bond was formed.

African Chess

To the disappointment of the hotel staff all bets were cancelled the next day.

From the very first day everyone at the hotel treated the two boys as twins, they were always together.

They were sent to a private boarding school in Pietermaritzburg, their days at school were fun days and both achieved high sport and academic results.

Later at university, Robbie quickly learnt what it was like to have their colour difference tested and brought into sharp focus. Because of his parent's wealth, Mike was always in great demand by the other white undergraduates who thought he was the right sort of person to know. Robbie, on the other hand, because of his outstanding athletic ability and the fact that he was Mike's best friend was simply tolerated by them.

Mike would always shun any invitations that did not include Robbie. By the end of their first year Mike found himself being slowly ostracised for his friendship and became a social outcast among the white students. In their second year both men became active members of the student's union helping with anti-apartheid rallies organised by them.

One rally was held in the quiet town of Pietermaritzburg where the students gathered at the end of Commercial Road. All participants carried banners depicting their stand against apartheid. Sitting on a curb, Mike looked at the pretty town that lay on the main Durban-Gold Reef Highway. It's wide tree-lined roads, large thatched cottages and carefully trimmed gardens; this was not normally a hotbed of trouble for the government.

He had read somewhere that Pietermaritzburg was formerly known as Fort Napier, after an English governor, Sir George Napier, it was only later that the town was renamed after two Voortrekker leaders, Piet Retief and Gert Maritz, when it became the responsible parliament town of Natal in 1893. It still contained a mainly English speaking community. The town lay in the heart of Zulu territory, in a fertile hollow valley at the foot of a forested escarpment, rising some four hundred metres above it. A gentle river called the Msunduzi or, the pusher, from the surging power of its floods, wended its way quietly through the valley for most of the year. Into this idyllic setting with its green trees and wild vividly flowering azaleas, the hated police arrived to confront the students. They left their yellow police vans; all armed with shotguns, whips and tear gas and started walking towards them.

Michael and Robert were uncertain and remained at the back of the group when it surged forward towards the oncoming blue uniformed cordon. Shouting like banshees, the students raced into the group of advancing policemen. There was no option. They went into a well-rehearsed routine of arresting students without hesitation.

They quickly focused their attentions on three black students and four known white agitators. They bundled them into the waiting vehicles before taking them to the local police station. This was the most dreadful time of Mike's life and it was where Robbie received his first taste of white man's justice. During the afternoon and into the evening he was belittled, punched and ridiculed, while the four whites were released on bail within hours of their arrival.

He and the other black students were all placed into holding cells while their white counterparts were let free. The injustice affected Robbie's perception of his station in life.

Mike had quickly parted from the rest of the group when he saw his friend being arrested. There was not much that he could do to help, so he made his way back to the campus and immediately telephoned Champagne Hotel.

Nicole after hearing her distressed son contacted the company lawyer and instructed him to get the black youths out of prison. The three black students were finally released on bail the following morning; Robert came away with murder in his heart for the manner in which he had been treated during the night. Mike noticed the subtle change in his friend; he had gone from a normal youth to adulthood overnight. He keenly felt the sad passing of Robbie's youth in one stroke, what affected him most was that he had been unable to help his friend in his time of need. He felt unable to help him bear his pain and suffering. His friend was marked all over where the sadistic law enforcers had used him as a human punch bag. Robert doubled his work output at university feeling he had let the family down, but more importantly he realised that without a formal education he would not have a chance in this white man's world. At the same time he became deeply engrossed with the student's union, forging new underground links with the banned African National Congress movement. He was happy to remain inconspicuous in the background, conducting the white puppets, much of his spare time was spent on organising the will of his people. Never again was he going to be humiliated by these white pigs because of the colour of his skin. Even his strong relationship with Mike began to transform as they went their separate ways. Even when they met up the two didn't have much to say to each other and during the following two years the student's union changed dramatically. Every student was expected to join and its membership expanded considerably. Students were made to participate in its activities; those who refused had their lives made intolerable. Robert made sure that not one of the undergraduates entering the University slipped through the net.

Robert's efforts and potential were quickly recognised by Oliver Tambo, the outlawed fighting general of a prisoner called Nelson Mandela, the then accepted supreme commander of the ANC, who carefully and skillfully directed the struggle against apartheid from within the shadows of their lengthy incarceration on Robben Island. As a young influential leader, Robert was capable of commanding the utmost respect of his comrades. He was hoping to complete a degree in legal and political studies, this qualification he intended putting to good use, furthering the cause of blacks in South Africa. While he was still at university the ANC then invited him to become head of the Natal youth military wing in the heart of the Zulu area backed by a group named the Crocodiles, they were the ANC's union enforcers. Their actions were swift and their reputation for dealing with non-compliance was ruthless. They remained judge and jury in the people's court, justice being dealt out swiftly by the young legionnaires within the grasp of the ANC. In all these glory days Robert did not know that the tide was about to turn against him as he floated on the wind of power invested in him.

The Zulu leader, grandson of Dinazulu ka Cetewayo and most of the elders of the tribe were not happy with the situation developing around them. They preferred peaceful change and it was not in their interests to have a civil war even though most people felt it was becoming inevitable. His leadership was being severely tested and undermined by the ANC because people like Robert had become a thorn in his somewhat peaceful crown. They had been creating small effective pockets of resistance throughout his own heartland and he wasn't prepared to let these young Turks overrule his authority.

The supreme council decided that the time had come to give a taste of their power and a formal Indaba, tribal conference, was called. This meeting brought a large gathering of the tribal elders to Ulundi, the high place that was the central capital of the Zulu nation. It was a fitting venue where the great Cetewayo became king in 1879. It was also the final battle place of the Anglo-Zulu War. New battle plans were again drawn up by the group and carefully outlined. This was the Zulu bunker, controlling the war was to be carried out from here.

In a position contrary to that of the ANC and in line with his growing co-operation with the Government, the Zulu hierarchies were opposed to incoming anti-apartheid sanctions. As a Homeland leader, the leader's lifeline wholly depended on the South African state and economy. With anti-apartheid leaders inside South Africa and abroad demanding sanctions, the Zulu chieftain came to be regarded more and more as a Government puppet along with other Bantustan leaders. His tribal loyalties and focus on ethnic interests over national unity was also criticised as contributing to the divisive programme of the regime. This now was leading to a virtual civil war between the Zulu loyalist supporters and ANC members in that part of the country.

The tribe had chosen the venue carefully. What better place to start the next great battle against a new foe creating an unacceptable breed of Zulu?

This court knew the Zulu were the largest tribe in Southern Africa and that they had vanquished all tribes before them under the leadership of the great Shaka. In their time they had become a most formidable military power to grow from any primitive African people and traditionally the whole of this country was their ground. The only tribe to have beaten them was the white colonists and they respected them for that. It was the Zulu's destiny to recapture their birthright back from the white man, not a handful of troublemakers. Zulus considered themselves the elite amongst the Africans and were not going to be dictated to by this small band of pack rats from the north. The elders listened to their leader and agreed with him.

Like a time forgotten the all-conquering regiments were able to unify their ancestral pledge to new conquests with the salute to their leader, "Ngathi impi!" With a new flame alight in their hearts, they sent their regiments into battle shouting, "Because of us, war!"

The ANC was, meantime, creating an acute embarrassment to the white government by stretching their limited resources almost to breaking point. Training had started with the most easily led, the students. Both schools and universities refused to be taught in the hated language of Afrikaans, this rule of defiance was hurting the white man. Robert led the fight against the government from the safety of the university, he never projected his image as a leader and he was always in the background unknown to the state police or the Zulu leadership.

CHAPTER FIVE

'Son of dust and bone, rocked by a base of massive stone'

Robbie made sure that successes achieved by the Natal activist group were almost immediate; student action became a threat to government stability in the region. Uncontrolled white police forces were not helping matters by attempting to stamp out all resistance with punishment such as beatings, imprisonment and torture tactics.

Unbeknown to him, this action alienated parents and fuelled anger among a normally law abiding community which refused to stand by and watch their offspring being treated this harshly. The ANC was starting to gain the upper hand by achieving minor victories and always having the world media on hand to record police action. With this carefully planned strategy, Robbie's group managed to gain world sympathy for the plight of all black men in South Africa.

The Zulu leadership decided to step in and interfere with their plans by forming the Incatha movement. They supported dialogue with the government, instead of waging war.

Incatha quickly created a self imposed disciplining procedure on the students. Like the Crocodile movement they tended to be extremely harsh in their judgements. Those not heeding the leaders were effectively dealt with by their own kind. Thrashings, knifings and even death were the penalty handed out to the young black upstarts.

The government breathed a huge sigh of relief, hoping that the world press would turn its attention to the fact that the responsible black leaders were on the side of law and order. It also meant that the ANC and the leftist propaganda machine would have to defend the action, placing the government in an attacking position. To people in the outside world, events in South Africa were shown as being complete chaos with no form of law and order. Instead, Incatha started its own law which it imposed within the townships and soon, open warfare spilled onto the streets.

Unbeknown to all was that a deal was struck with the Zulu leaders. Promises of large financial investment from a ministry slush fund to the homelands were made, which would help strengthen their underlying economic position. Immediately the Zulu formed their Impis, regiments of soldiers around the country; each regiment being headed by a team of older men. At first, seeds of discontent were sown among the other communities throughout the land and young agitators were urged to stop flaunting their newfound authority. Orders came from the Zulu leadership and most of the rebelling young blacks belonged to the northern Sotho and Ndebele tribes that were grouped around the Reef area. The instructions continued to be disobeyed as the world saw the South African problem as a simple black and white confrontation. The fact is that South Africa is made up of eleven separate tribes with customs and cultures that vary greatly in complexity. They were as different in culture as the English are to the Germans, French, Japanese, or even Americans and this resulted in a community being out of harmony.

At 10.30 am on a crisp winter morning in June, the

township of Soweto exploded and forty eight policemen, forty of them black, found themselves surrounded by over six thousand fist waving, stone-throwing pupils just off Vilakazi Street in the district of Orlando West. Shots were fired and Hector Petersen, a thirteen-year-old student, died instantly; the first of many in the next few days. By the end of that day, a further twelve had met the same fate. Riots in Soweto spread quickly along the Reef and down to Cape Town but never reached the same heights in Natal. During the next eight months South Africa became a bloodbath, over five hundred people died in the ensuing riots. This was virtually civil war, the country had misread black feeling and the people like drunken boxers reeled from the attack. Then, the tide started to shift slowly in the opposite direction.

The government quickly imposed widespread bans and imprisonments for all agitators, including students and children, which further incensed most of the world's population.

The government promised concessions at first, better pay, education and facilities but the right to vote in Central Government was left aside. The young had had enough. All black newspapers were soon shut down so that they couldn't frustrate the population any further, editors were arrested, and they had gone too far, too quickly. Activist leaders throughout the country were systematically being arrested and jailed, killed or simply disappearing without trace. The net was closing fast, tightening against those who had been causing any embarrassment to the government.

Zulu leaders were now being helped by informers within their movement to reveal the whereabouts of all freedom fighters. Leaders and political agitators alike, who, for the last year had been able to dictate ANC movements were suddenly being victimised and nobody was prepared to help them.

Robert watched with growing discomfort his triumph of a few months ago crumbling before him. Street wars were now commonplace in townships and their own people were taking black youngsters to task in open warfare. The police did not intervene; in fact they were assisting the onslaught being aimed at the youngsters. The initial ANC plan was now in total disarray; Robert's carefully planned schemes were being demolished and no matter how hard he tried to rally his small, but effective band, he found himself unable to do so. His people were frightened because this was not white man's revenge; the Zulu was systematically controlling it. Stories like those of Shaka Zulu, their great leader who marched thousands of his own soldiers and enemies off the Hanging Rock into a four hundred metre ravine, who slaughtered seven thousand soldiers as a mark of respect to his mother's death, still held sway within the tribe. Robert was nervous as his friends were systematically pinpointed by his leaders and severely dealt with. His authority was diminishing rapidly and he knew it was only a matter of time before they found out the truth about him. There were daily reports of stabbings, clubbing and fire necklaces, the last of these punishments being a particularly unpleasant and cruel method of revenge which involved petrol doused tyres being placed around the conscious offender's neck then set alight. Atrocities became widespread with more and more comrades simply disappearing without trace.

Robbie tried in vain to contact ANC leaders who had taken

fright and had crossed the borders to Botswana, Zimbabwe and Zambia to try and regroup.

One late afternoon a black student burst into his room. He had a long gash on his cheek that bled profusely. "Robbie! I'm sorry"

"What happened to you?"

"Some Incatha bastards stopped me and started to question me," he said as blood poured out of his open wound splashing droplets onto the floor.

"What did they want?" demanded Robbie earnestly.

The man dabbed at his face with his blood-soaked handkerchief, trying to stem the flow, "They want to know who our leader is. I didn't tell them so one of them cut my face with a knife"

"Do they know about me?"

"Not yet. But they know that someone here is the leader of the crocodiles and it won't be long before they find out who it is."

"Tell me everything!"

The youth related to Robbie all the questions asked and answers given to the members of Incatha. They had sent him on his way and tried to follow him. He thought he had managed to give them the slip, but they weren't far behind.

"Right you must leave now. They're probably following your trail of blood. Its one of the oldest known tricks and you've fallen for it."

"What do you want me to do?" asked the student.

"Try continuing in the same direction. That way if they're following you, they won't realise that you've been to see me." Quickly Robbie raced to Michael's room and found him busily preparing work for the following day. In utter despair and desperation Robert hurriedly confided all the facts to him. Mike immediately recognised the perilous danger that his black brother was in. He also realised that he could be linked with Robbie. They quickly packed most of their belongings and made hurried last minute arrangements. That same night, taking care that nobody saw them, the two hurriedly left the campus and headed inland to Champagne Castle and relative safety.

Mike insisted that Robbie tell him everything from start to finish, he wanted to know exactly what had been going on. Robbie held nothing back and told everything since his arrest, his union role with the Crocodiles and how earlier that year he had been promoted to Natal leader of Umkhonto we Sizwe, the military wing of the ANC. Michael couldn't believe his ears, he was stunned.

Sitting next to him was his best friend explaining that he had become one of South Africa's most wanted men. All this time he had thought that Robbie was nothing more than a silent protesting student.

The little car turned off the main road at Escourt, a sleepy little town with a large co-operative farming community. Nothing moved; the town died at midnight except for the lone petrol station serving overnight travellers to the Reef. There was no traffic on the sand road, as they watched the scenery changing in the golden circle of their bright headlights. Changing from flat grassy plains to dense pine forested woodland, as the car climbed into the foothills of the Drakensburg, heading towards the hotel.

The only witness to the late arrival of the fugitives was old Daniel, the night watchman, who saw the lights approaching long before he even heard the vehicle. It was unusual for any traffic to be on the road at this time of the morning he thought; nobody had informed him to expect late arrivals. He watched from his high pedestal as the fast approaching vehicle started its tortuous climb up the last winding hill below him. There were plenty of rooms available and the old man eased himself off his stool and prepared to greet the latecomers. He went to the office to collect room keys, then he started walking across the wet grass towards the car park; but instead of heading straight towards him the vehicle swung down the track towards the main house, which was lit up with a bright halogen lamp. Daniel cursed, thinking that the city fools had been attracted by the bright light like a moth to a candle. He turned towards the house and could see the cars red tail lights winking at him in the distance as they suddenly became brighter glowing like two red embers in the ebony darkness.

The dark intruder stealthily coasted the last hundred yards like a silent owl gliding towards its prey.

He recognised it was young Michael's car as the light from the house shone directly in front of the vehicle, clearly silhouetting two figures inside. He could do without all this extra work he thought, turning back towards the hotel, but not before noticing the two occupants leave the car and walk around to the side of the main house. He wasn't sure whether or not it was the young master, as he called out in friendly greeting. The figures disappeared around the corner without replying and the old man sauntered back toward the hotel, he was not at ease.

Normally he would have been told to expect Mike but nothing had been said and if it were Mike, he would normally go straight to his shack rather than disturb his parents.

Daniel wasn't sure whether the other man was black or white. If it were Robbie he would have at least acknowledged the old man's greeting. Robbie would have gone to his quarters and not inside the house. Something was amiss and Daniel could feel it in his weary bones, they never lied.

The old man mounted the stairs and looked again toward the half hidden house below him, the kitchen light had come on so the family was safe but he couldn't help pondering what mischief was afoot.

In the passageway the two guarding Rottweilers confronted them; they had bounded through from the back of the house where they normally slept when they heard the two men enter the side door. Mike quickly reassured them.

"Hello! How're my two lovelies then?"

The two were overjoyed, both attempting to jump up and lick his face at the same time. Mike was thrown off balance and forced backwards against Robbie, who bounced off him against the wall. Nicole awoke to find her husband leaving the room having heard the commotion, she also arose from bed and made her way to the kitchen.

She found the three men already talking earnestly in hushed tones.

"Hi mom!" Mike said, rising and giving her his usual bear hug. "Sorry to wake you, we didn't mean to, but we've got a bit of a problem and needed to talk to you two".

She released herself from her offspring, she was always glad to have the two boys home.

"Well, I expect you two want something to eat, but first, none of us can think until we've had something to drink."

"Okay! What's happened, where's the fire this time?" She knew that they would tell them everything; she had her suspicions, instinctively knowing what they were going to tell her. She'd already heard whispers.

The four discussed the problem well into the small hours of the morning, knowing that they would all be suspect once it became well known that the boys were missing from Pietermaritzburg. Eventually Ian told the boys to go to bed.

"Make sure that no one knows you are here, I don't want you to be seen by anybody, do you understand?" He warned sternly. By midday he had delivered his verdict, it had taken the boys by complete surprise, especially the speed and clarity at which his plan had been transacted.

"You two are being sent to England as quickly as possible, to complete your studies at Oxford or Cambridge, I'll know later today," he said.

Mike knew that both his parents, as well as his uncle Peter, had very strong friendships in England; his father originally came from Surrey somewhere.

"This will get you away from the immediate spotlight and give you both a breathing space," he continued, "and at least you will be able to complete your studies in peace."

Mike knew his father well; he hated weakness and disliked the government policies. This had given him the ideal let out without having lost face.

Nicole interjected, "We think that we can get you into Oxford. The company has been funding one of their science projects for some years now, so hopefully this will help to get you places there."

Ian and Nicole Roberts spent the rest of that day and part of the following morning, constantly making and receiving telephone calls; the antiquated telephone system objecting to so many long distance calls. By mid-morning Nicole had received a call from the Vice Chancellor at Oxford University confirming their two places; the Robert's trust fund having doubled the amount of their present research grant. Peter Roberts had arranged for suitable lodgings somewhere, together with a letter of introduction to the manager of Natwest Bank in London. The whole operation had stunned the boys. Mike looked at his parents in a new light, he had seen a side to them that he never realised existed. Robbie couldn't believe his good fortune and was equally astounded at the breathtaking speed that events had unfolded during the previous twenty-four hours. The only thing that bothered the Robbie was that he wouldn't be allowed to see his mother before his departure. He knew that her tribal links were too strong and that if she found out she would have no compunction in letting him face the Zulu elders for his part in the uprising. He had his white family around him, but bloodlines were stronger, he dearly wanted to talk to his own people but knew it would mean certain death for him. He wished that he'd listened to the tribal stories his mother used to tell.

CHAPTER SIX

'Duty of conscience, arrives fresh from conference'

<u>Drakensburg Resort - South Africa</u>

Ian entered their room at five o'clock. Mike was at the small desk playing Knight Chase on the computer; Robbie was sprawled on his bed reading a book.

"You will be off within a week, everything has been prepared and the only thing that hasn't been taken care of yet is a new passport for Robbie," he said. "It will take a couple of days to fix. I've sent George to Johannesburg with the documents and thank God we still had those driving licence photographs".

"A passport takes weeks!" exclaimed Mike.

"No! It will be ready by tomorrow afternoon. The thing that takes time is to get the necessary visas for you both".

"Is that difficult?" asked Robbie.

"It took some negotiating, but the British Consul has agreed to give you both study visas and everything will be ready in two or three days," replied his father with a slight grin. "Meanwhile, until you go to Johannesburg, both of you are grounded. Nobody and I really mean nobody, must know that you are here. Not even your mother has been told," said Ian to Robbie. He could see that he had been hurting but he also knew that the stakes were very high and they didn't need to take any unnecessary chances. Ian had placed Mike's car in the double garage out of sight. Both men were made to stay in the house, because Ian knew that bush telegraph was far more effective than any white man's system. If anyone suspected that they were at the hotel, a message would very quickly filter across the valley and the Zulu leadership would soon be notified.

Then it would be a matter of time before either the Impi or the police arrived. The local police have already been to the university and this afternoon they called to find out whether you were here."

"What did you tell them?" asked Robbie anxiously.

"I said you weren't here and played the concerned father bit," Ian said, "But it won't be long before somebody arrives to check because the word's out. That's why nobody here must know of your whereabouts."

"The fewer people who know where we are, the longer we can stay hidden. Is that what you're saying?" asked Mike naively, looking from Robbie to his father.

"No!" Ian replied firmly.

"What I'm saying is if anybody sees you, your chances of getting away are reduced considerably. At present we still have an advantage over them."

He knew that the two must be feeling like frustrated beasts but he could only sympathise with their requests to go on one last hike. To leave without seeing at least the mountain pool and cave was extremely hard for Mike. Robbie couldn't even walk the short distance to bid his mother farewell.

For many years Phineas Tlana, the hotel gardener, had carried out a standard ritual when he finished his day's work. He would return to the hotel compound and have a warm shower changing and going to his friends' rondavel to wake him for supper. The two would share dinner and a gossip before he retired to his own quarters for the night. The two old men had been doing this every day for twelve years ever since Daniel had fallen from a rock and injured himself. Daniel would cook their evening meal. Kitchen staff always left their food in heavy pots and the two would discuss events of the day. Then the old men would always shake hands and go their respective ways. Daniel reported for his night duty at six o' clock and would not meet Phineas again until morning.

This particular morning Phineas, after everybody left the house for the hotel, made his way towards the double garage with its lean-to workshop. He needed weed killer because the thorn grass was growing fiercely at the top end of the garden.

For a while he wandered around the house, glancing into each window, hoping to catch sight of the visitors that Daniel had told him about.

Sheba was lying in the sun on the front veranda; she lifted her head and growled. She knew who was allowed near the house and didn't accept anyone readily.

There was no sign of any movement from within as Phineas ambled towards the cottage skirting it in the same fashion. Seeing nothing he walked over to the shed, as far as he could make out nobody was at home.

Only he and Ian Roberts had keys to the shed, mainly because all the tools, poisons and fertilisers were kept there. He fixed the hand pump onto a forty-five gallon drum marked in red 'PCP Poison, Handle with Care'. Phineas pumped the cloudy liquid into a copper jug, being careful not to spill any.

Then he walked across the shed to the full length bench against the garage wall. The brass spray gun hung from the roof trusses above the bench and Phineas used the small steps to climb onto the wooden bench to reach it. There was a small window in the wall above the workplace; this had originally been the outside wall before the shed was added. His hand stopped in mid air as he reached for the spray. Through the window he saw the young master's Volkswagen on the far side of the garage; they hadn't left the house as he had first thought.

The old man emptied the poison into the canister then wandered towards the house where he slowly filled the spray with water to dilute it. All the time his eyes searched for traces of life within the house; he now knew that somebody was there. Perhaps they were upstairs so he decided to keep an eye on the house as he started back towards the vegetable garden, with his killer load strapped to his back.

John Tlana, another of the old man's nephews, arrived at the hotel at about three o'clock for his regular visit to his uncle on Wednesdays and Saturdays. He had arrived from Escort and after delivering a post bag to the main hotel building, he sought out the gardener. John was the local postman and he would collect two mugs of tea then seek out his uncle for a chat. The two chatted earnestly for about an hour as John brought the old man up to date with the latest tribal gossip, reporting news about old friends, family births and deaths from all over Natal. He told his uncle what he had heard about his cousin Robert and the problems in Pietermaritzburg.

John calculatingly questioned the old man, asking him whether he had seen the young student. The gardener laughingly played down any suggestions that Robert was involved.

"Robert is playing with fire," said John.

"But he's done nothing!" protested Phineas. "Uncle! Robert was the leader of these people in Natal. Our leader wants him dead."

"What can I do to help?"

"You are his favourite uncle and he and the white boy are going to be here soon. I want to know the minute they arrive," said John.

"I think you are wrong. If he has committed this deed then he won't come back here."

John stared long and hard at his uncle trying to understand his reasoning.

"Why won't he?" asked John.

"Because this is the first place everyone will look."

"That makes sense."

"Anyway the boy isn't at the hotel because he's still at university somewhere. He wouldn't betray his own people. I know him too well," the old man suggested.

The postman wasn't certain about the whereabouts of his cousin, but knew that he must be in the vicinity somewhere. As far as he could tell his uncle hadn't lied and had spoken with a clear conscience.

John left the hotel satisfied that the students weren't there as nobody had seen them; so they must have gone elsewhere first, he thought. He would report to his elders that he had questioned the cook, one of the maids and his all knowing uncle who knew everything going on at the hotel. John was almost certain that his cousin was not there yet, he had alerted the entire area and the bush telegraph was in operation; sooner or later the student would have to break cover.

Yet the hairs on the back of his neck told him differently and he strongly felt that Robert Molefe was close by. A tinge of jealousy crossed his mind; it would be a pleasure to report that he had found

Robert.

The gardener related his story to Daniel, who praised his friend's presence of mind in not revealing his suspicions to anyone. They decided to keep it to themselves, at least until they knew the full facts.

Sitting thoughtfully watching the sun disappear behind the high granite wall above them, the two knew full well that their lives could be forfeit if it were ever found out that they knew of Robert's whereabouts and had protected him. Long fractured shadows were quickly spreading across the valley floor and like their fear, crept outwards to envelope all in its path. They were both certain that Robert was here, but they weren't about to betray his and especially Mabel's trust.

That night old Daniel went on duty with a heavy heart. Tribal law was always paramount. He had always respected it and if he did not obey, he would suffer the consequences. His loyalties were divided between family ties and his allegiance to his people.

On his final examination round that night, Ian approached the old man. Noticing his troubled expression he asked with concern in fluent Zulu, "What's the matter Daniel, you seem troubled?"

"There is much weight in here," Daniel said pointing towards his head.

"Why?" he asked, genuinely interested.

"Robert and Master Mike are here. I saw them the other night and today a tribal courier has told us to inform on them," he said quietly.

Ian Roberts was visibly shocked. If the people here had told the courier, by tomorrow morning the police or elders from the tribe would arrive.

"What did you tell them?" he demanded impatiently.

"Nothing at all, it is not in our hearts to betray them; but soon somebody will come and we will not be able to stop them. The boys must leave for a safe place," the old man replied.

"Tell me Daniel, do you think that I can talk to the elders?" asked Ian.

"No! The tribe has been disgraced and the penalty is death. You will be unable to persuade them differently as the command has come from the highest level," replied the porter. He continued "You have many white friends, please get the boys to safety tonight. If you don't there will be blood on your hands," the warning was very definite.

"Thank you for not betraying their trust old friend. If you would like to see Robbie, I'll arrange it later. Mabel doesn't even know they are here."

The old man moved close to Ian and in a low voice said "You are very wise not to have told her. She would not betray her own son; a mother's love is too great. She would be duty bound to kill him herself. She must never suspect, otherwise we will all suffer," Ian could feel the terror exuding from the old man's eyes as he spoke of Mabel and her powers. "Do not worry, they'll be gone by morning," he promised.

Out of a long and trustful friendship the old man readily promised that neither he nor Phineas would readily part their acquired knowledge to anybody.

The two young men left for Johannesburg in the early hours of the morning. Both Daniel and Phineas wished the two well on their journey. Both young men knew that this was probably the last time that they would ever see their lifelong friends alive. Ian and Nicole promised to visit the boys before Christmas in England, where they normally took their business holiday break, as they had done every year for as long as Mike could remember. As they left the place of their birth, both young men wished that it had been daylight, so that they could look upon the Drakensburg Mountains for the last time.

The drive took them along sandy back roads to Harrismith, where they joined the tarred highway which would carry them to the Gold Reef. They were on their way at last, the endless straight road carrying them along through the grain belts of Orange Free State. As dawn broke the little grey Volkswagen crossed the Vaal River, just like the white settlers had done many years before, heading towards the unknown.

CHAPTER SEVEN

'Watch the strike, for the wounded animal reigns terror'

<u>Johannesburg - South Africa</u>

The Volkswagen encircled Johannesburg with its gold coloured mine dumps scarring its outskirts; these bleak defoliated humps dotted randomly where men had extracted rich ore from the earth. Unlike the natural green surroundings of Pietermaritzburg, which Mike knew so well, he thought Johannesburg had a gold brown look about it; the landscape was stark by comparison. The city was built upon the richest gold vein in the world and it didn't have any of the attributes associated with most natural cities. From a shanty gold mining town, it had become an ugly duckling with high rise buildings and mining headgears shooting out of the flat earth like tentacles reaching toward the clear blue sky above. Architecture, it seemed was to be judged by height rather than natural beauty.

The Volkswagen made its way up a park-like area with luxurious homes hidden behind the closely guarded and high walled gardens of the white rich. Reaching a white-walled, thatched, double-storied house, they found they were able to drive straight into the multi-car garage adjoining it. Peter Roberts was there to welcome them and as Mike and Robbie got out of the Volkswagen, Peter busily closed the garage doors behind them. Robbie opened the boot and they collected their belongings out of the car.

Inside the house, Mike immediately noticed the similarity between the hotel building and this house with its thick dark timber beams.

"I'm going to have a large breakfast, the full works," said Peter. "Are you both going to join me? I suspect you're both starving."

Mike and Robbie brought Peter fully up to date with everything that had not been explained by Ian on the telephone.

"I called Sharon two days ago and told her of your impending arrival," said Peter.

Mike looked through bay windows at a beautiful rising sun; he realised that he was looking forward to seeing her again. She had been an undergraduate at Oxford for two years.

"Hopefully we will have all the documentation completed today, if so, you fly out tonight or latest tomorrow, now I'll get Nellie to serve breakfast," he said.

Mike and Robbie were called for breakfast which was being served next to the swimming pool at the back of the house. The garden was laid out with meticulous care; high bamboo reeds screened them from the surrounding properties and from the servant's quarters at the bottom of the garden. For the first time in days, Mike felt relaxed among his family and seeing the place now remembered that the house and its lovely garden had regularly been photographed by Home Magazine. The early chill had melted away and the morning heat was nicely comfortable, the air hung fresh from the overnight thunderstorms. They seated themselves around the white wrought iron table at the edge of the swimming pool.

Nellie's short and very fat body wobbled around the table as they were served breakfast. Built like most of the women of her tribe, hers was an admired African shape, said to be a sign of wealth. As far back as Mike could remember Nellie had been as much a part of this household as was Peter. He knew that she and Mabel had not seen eye to eye; at one time Mabel had threatened to bewitch her. When Peter and his family left the hotel to settle in Johannesburg, they asked her to accompany them; she grasped the opportunity with both hands. She still missed the country life and her friends. Every year Nellie would return to the mountains for a month's holiday, invariably this was spent helping at the hotel where she was able to renew old acquaintances. Mike and Robbie watched affectionately as she finished serving the large breakfast and scurried to the gate; where she collected the milk from Petrus the milkman each morning. She badly needed to talk to him.

In a small house in Bryanston, Shorty Majozi had just finished talking on the telephone to Petrus Malahele. He returned thoughtfully to the sitting room where four older men, one white, one of mixed race and two black, were seated. The four men were all part of the joint operation set up in the Transvaal by the Government to find and stamp out all ANC. activists.

"We've found Robert Molefe," he said. "He's at the house in Melville. We must get somebody in there quickly." Dirk Lemmer the white man and provincial head of the dreaded Bureau of State Security, BOSS for short, said arrogantly. "I'll take some men and arrest that bastard now!"

"No!" exclaimed one of the black men, his greying hair and whiskers, bristling as he spoke. "This is not for you, the white family is one of the wealthiest in the country, you wouldn't get very far before they had top legal men getting him released for a so called fair trial."

He was happy to leave it to them. The white man knew full well what that meant. Many times before he had experienced black man's justice upon their own kind and it made him shudder, they were worse than animals he thought.

The men made arrangements, then all four set off on their respective missions. The net was closing tight on Robbie again.

The two boys took to their beds immediately after breakfast. They were housed in the self contained flat for visitors which extended full length across the top of the long garage. It had a big brass double bed in the main room, on the other side stood a smaller room with a single bed; either side of which was a small bathroom and kitchenette. Leading from the little kitchen was an outside door with a stairway leading to the back of the garage.

The flat was built for privacy in case any visitors didn't want to walk through the main house when coming or going. Before going to their room, Peter's wife Jane, dressed in a full length Japanese kimono, joined them as they finished their breakfast. After initial formalities and greetings had been exchanged, the two boys left and she stayed on at the poolside with her husband. Nellie served her madam a light fruit breakfast with orange juice and Darjeeling tea. Jane and Peter talked for a while longer and didn't notice Nellie slipping away down the driveway once again. She knew from experience that the two would remain talking for some time as she waddled to the end of the drive where she met the men from Bryanston.

Three men were waiting for her outside the large gates. Two greying old men dressed in fading dark suits and a younger man of about thirty in jeans and open necked shirt. Nellie knew who the two older men were; but she carefully examined the third, sensing something evil about him. His shaven head showed several old knife scars. His dress was casual but the eyes were extremely alert. She knew the type of man he was and exactly what he was here for. Nellie quickly described the entire layout of the house, laying special emphasis on the area where the two could be found. The younger man asked whether the outer kitchen door was unlocked as a hurried plan was hatched and put into motion.

They instructed her to go and check the door then to let them

69

know the movements about the house, making sure to keep the Rhodesian Ridgeback dog indoors for the next hour. It didn't take long for the three men to form a plan; these were all professional killers and had been doing this type of work for a long time.

Shorty Majozi rubbed the top of his shaved head and then set off in the direction of the garage. The old men watched as he moved away from the driveway into a green area of foliage, disappearing from sight like a vanishing shadow into the dense undergrowth. They knew that the killer understood the task ahead of him and how to carry it out with maximum efficiency.

Nellie entered the flat trying to be as unobtrusive as possible. Mike was asleep on the double bed as she quietly passed the room and reached the kitchen. Unlocking the door she descended the back stairs; walking around the garage down the drive again.

Mike heard the gentle footsteps padding past his room; he pretended to be asleep until the outer door closed softly. He had never been able to sleep during the day and now sunlight was streaming into the room and he felt the heat of the morning starting to build.

Getting up, he went to the bathroom and had a cold shower after first checking on Robbie, who was fast asleep and comfortably stretched out on his back on the bed. Towel wrapped around his midriff, Mike busily brushed his teeth, while admiring his supple young body in the full length bathroom mirror. "God, you're beautiful!" he whispered softly to himself as he finished his ablution. He opened the door in one quick movement to stop it from creaking and waking his friend. "It must be Nellie back again," he thought.

Light entered through the opened kitchen door, directly across the passage from the bathroom. He automatically looked to his left into Robbie's room. His heart skipped a beat as he realised that it wasn't

Nellie that had entered the flat. Outlined by the large window was a bald-headed African looking down upon his sleeping friend. The man looked slightly startled at the sudden sight of Mike across the room. Mike knew immediately that he was in two minds and unsure of his next move and was rapidly considering his options. In the sunlight Mike saw the glint of a steel blade in the man's hand. He shouted loudly, hoping that Robert wouldn't freeze in panic as he woke.

"Peter! Bring the gun, I've caught a thief!"

Afterwards he wondered why he had chosen those particular words. They were the first thing that came to mind when he realised that their lives were in danger.

Then Mike let out another blood curdling yell.

"Peter! Come quickly!"

The stranger turned. He now faced the white man head on as he moved menacingly towards him.

The young man held his position until the very last second and then moved backwards into his room still facing the black man, giving him the chance to escape through the gaping kitchen door to his left. Shorty Majozi flashed the knife at Mike, who had moved out of range of the lethal weapon in the killer's hand. The black man turned and fled down the stairway like a cat, taking three steps at a time. He raced down the drive into the street and jumped into the waiting brown Datsun car with the other two black men.

"Drive!" he screamed.

Peter heard the shout and raced towards the house, he was panting heavily by the time he reached the main bedroom of the flat.

Mike appeared through the doorway of the smaller room.

"There was a man in here with a knife!" he shouted excitedly.

"Shit! They know your whereabouts already."

"How?"

"They must have had the house watched; I'll have the grounds searched."

No one considered the faithful old servant as being a collaborator.

By this time Robbie had surfaced.

"You were almost bloody dead meat!" Mike shouted at his friend. Robert stared long and hard at his white brother. This was the second time that his life had been saved by him, the first when he had been bitten by a puff adder. He silently vowed to repay the debt as soon as he could. He did not enjoy beholding his life to white men, even his best friend.

Within an hour, a courier arrived at the door carrying the prized documents for both men.

"You can't leave from Jan Smuts Airport now. If they know you're here you can be sure that the police won't be far behind," said Peter. "We'll get you out via Botswana, go and get your things now! We're leaving right away!"

While they gathered their belongings, Peter called the airport to get his Baron aircraft ready immediately for a flight to Botswana. He made a second call, threatening the recipient. Peter was not used to having anyone endanger his household. He was as mad as a hornet; someone was going to pay for this intrusion.

The trio left from Lanseria Airport within an hour of the call. Peter regularly flew himself to Botswana because the company had extensive mining interests in the country. He had arranged for a company car to collect them on their arrival. An hour after takeoff they landed at the desolate airstrip and passed through customs. Ten minutes later, three men had booked into the Holiday Inn on the outskirts of the town of Gaberone. Peter had arranged everything for them as they booked into rooms held permanently for company staff or overseas visitors. He stayed with them all day until that evening, making sure that they enjoyed themselves. Most of the time was spent beside the hotel pool.

It was seven o'clock in the evening when he took them back to the airport and checked them onto flight 249 from South Africa via Gaborone to London. It was not until the huge orange, white and blue 747 short bodied Boeing left the ground that the two relaxed and the burden of weight carried during that day floated away. They had first class seats; the aircrew bustled around feeding them drinks and food. They relaxed into their fourteen hour flight around the bulge of Africa. Robbie stayed awake to watch the in-flight movie; Mike was exhausted and dropped off to sleep almost immediately.

The following morning at nine o' clock, the big steel bird made its approach on its final flight path over the congested city of London and onto Heathrow Airport. They entered England without any problems.

Waiting for them as they passed through the arrivals door was Sharon. A new chapter in their life was about to begin, they were all looking forward to it.

CHAPTER EIGHT

'A learned man can always rile, when life becomes infantile'

Oxford - England

Sharon was standing in the arrivals' hall of terminal number one at Heathrow Airport. The passengers from South Africa started appearing through the doors and there was no mistaking them with their suntanned skins against the paler European complexions. She carefully watched the electronic doors slide open and shut each time they ejected a cart-pushing passenger. It had been nearly four years since her holiday and she wondered how Mike had changed in that time. Smiling to herself as she remembered that first day and feeling a slight stirring within her loins. She thought that she'd prefer being there now instead of in this wintery Britain. She recognised them at once and lurched forward out of the crowd in their direction. The two young men were transfixed as the black caped woman came straight at Michael and threw her arms around his neck with such force that both of them almost toppled over.

He hugged her, kissed her, hugged her again; the joy within him knew no bounds as he slowly released his grip and held her at arms length to have a good look at her.

She suddenly turned and dived at Robbie in the same fashion hugging him violently. He wasn't quite sure how to react as this was the first time that any white woman, other than Nicole, had dared put their arms around him in public.

She sensed his embarrassment immediately and whispered laughingly in his ear, "Don't worry its quite all right to do this in public here. You won't be arrested you know."

Only then with the spell broken did Robbie give her a bear hug. It felt great; he could see that nobody around them was even taking a blind bit of notice. He would have been arrested in South Africa for what he was doing now, as he hugged tighter. The three bubbled laughingly as they made their way from the terminal building across the walkway towards the multi-storied car park where Sharon had left her car.

During the drive from the airport they related most of the details of their escape to her. She was thoughtful and tried to dismiss the subject by telling them about the university. She had been told some of the facts by her father, but not being a liberal, she preferred to think that South Africa would remain cocooned in its present state forever.

The traffic travelled nose to tail until they left the M25 and turned onto the M40 motorway under a sign marked Oxford. Only then the traffic began to ease and they were able to drive faster. Robbie had never seen such concentrated traffic and wished that they could be lifted back to South Africa.

The road narrowed as they moved away from the motorway and he felt they were now in the real English countryside. Sharon turned the vehicle off the main road and onto a winding country lane towards her home.

"I've got a cottage here but you may not like it because it's a very quiet little village," she said.

The car slowed down around a large "olde worlde" village green with a duck pond and cottages and even older oak trees. To their right was an old fashioned pub called 'The Seven Sisters' with a tiny car park beside it. At the far end of this delightful green, Sharon edged off the road and went through a narrow gateway to halt under a rickety lean-to which extended outward from the side of a red-bricked house.

"Here we are; come on I'll show you around and then we'll go and have a pub lunch."

She bubbled with excitement, glad that they had finally arrived home and wanting to impress them.

Mike was surprised to see that the view at the back of the little house was overlooking open countryside and not surrounded by other buildings; which was the impression gained from the front of the house. A large open paddock spread across the width of several houses. Two magnificent looking stallions, one bay the other grey, stood quietly grazing in the field. The paddock had a freshly painted timber fence running the full length and passing behind the stable; while the other three sides enclosed the field with a thick privet hedge. Michael also noticed that the house was on a slight rise giving them an uninterrupted view of the distant hills.

The furnishings were tastefully expensive and could have been planned by an interior designer. There was deep piled wall to wall grey carpeting and heavy armchairs gracefully filled this entrance room. All the walls had been covered with warm autumn coloured wallpaper interspersed with several full length aged mirror strips, which helped to emphasize the tasteful decor. He noticed stairs led down to a cellar from an open kitchen and a new spiral staircase all in polished teak went upstairs.

"This is lovely," he said, genuinely impressed with the modern look given to the old house, "have you been here long?"

"You should have seen it when I bought it last year, it was a wreck and I've had to gut it and start from scratch; it's been a labour of love though," she replied.

Obviously proud of her achievements, she gave them a guided tour of the recently revamped cottage. Inwardly though she was starting to question the decision to let them both stay and suddenly feared that her freedom was going to be sacrificed. They followed her up the winding stairs onto a small landing leading to two large rooms in the front and a large bathroom with a massive linen cupboard, at the back.

Mike noticed that a similar pattern of decor had been extended to the upper floor, the aged mirrors were very effective, but he felt like a goldfish in a bowl with so many of them about. "You can share this room or one of you can have the spare room below the kitchen," she said pointing to the smaller bedroom of the two.

"Let's see the other room," said Robert. Since boyhood the two had had separate rooms and he preferred having his own space. They went downstairs into the basement. There was a computer and television in the room. A floral covered sofa bed stood in the corner and he noted a guest toilet at the far end.

"I'll stay here, I don't want to share a room with someone who snores," Robert said jokingly, as he was pleasantly surprised with the room.

"Fine, you'll have to help me get the spare bed and one of the wardrobes down here," she replied.

Very quickly they had manoeuvred the furniture into place, unpacked and organised their living arrangements; Sharon directing and the two men labouring. When they finished she phoned South Africa.

"Hello daddy! They've arrived and we're getting ourselves sorted out."

She had curled her long legs underneath her on the chair her manner exuding total confidence and giggling seductively as the voice at the other end said something to amuse her. Suddenly the laughing face became serious.

"Why, what's happened?"

"When?"

Again she listened and tears began to appear. "Oh God!" she exclaimed "Do they know how it happened?" She was now crying openly.

Both men were sitting opposite her, mouthing anxious questions.

Eventually she slowly replaced the receiver in its cradle. "Nellie's been knifed to death, the police found her body in the park this morning. Who would want to do that to my nanny? She was such a harmless old soul."

Openly distressed by the news just given to her by her father, she sobbed aloud. Mike and Robbie looked at each other, their matching thoughts not having to be spoken aloud. Both knew who had done the killing, the only question was why. Suddenly as if nothing had happened Sharon got up and said "Give me a minute to clean up and we'll go and have something to eat; you two must be exhausted"

It caught both of them by complete surprise as she quickly mounted the stairs two at a time.

That evening, after a light supper, they sat quietly watching television feeling absolutely drained. Sharon moved her computer into the conservatory and was hard at work on a project. The two boys retired early. Michael had a shower in the large bathroom then went to bed. He picked up his unfinished novel and started to read.

About an hour later his door opened gently.

"Are you asleep?" she asked.

"No, come in."

It was obvious to him that she had been crying as her eyes were swollen and red. She sat on the end of his bed, "Why, would anybody want to kill old Nellie?" she asked; her powerful inner strength seemed to have deserted her.

Mike looked at his cousin, she was like a little lost girl; he simply shook his head and said. "I really don't know."

Sharon lay down on top of his bed and put her head on his chest "I'm so glad you're here. I've missed you and when dad told me you were coming it was the happiest day of my life. Now this!"

He put his arm around her "It can only get better," he said, "Just lie here and cry if you want, it's good to get it out of your system."

"Another thing," she paused, "I didn't tell you earlier but my dad asked me to give you both a message."

"What is it?" he asked.

"Quoting him verbatim, 'tell the boys, especially Robbie, never to let their guard down; because the people here are like African elephants, they never forget' end of quote. What does it mean?" she asked.

"Aah! Nothing really," he stalled, suspecting she already knew.

The two fell asleep as they were; Sharon woke feeling cold in the early hours of the morning and wondered whether or not to climb into the bed. She decided against it, knowing there would be other nights. Moving very slowly so as not to waken her cousin she lifted herself off the bed, switched off the bedside lamp and crept to her room. She went to bed with mixed feelings as she wanted desperately to revive her holiday experience with Mike; but she had had a very emotional day, first with the joy of his arrival and then the news of her old nanny. She was confused and sleep didn't come easily that night with her mind in turmoil.

CHAPTER NINE

'African harvests and distractions, serve bitter mood reactions'

They drove a short distance into Oxford the next day to enrol at the university. Entering the city for the first time would remain in Mike's memory for a lifetime. The experience, he imagined, was akin to walking amongst the Pyramids, climbing the Matterhorn or seeing the Great Wall of China. The brown Honda moved slowly across Magdalen Bridge into the High Street, where the two boys had their initial close-up sighting of the University town. High yellow-brown, ivy-clad sandstone walls surrounded the magnificent old buildings and were breathtaking in stature, size, age and architecture. Ornate gateways that led to minute cobbled alleys and imposing churches seemed to abound everywhere one looked. The University College rumoured to have been established by Alfred the Great, or Magdalen College, Queens College and Jesus College had simply been famous university names to the two. Now they were actually seeing these historical buildings, some dating back from 1263, for the first time. Mike remembered reading that scholastic tradition had existed here in Oxford since 1096 and then had rapidly developed from 1167 onwards with the closing of the University of Paris to Englishmen. They made their way from St John Street to Wellington Square and the admissions office. Sharon handed the grey headed woman a letter of introduction from the chancellor. They met their tutors and were shown their Junior Common Rooms, sports field and generally spirited around, gaining a minuscule idea of their home for the next two years.

Robbie stretched out full length on the back seat of the car on their way home; the effects of the previous two days and a slight attack of jet lag finally caught up with him. By the time they had reached the cottage they were both flagging miserably and went straight to their beds. While they slept Sharon buried herself in her studies, trying to catch up with her interrupted project.

After that memorable holiday with Mike she had arrived in England and spent five months touring through Europe before settling down to study. Her father had decided many years before to send her to an English university and had entered her into Oxford well before completion of her South African schooling. Coincidentally the head of her college, a very determined lady called Daphne Parks, had been born in South Africa and until the age of eleven had not attended any form of school. The two had developed a liking for each other shortly after Sharon had entered Somerville College, one of the only two colleges for women at this great university. At the end of last year she had completed her undergraduate studies, obtaining her matriculation, which meant she could enter the university as a graduate and decided to complete a degree in Physical Sciences. This was in preference to using her father's connections and entering the business world.

During her second year she had a torrid love affair with one of the married tutors. Because of his dubious 'high moral' principals, he wanted to leave his wife in order to be free to marry Sharon. This was never her intention and she refused to see him or have anything to do with him once the relationship had soured. He tried for weeks to contact her, then finally returned to his wife who gladly took him back. The heartbroken man became depressed and committed suicide two weeks later.

The affair was eventually forgotten but she slipped up again a year later when she found herself at the mercy of an unscrupulous adventurer from whom she was lucky to escape; all this left her determined to never trust men.

She looked at her watch and muttered. "Oh hell!"

Time had flown and she realised that she hadn't taken the steaks out of the freezer and now wouldn't have time to defrost them. "Better wake the boys," she sighed to herself.

Robbie was lying on his back with the sheets unknowingly kicked free of his ebony body leaving him stark naked. "Good God!! He's been concealing a black mamba and poisonous snakes aren't allowed in Britain," she giggled to herself. Sharon then went upstairs and woke Mike by gently rubbing his forehead. His eyes flickered open.

"Hello beautiful," he said as his hand stretched up to stroke her golden hair.

"Time to rise and shine lazy head; we're going for a meal at a super place I know near Abingdon."

Leaning forward, she leaned over and gently kissed him on his cheek.

"Up and dressed, then wake your friend while I go for a quick shower, I won't be long."

They entered the restaurant and Sharon seemed to greet everybody in the place as they moved to their table. Everyone appeared to know her and wanted to chat. "Not surprising," thought Mike.

She was looking extremely exciting and gorgeous and he was proud to be seen with her he thought as he held back the chair for Sharon. The two men had been introduced to all and sundry on the way towards their table. It was obviously that she led a hectic social life and was well liked. Everyone they were introduced to asked them the usual polite questions and wished them luck with their studies.

Mike and Robbie had been assigned rooms at their respective colleges and decided to move into the residencies during the weekend.

They also realised they had to go into London to sort out their finances at the bank and after discussing this with their tutors, it was arranged that they would go the following Friday.

The two boarded the blue and grey British Rail train for their first experience of rail travel; the train was hot and overcrowded and arrived in London at nine thirty that morning. Having never been on an underground metro system before provided great amusement and they became lost on numerous occasions, whilst trying to find their way out of the maze. They were fifteen minutes late for their appointment and a policeman courteously directed them around the Bank of England building to their destination at the National Westminster Bank headquarters. The manager, James McGregor, sat at a large circular rosewood boardroom table; he was used to overseas visitors getting lost and arriving late. He stood up to shake their hands

"Ah! Time for elevenses," he said, "This is something we British have institutionalised. Now I have instructions to let you both have funds and have arranged for the branch in Oxford to provide a monthly living allowance, they are also instructed to settle your university fees and accounts."

"Next," he continued, "I have also arranged for them to provide funds to enable you each to purchase a small car. We did the same for Miss Roberts as you will need transport to get around."

"Students seem to cycle everywhere in Oxford," said Mike.

"Yes, but that is only around the campus area, you'll find that a lot of them have additional transport," the manager replied.

He lifted the teapot to pour himself a second cup. Setting it down he continued to outline what else had been done for Sharon when she had arrived and explained that they were to be treated exactly the same way.

Both noticed that his entire instruction was directed towards Mike knowing that both he and Sharon were heirs to vast fortunes. He'd sort of dismissed Robbie as a hanger-on and of little subsequence as he continued with his brief.

Finally, drawing matters to a close, he got up to indicate the end of their meeting, saying "Well that's everything. When you need us, just call and I'm sure that we can accommodate you while you're in England."

He walked them to the lift and shook hands with Mike first "Please remember me to your parents when you next talk to them." After shaking Robbie's hand he strode back towards the office.

They immediately headed for Soho. Their first stop was to view the blue movie parlours, something South Africa and its high moral churchmen would never allow. They continued wandering aimlessly through the streets admiring the old town with its strange sounds and shops revealing a whole new world to them. They reached Trafalgar Square and saw South Africa House with a small demonstrating crowd urging passers by to sign petitions against the apartheid system on the pavement outside. Mike didn't want to become involved and crossed the road, leaving Robbie on his own as he busily looked at the inscription on Nelson's Column. He didn't see his black friend start talking to one of the demonstrators.

When Robbie re-joined Mike they carried on walking past

Piccadilly Circus and up Regents Street; looking into shops like two children with their noses pressed against the window at Christmas time. They followed their torn little map and even though they lost their bearings on several occasions, it didn't matter to them because they were having fun.

Finally, after arriving back Oxford station, they took a short taxi ride to the cottage; only to find Sharon surrounded by books and papers as she had spent the entire day studying to catch up on work.

"You look busy," said Robert, his teeth flashing white against his darkened skin, as he offered her a carefully wrapped present that they had bought for her. In the neatly folded package she found a Gucci silk scarf and a small bottle of Chanel tucked inside.

"Oh this is very sweet of you, you shouldn't have wasted your money on me," she said trying to hide her delight. "Thank goodness you're home, I can stop working now."

She was wearing a gold coloured kaftan and looked like the phoenix emerging from among the ashes as she stood up amid the white papers surrounding her workplace.

"How did your day go?" she asked as she stretched her body upwards to relieve slight cramp. The kaftan danced under the single light and spread away from her like a giant bird in flight. For a while they spoke about their day in London, then Mike and Robbie changed while she busied herself preparing evening dinner. Mike was the first to return to the kitchen. He crept up from behind and put his arms around her waist while nestling his head on her shoulder, as they continued to talk about his trip to London.

After dinner the trio made their way to the pub for a drink. This was the beginning of the weekend for them and the place was packed out with young people. The quiet car park overflowed onto the central green with an array of highly expensive cars parked everywhere. From the back room of the pub came the throbbing sound of disco music.

They drank too much and again they noticed that wherever Sharon went a constant flow of people would greet and chat to her. Mike found this continual attention disconcerting and he slowly found himself becoming slightly jealous.

Robbie disappeared to the disco several times during the evening with a small waif named Joan who had attached herself to the group at Sharon's invitation. According to Sharon this short girl, dressed in tight jeans and a sweater, was the local bicycle – ridden by everyone. That didn't worry Robbie as he hadn't had the opportunity to feel so free and express himself this way for a long time and he was going to make the most of it.

The cousins eventually made their way to the flashing lights of the disco, where Mike watched Sharon move with the grace of a swan to the pulsating beat of the music; as she teased and tempted him like a nymph. Her golden hair swung loosely around her face as he envisaged her body and long legs beneath her clothes. The unanswered burning question that had been with him for the last few years had been answered at the airport by her body language and was now being re-enforced. They had had many opportunities during the week but neither had dared make the first move; Mike was now certain that the time had arrived.

Robbie watched the couple on the dance floor and said he was going to walk Joan home; they both knew that they wouldn't see him until the following morning.

When they left the pub, Mike and Sharon walked arm in arm along the potholed narrow road, stopping several times to lock in embrace.

Both knew that they felt absolutely right and were glad they had waited and not rushed into the moment.

The two kneeled on her bed facing one another and in slow, but deliberate movements, they removed each other's garments piece by delectable piece. Treating each other like china dolls they delicately savoured the long slow build up for what was to come. They stayed awake all night and each took their fill not wanting to sleep until their appetites had been fully sated.

Later, Sharon showed Mike a secret compartment behind the linen cupboard in her bathroom.

"This house used to belong to a voyeur and the mirrors all conceal lenses. He unfortunately got killed in a motor accident and it was only when I wanted to remove the old mirrors that I found all this equipment."

Mike looked at the bank of video machines.

"Why didn't you remove them?"

"I don't know, probably because it would have been a costly task; anyway, I should have put them to good use last night."

"You didn't did you?"

Sharon gave a wicked smile, "What if I did?"

He could see that she was teasing him. He pulled her towards him.

They both laughed.

The four finally got together at lunchtime. Robbie had Joan in tow and that afternoon was spent at a local fair.

CHAPTER TEN

'In the boding breast, jungle law creates a lasting feast'

Pretoria - South Africa

Michael's mind drifted in and out through grey misty patches, reminding him of flying down between wintery cloud filled skies. On his journey to hospital in the ambulance the continual bumping racked his body with pain, causing every jolt to feel like a hot spear piercing him. He tried hard to keep himself from falling unconscious again. He had seen the person responsible for the bomb and knew that it was only a matter of time before they would try getting to him. Jay was in the ambulance with him, she was seated on the stretcher across the narrow aisle and Michael felt slightly comforted by the fact that she was there.

"How long before we reach the hospital? The pain is becoming unbearable," he mumbled.

She leaned over and pressed a dampened cloth to his head

"Just a few more minutes Mike. Keep hanging on in there, it won't be much longer," she urged. All colour had drained from his skin and there was nothing more that she could do until they reached their destination. "I told you that I'd stay with you," she said.

He could hear the loud wailing of the siren and saw the skinny ambulance man having difficulty keeping his balance as the vehicle swerved from side to side, carefully picking its way through the afternoon traffic.

Jay had decided that there wasn't much more that she could do at the Union Buildings and hurriedly left her name with the police after telling the doctor that she would accompany the ambulance to the hospital. She had helped to keep him alive so far and now she felt it her duty to keep this fighter going. Many lesser men would have given up by this stage; but years of experience had taught her how to identify those individuals who would not give up easily. She was sure that this one would cheat death against all the odds stacked against him.

"Mike is there anybody you would like me to call?" She asked. He slowly sucked in a deep breath before painfully answering her question.

"Not yet, but if I should make it then we'll see, Aaah!" A stabbing pain passed through his chest as he tasted blood in his mouth once more.

"Please get my case, it is very important not to let anybody near it and make sure..." Again he paused while battling to clear the enveloping mists reaching into his brain.

"What!" she said impatiently. Mike summoned the last ounce of his fading strength together with superhuman effort.

"Get hold of all my clothes, take them with you and keep them safe," he gasped and passed out.

Jay clearly understood his answer and accepted it without another thought. When she first found him, he was holding onto a brown leather briefcase which she had placed in the ambulance alongside her bag.

They arrived at the Pretoria General Hospital a few minutes later. The staff had been alerted to expect them and the ambulance-men quickly wheeled the stretcher into the casualty ward, where a burns doctor and two specialists were waiting. The three experts quickly stripped away all clothing to inspect the damage as Jay stood in the background watching them carefully probe the unconscious figure.

Johannesburg - South Africa

Dirk Lemmer was again sitting at the kitchen table talking to the four grim Askaris seated with him. Tempers flared in the small bungalow where they regularly conducted their meetings and which was set among the opulent homes of the rich white northern suburbs. This house, well hidden from the street, was convenient as well as inconspicuous; being situated almost halfway between Johannesburg and Lemmer's headquarters in Pretoria. He was in his late thirties with closely cropped fair hair. His face revealed hardened features from years spent in the South African police forces. In typical Afrikaner fashion, he was dressed in a pale blue safari suit.

Listening to the others, he did not speak but occasionally interjected with carefully posed questions to try to understand what had gone wrong.

His life was not a happy one that afternoon as he thought of the earlier events that had led to this meeting; when the radio in his car buzzed loudly.

"Ja! Lemmer here," he answered.

"Commandant Roux wants you come in immediately," barked the woman's crisp voice across the airwaves. "He said you must stop whatever you're doing and get back here."

"I'll be there in about eight minutes, over and out."

Dirk was puzzled as his counterpart in the police force never called him this way; it must be serious he thought. Swinging his maroon Ford down into Main Reef Road he headed back towards

Johannesburg, fortunately for them he had not travelled very far and was reaching the outskirts of Crown Mines when the call came. It took five minutes before he turned left under the concrete overhead freeway and immediately right into the parking garages of John Vorster Square Police Headquarters. There was a permanent place reserved for him to park his vehicle and he eased the Ford forward very gently until it stopped against the wall.

Bennie Roux, a short dumpy man in his early fifties, had waited impatiently for Dirk's arrival. He rose from behind his large desk when the younger man entered and shook hands with him.

"What the hell is that killer kaffir of yours up to?" he stormed in Afrikaans.

He didn't wait for the security man to sit down before releasing his attack. It was not the first time the two had met in such circumstances.

"Why, what's happened?" Dirk stalled. He needed to know the facts first.

"That black bastard entered the house of one of the most important business men in this town. He had a bloody knife in his hand but luckily he was seen and ran away before he could hurt anyone."

The man sitting across the desk was livid, his cheek and jowls puffed into a strange combination of purple and red.

"How do you know it was Shorty Majozi?" asked Dirk.

"Hey! Look man, he was seen and described by the owner of the house. I know it was that evil bastard that works for you."

The men didn't like each other because Roux had been passed

over for the security job. The younger man was now senior in post but not in rank. Dirk was in the position of being the most feared and hated, of all men. It was a lonely job and contained power which he constantly had to use to achieve his goals. Roux was jealous of the power, it should have been his, or so he thought. Both men were Afrikaners belonging to the Broederbond; meaning 'bond of brothers' and was set up to protect their own language from extinction when the British took over the Union of South Africa. Now all government senior posts were carefully delegated to those Afrikaners within the Broederbond and no Englishman was ever allowed entrance into their haloed brotherhood.

"Did he see the man himself?"

"He just said that someone had seen him in the house and that he had a knife in his hand; when he described him, I knew straight away who it was."

"You didn't say anything, I hope," knowing that Roux would be vindictive if he could.

"No man, what do you take me for?"

"You know nothing! You say nothing! You won't help them find my man, do you understand?" Dirk ordered.

"The crap will hit the fan over this, you mark my words," warned Roux.

"They can't prove anything and we don't even know that it was him, do we?" Dirk knew that this man would scheme his downfall if he had hard evidence.

Dirk had then called the meeting for later that afternoon; he wasn't sure what had happened, but whatever it was had gone terribly wrong. He knew of Peter Roberts, from his many newspaper photos and that he had connections in high places.

The four black men were ex ANC guerrillas who had been forced to switch allegiance to the police and were now used as killers for the security forces. They were highly trained Askaris, each having a particular speciality including the use of explosives, small arms and poisonings.

The five men in the room were all experts in death; they formed the nucleus of undercover hit men for BOSS, the Bureau of State Security and travelled long distances to covertly deal with ANC troublemakers.

Dirk faced one of the older men.

"You said that you would deal with the matter and now look at the problems we've got."

"We were given false information, there is no way that they can trace it to us," came the confident reply.

"The police already know who it was; they were given a full description by somebody."

He stopped speaking and watched their reaction, slowly tapping out loose ash from his pipe into a large ashtray. "I don't think it was the white boy either," he continued.

This took the four by surprise, as the only other person was Nellie the maid who had called them in; so it was unlikely that she had given the police any form of description.

Refilling his pipe with brown pungent tobacco, Dirk continued

"The only trace back to you then is this black bitch. Something must be done to silence her before the police put the puzzle pieces together."

Realisation shot through the four and Shorty spoke their thoughts aloud.

"She could point a finger at three of us and if they think she was involved they'll soon get the truth from her."

Dirk lovingly lit his pipe and the aromatic smell quickly filled the room as grey puffs of cloud belched from his mouth and curled upwards to the ceiling each time he sucked.

"Exactly," he said, "and if they do find the truth, it will be your necks on the line."

He knew how Roux felt about him and he also knew that the commandant of police would have no compunction in sabotaging his efforts by leaking snippets to the media; they didn't have much time in which to complete their task.

"Now let's remove this woman from the scene so that she can't tell them anything. We have to do it today and without any foul ups this time," he said.

They left together just as day began to drift into night. Three cars all headed towards Melrose and Peter Robert's house.

Nellie finished serving supper in the large dining room. She could never understand why her employers always insisted having their meals here, with its long dining table. They usually sat at opposite ends of the table, a long way apart; it was only when they entertained guests, that Nellie could see the reason for this monstrous table. It and its chairs had been ornately carved from stinkwood - a rare timber obtained from the Knysna forests. The rest of the room was panelled in dark mahogany, as was the drawing room next door. Nellie was summoned by a brass foot button on the floor, which chimed a bell in the kitchen. This meant the end of a course; tonight, when she went to clear the dishes from the table, her madam had told her to go to bed because she didn't need her again until morning. Collecting the remaining empty dishes Nellie returned them to the kitchen and placed them in the dishwasher. Before this lifesaver had arrived she would have to stay late washing the dishes. Sometimes, after a big dinner party, she would have been washing-up into the early hours.

Nellie gave the kitchen a final check, to make sure that there was enough food in the animals' bowls; switched off the lights and let herself out, locking the heavy outer door behind her. The tiled pathway to her small house was brightly lit by a spotlight shining from the main house and which was left on all night as a security precaution. She walked along this pathway which took her past the swimming pool at least three times every day.

As she passed the tall bamboo thicket a male voice called her name from the dark. It startled the fat black lady and she stopped dead in her tracks. Calling out loudly for the owner to identify himself, she heard a rustle in the bamboo which revealed a greying old man. He spoke her name again, beckoning her towards him and into the deep shadows.

She recognised his silvery grey features in the dark immediately and with relief she sauntered towards the undergrowth.

"What happened today, after we left?" the old man enquired.

"The master and the two boys left straight afterwards," she replied.

"Have you told them anything, or have they asked you anything?" he asked.

"No! Nothing has been said; but two white policemen arrived late today asking for the master. The madam said he would be back later, so they are returning tomorrow morning," she answered.

She knew he could see the look in her face and she was scared; not used to dealing with situations like those experienced today.

"Don't worry," the old man said touching her arm trying to allay her fear and calm her down, "we need to discuss this and make plans."

"Why?"

"Come to the park at the end of the road. We will tell you what to say to the police if they ask you anything."

"Let me go to my room, I won't be long but I must go to the toilet and then I will come to the park."

Nellie made her way along the road, she never walked very fast, her bulky stature prevented it. She was glad of the circular beams thrown from the overhead street lights, they reduced the chances of being mugged at night.

As she crossed the road to the park, she could make out the familiar silhouettes of the swings and slides in the play area for the white children during the day and the young black maids at night. The lights at the far side of the park also revealed two black men, but at this distance she could not make out who they were, although she suspected the old man was bound to be one. One man paced up and down like a leopard, his gait carefully measured like that of a trapped cat, while the other stood quietly talking to him. She could faintly hear the distanced voice of the old man who had earlier been in the garden.

She waddled through the park towards the two shadows, making sure not to trip on anything in the dark. Not until she was within yards of them did she realise who the other person was. She stopped; panic overtook her squat rounded frame and a tingle of fear ran down her spine. The man pacing up and down was Shorty Majozi, the evil one. Instinctively she moved toward the older man.

They'd watched her coming down the brightly lit street and across the park. The two had purposely switched their discussion to a local football team called the Kaiser Chiefs, to hide any suspicion of their real intention from the cuddly figure steadily making her way across the park.

"Sawubona," she called her greeting.

"Eh' he," the two replied simultaneously.

For a short time the three exchanged niceties as was African custom, then Shorty asked her about the day's events. He really just wanted to get the job over and done with.

She related everything to them, not missing any details. She had wanted this traitor out of the way, as any offspring of the Induna, Mabel, was dirt she said; still feeling animosity towards the Zulu diviner after all these years.

"What of the white boss man at the house," continued the grey haired man, "where has he gone and will he be back tonight?"

"I heard him talking on the telephone. He has an aeroplane at Lanseria and told them he would fly within one hour," she said in her African dialect.

"Then he made one more call to the police, I think and the three left the house. That's all I know."

The men pondered for a short while; if Roberts flew they could always find out the destination. He'd got the black man away and they may have to deal with him as well, only Dirk Lemmer would decide.

Nellie watched the old man intently as he deliberated. Shorty was still ceaselessly pacing back and forth, only stopping in front of her when asking a question or requesting an answer. Suddenly he stopped in front of her and she saw the glint of steel then felt the thrust against her chest like a hammer blow. She watched the arm raise and drop again and again and again.

"Yaaach!" she shouted as a hand covered her mouth and blows kept raining onto her. The last thing she saw was the old man's face, the grey hair slowly disappeared into blackness as her life ebbed away onto the ground. They quickly emptied her little purse to make it look like robbery; the fat lady lay sprawled on the ground, blood stains from her white pinafore mingling with the dust. The two men walked across the park where, in the shadows at the far end, they found two cars carefully parked amongst some tall bushes. Dirk Lemmer was seated at the wheel of one of the vehicles. He saw the two men and asked uncaringly. "Any trouble?"

"No! It's all done and nobody will finger us now" replied the older man.

Two vehicles pulled away and sped off into the darkness, in the direction of Bryanston, the post mortem of their night's work still had to be assessed. Dirk Lemmer was furious, they had let one of the main ANC people slip through their grasp that day. He would track him down like a wounded dog and finish him off, no matter where he was or how long it took.

As far as he knew the white kaffir brother had nothing to do with the ANC. He was only interested in the black one and he made up his mind there and then to follow the route taken by Roberts and the two boys. Their work at Melrose was complete and Roux wouldn't be able to prove anything now; his Askaris were once again safe from prying eyes.

The following morning a young servant girl crossing the park on her way to work discovered the blood soaked body of Nellie; she ran screaming to the nearest white man's house. The police were called in and a young constable taking notes pointed out that she was just another dead black. He joked to his colleague that it made one less to worry about; they bred like flies, so one wasn't going to be missed.

Back at John Vorster Square Police Station, the constable filed a normal report, thinking that that would be the last that he heard about the matter. That was a mistake on his part; because first thing the following morning he was summoned to see Commandant Roux and was told to file an extensive report this time.

Roux felt cheated because he was certain that he knew the identity of the killer, or killers; but he needed concrete proof.

This vendetta against Lemmer had become an obsession with him; so he put his best detectives on the case. He knew that he had to trap Dirk Lemmer through mistakes made by his Askaris and was determined to get him this time at all costs. By that afternoon he had two comprehensive files in his possession containing facts about the murdered servant woman and also about attempted murder on one Robert Molefe.

He was positive that both cases were linked and that the evil killer working for the security chief was the man to watch.

CHAPTER ELEVEN

'Hate, like trees, can shed it's summer mantle with ease'

<u>Oxford - England</u>

Robbie was lying naked on the big double bed as Joan snuggled up to him still fast asleep, they had spent several hours making violent love. She had brought him home and offered him something to drink and he had asked her straight out whether she wanted to make love.

Joan had never slept with a foreigner before, let alone a black man. This is a first for me, she thought, so let's go for it and have some fun... Ever since her school days she had had an insatiable sexual drive, which nobody to date had been able to satisfy.

Before entering her bedroom, Robbie insisted on going to the bathroom for a shower, which she considered rather unusual. After undressing she got into bed and being a warm night, threw the blankets onto the floor leaving only the dark blue sheet covering her small body. Within minutes Robbie emerged from the bathroom with a small white hand towel tucked around his midriff which barely hid his black manhood. At first he strolled around the room, looking at her vast collection of teddy bears with interest, commenting occasionally when something specific caught his attention. She watched the slightly coffee coloured man move like a panther, perfectly balanced, each step deliberately paced as his eyes missed nothing. It was as if he were making sure that his resting place was safe before settling for the night. Studying his body she noticed that every sinewy muscle was almost perfect. His facial lines were slightly European and she could see small peppercorn hairs covering his young chest and wondered if it would be the same

101

below.

He stopped and gazed down at her and as her eyes moved from his body back to his face, she noticed a look that momentarily frightened her. His beautiful brown eyes had taken on an amber tinge and for a split second, they seemed to be hooded and evil; like a snake about to strike.

In one swift movement he whipped the sheet away from her body to reveal her nakedness. She could feel his powerful gaze searching her inch by inch, whilst she could not look away from his hypnotic eyes. Only when his hand dropped and released the towel did she dare move them, travelling down his torso until they rested on his relaxed member.

"Christ!" Her thoughts screamed out. "Why haven't I aroused him? But when I do and he puts that inside me, it'll kill me." Joan trembled at the sight of him looming up over her, not knowing what his fantasies might be. She watched him take his palm and with fingers spread wide, run it up over her mound. She shivered in anticipation as he gently squeezed his fingers closed and pulled at her dampened hair. She felt herself relaxing into a rhythm as he massaged her with both hands for a while. It was delicious and exquisite. She felt her legs being spread apart as wide as she could manage.

Robbie then leaned forward and inserted his tongue as deep as he could and she had the first orgasm as he licked and sucked at her tender sweet flesh: Her whole body being eaten alive as she shuddered with release. He stood up and her eyes were riveted to his rampant manhood; it looked like an enormous flagpole protruding from his thighs. He lay down and rolled her on top of him; with one hard thrust he drove into her. He filled her as he moved in and out of her again and again very slowly. Suddenly the animal in him took over, ramming into her time and time again until she couldn't take it any longer. She exploded in a long orgasm that seemed to go on forever; he didn't stop but carried on and on. It was sex with a desire to please her; her whole body contorted and racked as her vaginal muscles squeezed the massive intruder. It was glorious and when she heard his deep throated cry at release, they were both spent and worn out.

"Never in my life did I think it was possible for someone to satisfy me to the point where I couldn't go on," she said, "I passed out with pleasure several times."

"Well now you've met that someone and if you're a good girl, you can have more where it came from."

For the first time in Joan's life she felt completely contented and immediately fell asleep, totally exhausted.

Robbie remained awake for some time, thinking to himself that this white girl would serve his purpose well. Not only was she pretty, she would also help him gain social acceptance. He knew that he now had a white girl to tend to his needs, political or otherwise.

Joan woke early, feeling as if somebody had exploded a bomb between her thighs. She rolled over and lightly scratched the dark man beside her

"Never will I have to search for anyone else," she whispered to the sleeping figure.

Instinctively she knew that this was the man for her and would do anything for him; the only problem was that she would sooner or later have to tell her parents - they were in for a shock!

Joan was afraid of her father, the respected General Sir Honourable with his high military breeding. What the outside world didn't know was that her fear of him was because he was a child molester. Joan often thought that if people knew what he was really like he would suffer from the embarrassment. She hated him for what he had done to her; she was only twelve when he first sneaked into her room. She had vowed to herself that one day she'd destroy him; revenge would be sweet. The only reason for not doing anything about it so far was that her mother would also suffer and Joan didn't want to hurt her.

Over the next few months Robbie indoctrinated Joan in the workings of the ANC; explaining how bad and unfair life was for the blacks in South Africa.

Because her parents were strict Conservatives Joan had become a Young Liberal, just to rebel against them. On entering university she had quickly learnt that not everybody came from wealthy backgrounds and found herself supporting all the underdogs. Traditional values nudged at her conscience, telling her that she should be doing more for the underprivileged of the world and now she had found a cause that she could fix her banner to. Always at Robbie's beck and call, demanding a reward like a small child or a trained animal each time she did something that pleased him, Joan followed him everywhere from that night.

They went to London one Saturday where Joan met George Mxenge, one of Robbie's friends and they stayed there overnight with several people who came to the basement flat. Most of the time she couldn't understand what they were talking about in their African tongue, although she guessed that some of the talk was about her by the furtive glances in her direction. Such a happy people, she thought, they were always laughing and joking; she felt they had accepted her and two other English girls into their inner circle. It never struck her that there were no white men in attendance at this, or any of the other, gatherings that were arranged by Robbie and

George.

As each week passed, they became more engrossed in a campaign against the hated South African Government policies; taking turns standing outside the embassy building in Trafalgar Square. Robbie never stood outside the building because he was too busy at the ANC headquarters in Penton Street; Joan only knew that he was made the chief officer responsible for making contact with other underground movements all over the world. Most of them had connections in London and it was his job to find them. Robbie kept it from Joan that he was trying to meet group leaders who would be able offer arms and explosives; the mainly Communist countries needed funds and were readily able to offer this help.

Every weekend the pair would make their excuses to Mike and Sharon and slip away to London. The ANC really needed him to work full time, but he refused to compromise his degree for anything and insisted that he could serve them far better by completing his studies before permanently joining them. One thing that nobody realised was how much Robert missed his mother.

One evening Robbie was informed that Oliver Tambo and some of the major ANC members, was going to be in London for a television interview. To get maximum publicity for the TV appearance they had planned an attack on the Carlton Centre; one of the largest hotel complexes and shopping malls in Johannesburg. His idea was designed to be twofold; first it would give added coverage and would also provide a talking point for the interview.

The gold city's first taste of terrorism happened in the afternoon to coincide with the leader's arrival in London. Media stations worldwide carried full reports and any 'expert' who could put forth a view was contacted by television and radio stations; giving the leadership a field day explaining to the world why they had ordered the attack.

At the Carlton Centre a powerful bomb exploded beneath a flower pot on the south side of the underground mall system. Sixteen people were injured, none seriously, but considerable damage to shop windows and property resulted. The area was sealed off in seconds by the security staff and forces who had been preparing for an emergency of this nature. Oliver Tambo gained considerable media coverage for his cause and Robert Molefe became the hero within the group.

More often than not Robbie and Joan went to London for the entire weekend; leaving Mike and Sharon to their socialite friends. Robbie had tried hard to become accepted by them but found the racism barrier was never truly let down. After several months he gave up, preferring his own kind in London and realising that racial feelings were as inherent in this wealthy society as it had been back in South Africa. This began at a party given by Joan two weeks after their arrival when Sharon introduced them to Colin Baird, a mountain of a man with a square jaw and ears that looked like pink prunes stuck on the side of his head. He was an Oxford rugby blue and a potential lock forward for England and was always on the lookout for new players with potential around the university campus.

"Do you play rugger like most South Africans?" he tentatively asked Mike.

"I used to play centre at school, but haven't played since then."

"Why don't you come down to a practice session on Tuesday?"

Mike pointed at Robbie "If you want a star wing three quarter, there's your man."

"Well I'm not sure as we have some very good men there; but why not bring him along and let's have a look at him and see."

As promised the two joined practice and Robbie thoroughly enjoyed the workout; he was a natural athlete while Mike had found the going hard because he was a little out of condition.

"Your man can run some, I'll give you that," said Colin Baird in the pub afterwards.

Robbie just laughed. All of them knew that he had outstripped everybody on the practice field while running-in four tries. Very few players could touch him and as the weeks of practicing passed it was made obvious that Robbie was not going to make the first team. Even though his abilities were far superior to anyone else's, they told Mike that his friend was a loner and that rugby was a team sport.

For Robbie, no matter how hard he tried to become one of them, their ranks were closed to him because of his colour. Eventually he gave up trying and didn't attend practices any longer, much to the relief of the other players; he was a threat to the dominantly old school tie brigade. Not only was he ostracised on the field of play, but the cold shoulder given to him on social occasions as well. He was treated with indifference no matter what the occasion was.

On the other hand Mike was welcomed into the close confines with open arms. The fact that he was South African didn't seem to make any difference at all, his parents were from first class English stock and he was white; that's all that mattered.

As had happened in Pietermaritzburg, Mike and Robbie started drifting apart again, meeting each other less frequently as the months passed.

Robbie became very active within the student's union and spent all his spare time in their offices at Frewin Court across the road from Jesus College. Mike obtained blues in rugby and rowing and attended all the major functions such as the Henley Regatta, Ascot and various other social elite gatherings. Both men excelled at their studies, as their respective paths set them further and further adrift from each other, yet their loyalty to each other still remained firm and true as it had always done.

CHAPTER TWELVE

'Not all learning creatures, gain from mortal teachers'

London - England

Nine months after Mike and Robbie had left South Africa, Nicole and Ian visited England and their first reunion with their young was a staggeringly happy affair.

Every year the company booked a large suite at 'The Inn on the Park' in the West End of London, which meant they were centrally located for their meetings, the theatres and dinner parties. This time a further three rooms were reserved close to theirs for the three young people to stay in, so that they could make the most of their visit. Every evening they would all go to see a West End show and afterwards dine at one of the best restaurants. During the day Nicole and Ian would attend board meetings in the city, catch up on their share holdings or revise their portfolios; the youngsters would take the train back to Oxford for the day. It was a non-stop merry go round for everyone while they were visiting.

Michael wouldn't go to Sharon's room; they had decided that it would be too risky. Visiting London with Sharon and Mike each day, Robbie had hoped that his mother would have come to London; but he discovered she had refused the offer. When Nicole and Ian first saw him at the airport they threw their arms around him, making him feel good but it wasn't the same. On the second evening he had a long private discussion with Nicole, to confide his feelings about his mother; she promised to try to make Mabel see sense, as Robbie had seemed so near to tears. On their last night in London, Nicole called them together and told them that Peter and Ian had been discussing their futures before they'd left South Africa. Individually she questioned them, asking what their intentions were after their studies at Oxford were completed. All three were slightly uncertain and taken aback by this sudden questioning.

"We have just acquired a promising old family business," she said, "how would the three of you like to own and run it for us?"

"Doing what?" asked Sharon.

"As you know, there are various embargoes already placed on South African goods," Nicole replied. "Well, there could be the possibility of all-out sanctions against us, so we need to expand our trading base abroad."

Ian, who was seated in a large chair reading, spoke up from behind the Financial Times.

"We need a strong London operation entirely under our control to divert attention from our present activities if needs be," He lowered the newspaper slowly for the first time, to examine their faces in response to his proposal.

"It will need the skills of all three of you," interjected Nicole.

"You each have separate capabilities and potential to take a business to the very top."

Stunned, the three just looked at each other, no one sure how to answer the questions and waiting for one of the others to take a lead. Each one realised for the first time that their lives had been carefully orchestrated and that their destinies had been mapped out many years ago.

Ian laughed "Your direction of training, economics, maths and law constitute the makeup of any good business and you're a perfect partnership without knowing it."

Sharon was the first to answer after the long silence.

"Tell us about the business and what is expected; because we can't just make up our minds like this. Does it mean that we won't be returning home?"

"You have already made a start here so it will be easy to continue." Ian added.

"If things keep going in their present direction then our stupid white population will find itself cut off from the world." Nicole said. "Think about it for a while, because we don't need any decisions right now."

There was not much opportunity left to put up any major arguments to this sudden ready-made plan before Nicole and Ian left for America at the weekend and the youngsters quickly got back to their daily routines and studies. There were a lot of questions and talking to do about the proposal made by their elders which had come out of the blue.

They were constantly busy. Oxford had an atmosphere of its own, which most students really enjoyed. Robbie loved spending his free time with Joan walking among the old buildings; while Mike concentrated on his sport.

During the Christmas holidays Mike and Sharon went on a skiing trip to St Anton in Austria at the invitation of Andrew Burberry-Taylor. They were part of aristocratic society and had entrée with the very best families in the land. Sharon didn't really like Andrew, but had agreed that, in order to go places with their intended business, they were going to have to hob-knob with these people.

Their friends were now all going to have to come from the top drawer of society and they only had eighteen months to cultivate friendships before finishing their studies to take over the business. They both enjoyed learning to ski, they had natural balance and it didn't take long to get the hang of it. Within six days the two had started to ski from the Valluga, at the summit of the St Christoph mountain range. At après ski dinners and parties they continued cultivating solid companionships with a whole range of the elites who they intended using.

Mike spent a night trying to persuade Robbie and Joan to join them; he felt guilty and wanted his black brother to share Christmas and all its trappings with him: They had never missed this time of the year away from each other.

"Why don't you come with us, there's plenty of room."

"No, we're going to stay in England because I want to spend Christmas in London to see what its like here and to feel the traditional Charles Dickens Christmas." Robbie replied.

After Mike and Sharon's departure, Robbie and his girlfriend went to London and spent the week there with other members of the African National Congress. He had refused the Burberry-Taylor's invitation because he wanted to share Christmas with Joan. He felt that they had more in common, both enjoyed working actively for the student's union and now the ANC.

By this time Joan had realised that Robert was far more involved with the ANC hierarchy than he had originally made out. Later, when she questioned him about it, he told her his full role; not withholding anything. At first the thought of killing people alarmed her and only the thought of him leaving her and losing the genuine friends she had made through him, persuaded her to become more actively involved.

She went home for a week and spent lengthy periods renewing

old acquaintances. Most evenings found her talking with her mother because she felt the need to get closer to her. One afternoon, while her folks were out, she searched through all of her father's papers; finding and copying lists of names of outlawed gangs and vigilantes worldwide. Joan knew that one of her father's old bibles contained the combination to a wall safe hidden behind a bookshelf. She had secretly watched him open it enough times to know the routine.

Carefully, so as not to disturb any dust on them, she opened each of the ancient bibles, inspecting inside covers until finding the correct name and number. As she pulled at an old book, a mechanical action swung back the entire bookshelf in concertina fashion, to reveal a large safe. Fully aware that her father was a stickler for tidiness, Joan didn't enter the hidden room at once but slowly moved forward, examining the position of all the documents. Satisfied that all papers were correctly placed in her memory, she slowly sifted through them one by one, book by book, until she found what she was looking for in a small leather diary.

It was all there; a complete dossier of names compiled by the SAS containing Iranian Hezbollah, the Red Brigade, Libyan, IRA and the rest of the world's freedom fighters.

Estimating that she had about three hours in hand she carefully closed the bookcase and drove to the library, where she copied the entire book. When she returned home she replaced the vital book; leaving everything exactly as she had found it. She closed the bookcase and checked once more to see that everything was in order.

She left a short note for her parents, telling them she'd gone back to Oxford and wishing them a happy Christmas. On her way back she couldn't help feeling pleased with herself. She now had the means to keep Robbie interested in her and she calculatingly decided to feed him the information slowly. When back in her digs, she removed one of the loose ceiling panels above the bath and slid the papers behind it, keeping just one aside. She felt buoyant and pleased with her day's work; this weekend he would thank her in his special way.

Christmas week became one of significance to Robbie because of an unexpected surprise when he arrived at the ANC London headquarters. Oliver Tambo, the military General of the ANC and other leaders were supposed to arrive in London and his group of friends were busily preparing for them.

On the pavement outside the South African Embassy, Robbie had seen Roger Mxenge, an old friend who had once been the up and coming leader of the ANC in Natal, who had also been forced to quit the country because of his stand against apartheid.

On Christmas Eve all helpers were invited to a small party given in honour of the leader's visit which was to be held at the ANC Headquarters in Penton Street. Robbie and Joan walked slowly hand in hand along the Pentonville Road, stopping to look into shop windows which were all brightly decorated with Christmas trees, lights and presents, even in this down-trodden part of London. The area was alive and pulsing around them with last minute shoppers all scurrying around trying to complete their final chores and they felt relaxed and happy.

Robbie could see that people in the area were not wealthy, most of them struggling to make a living, yet not losing an inbuilt friendliness as they willingly chatted to anybody who would listen. This was a totally different world from the one that they lived and studied in at Oxford.

They were still a little early when they reached the green, yellow and black painted frontage with its locked door. Robbie pushed the buzzer, the door opened and Roger Mxenge welcomed them inside with a low bow from the waist. They could see that he had started his party much earlier in the day.

"Good evening, comrades," he said, stepping aside to let the couple through. Joan still flinched at 'comrades' so Robbie didn't repeat the epithet as he and Joan entered the building. ANC groups were Russian trained by the KGB in the USSR at special training camps. Robbie knew of the alliance, but he suspected Mike's friends would dismiss it as being in the superpower's interest to overthrow governments such as South Africa. For many years it was suspected the communists had envied the strategic position of South Africa, knowing that whoever controlled the seas off Cape Town at the base of Africa effectively also controlled the movement of east-west cargo. Furthermore, some of the strategic metals supplied by his country for weaponry and space travel were not available from anywhere else on the planet; so possession of the country would stop the Americans from dominating these technological areas. It was believed that the Russians had thrown their full weight behind the ANC in the hopes that they would eventually be able to secure the country for themselves.

They knew everyone at the actual party; in the back room, however, the leaders discussed various operations still to be carried out.

Parked about thirty yards down the street was a red Vauxhall; inside were four men, two white and two black, busily taking photographs of all the people entering and leaving the building. They had been there for four days; the old black man with a shock of grey hair and matching beard looked at his closely cropped white companion and said

"They're all gathering today, that one was Robert Molefe."

The white man's face broke into a semblance of a smile

"Got you! I knew I'd find you somewhere around these other black bastards." He turned to the others, cruelly savouring the moment of triumph and whispered "Maybe the trip hasn't been a waste after all, we're going to have some sport tonight."

CHAPTER THIRTEEN

'Evil comes from within, one is never born with sin'

<u>Pretoria - South Africa</u>

"Hurry up! Let's get him to theatre. There's a lot of work to do here."

Jay watched them feverishly attempting to save what they could of the broken man on the bed. After inspecting the X-Rays the doctors knew that they had done enough to stabilise his erratic breathing and had to operate quickly to release the pressure being exerted on his diaphragm by several broken ribs.

"That is only part of the problem; there are other complications that have to be rectified as well. It's going to be a long hard night," one doctor explained.

She approached the chief surgeon and asked whether she could help, explaining her position and qualifications. He immediately agreed, because he could do with all the help possible with all the cases from the explosion.

Jay phoned excusing herself from her normal duty; but they had been alerted to expect victims from the explosion and she was told to stay on to give what assistance she could.

Two doctors, an anaesthetist and three theatre sisters prepared for Mike's operation as they scrubbed up. One of the largest problems facing the operating team, in emergencies such as this, was lack of blood. Mike was luckier than most in that his blood group was RH Positive, the most common type. Whilst an anaesthetist was busy searching for an artery, Mike opened his eyes and immediately recognised Jay. Though wearing a mask and head cap, she could not hide her deep blue eyes.

"Make sure they cut in the right places," he joked, "and remember what I asked you to do."

She nodded and lightly touched his forehead with a cotton wad.

"Don't worry, soldier. Consider it done; I'll see you later in the ward." He battled to stave off the penetrating pain as it attacked his insides with vicious ferocity.

"Stay with me until I wake up, I er I," his confused brain was making it difficult to talk. "I think the killer is going to try and kill me because I recognised hi..."

"He's all yours!" called the anaesthetist to the doctors who were still busily studying the x-rays in the frame on the wall. Mike didn't fight sleep when it again overwhelmed him. His little angel was watching over him and nothing could go wrong.

"Ladies! This is going to be a marathon session, so be prepared to work overtime today," said a doctor.

Johannesburg - South Africa

Sitting at his desk, the man sucked deeply at the wooden shaft. The pipe had gone out a long time ago, but he didn't seem to notice it. He couldn't come to terms with failure; it wasn't in his vocabulary. He'd had one of the leading dissidents within his grasp yesterday and today the black man was an eternity away from him. His large desk was fronted by two old red leather chairs and against the opposite wall a grey filing cabinet gathered dust. Half covering the cold blue vinyl floor lay a withered grey carpet. It had never worried him very much that his office was sparse, because most of his work was carried out elsewhere. He only used the office as a base when he wasn't at one of his many secret locations. Most of the security files were kept in a special safe in the main filing room and the rest of the secrets remained guarded inside his closely cropped skull.

Reflecting on their evening's work, Dirk Lemmer made a mental note to threaten the Askaris because they had been slack and not up to their normal standard. They had disposed of the evidence and that was a plus factor as Bennie Roux wouldn't now be able to hold him to ransom. Dirk permitted himself a sly chuckle, thinking that the little fat policemen would be spitting blood by now.

"God help those working for him today," he thought. On the desk in front of him lay a police report mapping out the movements of the small plane belonging to Peter Roberts; it particularly detailed the previous day's flight plan. He pondered whether or not to try and arrest Roberts because the man had helped fugitives escape from the country; but he knew that it would be futile and would probably attract suspicion towards his activities. He filed the papers in the top drawer, where he always kept any current information; his staff knew that he was a natural hoarder. He always said, "You never know when a piece of evidence will be needed".

Dirk's attention switched as the door to his office opened and a thick set woman with dark hair entered. His secretary's clothes always looked as if they had been acquired in a local jumble sale. She was short and stocky by South African standards and had come to him straight from police training college. He had picked her personally; not for her looks but for her deadly ability and skills - she could also keep her mouth shut.

Annemarie Bezuidenhout had won the forces' self defence championships and could shoot to kill a dove in mid-flight at a hundred yards. During one of his regular training sessions at the college Annemarie had nearly killed him, even though he was a black belt in unarmed combat.

"Hello Dirk," she said, being one of the few in their building permitted to use his first name. He nodded to her and laid his pipe to rest in a large glass ashtray.

"Are there any messages?" he asked.

"Ja! Commandant Roux has called twice this morning and you have an appointment with the minister of police at the Union Buildings at two pm.

"What does he want now? Doesn't he know I have a lot to do without having to jump every time he clicks his fingers?" He lifted his pipe to signal the end of their meeting.

"Get me Roux!"

As she reached the door, Annemarie looked at Dirk with slight affection. He had made love to her in this office twice, both times at the conclusion of a difficult case. Once he had finished a case he would never reveal the details to anyone, however on those two occasions he had explained the gory details to her. She thrilled to hear about the violence and they had ended up on the tattered carpet making love. His stories were better than any sex drug to her and on each occasion she had been the one to instigate their lovemaking. She closed the door, still looking at him and wondered why he didn't allow her into his closed life; she would do anything for him and he knew it.

Dirk left his office and drove to Union Buildings, the heart and pulse of Afrikaner government. He skirted the east tower because he preferred entering through the front door rather than through the back of this magnificent building. It always impressed him that in here worked the prime minister and most of his cabinet, making plans and preparing for the future South Africa. The feeling of power generated from within this stone building gave him great satisfaction; because he was a part of it all.

One day he would be able to openly take his place here and not have to lead this clandestine existence. Massive stone columns stood, like guarding sentinels, along the impressive semi-circular frontage; which connected the two clock towers. He turned to glance backwards before approaching the main entrance; enjoying the distant view of Pretoria from this hilltop vantage point.

"Room 217 on the second floor, he's expecting you," said the khaki-clad security man seated behind the reception desk after Dirk had signed in. He could have taken the elevator but he chose to walk up the wide marble staircase. Apart from needing the exercise, he liked to study the various statues and paintings on the way up.

"Kom," beckoned the Afrikaans voice beyond the large teak door, as a secretary knocked and led the way into a large office; announcing the visitor.

"Aah! Lemmer, how are you?" said the portly man behind the desk, rising to greet his trusted security man

"Goed meneer."

For a while the two chatted comfortably in their native tongue, the security man relating the events of the week to his boss; making sure to reveal only the hard facts, without any of the sordid detail. The minister listened intently, he was the general in charge of the war against the communist threat and his duty was to the motherland; to keep it safe.

Dirk had been his personal choice. The minister didn't know of the

Askaris, nor would he have wanted to. His man was getting the job done, that's all he needed to know.

Dirk was taken aback with his superior's next remark.

"Now the reason for this meeting is I want you to take a little holiday, all at our expense. Don't worry; this is a working holiday in London."

"London! What's going on there?"

"The ANC leaders, such as Tambo, are going to be there for Christmas. We need to be there to record the fact." A broad smile creased round the minister's face as he continued

"No heroics please, the British will go mad if we try anything and we need all the allies we can get. However, we won't get a better chance to see the opposition's strength."

Dirk walked slowly down the marble staircase after he was dismissed; thinking that fate dealt strange hands. He could go and look, but couldn't touch the enemy!

It was the fifth day of the four men's vigil; working in shifts outside the ANC headquarters in London. It was a boring task, carried out in pairs; one black man to identify suspects and a white man to record all the movements to and from the building. The dossier was growing daily because there were a lot of faces familiar to them. There were also many faces that they had never seen and they religiously documented and photographed them all. It was pitch dark outside, except for the flickering shop window lights; all four were sat quietly in the Vauxhall on Christmas Eve observing the constant movements around the colourful building. Each would have preferred to be at home with their families in the sunshine; they found it difficult to come to terms with winter night's darkness starting at three thirty every afternoon.

The men switched the cameras and binoculars, which had been acquired by the embassy for them, to night vision mode. Dirk Lemmer and the old man were due to go off duty at six. The backup team had arrived a little early to pick up their nightly brief and now the four drank hot coffee together. During the afternoon all the main players had arrived and were still inside. There seemed to be a gathering of vultures taking place, thought Dirk. A young couple passed below the orange streetlamp and stopped outside the building. The man reached out and pushed the buzzer, then turned and wrapped his arms around the girl. Inwardly the security man cringed as the black man kissed the white girl long and hard; he swore silently under his breath. The old man, seated at the steering wheel, put down the camera after taking several photographs of the couple.

They waited for several hours when, eventually, the two people he had been waiting for emerged. Robert half carried half dragged another black man; who was in no fit state to walk unaided. Robbie had to combat the friendly protestations from the drunk, who wanted to return to the party.

Dirk and the grey-haired man left the Vauxhall and got into the backup Celica parked behind it. The two cars travelled through the noisy streets of London as if attached by an invisible thread. They slackened to a snail's pace outside Harrods as the road ahead was busy with night late revellers. They sped onward along Cromwell Road; Robbie's car had been allowed to stretch its lead. Dirk presumed it was on its way out of town when, without warning, the car indicated a left turn.

The old man put his foot down to the floor and the Celica sped into the Earl's Court Road. The other vehicle was nowhere in sight; Dirk screamed to the driver "Take the next left!"

The Celica cruised like a shark seeking out its prey; Dirk felt that they were here somewhere. Suddenly the old man pointed to the car they had been following; it was stopped at the side of the road. After parking, the two sat for a moment trying to familiarise themselves with the surroundings. Dirk got out and went to check and identify the number plate. The old man had the engine turning over in case it was a false alarm, keeping his eye on the white man, who quickly returned to the waiting car.

"That's it all right and guess what? That drunk is still in the car! They will come and get him or he will lead us to them when he wakes up. They are probably screwing somewhere near here," he said.

The older man leaned over to the back seat to retrieve his flask of hot coffee. "Happy Christmas, Mr Lemmer." Dirk scowled. In his mind he was running through all he knew about the comatose man in the car. George Mxenge was the head of the ANC London office. Three years previously he had caused problems in Durban with his little gang based at Cato Ridge, the Soweto of Natal. A Zulu informer told the police of his activities but they had arrested his younger brother by mistake.

George knew that when they found out it would be jail for him so he fled to Johannesburg where the ANC had an escape network set up through Botswana into Zambia and on to London. This was the same route that was used by key ANC members to get out of South Africa and on to communist training camps without being noticed by the authorities.

To help them stay in England, the ANC had persuaded impoverished Zambian Government officials to issue false student passports and documents. So Mxenge had come to London to study at the Queen Mary College on the Mile End Road; just long enough to avert suspicion. He then stopped his studies to work for the cause and after moving home several times, nobody knew of his whereabouts. He was safe unless he did something wrong and fell foul of the law.

He awoke, limbs stiff as boards from the cold. Groaning loudly he tried to move.

"A cigarette, that's what's needed," he searched his pockets.

"Keys?" he thought and realised that he must be in his car.

Dirk tensed inwardly as George stepped out of the car slowly and gingerly; the ground was slippery but his rubber soles held firm.

He locked the car and started walking towards his little basement flat. He did not notice the two shadows moving in behind him, the snow muffling their footsteps.

Staggering and lurching from side to side, he battled his way down the stairs, holding onto the railing to reach the bottom. He shook visibly as a voice above him said "Excuse me brother, can you show me the way to Earl's Court Station?" As George focused upwards, the figure slowly descended the stairs.

"What a time to get lost!" he mouthed. His head nodded back and forth as he tried to concentrate. The old man stopped at the bottom and held tightly onto the rail feigning a breathing attack.

"What's wrong?" asked George.

The old man leaned forward and said something that George couldn't make out. George moved to help him, but instead swayed against him trying to steady himself.

He looked down at the snow which was turning red

"The old man is bleeding, he must be in a bad way."

George looked up into the cold eyes of the grey bearded man

"What's happened to you, why are you bleeding?" he demanded shakily.

Suddenly he knew that the blood spilling onto the ground didn't come from the stranger. George dropped onto his knees as the white man descended the stairs, then fell forward face first into the snow.

"How warm it is," was his final thought.

"Why so quick! You should have gutted the pig and made him suffer," said Dirk.

The white man moved forward and used the sole of his foot to roll the dying man onto his back. His face now contained a hard mask of hatred.

"This will teach you to try and take over our country and bomb our people. Death begets death." Hurriedly they took the keys from the dead man's pocket and entered silently into the little flat finding one occupant asleep on the couch. He had obviously passed out from too good a night as well.

They searched drawers, cupboards and the sleeping man with such skill that nobody could tell that the place had been ransacked. Among the papers were various names and addresses of known activists and Dirk photographed the relevant documents with the miniature camera that he always carried. As the two left the building they took the dead man's valuables, after replacing the keys. The old man found a broom under the stairs and cleared their footprints behind them.

It was nearly five o'clock and still pitch dark as they set off in the direction of their hotel in Bayswater Road. They had expected to find the couple naked and asleep and were disappointed that again he had slipped through their fingers.

"He could be anywhere by now," said the old man.

"Next time for sure Mr Bloody Molefe; next time you die!" Dirk venomously spat the words out then placed his pipe in his mouth.

After watching the headquarters for four more days, they decided to pack up. Dirk Lemmer paid a courtesy call to the embassy, to hand back the borrowed equipment, before leaving for Heathrow airport.

CHAPTER FOURTEEN

'Go boldly forth with disaster, do not blame thy master'

Johannesburg - South Africa

Aabel Smit had seen to the last of his drivers and as always made sure that all the on-site equipment was loaded on board the vans before leaving the factory for the day's deliveries. He walked through the large workshop to the fever pitched zinging of a timber saw; as always the area was a scene of constant activity. He picked his way through the bustle and cheerfully greeted each person by name, firm in the knowledge he had the understanding and trust of everybody on the shop floor.

During his first hour Aabel had to make sure that all the sites had their requirements and he inspected and checked each vehicle personally before it left on its journey. Aabel had done the same routine every morning since he had begun as a dispatcher at PIP Design; quickly working his way up to become the contracts director.

It didn't take long for the owner, Raymond Morley, to realise his potential and managerial qualities. Furthermore, Aabel had a formidable command of languages and a persistent eye to detail; it wasn't long before Ray gave him a five per cent shareholding in the company.

Ray knew that he could leave the working side of the business to Aabel while he spent his time developing contacts, which suited both of them equally well. When all the vans had been despatched, he could start to relax and catch up with the day's paperwork. Everyday as he entered his office, he called through the door to Rashida to bring him his usual morning tea; he couldn't start his day without it.

From his office Aabel could keep an eye on the workmen and the main factory door without anybody knowing whether they were being watched or not. He casually flicked through his morning mail and discarded the junk with the expertise of a card dealer at a casino; tossing it into the bin beside his desk. The remainder went onto his desk in various piles. This particular morning one blue unopened envelope, posted from England and marked Private and Confidential, immediately caught his attention because he recognised the handwriting.

Rashida entered carrying an enormous mug of steaming tea. She had often remarked to him that the mug should be under the bed because of its size. She set it down in front of him and did it noisily, because he seemed to be miles away.

"Please contact Mr Miller at Standard Bank because he wants an extra extension made to the counter that is being built in the Hillbrow branch," she announced as she left the office. Both Aabel and Rashida had originally come to Johannesburg from Cape Town; they were of mixed race but scarcely knew their hybrid origin except that they were not Indian, Chinese or Malay. Interbred by white or black, they only knew they belonged to neither. In the three tier political system of apartheid, it was whites at the top, blacks at the bottom and the mixed races in the middle. Nobody but the whites were allowed to vote in South Africa, although the mixed races could own land, own businesses and generally do most things offered to the privileged white class. Blacks could not own land because they were expected to return to their homelands; the various areas tribally owned before the arrival of outsiders. The only flaw in practice was that the cities held all the big businesses and life within the homelands was dismally poor. Staying in the homelands meant no real money for the families, so blacks tried to move to the cities in droves. They knew that the reason for the hated pass laws was in order that the government could control the movement of the black tribes. Happily for Aabel and Rashida, Coloured and Asian people were not restricted to the same measure. They represented a small minority and the whites did not fear those swamping cities.

Both Aabel and Rashida spoke Afrikaans, a language that had stemmed from a mixture of Dutch, Indian, English and Xhosa. An irony not lost to these two was that their race, although looked down upon, had given birth to their country's official language. The mixed races created this bastardised language in order to be able to communicate with each other and which the whites had later commandeered as their own. Most white Afrikaners wouldn't dare accept that their mother tongue was born of dark skinned people.

Aabel sipped noisily at his tea as he extracted the letter from the blue envelope and started reading through the contents. It was an instruction from ANC Headquarters in Zambia, which had been routed via their London office. The coded message hidden in among the lines made Aabel lean far back in his swivel chair and release a long low whistle. His mind did a double take as he read it again, slowly this time to make sure that he had understood the contents correctly. He had missed nothing, he whistled again.

During the day he had to try hard to concentrate on the normal activities of the shop fitting business because the letter had thrown him out of his confident stride. He called two friends asking them to meet him that evening at the small factory in Nursery Street in Fordsburg, an older and more run down borough of Johannesburg. After all the vans had returned and loaded for the next morning, everybody left the premises; except for Aabel, who usually stayed late anyway.

He busily worked away at his desk until after seven o'clock when the front doorbell rang and he unlocked the door to Solly and Getieb

Abrahams.

The three sat in his office discussing the letter and its contents, their voices remained hushed and secretive, the brothers were also taken aback from shock. This instruction from headquarters asked them to set up a bomb, possibly in a public place to draw attention to the cause. This was to be carried out before Christmas Eve.

One of the brothers was an expert in explosives and his job brought him into daily contact with detonators and dynamite. He worked at Rand Leases Gold Mine, one of the older diggings on the Reef. For several years he had been the store man in charge of explosives used at the underground rock faces. Every week Solly stole small amounts of the lethal material; no one ever noticed the loss of these minute portions, because so much was used on a daily basis. Over several years the three had steadily built up a large stockpile, which they hid under a floor in the tool store at the back of the PIP Design building. Aabel was the only one with a key and he always made sure that he was in attendance when any tools were required.

All three became very proficient in handling the explosive materials. Driving to a quiet area on the weekends in the Highveld bush, they practised regularly by manufacturing various types of bombs. Solly primed the charges and Getieb, being a watchmaker by trade would make and fit the specially designed timers. Aabel would use different types of container to check their efficiency after exploding the devices.

Finally, after much deliberation and soul-searching, the three decided that they would place a bomb in the Carlton Centre. It was South Africa's biggest office and shopping complex; what better place for their first attack in Johannesburg.

Aabel regularly visited some of the sites that the men were

working on. So it caused no suspicion when he left the office to go to one of the shops in The Carlton Mall to carry out an inspection.

The grey building projected out of the ground like a rocket ship about to blast off. It rose up over fifty storeys high and within the two and a half hectare site, was the main office block, a hotel, an ice rink and a huge departmental store.

Aabel was only interested in the multi-storied mall with over one hundred and sixty shops below ground level. Tens of thousands of workers and visitors entered the complex every day.

He walked around the mall going from level to level. He was seeking a discreet place in which to set up the explosive charge. Security men patrolled the mall continually, on the lookout for anything suspicious; they would be a problem, so he needed to find somewhere safe.

While strolling through the south side of the mall his eyes rested on a large oblong flower arrangement against one of the main columns. His men were working inside an empty shop situated to the right of the column, getting it ready for new tenants. The flower arrangement was in a large flowerpot; the ideal place, he immediately photographed the target. The question was how to place the explosives, "from beauty comes destruction," he said to himself.

At seven o'clock that evening the doorbell rang again and the three came together in Aabel's office; he related and showed the pictures he had taken to the others of what he had seen that day. He carefully explained the problem of moving the flowers. Solly instantly had an answer; his nephew Paul worked for the florists contracted to maintain the vast jungle of greenery and flowers in the mall and he was sympathetic to their cause.

Two nights later the three entered the empty shop after they had shown the security man on duty their passes, which had been arranged by Aabel. His two friends were dressed in workmen's overalls as they pretended to work in the empty site. A security man hovered around in the passageway outside, mainly because the mall wasn't very busy and he didn't have much to do. Paul Abrahams walked past the shop twice awaiting the signal from his uncle. The security man barred their way and Aabel knew that it had to be done that night because there wouldn't be a second chance.

He left the shop and started talking to the security man, trying to find a way around the problem; he needed to get him to move. The man complained incessantly about the things people got up to and how he had to sometimes take the law into his own hands; Aabel soon realised that the man suffered from an inferiority complex.

Luck suddenly smiled down upon them when, without warning, four youths started chasing each other through the corridors of the mall. They were jostling each other, shouting and screaming in a jovial tag game; bumping into the few bystanders as they ran.

The guard gave chase and Paul and Aabel hurriedly lifted several pots within the large flower stand and the other two men from the empty shop quickly walked towards the arrangement. Solly extracted two forty five pound bombs from a duffle bag and placed them in the cavity below the pots while Getieb leaned over and set the two clocks attached to it. Aabel kept guard watching out for the security man's return while Paul replaced the pots and quickly rearranged the flowers. They finished the whole exercise in less than four minutes, one minute longer than practised the night before.

When the security man returned from remonstrating with the over zealous youngsters, he found Aabel busily locking the shop as though they had finished their work for the night.

The explosion had been designed to maim and kill innocent bystanders. It didn't quite work out that way as, fortunately, nobody was killed because coincidence intervened.

A security man was grappling with a handbag snatcher about fifty yards along the corridor from where the lethal parcel had been placed. There was a lot of shouting and everybody wanted to see what was going on. A crowd collected in the passageway and this had drawn even more onlookers towards the swelling group. Sixteen people were slightly injured by the flying glass from the shop fronts as the explosion rocked the mall.

Raymond Morley called Aabel into his office that afternoon and told them to get ready to work all the hours God gave them.

"There's been a bomb at the Carlton Centre and we have to replace all the shop fronts with shatterproof glass. We'll make a fortune out of this."

Aabel smiled at his white partner, although he was upset that nobody had been killed. "From destruction, comes beauty," he commented. The men laughed because only the coloured man knew the real meaning of his disguised statement.

The ANC took full credit for the action and the world silently applauded as some applauded the IRA for bombings carried out in England. It seemed to the innocent bystanders involved in the explosion that they were the only ones to feel the total injustice of the war being waged in South Africa.

CHAPTER FIFTEEN

'The unknown fear from within, groan and quake sharply'

London - England

As he rounded the corner from Cromwell Road and into Earl's Court Road, Robbie received the strangest sensation which sent small shock waves up and down his spine. On two previous occasions he had had this strange sixth sense feeling - like a hunted animal. First when bitten by a puff adder and secondly when Ian was about to be attacked by a leopard. His mother told him that he was blessed with her vision.

He immediately turned left into a small winding side street behind George's flat, which fronted onto Cromwell Road.

"What say we go back home tonight? I don't feel like being around when he comes-to," he said to Joan pointing towards his comatose backseat companion.

"Lovely! Then we can relax tomorrow. I want to make love to you all weekend."

Robert parked the car and they both tried to get their passenger out of the back but he refused to wake up. He was in such a drunken stupor that they had to give up trying; Robbie placed the keys in George's pocket before locking the doors from the inside and leaving him to sleep it off.

Joan felt in total command of her feelings for this new man in her life, for the very first time since their initial encounter, he had told her how much he had enjoyed the evening. He wanted her to think it was because of her; but it was really because the ANC command had informed him that his proposed plan had been given the personal blessing of Nelson Mandela, their supreme commander himself. When they reached home they lay quietly on their bed for a long while, watching the snow falling softly outside; lit up by an orange street light. It was Christmas and what a perfect way to end a day, Robbie thought.

A shrill ring from the telephone woke them simultaneously and Joan moaned as she fumbled for the receiver.

"Yes!" she barked, irritated that someone would call them this early on Christmas morning. Is nothing sacred, she thought irritably?

"It's for you," She pushed the receiver into Robbie's hand.

"Don't your friends ever sleep?"

She heard him talking in his own language as she rolled over and tried to get back to sleep. She soon turned back again though as she didn't have to know the language to understand grief when she heard it. Robbie handed her the phone, which she replaced in its cradle. She lay back against the headboard looking at him; he was panting strangely in short sharp breaths.

"What is it!" she demanded, feeling the grief pouring out of her lover.

"That was Titus, George's flatmate. He said George was found dead on the stairs of the apartment this morning. Someone stole his money and knifed him to death."

She cradled him like a baby, slowly rocking him back and forth, allowing him to share his heartfelt grief at the loss of his friend. This was the first time in his life that Robbie had accepted somebody else to share anything like this with him. He realised that his instinct had been correct and that the hunted feeling from last night was real and those killers were out there looking for him. He now regretted not having gone to Austria with Mike; if he had, then maybe George would still be alive. The two lay on the bed for a long time, comforting each other.

Somehow, he couldn't accept that their drunken friend was now in the morgue, his happy life dramatically snatched away during the night by some unknown marauder. His brain was working overtime, if the murderers weren't simply thieves they were probably security men, then he had been their intended target. He wondered if they knew his whereabouts or whether George had told them anything before his demise: He got up and went to the window.

Being careful not to be seen from outside, he cautiously looked out from behind the curtains, his early hunter trained eye searched the surrounding area, seeking out any sign of something amiss.

"Are you out there waiting?" he questioned, as his eyes checked every car, building and blade of grass that protruded from the white snow-covered surface. It was Christmas morning, nothing stirred. The little hamlet was fast asleep and if anybody was out there, he couldn't see them. They were either very good or weren't there at all; he wasn't sure. He couldn't feel any sense of danger whatsoever.

Joan watched Robbie's cautious cat-like movements again, not standing in front of the window but peering through it from the side; because he didn't want to be seen naked by the neighbours. She smiled at his buttocks, shining like a pair of freshly roasted coffee beans against the white net backdrop.

"What a magnificent body," she whispered audibly.

Turning away from the window he glared at her with the same look that he had when they first made love; she didn't move a muscle.

Robert turned back to the view outside; everything was as it should be. No tyre or foot marks on the blanketed road, covered with a light flurry of snow. Even though the heating was on and the room was reasonably warm, a cold chill ran through his body. He returned to bed and she heard him sigh deeply as he relaxed; his eyes had returned to normal. Slowly stretching out she started teasing him, he felt her sharp fingernails starting at the head and working down toward his scrotum. He needed to make love to her but pretended to remain indifferent; however, his manhood had a mind of its own as it disobeyed his commanding brain. He felt movement on the bed and expected to feel her settle down on him, but instead he felt and heard something strange being pushed onto it; it felt like a paper condom.

"Happy Christmas my darling!" she shouted loudly.

He opened his eyes and saw his proud shaft now wrapped in Christmas paper and tied around with a giant red satin bow. He screamed with laughter his fears momentarily forgotten as tears flooded down Robert's cheeks, it took him several minutes to finally regain some form of composure. Carefully undoing the red bow she unwrapped the brightly coloured Christmas paper and showed him a piece of plain paper inside

"Look at it. It's something you've always wanted." His eyes scanned the white sheet until realisation struck him like a hammer blow. He pulled himself up the bed to get a better view of the valuable document in his hands

"Where the hell did you get this?"

"Did I do well?" He leaned over and kissed her upturned forehead. In front of him was a complete contact list for the Arab Liberation

Front including addresses and telephone numbers for their worldwide network.

"You have saved me months, maybe even years of work," he said, unbelievingly, "But where did you get it?"

"Don't worry there'll be more." His estimation of Joan's capabilities had suddenly soared to a different level; this present was her bonding gift to him. Robert carefully placed the paper down on the bedside table, then moved down the bed and slid his hand between her damp thighs. In their exhaustive lovemaking he tried to convey the immense gratitude that he felt for her; she gladly accepted everything with pleasure.

Later that morning the two eased their way into the lounge to open the presents gathered under the small fir tree. Because of family gifts her pile was understandably much larger than his; but, unknown to each other, the two had been buying small gifts throughout December. These were placed in bulging red Christmas stockings that hung over the mock gas fireplace. They giggled, squealed and laughed like children as each present was carefully extracted from its red womb and opened to reveal its contents. Mike and Sharon had left a host of larger presents for both of them, Mike having acquired Robert the newest computer, printer together with several software programmes and games. Each piece had been lovingly wrapped and it seemed to take forever to get through the unwrapping procedure of the pile of packages. It was a present that Robbie hadn't expected and he enjoyed putting it all together.

When the telephone in the hall rang, Robert quickly stopped what he was doing while Joan answered the call. He was relieved when she laughed happily at the caller.

"And a Happy Christmas to you as well; how are you both getting on? Haven't broken any bones yet, I hope?"

Robbie raced upstairs two steps at a time and picked up the bedside telephone extension.

"Hi!" he shouted down the line almost deafening Joan. "Happy Christmas and thanks for the present, it's fantastic."

"Hi Robbie, how are you?" came Mike's clear voice through the receiver. At that moment Robbie longed to just see his lifelong friend, his voice sounding as if he was talking from the next room.

"When are you two coming back, we're missing you?"

"We'll be back on the British Airways flight arriving at six in the afternoon on the twenty ninth. Could you collect us from the airport?"

When Robert replaced the receiver, he realised just how much Mike really meant to him. The white family treated him better than his own mother. Remorse suddenly set in and he cried softly

"Oh Mamie! I miss you, please forgive me, I'm still your only blood son."

Joan took Robbie for Christmas lunch to Biscuit's Carvery in Oxford. It was a sumptuous affair with all the trimmings, hats, crackers and everything. They had both enjoyed the lunch but the tragedy of George's death overshadowed them. Robert watched the movements of everybody, deeply seeking some clue as to why he felt somebody was following him. Nothing was amiss; people were simply enjoying their Christmas lunch. The next four days passed uneventfully and Robbie started to convince himself that the feeling had been a figment of his imagination. He thought about the security men from South Africa; if George had said anything to them they would have shown themselves by now. When George Mxenge was buried, Robert did not attend the funeral; he offered his apologies but didn't say why, just in case his suspicions were justified.

Joan and Robert set off from her little house at four thirty on the twenty ninth as arranged and bound for Heathrow. They drove carefully and slowly through the heavy fog, with visibility down to less than fifty yards and the roads were like an ice rink. Traffic was down to a crawl, not helped by a multiple pile up on the motorway. Fortunately when the accident happened ahead of them they weren't very far behind it, so they managed to get by before a massive queue had built up. As the little brown car picked its way through the motorway debris they were appalled to see other drivers passing them at high speed. It represented a cocktail for disaster as they tried to get away from the collision as quickly and safely as possible.

With great relief they eventually moved off the motorway and soon passed the sign welcoming them to Heathrow Airport. The only parking space available was on the open-topped floor at the very top of the multi-storey car park. Locking their car they made their way towards the lift that would take them down to the first floor arrivals hall. The doors were about to close when Robbie shouted for them to hold the lift as he didn't fancy the thought of waiting in the cold until it returned. Someone in the lift heard his shout and the doors reopened, the lift was filled to capacity but the two gently squeezed their way in. Robbie faced the doors as Joan was squashed in beside him, her hand locked into his gloves for warmth. Suddenly and without warning that hunted feeling struck him again; the hairs on the nape of his neck bristled, his muscles tensed, his brain suddenly became an extension of his sixth sense.

He turned to find where this feeling was coming from, but all he could see was a family of Indians. They were all bubbling excitedly, six adults and about fourteen children of varying ages. Three teenage girls were standing abreast directly behind the couple, they spread across the full width of the lift. Each girl had obviously been left in control of an overdressed infant in the three prams which pushed tightly against the couple's legs.

Robbie guessed that they were here to meet someone and not going to be travelling. Then his searching gaze suddenly picked out the misty blue eyes of a white man at the back of the lift. He had not realised that the man was standing in the far corner and was partially obscured behind the men of the lively Indian family. All that he could see was the closely cropped head and the ice cold eyes of the man's stare.

"That's the one"

Robbie instinctively knew where the feeling of evil was coming from; he was looking straight at it. His bush sixth sense worked overtime, he had never seen the man before but knew that this was the hunter and that some fate had placed them in the same arena. Next to the white man and virtually hidden from view, Robbie realised another person was crouched behind the tallest Indian.

Dirk Lemmer had met his companion, as arranged, outside Piccadilly Tube Station on the corner of Regent Street.

"Bloody coolies, they're everywhere in this god forsaken hole," he said quietly to the old man as they were pushed to the back of the lift. When two more young people entered, he couldn't believe his eyes; here he was stuck behind this family and unable to move, whilst only feet away was the enemy.

"Maybe third time lucky," he thought to himself. Neither of them had any weapons, because they had to clear through British security to board the plane. It didn't take long to figure out that he would have to use his bare hands if he could get this one alone. Looking at his watch he gauged that they still had time before their flight to see to this troublemaker. The lift stopped and he saw Molefe pull at his white trollop's hand with great force, he saw them running towards the safety of the main building along the overhead passageway and he was still stuck at the back of the lift. The two could move quickly because they weren't handicapped by the weight of any luggage and youth was on their side. They were out of sight before Dirk Lemmer had managed to force his way past the Indian family.

"Why are we running?" puffed Joan as they crossed the road.

"Just do as I tell you, we're in danger and I'm not going to end up like George!" Her legs could not carry her as fast as his could, he didn't slacken his pace until they passed through the doors of Terminal One. He knew they had to find somewhere public yet out of sight. Robert's eyes searched frantically around the crowded building with its unfamiliar territory. Knowing the rules of the game, any animal caught in open ground away from its lair was always an easy target. Open ground meant death; he either had to find a substitute lair or try to camouflage themselves amongst the crowd - while still being able to keep an eye on the hunter.

CHAPTER SIXTEEN

'Fortune and Hunters gain, is lost in empty flight'

Pretoria - South Africa

"This man is very lucky to be alive," the masked doctor said. They were examining the X-rays mounted on the glowing blue light frame on the wall, the black and grey negatives showed the extent of damage to the recumbent body on the operating table.

"The rib cage has been hit by a fast travelling missile; internal damage has caused extensive haemorrhaging, look at the way these two ribs have broken." Jay was still hovering in the background, looking at the pictures over the three men's shoulders. She understood perfectly what was being discussed, her charge had three broken ribs; one of them, situated directly over the heart, was causing the consternation. The two doctors decided to operate on the ribcage first. It didn't take a genius to see that one of the shattered ribs was poised like a sharp scalpel, ready to plunge into the overworked heart. This had to be the luckiest man at the accident Jay decided, as she knew that the missile had been a heavy chunk of masonry that had bowled him over, onto his back, before the main blast had reached him. Luckily for him, this had prevented first degree burning or high intensity shrapnel damage to his body. The searing heat and the blast had been propelled outwards and upwards from its epicentre and had not reached the victim. Others had not been so lucky, projectiles from the blast had torn them apart and the searing heat had cooked and singed their bodies. Due to the masonry pinning him down he had been unable to sit up; otherwise, the rib would have punctured his heart. Luckily too, he had passed out when he was admitted into casualty and the hospital staff had not wanted to turn him over.

"You are one lucky beggar." She whispered softly.

His burns were not very severe, although at first glance they had not been sure and nobody wanted to touch his skin for fear of aggravating the burn area on the front of his body. Faced with these facts, the radiographer decided against turning him over to complete the X-ray procedure. Instead she had manoeuvred the lens around his body and took pictures from various angles. The vital work to save him had not yet started and the doctors were still considering their options.

One slight slip, or pressure in the wrong place from them, would certainly mean instant death. They needed to know exactly what they could or could not touch before entering the broken body.

Jay turned away from the pictures and looked towards him. He had put up a good fight and the gods were smiling on him; she hoped they would be smiling kindly on the two surgeons. The other problem was that his breathing was erratic; Jay gave him no better odds than thirty-seventy of making it through the operation: By morning he might be in the morgue.

"That would be a total waste." she thought bitterly.

St Anton - Austria

The cousins entered the hotel feeling tired yet comfortably relaxed; it had been a superb final day. The sun was high in the heavens and a crisp blue sky formed a breathtaking backdrop to the white background, when the two flowed off the top of the steep embankment for the last time.

Mike desperately wanted to attempt powder skiing as he had now mastered the pistes, which had been flattened by the growling red snowmobiles. In order to reach the untouched virgin snow meant leaving the marked trails, Sharon had also felt confident enough to tackle the powder. The two hurtled down the slope at breakneck speed, Mike in the lead; they had both become reasonable skiers in the week. Further down the mountain Mike suddenly turned left, off the flattened piste and entered the fresh powder snow that had fallen during the night. Instead of placing his full weight on the back of the skies, he tried to ski normally by leaning forward to centralise his balance. The weight of snow above his unsighted skis prevented him from turning; instead he rocketed straight towards a large protruding boulder. He had no choice, rather than be dashed against the onrushing grey sentinel; he dived sideways into the deep snow.

"Mike!" Sharon was in two minds as she followed Mike into the thick snow, the moment she entered the powder field she took fright and decided to sit down; but she couldn't guide her skis, they weren't responding to her any longer. To her surprise the curved tips rose upwards through the snow, emerging like two miniature submarines breaking through the surface of a white wave and she found herself back in control again. She looked up just in time to see Mike hurtling towards a large grey rock and then a miniature snowstorm erupted around the tumbling body. Mike bounced and then disappeared below the surface. She saw the two planks above the white surface and was thankful that the skis had broken free of Mike's boots knowing that if they hadn't he surely would have broken a leg.

"Are you all right?"

She drew level with the emerging red, white and black snowman he didn't answer her as he simply flopped backwards into the deep snow laughing uncontrollably. She stopped and sat down awkwardly; her skies sank deeply below the white snow as she tried to untangle herself from her poles. Mike came bounding towards her and grabbing her around the waist, they both tumbled backward.

The two were covered from head to toe in white ice and snow; laughing uncontrollably they hugged each other as they sank deeper into the feathery surface. It took them a while to get back onto track but they finally returned to the Bergheim Hotel for the last time, feeling a bit sad that their holiday had reached the end. Back in their room, they quickly stripped and plunged into the shower together, both bodies ice cold to the touch. The hot water hit their bodies and stung life back into the soft flesh she teasingly soaped her lover's back, letting her hands dwindle enticingly between his legs before starting the same procedure to the front of his sinuous body. By the time she had completed the agonisingly slow ritual, he was rampant. He took over, slowly but seductively foaming every particle of her long body and they made love standing up in the shower.

The aircraft circled above England in the stack awaiting its turn to make its final approach over Heathrow. Light breezes tugged and blew at the fog. All of them had to wait their turn until Heathrow cleared. At last the steel blue and white bird was given permission to land, it banked sharply over London making its final approach. When the aircraft landed Michael looked at his watch; they were nearly an hour late. The small group sluggishly made its way through the passport area into the baggage hall to collect their luggage before passing through the arrivals door.

They searched the sea of faces looking for Robbie and Joan but they were nowhere to be seen.

Sharon looked at Mike "Maybe they're upstairs," she said hopefully.

"Yeah, more likely they got tired of waiting and went home. You stay here with the luggage and I'll go and see if I can find them; if they turn up, stay here." He moved away, leaving her seated on one of the long blue seats. He couldn't find them on the ground floor, though he walked through the area twice to make sure.

"Where the hell are you Robbie? I'm knackered and just want to get home," he muttered.

The fog had caused chaos to the scheduled flights and there were thousands of travellers and well wishers mingling around on the upper floor. Mike looked at the hoard of people and realised that he was looking for a needle in a haystack.

"Oh no!" he sighed "you could be anywhere."

He stood still for a while trying to gather his thoughts. Sanity told him to collect his girlfriend and take a taxi home; but an inner feeling urged him to continue looking for his friends.

CHAPTER SEVENTEEN

'A hunter takes flight, to live for another day's fight'

London - England

As children, they would be woken in the early hours of the morning by their father. Dark and bitterly cold with white Highveld frost covering the brown bush - after a quick hot breakfast - the party would leave in convoy heading towards the Magaliesburg Mountains. The mood always grew in intensity as they neared the killing fields.

Dirk's mood was the same today, he was heading for a different killing field except that this time the hunted could fight back and he wouldn't be able to destroy a life at long range. During those early days the party would spend long periods searching for the sacrificial beasts; sometimes hours went by before they sighted a herd. This had always been the moment that he had enjoyed most; his adrenalin count would soar as he anticipated the final result of his handiwork. Then, as now, the party would skilfully skirt around the unsuspecting prey until they had secured the best position of attack, before pouncing and destroying the lives of the animals. The finest site was always obtained by stealthily gaining ground towards the herd and not alerting them; leaving them unaware of their intended fate.

Several golden rules were learnt from those boyhood hunting trips, skills such as always being upwind, trying to secure a clear view and getting as close as possible to the prey before attempting a kill. Destroying a life had never been part of the excitement; that was simply the reward for his skilful stalking prowess. The same approach and attitude had always been applied to his work, these same rules had worked on humans as well as they did on animals; his conquests were always carried out when the prey was least expecting it and their defences were down.

They strode across the road and into the departure hall; the place was alive with stranded passengers and he walked ahead of the older man. He made his way to one of the many check-in counters; his flight to South Africa was due to leave at seven forty. He checked his watch; they still had slightly more than two hours in hand. His companion had gone to another counter as he had instructed, they wouldn't be looking for a harmless old man.

The old man left the check-in counter, turned left across the hall and walked towards the coffee shop at the other end of the crowded building. Even though his frame seemed old, his brown eyes were keen as they searched every black face trying to locate the two fugitives.

The white African security man showed his boarding pass to the guard at the entrance of the departure lounge and quickly walked through the archway out of sight behind the entry screens. He put his brown carry-all on the floor and started rummaging through it before he had reached the security desk; he gave the appearance of seeming to have forgotten something. Knowing the full workings of an airport's security, he knew that he would still able to exit the departure lounge area at this point. Nobody paid much notice, he was simply another passenger, the carefully planned ploy wouldn't draw any attention to him. He played for time.

Robbie entered the building with Joan; he had to gain higher ground unnoticed and be in position before the white man arrived in the building. Looking around, he spotted the bar and restaurant on the mezzanine floor across the hall a likely vantage point.

"Come on," he shouted at the young girl, trying to keep up behind him.

The two walked quickly towards the mezzanine bar which seemed to take an eternity then, just as they approached the open wooden stairway, Robbie decided against this position; it didn't feel as secure as he first thought. The time taken for them to cross the large hall might allow their followers to spot them; so he turned to the left and started climbing the stairway to the offices situated above the restaurant. These stairs were enclosed in concrete, not open like the others; they felt a lot safer.

Robbie also tried to think of what animals in the wild would do. Their best protection would be to remain hidden yet be fully aware of the other movements. This meant that his first thought to gain height was the correct thing to do; especially with all these passengers milling about. When they reached the landing and saw the human ocean moving around the enormous hall below them, he was satisfied for the moment with his decision. Robbie pointed to the top step

"Sit there, until I come back," he ordered Joan.

"What's going on?"

"I think we're being followed, possibly by the man who stabbed George."

"What!"

"We're safe here for the moment, just trust me." He placed his hands on her shoulders, pushing her gently into a sitting position on the top step. She looked into his face; those hooded eyes had appeared again. She sat down, placing herself in his care, not knowing what was going on except that her safety depended on him. Robbie moved to the beginning of a long open balustrade walkway, the right side opened to the main hall and on the left the narrow corridor led to a series of airline offices.

"Not the best hideout," he thought; the corridor ended against the far wall, so there was no means of escape from this position. His prime objective now was to locate the pursuer, or pursuers, from this vantage point. From here, he could survey the entire hall; his keen eyes searching the hundreds of people on the concourse below. He knew that he was not entirely hidden from view and eventually he would have to expose his position if he wanted to look towards the coffee shop at the other end of the hall.

Suddenly Robbie spotted the man; he was wearing a light brown mohair coat, a brown hold-all slung over his shoulder with a matching suitcase following him like an obedient pet. The man's closely cropped hair had betrayed him; it was unmissable in the sea of people below.

The tingling feeling was unmistakable as the immense power of evil was reflected by this white man; yet Robbie had never seen him before. Had he inherited his mother's intuition or was this simply unprovoked fear, caused by the two recent deaths? What worried him most was that the man didn't appear to be searching for him; on the contrary, his walk had an element of purpose to it as he crossed the open space.

He watched carefully, seeking any telltale signs that the man was looking for him, there weren't any. After he reached the check-in desk, where he spent a few short minutes, the man headed towards the departure lounge. Robbie felt uncertain and he questioned his feelings once again; was this simply his imagination playing tricks?

Robbie was really bewildered as the man quickly picked his way through the throng of people, not even stopping to look around; he edged forward, up against the balustrade, to make sure that he actually entered the departure hall. He watched as the white man showed his ticket and then disappeared from sight. He couldn't understand it, yet the feeling was still there that they weren't out of danger. Not quite sure what he should do next he leaned against the railing in full sight of those below who cared to.look upwards. Robbie remained there for some time, just in case the man emerged back into the hall, his eyes continually flicked over the heaving mass, still searching through the crowd.

The old man walked around the coffee shop area, which was packed with customers trying to obtain refreshments for the long waits ahead, there were as many black faces as there were white. This was a cosmopolitan meeting place, his trained eye swept across the faces as he unobtrusively moved through the crowded hall. He noticed a toilet situated at the back of the seating area and made his away across towards it.

So many people he thought and even if we find them there would be too many bystanders. It would be better to wait outside in the car park for them, whatever Dirk Lemmer said. Returning from the toilet he passed a stairwell on his way back into the main hall and wondered where it led; so he moved towards it, trying to decide what to do next. The enclosed stairwell went up to airline offices and down to the arrivals hall. He went down, it being the easier option for a man of his years; on the mezzanine floor he saw the left luggage counter.

He considered handing his heavy hold-all in for safekeeping and then decided not to, because it was full of Christmas presents for his family. While he had been off duty in London he had hunted for unusual gifts, mainly toys that were unobtainable in South Africa. Reaching the ground floor he was amazed to see how packed it was with people awaiting friends, looking just like an enormous rugby scrum.

The old man was bumped and jostled as he tried to search through the arrivals area, his age was starting to catch up with him and he was tired, he felt helpless. No sooner had he examined a face when it was replaced in an ever moving wash; his chances of spotting the couple were very remote. The indicator boards flashed late arrival markers next to every flight due in that afternoon. He checked his own flight and surprisingly it was still on time, with no delay, all he now wished was that time would pass away, because at this moment all he wanted was to get home.

Heading back, he walked toward the enclosed stairwell, the same one that he had descended twenty minutes ago; he decided to take the lift to the top floor instead, to start his long searching sweep again.

Robbie waited for over fifteen minutes on the top stair with Joan, eventually the two walked down to the mezzanine floor; but Robbie wasn't comfortable as he went to the balcony edge and once again scanned through the heaving flow of bodies below. That's when he saw him; somehow the man in the mohair brown coat had doubled back and was walking through the doors in the direction of the parking garage. "There he is!" he said quietly to Joan.

The two watched the man exit through the doors and disappear from view for a short while as various airline booths blocked their line of sight. Nobody normally stalked around in that manner, Robbie now knew for certain that they were being hunted by this man. Then the man reappeared heading hastily toward the car park.

"We're safe for the moment," he told the scared girl by his side, but he knew that the trap was going to be set in there. Robbie wondered how he could reach the car; he would have to come up with a plan before very long.

"You go and meet Mike and Sharon; they'll be looking out for us.

I'll stay here and keep watch. Just the same, try to stay hidden, until they come through." He pushed Joan gently forward as she wrapped a scarf around her mouth in an effort to hide her face.

"Where will we meet you?" she asked.

"See the bench in that alcove between those two side doors in the corner of the building; go there, I'll be able to see you and I'll also be able to tell whether anybody is watching or following you. If it's all clear I'll approach you; but I must first make a plan to get away unseen."

Joan went to the ground floor and looked up at the indicator board over the exit. Their plane was late and it would be at least an hour before Mike and Sharon cleared customs. She turned around and realised that she was vulnerable where she was, so she circled the floor where Robbie could see her. She looked upwards and he beckoned to her; moving slowly she returned to Robbie to tell him of the problem. He was furious, this was an unwanted complication. He hadn't reckoned on the flight being delayed; the two stayed where they were, not many people appeared on this stairway as most of them seemed to be using the open stairs on the opposite side of the hall.

Robbie considered going back to the top where they had been before but then discarded the idea. From this position he could see most of the arrivals hall and he could also maintain his vigil of the walkway exit. If they moved, there was a possibility the pursuer might slip back unnoticed and he didn't want to take the chance. Time passed quickly when suddenly Robbie pointed,

"There's Mike. Their flight must have come in earlier."

They saw Mike slowly picking his way toward the opposite stairway, leading up to the departures hall, Robbie quickly spotted that he was walking with a pronounced limp.

"You go and fetch him." Robbie said to Joan, "take these stairs, then meet me as arranged." Joan hurriedly made her way to where she had seen Mike standing against the railing at the opposite end and raced across to him.

The old man was descending those same open stairs going down to the arrivals hall as Joan reached Mike and hugged him. She started talking excitedly, gesticulating with quick arm movements, the old man couldn't hear what they were saying. He carefully followed them down into the hall where they met a tall, tanned young girl. He could see by their expressions that something was wrong with the excitement of their meeting up quickly soured. The three made their way back towards him as he pretended to be looking at the screens above, they passed and he watched them reach a bench in a corner. Seating themselves there, as they did, meant he couldn't get any nearer; as he was standing opposite the local flight baggage carousel. The short girl started talking again and the others looked dumbstruck, as if they couldn't quite grasp the meaning of what she was telling them. For a while the old man watched them, whilst looking around in the hope of spotting Robert Molefe. Then, as if appearing from the shadows, he was suddenly with them. The four quickly gathered their luggage and went up the stairway out of the doorway at the top. The old man cursed the ageing process that had allowed his quarry to arrive undetected.

Dirk saw them coming, he was stationed against the wall and could see everybody entering the walkway. Under his breath he swore softly; there were four of them now, which would make his task more difficult.

He gripped tightly onto the screwdriver in his coat pocket; it was as fine a killing tool as any sharp knife and he could use it to good affect at close quarters. He walked towards the lift, timing his pace carefully to arrive marginally ahead of the four who had almost reached the end of the tunnel. He could also see the old man following behind them. Dirk reached the lift and pushed the button, he wanted to get in behind the two men. His man in front would complete a pincer movement. He was totally caught by surprise as the old man rounded the corner, immediately followed by that damned Indian family and their intended prey wasn't there; his eyes blazed toward the old black man.

"They'll be here in a second," the old man whispered.

From his balustrade vantage point Robbie had spotted the grey haired black man watching Joan greet Mike and Sharon. He was taking more interest in her movements than was necessary; he deduced that this was the accomplice of the man in the mohair coat. Robbie believed that the four of them together would be safe and able to reach the car. At the pay counter they encountered the same Indian family that had been in the lift with them except now there was the addition of an old man being fussed over; he was obviously their reason for being at the airport. As they walked and reached the end of the tunnel Robbie saw the mohair-coated man moving towards the lift and also saw the old man moving in behind them. He now knew the trap was set.

He was going to use the cover of the Indians once again and they slowed their pace until the family was right on their heels. He bumped Mike, a prearranged signal and when Dirk disappeared round the corner to the lift Robbie suddenly stopped and bent down to tie the laces of his trainers.

All four stopped and moved against the wall. The old man was taken by surprise and became confused by this sudden turn of events; he couldn't stop now as they were all facing him - he kept on walking.

The Indian family, battling with baby carriages and a luggage trolley, passed them. "Keep them between the old man and us," urged Mike; both girls were as nervous as the men. They knew what Mike and Robbie's plan entailed and trusted the two men to see them through it all. After the Indian procession had passed, the four gathered up the cases and turned into the stairwell, racing as hard as they could go to the top floor. Puffing and panting they burst out through the door and onto the slippery surface; they reached the car and Robert opened the back and then the two side doors. The luggage was bundled in as Mike took the steering wheel; the girls got into the back seat. As they drove towards the exit the white man emerged from the stairwell. They were safe, cheering and laughing with relief as the vehicle took them away from the danger.

As he passed through the door, Dirk knew that they had beaten him again, the brown Honda passed him on its way to the exit ramp; the four youngsters didn't even look his way. They had known he was there and like the animals of his youth, had bolted. He wouldn't have his kill today.

The old man came out of the lift closely followed by the Indian family, tumbling out in a never ending stream.

"Bloody coolies! They screwed us up." Dirk nodded towards the old man

"I'll get that bastard! Even if it takes forever and it'll give me the greatest pleasure to watch that kaffir die." The old man looked down sheepishly at the concrete floor. He knew that Dirk blamed him for this fiasco. They returned to the terminal, both wrapped in their own thoughts. The South African flight left London on time.

CHAPTER EIGHTEEN

'With deep precise meaning, antiquity must be taught'

<u>St Johann - Austria</u>

For several weeks all four moved around very cautiously checking each other's movements to make sure that they weren't being followed. The experience at the airport had scared them witless and only after the incident did Mike tell Robbie of the warning given to him by Peter Roberts.

He apologised and explained that he thought it had been irrelevant to tell him at the time, as they were in no real danger being this distance from South Africa. As life got into its hurly burly normal routine once again, the group began to relax.

Mike and Sharon once again became engrossed with the titled and rich attending every society function possible. Mike became a regular player in the Oxford rugby team and twice more sculled for his university in the annual Oxford and Cambridge boat race on the Thames. Because of his sporting prowess he was well known to most students and in constant demand, as he and Sharon carefully climbed the social ladder. Uppermost in both their minds were the link with moneyed people from around the world; essential contacts for their business. They began to make lists of the have's verses the have not; anybody with access to money was placed on the have's list and these people were carefully cultivated: Bankers, financial institutions, large manufacturing organisations, governmental departments and students with political contacts were carefully nurtured with delicate precision.

They gathered as much information as they could on each person, such as taking photographs of them at parties whilst they were taking drugs or smoking pot; always done in the name of fun. The two made sure that they were never shown in the photographs and these lists ended up in files for later use.

Sharon's little house was known far and wide, becoming notorious for its fantastic parties as the selected elite arrived to be greeted with gross amounts of food and drink. The local villagers frowned on the goings on each weekend, although turning a blind eye to it all. It was not unusual during some of these parties for guests to be found running unclothed around the common and on more than one occasion the police arrived to warn the students. By the following morning though, some diplomat or government minister had smoothed things over and charges were never pressed. The village was inhabited by a few old families and the balance of small houses were filled by rich young people from London. Most of them had open invitations to the parties, so weren't about to complain to anybody. The influence of these people was an added bonus and many a useful contact was made there. What nobody realised was that at all of these events video recordings were being made throughout the house, especially in the bedrooms.

Sharon had had the system reinstalled to her specifications when she had the house renovated. At first the recordings were used for her amusement; but later they were used for reference purposes or a study project before being carefully filed away. Their information records grew; Mike and Sharon soon realised what potential damage could be caused if they released these recordings so they kept them secret - not even Robbie knew of their existence.

As soon as Sharon logged all the information into her computer the hard copies were locked away in a bank security box. They both knew that in time they would profit from these tapes; parents of importance around the world took immeasurable precautions to protect their secrets but forgot that their offspring knew much more then they realised. Once these youngsters had had too much to drink or smoke, they would boast about their parents without realising that their admissions were being recorded. Mike and Sharon's power grew every time their friends opened their mouths, although they didn't appreciate the full potential of it yet.

During this period Robbie remained in the background, only occasionally going to functions when Mike insisted; but otherwise he spent time at the student's union headquarters. He tried to stay away from the ANC in London, contacting them only by telephone; he wasn't prepared to push himself into the limelight just to be shot at. It was agreed with the ANC leadership that until he had completed his studies he would control the contact with them on his terms; feeling he could safely achieve much more this way. To prove his case he used the list given to him by Joan until finally he was allowed to meet John Reilly; a Sinn Fein leader of the political wing of the IRA. It took nearly eleven months of negotiation before they met to discuss the acquisition of arms for their struggle in South Africa.

Robbie explained his position within the ANC; as provincial representative and head of the youth military wing he was empowered to make decisions on their behalf. He explained that the ANC wanted to create unrest in South Africa by creating civil disobedience and attacking the government to stretch their resources to the limit.

Members of the IRA met him and decided to take talks further once they were absolutely sure that Robbie was genuine. Nothing in life is free and in return he had to help the IRA by sending them lists of all registered students, together with addresses and occupations of their parents. They were looking to find military or government contacts.

Robbie didn't want to lose his friendship with Mike and when they were alone together he would often pour out his personal problems and how he yearned to get back to South Africa. A particular grief concerned his mother; he would do anything to gain her respect again. Mike undertook to become Robbie's intermediary and included a letter for Mabel when writing home. He never received any reply from her but kept writing in the hope that one day she would forgive her son for his beliefs. Neither Robbie nor Joan told the other two of their ongoing activities for the ANC, or at the students union, leaving them to think that all that was far behind them.

Mike and Sharon had so enjoyed their skiing trip that they convinced their friends to join them. This time the holiday took them to St Johann im Tyrol, near Kitzbuhl. On the fourth day Joan fell awkwardly and cracked her fibula, the long thin outer bone in the lower part of the leg. Being unable to ski she went touring to Salzburg, Innsbruck and Munich on day trips; she joined her friends at night for the après ski activities. A group from the hotel arranged to visit a chalet located high in the mountains; it was in the early evening when they made their way to the chalet for a fondue. During their meal, the small gnome like owner asked whether they would like a speciality of the house to drink after the meal. He explained that the drink was called Hexingeist, the witch's breath and this suggestion met with everyone's approval. Sepp Schroeder, the hotel owner, had warned them of the dire consequences suffered by others through drinking too much of this liquid. The little gnome quickly set out twenty thick liqueur shot glasses edge to edge across the table; he filled each one to the brim with the dark brown liquid then set alight to the first glass in the line and they were mesmerised as his precise method of preparation of the herbaceous concoction spread its blue flame to all twenty containers. After two minutes he carefully placed beer mats over the line of blue flame to extinguish it;

"Prost," he shouted and tossed the liquid to the back of his throat. The group ordered round after round; only two people took Sepp's wise advice to go carefully. Sharon, who wished to remain sober and Robbie who had never acquired a liking for alcohol, both were content to watch whilst the white people made fools of themselves. It reminded him of the Zulu rituals in South Africa when his peers stumbled around incoherently after drinking 'Skokiaan', a home made brew of varying substances. By closing time the group were dancing on the tables, most of them without any clothes; the singing, dancing and passing out parade eventually returned to the hotel after midnight.

Mike was violently sick in the mini-bus and Sharon was embarrassed by his behaviour, refused to help him to bed. Robert suggested that she and Joan share his room; he would see to Mike and sleep in the spare bed that night.

Sharon agreed and helped Joan, who kept passing out and coming-to again, to bed. Sharon lay back against the wooden headboard thinking about something that Joan had said; she had promised to give another sheet of names of the Red Brigade when they returned home. Sharon tried to work out the strange statement. Why would she need a list of names of the Red Brigade? It didn't make sense, unless Joan, in her drunken stupor, had thought she was talking to Robbie.

She got up and dressed again and went to her room where she woke Robbie and told him to go back to his bed. After he had left the room Sharon got into her bed and lay awake thinking that her two friends were involved in something sinister.

Her chance to find out more arose when Oxford were playing a friendly rugby match against St Andrews University in Scotland. She asked Joan to stay with her; they went shopping and arrived home tired and laden down with packages. That evening they dressed and undressed several times whilst admiring each other's new garments. Joan sat cross legged on the bed, admiring her friend's long body as she watched her through the open bathroom door as they discussed the day's shopping trip.

After supper the two had a light supper and got slightly tipsy together. Sharon opened a bottle of Hexingeist that she had brought back from Austria with her. She pretended to drink and it didn't take much to get Joan drunk enough to start answering the questions Sharon posed to her.

Joan woke up in the same bed as Sharon; she couldn't remember anything that had taken place on the previous evening. Sharon feigned a heavy hangover but now knew everything she needed to know. Later she carefully entered a new file into her computer and decided not to tell Mike of his friend's escapades. A special file was marked and entered; it was at times like this that she felt a twinge of evilness creeping into her. She locked the false panel into position and took two tapes down to her desk and locked them up with her computer tapes.

CHAPTER NINETEEN

'Cut in rock of living stone, is the mighty dollar throne'

<u>Johannesburg - South Africa</u>

Bennie Roux eased his Ford up the long tree lined drive towards the thatched house in Melrose; he turned around in the area in front of the massive garage and stopped. Seated next to him was Sergeant Andrew Murray, the commandant's crack detective who had solved more cases this year than anyone else in the police force. He reminded Bennie of himself in bygone days when he was the hungriest young detective on the force; like a terrier with a rag, he wouldn't let go once put on a case. To date, both men had perfect records; they had obtained convictions for every major case that had been placed before them, Bennie now badly wanted this one solved in a hurry.

While they walked towards the house, the commandant scanned the neatly terraced garden admiring the layout. There wasn't a blade of grass out of place.

"Man! This garden is beautiful, it must have cost a fortune to get it like this," Bennie expressed idly.

"Ja, but if you're rich, then you can achieve almost anything," both men spoke with heavy Afrikaner accents, as did most of the whites in the police and government offices. Bennie knew that Andrew's Scottish forefathers were missionaries teaching blacks and poor whites in rural areas and in order to make themselves understood, they had mastered various local languages and dialects; because they were not only tending the spiritual needs of the community but also educating them. Their children continued to speak the most accessible language of their playmates, who in the main were Afrikaans. This slowly became the children's daily vocabulary over a period of time and with each generation, the home tongue changed as did their Scottish accent.

The heavy door was opened by a Peter's wife; Bennie put his hand in his hip pocket and flashed his warrant card in front of her.

"Commandant Roux. This is detective Murray. We've come to investigate the murder of..." he flicked open his book to check the name "Nellie Mkube, may we come in?"

"Now we're getting somewhere," she said, recognising the short man's authority. "Come in. Can I get you some refreshment?"

"Black coffee for me please," replied the commandant.

"White coffee and two sugars," said his colleague. She ushered them into the lounge and left the room to get the drinks.

Andrew opened his briefcase and extracted a large buff folder.

"No shortage of money here," he remarked casually.

"This is how the other half live," Bennie mouthed to him from across the spacious room.

Peter came into the room and introduced himself before sitting down.

"Now gentlemen how can I help? I want you to catch those swines, no matter what the cost. I'll make it worth your while." He lifted a delicately carved onyx box and removed a cigarette for himself before offering it to the others. Andrew started the proceedings by asking Peter general questions about his deceased employee, her habits, her friends and mostly about her visitors. It was only then that Peter realised how little he knew of his trusted servant, even though he thought of her as almost part of the family. He found himself unable to help much, because he simply didn't know who her friends were, whether she had been meeting anyone, or what she did with her time off. Jane Roberts reappeared carrying a tray and set it down on a low table in the middle of the room. The two detectives stood up politely when she proceeded to pour the coffee, the policemen asked her the same questions that they had put to her husband. She was a little more helpful in being able to help them with the first names of some of Nellie's friends. Most of them were known to her only as *"the maid who works for Mrs Green two plots away,"* But the astute detective was used to this type of answer from white employers, he knew how to find his way around the community and with two of his black constables, to act as interpreters, he usually managed to find out everything he wanted to know.

When they had taken the questioning as far as possible, the two men asked the Roberts to show them the room where the black knife-man was seen. Peter explained his family connection with Michael as they went up the internal stairway that led to the flat.

"Can I see the young man? asked the older policeman.

"No, he now lives in Britain and is studying at Oxford or Cambridge, I'm not sure which." Peter lied.

"What about the other boy. Where is he now?"

"He is also studying in Britain, but again I'm not sure where."

Once in the room, Peter described in detail what had happened and the two policemen continually interjected with questions as they moved around. Finally they went through the kitchen door and looked down the concrete stairs with its metal balustrade stretching below them.

"He raced down here, around the garage and out into the street," said Peter.

They stood around for a while and suddenly Andrew asked "Did the fingerprint men dust the handrail?"

"I don't recall them touching it."

When the security men returned to the lounge, Peter asked them if they had found anything.

"Yes, we think we could have found some clues. But our forensic department will have to have a good look at them" Bennie replied.

"What did you find?" asked Peter.

"Well, we're not sure, but we may have found some threads of material which may prove to be of help."

Andrew asked about the gardener; what days he worked, how long he had worked for them, what he normally wore on duty. Without warning he switched his questions concerning Robert and Michael. They answered as best they could and Andrew carefully noted their replies in the buff folder.

Suddenly Bennie, who had been quiet for some time, spoke up "Mr Roberts, we know that Robert Molefe is actively involved with the ANC. This may be a tribal vendetta, but we must warn you that he is in grave danger."

"What do you mean?" Peter hoped his surprise sounded genuine.

"We think he is on a hit list and even in England, there is no guarantee of his safety."

"Somehow your servant saw something that she shouldn't have and they killed her. Life is cheap in this war."

"What should we do?"

"There is nothing you can do except, when you next speak to them in England, warn them and keep your own eyes and ears open... they may be back."

Bennie knew that this was no tribal feud and that the security police were behind the killings.

Peter lit another cigarette thoughtfully.

"Commandant Roux, I am a wealthy man and want these bastards found and stopped. I will pay you both a substantial amount to find them. They have attacked my house and family and nobody gets away with that."

Peter was pleased to see that his incentive was not rejected or thought of as some sort of a backhander.

Andrew too, watched the greed and eagerness with which his superior readily accepted the offer from this businessman. He didn't say anything, when they rose to leave; he casually asked Peter whether he thought that Michael was also involved with ANC activities. Peter simply shrugged his shoulders "I shouldn't think so; he isn't a fighting type of person."

When Incatha issued the death warrant, it was Robbie's ANC members, who had infiltrated the Zulu leadership that advised him to flee. His underground movement had grown so fast that the Incatha movement had not been able to control it by mere threats - they had to go to a street war with their own people.

Andrew couldn't help admiring the work of this young man; was Molefe taking all this trouble hiding behind the ANC in order to use them as a shield? Was his ambition to become one of the most powerful men in South Africa? Andrew suspected that Robbie didn't give a hoot for the black activists; but was using them simply as a means for his own end.

On their return to Johannesburg, Andrew placed the buff document in front of Commandant Roux. They knew that they had grabbed a tiger by the tail because this was no ordinary murder as far as they were concerned. Bennie Roux smiled at the younger man as he explained a plan to try to get this young entrepreneur to work with them; perhaps they could kill two birds with one stone.

CHAPTER TWENTY

'Their father's castle has now been won, another venture begun'

<u>*Pretoria - South Africa*</u>

The surgeon made the first steady incision into Michael's chest, along a red line across his breast like a road on a map. As some of his blood oozed gently forth, the scalpel penetrated again into the line. This time deeper as the cut parted like the Red Sea before Moses and the theatre sister efficiently dabbed at the cut with a reddening swab. The cleaned area was again delved into and sliced deeper through the muscle of the chest; once more swabs cleared the blood, which was now flowing freely from the wound.

The anaesthetist watched the breathing level drop and knew that a powerful strong mind was unconsciously at work.

Jay was busily inserting another cannula into Mike's arm; he had already used the first few pints of blood and was going to need many more before the operation was through. She kept her eye on the regulated speed of entry, knowing that too little and his brain would be starved of oxygen while a third sister was helping handing the two surgeons their lifesaving instruments and making sure they were all returned.

Although Jay was an outsider she quickly tuned into the theatre routine.

All six members changed from separate individuals into a highly efficient team working as one unit, nothing was being said and the theatre was silent except for the loud gurgling breathing of the patient and the louder sound of the respirator assisting him in this. The sister applied several clamps to the newly parted skin, laying them backwards onto the body so that they opened the wound more widely, in order to reveal the internal damage to the surgeon. Both surgeons found it difficult to comprehend how the splintered bones had not punctured the heart or lungs; the team felt that somehow had been extremely fortunate to still be alive and that this man must have also walked in the shadow of God.

For a short while they discussed the best way to tackle this delicate problem, knowing that if they tried to lift the ribs back into position and misjudged the pressure, the man would be dead in seconds. Finally both agreed that they would have to open the breast and tackle the problem from inside the ribcage. The surgeon lifted the scalpel and made a first incision from the base of the throat to below the solar plexus; Michael now had two cuts in the shape of a cross on his body. The team again settled into their routine until the surgeon was satisfied that he had the skin and muscle separated from the breastbone. He rapidly gave his theatre sister instructions on what instruments were going to be required for the next stage of the operation.

Jay watched them working furiously and thought that if he lived after this, he would have to become a believer always reminded of a cross each time he looked at his body. Fortunately for Mike, the lead surgeon was also one of South Africa's leading heart surgeons and had done quite a few bypass operations and what he was about to do was not new to the team.

The sister produced a miniature rotary electric saw; its little blade spun furiously each time the surgeon pressed the black button. He tried it several times in order to gauge the weight and effect of the fast spinning blade. Then, in a similar fashion, he tentatively made the first downward cut to the wound.

The sister quickly cleaned up the bits of white debris left behind; several times he swooped, cutting deeper into the bone, leaving a single track into the chest as the sister applied a dampened swab to get the dry bone particles to adhere to the cloth.

Making a third cut, with delicate precision, he reached the base of the hard resistant gristle: allowing for the natural curvature of the bone and being careful not to penetrate too deeply. Under normal circumstances he would have parted the last bit, with a tool not unlike a carpenter's chisel, by cleaving the bones apart.

He didn't want to take any risks, knowing full well that a downward force could bend the resilient ribcage in toward the organs. On the other hand, if he cut too deeply at any stage it would be like pushing a knife straight into the man. Silently he prayed for a steady hand as he continued his delicate work.

Finally the second surgeon managed to lever the two halves apart and the cutting was done as the first man handed the machine back to the sister. Very carefully they inserted a spreader into the narrow cut and slowly turned the screw until the ribcage separated; a fraction at a time as the tendrils forced Mike's bones apart.

Oxford - England

As usual on Sunday mornings, Sharon and Mike relaxed by reading through an enormous pile of Sunday newspapers - which the paperboy had delivered earlier in the morning. The exams were now behind them and all they could do was wait for the results to be published; they both felt confident that they had attained their degrees.

Mike was scanning the paper for news from South Africa, although there was not much to be found that day. He searched for anything that might help him understand what was happening in his country.

"Mike, let's go home for three weeks." Lounging at his side, Sharon whistled softly

Mike hesitated in answering, as the truth of the matter was that he was uncertain of returning to South Africa since the attack on them at the airport. Which he suspected was engineered by the security police. However, Mike too was homesick and he would have given anything to return to South Africa to visit his beloved mountains and Champagne Castle.

The thing that he missed most about home was the warm sunshine; because, unlike the UK, it was never bleak and cloudy for days on end. Even in winter the sun would shine, although the nights were sometimes bitterly cold.

As Sharon went on about going home he presumed that she had already made up her mind; whenever she decided something there was nothing that would sway her. Mike had got to know all sides of his cousin and knew that she was strong willed, having a callousness about her that was totally unbending. She could be gentle and cuddly but he had seen a wild cat side of her which sometimes scared him. By the afternoon she had called South Africa and made the arrangements with her parents for her homecoming at Christmas.

That evening she tried everything in her power to persuade Mike to take a holiday but he invented a thousand excuses for not wanting to travel to South Africa. She felt he was being a little paranoid about the underlying cause of his reluctance to go; but, no matter how hard she tried, she couldn't get him to change his mind.

The following morning they agreed that she would go for three weeks and he would stay and spend Christmas with Robbie and

Joan.

One of the things that the couple wanted to do before Sharon left was to inspect the house that Mike's parents had acquired as an investment in Surrey on their recent trip to England.

Mike called James McGregor at the bank to make necessary arrangements with the estate agent for them to collect the keys. Sharon suggested stopping in Virginia Water on their way to Weybridge, at the home of Diane Hicks-Brown who Mike knew was the rebel daughter of a wealthy family and a playmate of Colin Baird.

"Diane's given me directions and wants to come with us to the house; says she knows the area well."

"Why do we have to drag her along?"

Sharon was wearing a long silk-lined white gown with a hood hanging loosely down her back; she looked so beautiful just then that he resented any intrusion by Diane.

"We can't refuse her now as I've already agreed," replied Sharon.

They travelled on the M25 until they saw the signs for Staines and Windsor. "Should we quickly go and visit Her Majesty at Windsor Castle before we see Diane." Mike said without looking at Sharon.

"Yes! Let's... it will be a ripping affair," she said, contorting her face in highbrow fashion.

They both burst out laughing, this was the best thing about their relationship; they were always teasing each other and laughing together. Diane's home had extensive paddocks containing polo ponies; Argentinean, they decided. The grounds were vast and they calculated that there must be at least twenty to thirty rooms in the opulent mansion.

Sharon smiled wickedly at Mike and he immediately knew what she was thinking. They had this friend on tape and he could almost see the dollar signs in Sharon's eyes.

Diane had been keeping an eye open for their arrival and ushered them through to a large games room at the back of the house, with a large snooker table set in sixteenth century splendour. Shields, spears and coats-of-arms adorned the walls while suits of armour were carefully placed around the room. Off to one side of a large open fireplace was housed a gym and as far as Mike could see, contained everything that any modern gym club would be proud of. The whole area was carpeted and curtained in deep red against the grey stone walls. The only thing out of character was a pair of glazed doors at the far end of the room which Diane explained led to their indoor heated swimming pool.

Diane pulled at a long silk cord suspended from the ceiling before sitting down with her guests to chat away about their finals. An elderly woman entered the room "You called, Diane."

"Yes, Amanda, could you bring some tea for our guests?"

Like Nellie, Amanda was obviously treated as one of the family. It hadn't gone unnoticed by Sharon that Diane used the girl's first name and she suddenly felt a moment's bitter grief for her lost friend.

Mike couldn't help admiring this beautiful lady of the manor now entertaining them. She was a changed person from the shrieking dark haired ball of fun attending their parties. She was now elegantly dressed and her manners were impeccable as she carried out the role of hostess with grace.

The glazed doors swished open and a young woman entered, they immediately saw her striking resemblance to Diane. She wore a long red towelling gown and her short hair was wet.

"Vicky! Had a good swim? Come and meet the South African friends I told you about."

Vicky appeared somewhat stiff as she changed direction towards them.

"Oh, Di! Look at me! This isn't the way to be dressed to meet strangers," Her eyes shot daggers at her sister.

"Don't worry about that. We are very informal friends," Sharon said cheerily.

Vicky relaxed, settled herself on the floor in front of the fire and started to rub her hair with a towel. Slowly it became like Diane's short curly dark hair. Both had moonish faces and slightly upturned noses which gave them the same impish looks. Mike thought that they could be identical twins they were so alike and wondered whether they had similar temperaments. The four continued talking for a while, until Sharon suggested that it was time for them to leave to inspect their house when she noticed that Vicky was becoming over interested in Mike. Vicky, so diffident in the beginning, now seemed reluctant for them to go. She asked Mike whether he was interested in playing polo. When he explained that he was a good horseman but had never had the opportunity, she suggested he might like to give it a try sometime.

Sharon changed the conversation to her forthcoming holiday and then wished she hadn't when Mike explained that he was staying in England for Christmas. She took his arm and moved towards the door, bidding Vicky an abrupt farewell. As they drove to Weybridge, Diane gave a running commentary on the countryside they passed.

Diane had a map of the area as she navigated through the rich estate, noting that all the houses were hidden from view behind walls, hedges and trees. The homes belonging to the rich and famous, mostly film stars, pop singers or television personalities, all tucked away from sight.

The estate they sought was immaculate and it didn't take them long to find the narrow road where their house was located. Neither Mike nor Sharon could believe their eyes when they first saw the huge red bricked house; they hadn't expected anything quite as ostentatious. An old gardener was busily attending a climbing rose at the side of the front door. He greeted the three sombrely, but immediately continued with his work as they let themselves in. The house was fully furnished and ready to move into. They wandered through the rooms on the ground floor and then up to the first floor.

There were eight bedrooms, most of them with en-suite bathrooms. The basement contained a billiard table, a dart board and a small gym. They trooped out through the large kitchen and at the back they saw two large heated conservatories. One was used for plants but the other had been converted to house a sauna and Jacuzzi. The place left Mike and Sharon almost speechless. They made up their minds to persuade their parents to let them move from Oxford to this house. For one thing they could oversee the renovations Nicole had insisted on, for another it was much closer to London and their soon to be new workplace.

As soon as they had driven Diane home, the two began to make plans.

Mike was so overtaken with his enthusiasm that he forgot about Sharon's impending holiday and even all thought of Vicky provocatively dressed in her towelling-gown by the fire, went out of his mind.

CHAPTER TWENTY ONE

'Forgive fidelity, as parting lingerers bid adieu'

<u>*London - England*</u>

In between Christmas shopping trips, the three young South Africans, sometimes with Joan, visited the house in Weybridge. Mike had convinced his parents to let them move into the house initially as caretakers and if they succeeded in getting the new business off the ground they could then consider the three of them as tenants. After much persuasion, Ian and Nicole reluctantly gave their permission; Nicole pointing out to Ian that it would eventually become Mike's anyway. However, they set certain provisions such as insisting that James McGregor be allowed to inspect the place regularly. They also stipulated that, if they had not made a go of the new business within three years and could not afford the upkeep, then the house would be rented as previously planned. Mike agreed with Robbie when he suggested that Joan would move in with him as she was now very much part of their group.

On the eve of her departure, Sharon gently pushed Mike onto the large sofa and placed his favourite drink in his hand.

"Mike, I have been thinking about the new house. I think we should do the same thing to it as this house."

"Hell, it's another thing wiring up a house of such mammoth proportions."

"We can use the same man who did all the work here" Sharon crossed the room to her desk and searched through some papers before extracting a card. She closed and locked the drawer before returning to give him the address. She always did this and Mike became more than interested to know what she kept in that drawer. All the others, where they kept tapes and files, were equally securely locked, but he had duplicate keys; this drawer she considered her private domain.

"Here, speak to Barry Reynolds, he'll do the work privately."

"How are we going to pay for it all?"

"Don't worry, I'll speak to McGregor and tell him it's for security reasons. Leave it to me."

Mike walked Sharon to passport control, where she turned and hugged him tight.

"Don't worry darling, I'll be back before you know it. Next time we'll do it together."

"Have a great time and wish your folks a Happy Christmas."

Mike didn't want her to go and would have given anything at that moment to stop her. But knew any attempt would simply end up with an argument.

"Just remember, I love you lots and am going to miss your funny face around here," he said, hugging her more tightly. For a short while neither wanted to be the first to let go; each inhaling the final smell and feel of the other. They held their lips together, as if passing a discreet communication between themselves, before breaking the magical embrace.

He watched her show her ticket and turned and waved one last time before she disappeared behind the screen. He felt he was the loneliest person and his only real friend was somewhere in London with Joan. For a while he stood watching total strangers melting away through the screen; longing that Sharon would reappear.

As he wandered slowly towards the exit, he passed a bank of telephones and suddenly had an idea. Calling the operator and giving her a name and address, he waited and then quickly dialled a number; after speaking for a short time, he hung up and headed back towards the car park.

It was a short drive from Heathrow to Virginia Water. Diane, dressed in jodhpurs, black boots and club jumper, was waiting at the door when he arrived. Moving forward she took his hand then offered her cheek for a kiss in the Continental greeting style. She didn't release his hand as she led him through the house to the fire which glowed brightly behind a roomful of guests. The majority of them were young women dressed the same way as Diane and several men who had obviously just come in from a polo match. It was too late for Mike to back out, now that he was halfway across the room, in tow behind Diane. The conversation quickly died and all eyes turned towards them

"Everybody, this is Michael Roberts a very good friend of mine from university."

Anybody introduced as a friend of the Hicks-Browns was worth knowing and conversation immediately started up again. Vicky then came up to Mike, both hands held out in front of her, taking both of his hands in hers she also offered her cheeks in welcome.

"How lovely to see you again, where's Sharon?"

Mike thought her question unnecessary because she must have remembered her holiday. But he explained "At this moment she should be in a Jumbo about to take off for her South African holiday. Seeing I was in the neighbourhood, I thought I would just pop in."

"Oh! How lovely, do come and meet some of the others."

"Really Vicky, I feel too much of an intruder; I didn't realise you had company, otherwise I wouldn't have come."

Both women pulled long faces at him.

"What stuff and nonsense you speak Mr Roberts, we're so pleased you decided to come, aren't we Vicky?"

"You must stay to dinner, we won't take no for an answer."

"What's the occasion?"

"We beat the reserve men's team today in a not so friendly match. They keep saying we women are weak, so we had to show them otherwise. Would you like something to drink?" Diane said decisively.

Mike momentarily forgot his loneliness and accepted.

"Great. I'll leave you in Vicky's capable hands for now."

"Well Mike, what are you going to do with yourself for the next few weeks?" Vicky's voice was teasingly wicked and she smiled. Mike smiled back, but didn't answer. They both understood what the other meant and burst into laughter.

Dinner was an informal affair served as a buffet in the games room. A long table was magnificently laid with cold lobster, pheasant, smoked oysters and caviar. Wine flowed and the dull murmur of conversation raised itself to a loud pitch as everybody became more and more intoxicated.

Diane told everybody within earshot about Mike's house and its address in St Georges Hill raised more than one eyebrow in the room: It was known locally as the Mecca of Wealth. During the evening there was a noticeable gravitation towards Mike. He felt only a slight pang of guilt at not mentioning that it really belonged to his parents and encouraged the young women to think that anybody this young and good looking owning a house in St Georges Hill would make a fine catch. Several telephone numbers were thrust at him and some invitations were offered to events over Christmas. Mike promised to be in contact, knowing from past experience that he would first find out which ones would be of use to him. The party was becoming more and more boisterous when Vicky asked Mike whether he would like to stay the night. She told him that he was in no fit state to drive back to Oxford and that they had plenty of spare rooms.

"What about your parents, don't you have to ask them?" he replied.

"I can ask who I like, even if my parents were not away in Argentina for six weeks."

Just then one of the men passed, half carrying, half dragging one of the female polo players toward the glass doors. Two of her friends were trying half heartedly to stop him.

"Oh! Oh! Here we go," exclaimed Vicky. "It generally starts this way, and then everybody ends up in the pool. It's a ritual at our parties."

"It probably helps to sober them up, but it can't do their boots any good," laughed Mike.

"By the time he gets her to the pool she will have convinced him that her boots will be wrecked and that they will have to come off first. You should see the place when the girls are wearing expensive dresses; it amounts to nothing less than organised chaos."

They all followed the struggling group to the pool and as Vicky had predicted, boots, jodhpurs and top were removed before a ceremonial ducking took place. It wasn't long before many others had joined the solitary figure in the water, all the girls topless as they struck the water.

Diane came out of the pool wearing only a pair of see through white briefs and heading straight towards her visitor. Mike knew that it was his turn and that no amount of persuading otherwise would release him from the inevitable; so he started undressing.

Vicky watched him stripping and did the same; when she was down to only her briefs she took one hand, Diane grabbed the other and they raced Mike into the water. They surfaced laughing and Vicky tried unsuccessfully to duck him below the water again. He was too strong for her and he held her against him while Diane grabbed him from the back. He enjoyed feeling the naked bodies pressed hard against him as they romped in the warm water. The entire group fooled around in the pool for some time before dragging themselves out. Everybody went back to the playroom to dry off in front of the fire before the party started to break up and people started leaving.

When they were alone, Vicky, Diane and Mike sat side by side in front of the open hearth, soaking in the warmth of the fading fire.

"Would you two like a nightcap?" Vicky asked.

"Let's have Irish Coffees," suggested Diane. She got up and pulled the silk cord and Amanda came in.

"Please bring coffee in a flask Amanda, a bottle of Jameson Whiskey and a jug of cream. Then you can go to bed."

When it arrived, Diane was heavy handed with the whiskey. The three hadn't bothered getting dressed and were still wearing only their briefs. They spread themselves in front of the glowing hearth and chatted aimlessly, whilst subtle warmth slowly crept into their bodies; more from the strong coffee-mix than the heated fireplace.

Vicky spread herself lengthways in front of the fire and used Mike's upper leg as a pillow. Having had more than usual to drink he was at that stage where he was past thinking about Sharon finding himself slowly running his fingers through her thick black hair. He eased her head up and then stood up to go and drag one of the massive chairs towards the fireplace; sitting on the floor again, using it as a backrest.

Vicky replaced her head back in its previous position as the little group continued talking. Diane, not wanting to be outdone by her sister, did the same. Mike now had a head resting on each thigh as he sipped the sweet concoction of coffee and cream. "What could be better?" he asked himself smiling "how many people do I know who would be sitting in front of a warm fire with two semi-naked sisters?"

He continued gently stroking both heads. His bravado increased as they let his exploring fingers move down to their backs and back to the hair again. Vicky started running her hand up his leg gently tickling his inner thigh. Michael felt sensation building, as she eased her hand inside his briefs and started caressing his now hard member. He wasn't sure if Diane had drifted off to sleep and didn't want to move to find out. Carrying on with his movements down their backs and then cautiously moving his hands onto their breasts he noticed that both girls had hardened nipples. Gently but persistently fingering erect nipples in the stillness of the playroom he heard their breathing increasing in pace.

Diane suddenly got up in a hurry. Michael was about to apologise for offending her when he realised that she wasn't upset at all. She was simply removing her briefs. Then she knelt down next to him and pressed her lips fully onto his. As her darting tongue searched his wanton mouth he had a vague sensation that Vicky was removing her briefs. She knelt in front of him, tugging at his underpants until they were free of his body then returning to his waiting organ she gently started teasing it up and down.

Mike had occasionally fantasised about a threesome, now his first experience was actually happening with a pair of sisters, he leaned back and soaked in the sensation. His fingers explored both girls at the same time. Vicky moved around and placed herself to one side and Diane on the other with Diane working the top half and Vicky the lower. Without warning, Diane suddenly pushed Mike sideways so that he was flat on the floor. She then straddled over him and shamelessly lowered herself down to his mouth.

Vicky stopped attacking Mike's flaming passion and faced her sister as she eased herself onto his throbbing pinnacle. Lowering her hands, she touched Michael's lips and moved her fingers repeatedly from his tongue to her sister and back again as Diane moved forward to suck her sister's nipples.

The intensity grew in all three and simultaneously they reached their respective peaks. Vicky screamed

"Yes! Yes!" continually whilst Diane moaned and groaned in high pitched concert with her sister. Mike let forth deep throated grunts as his fluid shot up into Vicky. All three bodies resonated with vibration as the moment of impact reached them simultaneously.

Diane was the first to move as she dismounted and rolled over onto the carpet. Vicky eased herself up but didn't leave Mike alone. She once again sucked on his now limp penis, trying to draw last drops of liquid from him. Hardening again, Mike rolled over onto Diane, moving violently in and out delighting in her high pitched groan. Vicky helped him as she leaned over, starting to fondle and suck her sisters twin peaks as her hand disappeared between her own legs. Again their crescendo gained momentum until another explosion reached all three, who flopped down where they lay.

"Jesus," said Vicky "I've never had anything like that. In one night I've committed incest and had an enormous orgasm. We must get together like this more often."

After dragging themselves upstairs and having a combined shower they piled into a massive four poster bed. Several times during the night Mike awoke to find one or other beautiful sister fondling him or found himself making love to one of them. Each time any passion started up the ensuing movement woke all of them and ended up with all three making love yet again. They slept-in until late the next morning and when they eventually awoke, they showered together and went to breakfast in a wonderful community spirit. Amanda served breakfast in an alcove adjoining the kitchen, making no reference to Mike's presence. Afterwards Diane searched out some riding clothes for Mike among her father's things.

"Should we go for a hack or would you like to learn how to play polo?" asked Diane.

"Let's give it a go. I would like to see if I can hit a ball on horseback."

She knew from her time at Oxford that he was a natural sportsman but what she hadn't expected was for him to be such a superb horseman. All the horse siding gained at Champagne Castle automatically came to the fore. Here he had perfect balance and before very long he had mastered galloping flat out and striking the ball with the mallet.

Both girls coached him in the method of defence and by afternoon Mike had worked out the art of placing polo ponies between the ball and his opponent. He learnt to dribble the ball until he was ready to hit it.

The girls implored Mike to join their club, knowing that their father would be able to help him to gain membership. Mike promised to think about it because there was still some time to go before the season started and anyway he had his house and business to attend to, he told them.

When he returned to Oxford, he enjoyed a long hot bath and then climbed into bed and fell into a deep sleep, totally exhausted. He was awakened by the ringing of the telephone; it was Sharon phoning to let him know that she had arrived safely. She said she was tired after the fourteen hour flight; Mike didn't mention how tired he was!

CHAPTER TWENTY TWO

'When distant thoughts start to fade, an investment can be made'

<u>London - England</u>

Sharon, Mike and Robbie met James McGregor at his luxurious office in the City of London. Although having spoken to him several times by telephone this was their first combined meeting. He was seated at a circular table and his gentle Scottish burr held them transfixed as he spoke.

James had called the meeting at the request of both lots of parents to inform them of their responsibilities within the new company. His bank had been acting as the European investment advisers to the Robert's family estates for many years and he had personally been responsible for helping them to acquire the new business which the young people were to manage. At first Nicole and Ian wanted their two to serve a form of apprenticeship within one of their other companies, but Peter had suggested throwing them in at the deep end.

"If you have got to learn anything what's the quickest and best way to do it?" he argued.

"But they'll be eaten alive out there, it's a jungle," said Nicole, who was still the largest shareholder within the group. "What if we created a safety net in case they fall too hard," recommended Ian.

"How?" asked Peter.

"Any deals over a certain size have first to be discussed with James McGregor and every month, without fail, they must send a complete set of accounting figures to him."

With that basic plan in hand, they had then discussed this with James who had come up with an expanded idea. This placed a trustee of the bank on the board of directors, who would also be a working director (in effect a spy in the camp) who would keep him notified on a day to day basis. This compromise served to allay all the fears of those concerned.

James McGregor quietly explained a potted history of their newly acquired company, how it had been run before, as well as what achievements were expected. Like most banking men he carried out this duty systematically; finishing a section and checking that they understood everything, before commencing to the next item on his agenda.

There were three other people also seated around the table, two men and a woman who were all bank employees and who had all been involved in the initial purchase of the company. From time to time James would direct a question at one of them, who would carefully answer so that the three youngsters were fully clear on that point; James double checking to make sure. It was a long and laborious task but the banker had inspected all possible pitfalls before deciding to recommend the purchase. Any specific questions from the three were directed to each of the three individual bank experts.

One thing that really pleased James was the high standard of questions being put forward by the three friends; which made him realise that they obviously had a firm grasp of business management. This knowledge hadn't just been gained from education, but had been obtained through working with their parents; they each seemed to possess a good all-round business expertise.

Concluding their meeting, to adjourn for lunch at a nearby

restaurant, James brought up the subject of the extra director; expecting some form of resistance from them. However, they immediately accepted his proposal and in fact, Sharon welcomed the assistance, even suggesting that he employ a qualified accountant.

After lunch the bank arranged for two cars to ferry everyone to the premises of the company. They drove east past Bank underground station towards Aldgate and into Whitechapel Street. The areas, through which the route took them, became more derelict as they travelled past London Hospital towards Stepney. Just before reaching Mile End Road, both cars turned right down a narrow side street; crossing several small roads before swinging left into a cul-de-sac.

The large double-storied brick building was accessed via a sturdy set of gates. Sharon's eyes searched across the building and noticed that there were no company names anywhere on it. At the burglar-proofed re-enforced glass door, James pushed the buzzer on an external intercom; a voice asked their business.

"It's James McGregor," said the robust Scot into the silver box fixed into the wall. The buzzer sounded as he pushed open a glazed door and everybody followed him through into the building. They were singularly unimpressed by the exterior surroundings of the neighbourhood; where the ravages of time and war had turned this once proud east-end community into a virtual slum. However, the inside of the building was in stark contrast as they found themselves in a very plush reception area with thick gold-coloured carpets and modern partitioning.

"How can I help you Mr McGregor?" said the plump but efficient receptionist.

"I have an appointment with Mr Simonet," replied James.

"Please have a seat and I'll tell him that you're here," she said indicating to the party to be seated in deep leather chairs.

Alain Simonet appeared through a door at the end of a passageway and headed directly towards them. He was in his early forties, of medium height with dark hair and matching pencil-thin greying moustache that didn't match his rounded features. His redeeming feature was a broad happy smile which broke out and spread right across his face.

"James, how good to see you again," he said, shaking the older man's hand warmly before greeting the three other bank members with equal gusto.

"Alain let me introduce Sharon and Michael Roberts and Robert Molefe, the new shareholders that I told you about."

Alain Simonet greeted them like old friends but Robbie and Mike immediately sensed a hidden animosity towards them. Sharon, who had also taken a dislike to him, quickly made the man aware of her intentions.

"We're here to take a look around the place and to see what can be done to bring this company into the twentieth century," she said curtly.

"What do you mean by that?" he asked cautiously and now on his guard.

"Exactly what I said, would you now like to show us around please?" An immediate battle of wills had begun and she had won the first round.

Leading them through the swing door and turning right, into an enormous open-plan office that took up practically the whole ground floor, they saw about thirty commodity traders sitting in front of green flickering screens. This noisy trading room was generally filled with young people all competing with each other for valued business. All of them seemed to be shouting into one or more telephones at once as the place rocked with activity.

Michael immediately fell in love with this trading room the moment he clamped eyes on it; he wasn't quite sure what the traders were doing, but knew that this was his destiny. Alain guided them through the rest of the ground floor to the computer room where all the trading contracts were logged and recorded. At the end of trade each day, computerised statements and accounts of the transactions were posted out to their clients. Mike immediately recognised that this was the heart of the company and that their guide took great pride in this section. As they passed, people slaved away at keyboards and hardly even looked up; they were busily entering data as keyboards rattled to their pounding fingers.

It was quieter and less frenetic on the first floor; Alain explained that this was the physical trading division, whereas downstairs the traders were only dealing in futures transactions. They walked through this floor with secretaries, bookkeepers and administrative personnel in one section and physical traders in the other.

Sharon counted only six people in this trader's team, buying and selling goods for shipment from all over the world and which would end up in the company's warehouses. The last office and the biggest on the floor, was a combined boardroom and Alain's office.

"What about the rest of the building?" asked Sharon, as the man indicated to them to be seated at the table.

"This is it!" he retorted.

"Well, what the hell have we invested in then?" Sharon directed her question at the banker; who James played along because the

Roberts were his paymasters and they called the tune.

"Yes, there's also a large warehouse at the back where most of the investment is," he said half apologetically.

"Let's have a look at it then," she insisted, heading back out of the door.

The group followed her down the stairs as Alain made his way to the front in order to guide them out to the warehouse. This was a hell cat and he would tame her, he thought to himself hopefully. As they crossed a large courtyard leading to the massive warehouse, they saw the vehicle ramp with several container trucks being loaded with heavy brown sacks. The earthy fragrance hit them as they reached the steel sliding doors to the building; it reminded Robbie of distant maize fields and home; these smells could only come from dried produce as it permeated the air and penetrated his senses. He thought back to bygone days when he picked up fresh cobs in a field and placed them against his nostrils.

They entered the steel hanger-like building which was piled high with large brown hessian sacks and Kraft heavy-duty paper bags of varying shapes and sizes. They were stacked neatly on wooden pallets, in rows stretching out in long straight lines as far as the eye could see. Mike wondered how they managed to stack them this high without them overbalancing and falling over. In the distance they could hear the roar of machinery as Alain beckoned for them to follow; he guided them around the high stacks until they reached the huge pulsating machines at the far end of the warehouse.

"This is where we clean, sort, mix and bag the various products for the animal and pet trade," he shouted above the roar of the machines.

They watched as the product from large bags was emptied into gigantic bins sunken into the floor and then, further down the line, appeared re-bagged in white crisply sealed bags containing the company name. The process fascinated the group as they watched the bags being whisked along a large conveyor off to the next destination in the process.

For about an hour they wandered around the vast storehouse as Alain explained each phase of the process to the group before finally returning to the stillness of his office.

Alain extracted various files showing locations in both Britain and Europe of the company's silos as well as some smaller quayside warehouses where their products were housed. At the conclusion of the meeting all three youngsters were suitably impressed with the size and potential scope of the business and were all ready and keen to start work immediately.

On their way back to the bank Sharon spent most of the time asking James McGregor various questions. Mike wanted to get to grips with the trading side of the business. When they were once again seated at the round table Sharon was the first to speak.

"James, I'm sorry about the little outburst back there and I hope it didn't offend anybody, because it wasn't meant to."

"No lass, you quite rightly created the pecking order from the outset, we understand that," he replied. Noticing Sharon's slight frown the old banker wondered whether she thought him patronising.

He could clearly see the roles that each of the three were going to play and was happy with the way it was developing; although, secretly, he wished that it had been Mike rather than Sharon to take up the leadership mantle.

"It got my blood going to see how Alain decided to treat us like spoilt kids; but I think we'll be able to work well together," she said.

"Both Robbie and I want to learn more about futures trading, can the bank arrange for some expert help?" asked Mike.

"Yes, I'll arrange for you to spend a few days with some top traders. They'll toss you in at the deep end and teach you to swim afterwards," he laughed.

The three had agreed to start working on the following Monday week, giving themselves ten days to finalise work on their new house before setting out on the exciting business venture. Mike and Robbie were to spend four days at the bank's trading office and Sharon was to oversee the final arrangements for their move to the house.

"I don't like the name of the house, we must change it," said Robbie "to something that will bring us luck."

"Yes, I must admit that Granta Holly doesn't do much for me either," reflected Sharon.

Like parents bickering over what glorious name should be given to their new offspring, the three bandied names about; every one given due consideration before being abandoned. Then with sudden delight Robbie offered a name that the thought fitted the house perfectly.

"What about Champagne Castle? It can be our own little piece of home."

"Brilliant," said Sharon "You're not only a pretty face," she teased as she rubbed her hand hard against his head. "It'll never take the place of the mountain, but we're on top of a hill and it does look like a small castle. Yes, the name's appropriate," commented Mike.

African Chess

While Sharon had been in South Africa, Mike arranged with Barry Reynolds to remove the complicated array of cameras and video equipment from her small house and reinstall it in Champagne Castle. Together with the existing equipment, Barry needed to acquire several more items for the larger house and Michael arranged the finance from his trust fund; as agreed to with Sharon.

Mike started packing things into tea boxes for their intended move and it was then that he had stumbled across a key to Sharon's desk. At first he wasn't sure what the key was for and after checking everywhere he eventually found that it fitted her desk. He unlocked and opened the top drawer and would then have shut and locked it again if it hadn't have been for something that caught his attention. Her diaries were lying in the drawer and it took him two nights to read through them all. They started from her arrival in Britain and Mike found a side to her that he had never even suspected. While reading these books, he experienced a whole gamut of feelings ranging from intense love to overflowing distaste. Behind the gentle facade lurked a woman of immense ambition who would let nothing stop her from reaching her goals; if they were to remain together he knew he would have to accept that.

He went through everything as there was one particular file in the computer that he had been unable to trace no matter how hard he tried. Mike had mixed feelings about Diane and Victoria Hicks-Brown and his infidelity had given him sleepless nights; but after reading her diaries his conscience was cleared.

From then on he threw himself into preparing the new house for their move. Barry needed to rewire the large house in such a way that everything was concealed. He had chosen the little gatekeeper's cottage as the best place for the main consol of recorders and he lay extensive cabling under the ground between the two buildings. The only clue that any work had been done was a brown strip of earth leading from the main house to the cottage; Old Max, the gardener, had almost resigned on the spot when he found his precious lawn being dug up. Mike placated him and now, after working his gardening magic, Max had repaired the damage and no one would notice where the lines were hidden. With both Sharon and Robbie away, Mike had been able to add a few innovations of his own; which he decided to keep as a secret between himself and Barry.

The week after Sharon returned from holiday, they left the little house for the last time. All of them felt sad because their time there had been extremely happy and had seen them change from teenagers into adults.

Champagne Castle was ready and waiting. Sharon aimed her security remote control toward a black box as they approached and two large gates effortlessly swung open. Fixed above the archway, over the steel gates, was a security camera recording their movements as they continued up the circular drive to the house.

During the previous week Sharon had busied herself with rearranging the contents of the house and having a new name board painted. She tried to become friendly with the crotchety old gardener and had employed two elderly ladies to cook, clean, wash, iron, make beds and generally help.

Mike and Robbie went to the bank trading room each morning, returning with wonderful stories of their day's work as the household started settling into a routine. The grandiose property of Champagne Castle spanned nearly four acres of grassed and densely treed land which was situated on the crest of a hill. Dominating the pinnacle was the large house with its four garages, two conservatories and main garden carefully tiered and falling away steeply northwards from the house. Its long circular stone drive rose gently from the south side through a mass of carefully placed rhododendrons which screened the house from any passers by. A narrow passageway linked the side of the house to the two glassed conservatories. Heating from the swimming pool was filtered through to the greenhouse. The lawns and flowerbeds were immaculate and Sharon accepted that old Max had every right to be possessive about the gardens, because his love and devotion to them had considerably increased the property's value.

He, in turn, had to concede that it was amazing that someone as young as Sharon had the amount of gardening knowledge that she did and was suitably impressed with some of her suggestions. By the end of the week Sharon had organised the staff in their duties and got the house into shipshape trim. Every morning she went for a swim which enabled her to check and double check that the surveillance equipment was all working properly and had clearly recorded all her comings and goings around the property.

Champagne Castle was ready to show off to the elite and everything was ready for the young and rich to be suitably overawed.

Their house-warming party was a resounding success; the basement was turned into a discotheque complete with garish flashing strobe lights. This was their first event since completion of exams at Oxford. After the elaborate meal everybody moved on downstairs where the drink continued to flow as the party warmed to fever pitch. Some friends were openly taking drugs to heighten their enjoyment and by midnight bodies were scattered everywhere. Mike and Robbie had locked certain upstairs doors, leaving the rest of the house free to their guests; however the most popular attraction was the Jacuzzi area which was in constant demand by the young partygoers.

African Chess

By three o'clock almost all their guests had left as everyone respected Sharon's request to end the party by three. Anyone not respecting this simple request would be hard-pressed to be invited again. New blood, from outside the Oxford student set, was being introduced, with Sharon and Mike ensuring they acquired the addresses. By Sunday the useful names were entered into the computer in her private study; it then took them several days to view the recordings and select the ones with potential leverage.

CHAPTER TWENTY THREE

'The screen gave them visions wild and created spectre's child'

<u>London - England</u>

On Monday the three travelled together to start their first day at the offices of CCOE Export & Import Company Limited. These initials stood for Champagne Castle Overseas Enterprises. Alain was there to meet them; he had set up a smaller office next to the computer room as their combined office. Sharon immediately took charge, insisting that she was going to move into his office alongside him, because she wanted to see how the business was run. Mike and Robbie moved straight into the trading room wanting to watch the future's trading systems at work; especially in the light of the new ideas they had picked up at the bank.

On their way home they eagerly discussed the various changes that they wanted to institute into this old family business and the methods of introducing these changes. The staff had been forewarned that there were to be changes, but the speed at which the three moved in their first week ruffled a lot of feathers.

Mike immediately went out and acquired the latest computerised trading system and Robbie set about programming the new system to trade electronically. Mike also acquired two London International Financial Futures Exchange trading seats, known as LIFFE. This enabled them to trade in financial futures on an exchange floor as to date; all trading had only been done with commodities such as potatoes, grain or coffee. They were now going to be able to trade in almost anything possible. Robbie made enquiries about the metal exchanges and found that to become members they simply needed recognised traders to join the company.

African Chess

The company was originally formed in the late nineteenth century and had been one of the founding members of the Corn Exchange; principally trading in seeds, pulses and grains. Having survived two world wars and when it was evident that container shipping was going to be the order of the day, the company moved its headquarters from the London docks to the present site. Grain silos had been acquired all around the country near main harbours in order to handle the bulk movement of their product. For the rest, most of the products were shipped in containers from their storehouses in Rotterdam and Antwerp in Europe. These were taken straight to their various warehouses, where the product was cleaned, mixed, sorted and bagged, ready for delivery to their distributor outlets to sell to the market throughout Europe. Because of the fluctuations in different world currencies when the company bought and sold the products it became necessary to make sure that these rates were held firm. For instance; when they bought beans in a third world country at a fixed price of one hundred dollars per ton they exchanged the equivalent amount in sterling. If anything politically or otherwise, such as a natural disaster, exploded in that country while the shipment was on the water, they would still have the one hundred dollars to pay for their beans, so that they never lost money. As its global business expanded in size, the company opened a small exchange department and traded money for other smaller commodity traders not able to do so on their own account, taking a small commission for their work.

The company had always been owned by the same family and the two remaining brothers had reached retiring age with no children to follow in their footsteps. They had discussed this problem with James McGregor who was asked to find a suitable takeover partner; a marriage of convenience was inevitable.

Within two months they considered the business sold to the

Roberts family. The elderly grain merchants privately agreed that they were bowled over by Nicole, she was clearly a lady of breeding and they wanted their company to continue in good hands. Nicole was a superb horse trader and didn't tell the elderly brothers that the acquisition was a present for her family.

The old established and staid company had always proceeded cautiously into any new growth areas and suddenly there were three new owners creating utter havoc within the sacred portals. These wet behind the ears whizz kids had come into the company and started pushing the staff into the twentieth century; Alain was heard to mutter angrily.

Their parents had given them a free rein to spend on investment, the only proviso was that they kept the bank informed of their plans. Mike and Robbie had discussed their ideas with James McGregor and some of his staff during the previous week. The bank knew that restrictions in financial controls in Britain would change over the next few years. They had agreed with the two and it had been the bankers who had subtly suggested the LIFFE seats and the metal exchanges to them, as well as the up-to-date trading system.

Mike and Robbie had asked them to supply several metal and foreign exchange dealers to help them get to grips with the new systems and the bank made the necessary arrangements. Once the dealers and systems were in place Mike started contacting some of his well-to-do friends and arranging substantial fund investment with the company. Those not willing were gently persuaded to reconsider and in a few short weeks, they'd been able to convince their contemporaries, or their parents, to invest with the company. From being an old and reliable, yet comparatively unknown, commodity trading firm CCOE quickly became known as one of the most aggressive futures trading companies in London. Because of the amount of new and valuable business being acquired, this division grew at an unprecedented rate. Within three months the futures division had to move from Mile End to the City, to newer and substantially larger offices. These were based in Mincing Lane, around the corner from the Tower of London and the opening party brought snooping executives from the competition, wanting to learn their secret formula for success. Substantial sums were being injected into the business by means of trading profits from the futures side and Sharon started acquiring smaller allied companies; initially smaller British companies but quickly expanding these acquisitions into Europe.

Alain's fears of Sharon were soon history as he found himself working well with her. He admired her strength and commitment to CCOE and found her new ideas and management systems very beneficial. He happily conceded that her style of new management was more in line with the restructured company image and quickly realised that any argument would be utterly futile. Sharon was made joint managing director of the company and Alain became her backup man; his knowledge of physical trading of commodities being invaluable and like a kindly father, he guided her through the pitfalls of good and bad companies in the trade.

The actual ownership of CCOE was hidden in a maze of companies registered in Lichtenstein and Switzerland. So that anybody trying to find out where any injections of money came from wouldn't be able to locate the actual owner. Sharon quickly surrounded herself with two expert takeover specialists, supplied by the bank, who were carefully concentrating on companies around the world. Behind the facade of this old and respected company, the three youngsters started planning thievery on a massive scale. They were about to invade companies all over the world, with all the major investors in their company able to live easily with themselves as their funds were doubled. Just as long as the money kept coming in!

James McGregor held his breath; never in all his banking days had he seen a company grow at this rate. His main worry was that anything that shot up this fast could come down just as quickly. While keeping a watchful eye on trying to establish where the funds originated from, he was happy to let them come rolling into his bank.

Parties at Champagne Castle began to change in character; the guests were changing from spoilt children to wealthy parents, stockbrokers, diplomats, Arab sheiks and bankers like James. However, keeping their format the same, they became even more riotous; their fame spread and they became sought after as the place to be seen within moneyed circles.

Neither Sharon nor Mike actively took a great part in any form of licentious behaviour, knowing they were merely the instruments who helped create fantasy worlds for others. They reaped their rewards out of the weakness and greed of their guests. They merely recorded the fun and Mike had to admit he felt a little like an unclean voyeur peeking through a looking glass. Robbie never invited his own backers to these parties and he and Joan tried getting away to her house near Oxford each weekend, where he carried out his own plans.

Monaco - Monaco

During their meteoric rise the three were continually hounded to join some major function or other. One invitation taken up was from a member of one of the richest Arabic royal families. There was no immediate successor to this crown and it was fully expected that Mohammed would take up the role. They had met at Oxford, where he had been invited to the parties and had been recorded practicing unsavoury sexual activities on at least three occasions. From their many recordings the couple had approached about thirty per cent of the unwilling sponsors to participate in their business. For good reasons they had left the majority on the back burner, until they needed really big funds or services. If anyone refused their offer, it was within their power to have a salacious story plastered across the more receptive dailies; cheque book journalism would be a bonus!

Mohammed contacted them out of the blue to invite them to spend a ten day holiday with him. He needed to discuss a business venture while sailing in the Mediterranean after watching the Monaco Grand Prix. Mike and Sharon flew to Nice where a helicopter was waiting to collect them. In the shimmering blue Monaco Bay, a flotilla of millionaire's palatial yachts was gently rising and falling with the waves. They were surrounded by opulent apartments converging on the harbour and rising upward toward the castellated Royal Palace that pierced the clear skyline.

Mohammed wasn't aboard his super yacht 'Helius' to meet them, but had left specific instructions for them to make themselves at home in their luxury suite.

"Mike! Sharon! Welcome!" Mohammed shouted when they appeared on deck just as he was racing toward them across the gangplank. He grabbed Sharon and whirled her around several times. His ecstatic greeting took them both aback, especially when he turned his attentions to Mike and planted a firm kiss on both his cheeks. Mike was not used to this genuine Arab greeting and pulled back, embarrassed by the affectionate embrace.

They spent the afternoon and evening talking about the times they had shared in Oxford, the people they knew in common and catching up on events; they were treated like royalty. In the evening they left the boat and had supper at the Loews Hotel which overlooked the glittering sea. They went on to one of the famous casinos where Sharon and Mike gambled enthusiastically and enjoyed watching Mohammed lose vast sums of money. His inexperience showed at the gambling tables but it didn't seem to worry their friend.

The following day was Thursday and practice day for the Grand Prix competitors. Mohammed had obtained passes to the entire course and they freely wandered around watching the sleek machines being tuned and put through their paces, ready for the big day.

Sharon wasn't really interested in the racing and continually disappeared into boutiques surrounding the course. Although she fully intended spending a fortune on chic designer clothes, she found Mohammed following her, insisting on paying for anything that she fancied. She tried refusing but found that Arab custom was such that, once making an offer, she was not allowed to refuse. Eventually they reached the happy compromise that he would pay for the most expensive present that was bought. She acquired an ornate slim line Piaguet watch and he was upset that she didn't choose the most expensive one. Most of Sharon's shopping centred around clothes and accessories which she had sent directly to the boat. By the end of the day they were all exhausted.

The race day itself was the usual spectacular event with spectators and television viewers loving every bit of the hundred and sixty mile an hour thrills and spills through the streets of Monaco. Afterwards, all three attended several parties given in the town as they drank, ate and laughed all evening. Mohammed collected girls like butterflies, moving through the town and inviting hosts of people back to his boat for a party. Among them were several racing drivers who had been invited to all of the luxury boats in the harbour and having parties at the same time. Happy music drifted from the ostentatious floating mansions, each one trying to outdo its neighbour with pomp and ceremony on a grandiose scale.

'Helius' slipped anchor on Monday morning and moved slowly from the harbour towards the open sea. The sun was well up in the sky burning down upon the white canopy. Mike and Sharon had gone up to the covered deck where they were having breakfast served to them as they watched their slow departure from the harbour. Mike's plate was piled high with fresh red watermelon on which he had almost emptied the salt shaker as he had always done at home. When Mohammed appeared, he had three gorgeous French girls in tow. He had collected them for the trip during the party and invited them to be seated at a circular couch towards the stern before sauntering across to his friends.

The short Arab was already showing signs of running to fat thought Sharon as he moved towards them, his face breaking into a wide grin. He leaned over and kissed her on both cheeks, then sat himself down at the head of the table, his accustomed position. Edging forward he slapped Mike on the shoulder, almost forcing the fork through the side of his mouth in his usual jovial manner.

"Michael! How are you enjoying yourself?"

"This is the life. That was a terrific party last night; I need a week to recover."

Sharon had become used to Mohammed addressing Mike on all matters. It was as if she had become an extension of Mike and it was beneath Mohammed's dignity to ask her directly of anything of importance. She quickly realised that behind his English upbringing, training and education, Mohammed was still Arabic in culture and custom. She didn't enjoy the situation but accepted it as part of the man's makeup and he was after all, their generous host.

"Michael, my uncle has asked me to talk with you because we've heard wonderful things about your business."

Sharon put down the book she was reading as her senses suddenly came alive, knowing that they were about to find out why they had been invited for this luxurious holiday.

"He has asked me to speak to you, because we are always trying to find ways to invest our money. We would like to buy shares in your business," Mohammed explained.

Mike looked at his cousin and noted that her face was placid, giving nothing away. He turned back to his host, who continued;

"If you allow us to invest in your shares, we'll allow the company to trade some of our commodities which, as you know, have many trading offices worldwide."

Mike's head reeled because what the young man had just offered would realise the opportunity for them to become the most powerful trading house in Europe.

"We will invest a large sum for your traders to play the futures market and in return we will be able to trade substantial physical commodities through your company." Sharon mentally calculated the increased revenue to the company, carefully weighing the pros and cons as Mohammed went on.

"Our group would like at least a third share of your business for this to take place. What do you think?" he concluded.

Mike leaned back in his chair and whistled softly through his teeth. His mind was racing and he didn't want to commit anything without offending his host.

"Mohammed! What do you expect me to say? You dump something like this in my lap right out of the blue and then ask me for a decision in the next breath."

A smile crossed the young Arab's face; he had been horse-trading since childhood and had spent enough time considering how to approach his friend before deciding to take a direct line. Sharon could see that Mike was being hustled for a reply and immediately intervened to give him some breathing space.

"Mohammed, why is your uncle prepared to invest substantial amounts in somebody that he's never even met?" He hadn't been expecting her question; agreement or opposition, yes, but this question hadn't even been considered, as he twisted a fork over in his hands.

"It's not the people in the business but the fact that from nowhere your company has grown into a large trading house in no time. It shows excellent prospects and we want to be part of it."

He turned his attention pointedly back to Mike, who knew full well that he couldn't make a decision without consulting Robbie, so he leaned forward and stared hard into the man's almond eyes for a long while.

"Mohammed, we're flattered to know that you value our friendship enough to give us this opportunity. What I suggest is that you go back and formulate a proposal for us to inspect. No commitment can be made without Robbie"

"And one other who shall remain nameless for now," said Sharon, kicking her bare toes against her lover's shin; she was damned if she would be excluded.

"We know the full financing of your company because we have done our homework well. I have a completed proposal in my room which you can study. Let me know by tomorrow," stated Mohammed.

The cousins sensed danger to their business but they agreed to have a good look at the proposal. They remained adamant however that no decision could be made in less than twenty four hours.

"I must give my uncle your answer by five o' clock tomorrow; a positive reply will turn you all into multi millionaires immediately and your company will go from strength to strength."

That night Mike and Sharon carefully studied the proposal in the seclusion of their suite. Mike liked the idea but Sharon felt the hairs on the back of her neck rising.

"Put it off until next week, I know that Robbie will agree with whatever you say and the two of you carry the majority vote; but something's not right. Don't ask me what?"

The following morning, at breakfast, he informed his host that if his uncle was unable to wait until the following week he should inform him that the deal was off. They then saw another side of this young man who, not used to having his will rejected, was furious. All day he tried to convince the couple to change their minds until finally at five o' clock he radioed his uncle and gave him their answer; the subject wasn't raised again on the trip. As far as everybody was concerned the matter was closed.

The two flew back to Britain from Italy where they terminated their holiday. Far from being resentful at having the offer turned down, Mohammed ensured that the rest of the trip went on as if nothing had happened.

CHAPTER TWENTY FOUR

'Negotiating a curse of dread, he put it in his clansman's head'

Manchester - England

He sat in the darkened corner of the now familiar lounge at the Fountain Head Public House watching patrons order their drinks, playing darts and generally enjoying themselves. Robbie had been coming to this same pub in Manchester for the last four weeks without having met anybody; although he had been told that somebody from the IRA would make contact with him there. Each Saturday night was the same story as he waited there between seven and nine; up until last week he had not spoken to anyone. An old drunk had parked himself at the next table and started talking to Robbie. He reciprocated out of boredom and also his background demanded that he replied when spoken to. His conversation of the previous week had intrigued Robbie, the topic centring on the idiotic feuding of Scots, Irish and English. Some of the things said had been of interest while others were fanatical and the rest were downright ridiculous; but still, Robbie found the old man's conversation quite enlightening and entertaining.

He found it getting to him this week sitting there watching people drinking and making fools of themselves.

"Hello young man, I see you're here again," he said, as he slowly moved to sit himself down. Tonight the old man appeared again at the same table, just as intoxicated. This disturbed Robbie because he'd been given explicit instructions by the voice on the telephone that he was to sit alone.

"I'm really sorry, but you can't sit there, I'm waiting for someone to join me," he said apologetically.

"I'm the one you're waiting for," countered the man now firmly seated across the table.

"No! You don't understand, I don't mean to be rude but you mustn't sit there," replied Robbie.

"Why not?"

"Well I need to be alone until my friend gets here."

"Can't I sit with you even if I was sent here by the IRA to meet you?"

"You!" Robbie gasped.

The little old drunk with a lovely smile and talkative nature now facing him was the most wanted man in England and it appeared that he could go anywhere without being noticed. The man smiled softly "Yes, I'm the one you've been waiting all these weeks to speak to. We can't be too careful in England, you know."

Robert stared, surely this old drunk couldn't be the high ranking IRA leader he'd been waiting to meet, it just wasn't feasible?

"Drink up; we have a lot to talk over tonight. We'll go to a place where we can discuss our business in private," the old man ordered.

They sat facing each other in a small room of a house not far from the Fountain Head. There were several other men in the house taking instructions from the old man.

"Now, young man, we've considered your proposal carefully. I think that we can accommodate you and your people's needs," he was direct and to the point.

Robbie carefully studied the man more closely in the light, he was not as old as he tried to make out as his skin gave him away; the finely coloured wrinkles on closer inspection were more akin to middle age.

"There is only one question still outstanding and that is if you don't make the returns you envisage on the market...." he paused, "how are you going to pay for our hardware supply?"

"Quite simply I'm prepared to place myself up for execution within two weeks of the last payment date if I don't make it in time," replied Robbie.

"You feel that strongly about your cause?"

"Okay. Believe me if you double cross us we'll find you wherever you might be hiding." The old man waited for an answer but nothing was forthcoming.

"I won't let my people down; if I did, then life wouldn't be worth living anyway."

The older man pulled a 9mm Parabellum automatic from his old duffle coat and placed it against the young man's forehead

"One jerk from this cold steel and your brains will be spattered against that far wall; remember this warning well," he said threateningly.

Robbie parried his threat calmly, "there is no turning back for either of us from this point."

"Just you remember those words lad; at the moment we're friends, don't make an enemy out of me."

Robbie studied the man carefully, his eyes were points of steel and he knew that this gentle looking old drunk could kill as easily as he smiled. It had taken him almost a year of constant meetings, checks and double checks, to reach this stage and now he was with their number one and this man's word was law. Robbie still couldn't believe that this seemingly gentle Irishman was the same one who could order women and children to be killed in cold blood.

"We'll gradually transfer three million pounds with you, the funds will come directly from a Cayman Islands numbered account; you'll invest this for us."

His heavy Irish lilt came through strongly as he pronounced three as 'tree' and Robbie saw that he was now completely relaxed.

"Do you want us to return it to the same banking account?"

"No! Once it has passed through your system and is ready for payment, we will notify you where each tranche is to be sent."

Robbie had offered to launder their money through various accounts and by playing the market the profit would be split between them.

"Your contribution to pay for the goods will be paid to that account; all other funds will be used for other activities."

The hardware referred to by the man had cost Robbie one million pound sterling. He would receive three million to invest on the commodities market and hoped to realise the one million in investment profit over three years. He agreed to return the money at a rate of half a million per year, thus making it clean money and a profit of one million to the IRA for their investment. Robbie was sure that he could make sixty per cent return on the money which was two million, one for them, as profit and one million for his payment of the goods.

The Irishman realised that the commodity market was like being given vast sums of money and told to bet it on a horse. If you knew the horse was a sure fire winner, you made money. A simple difference between track and screen gambling was that your odds were far higher on the exchange. Robbie also knew that many a favourite had accidentally stumbled at the fences. On the outside he seemed cool and collected, but inside his stomach was turning to jelly. He was scared because he was taking the biggest gamble of his young life. If it came off he would be a hero; failure would be the forfeiture of his young life.

His plan was starting to fall in place and now all he had to do was arrange delivery of the deadly cargo to South Africa. He knew this would have to be via an overland route but there was plenty of time to make these arrangements because he wouldn't receive the goods until all monies had been paid. Robert had quietly renewed contact with several UDF friends to set up a different hierarchy within the United Democratic Front. This new group consisted of young men only and who were far more pliable than most of the tribal elders. They were tired of being pushed around by the ineffectual leadership working for the ANC and wanted a change of pace. Robert had given this to them and they knew that, with their backing he could do it again. From his base in England he masterminded everything in Natal, knowing that his strength and powerbase lay with the Zulu people and that he could trust his friends.

At first, like a general commanding a battle from a distance, he arranged his officers in order of seniority and suitability for the task; making sure that they would be effective in their posts. Stealthily, like the Mafia in America, they started recruiting younger members to their cause; each person having to take an oath of loyalty to the new regime.

They were inconspicuous because of their low profile and the group quickly built up its strength. The penalty for even whispering knowledge of the group was instant death by burning. Like the Mafia their silent tentacles spread throughout Natal, southwards through the black homeland of Transkei to the Northern Cape area of Ciskei.

The thrill of being part of a secretive movement, with little or no profile, intrigued young men and women and the fear of death from their own people kept them quiet. Robbie's organisation was quickly eroding the centre ground of the UDF and the Zulu forces, who were continually waging war against each other, without realising that this shadow was moving in their midst. They had completed the first phase of the campaign, which was to recruit the army and now Robbie had to find the means to arm them. Having finally met and agreed the weapons arrangements with the IRA the second part of his plan was completed and he quickly started planning the third phase of this operation. He was fully aware of the balancing act he had created; one mistake would be his last and there was now no turning back.

Always at his side was the faithful Joan, acting as a tower of strength. Robbie found the situation ironic that his white mistress and his white brother were both unknowingly helping him to destroy the white power in his country.

In Surrey, although one of the "lairds," of Champagne Castle, Robbie knew he was still a long way from being accepted. In their favourite pub, they jokingly told him that to become a local in any of the small villages in England one had to be a resident for ten years; because he was a different colour it would mean at least a further five years. He had laughed at the jovial bantering but, within, he seethed at the gibe; knowing that he had no intention of staying in this racist country any longer than he needed.

London - England

Within two weeks of his meeting with the IRA chief, Robert was summoned to a further meeting at the Hilton Hotel in Holland Park. He hadn't expected this call and because it was almost on his direct route home, he took his own car to work that morning. He left the office at three o'clock for his appointment and found a parking space in a small side street on the south side of the hotel.

"Dr Jamal Farouki, Room four seven nine" Robert instructed the commissionaire.

"What's your name?" asked the man disinterestedly.

"Molefe," offered the young man "Robert Molefe."

He spelt it out and told him to pronounce the last letter like 'l' in Farouki; but he still stumbled over it when he called the room to instruct the voice at the other end of the line of his visitor's arrival.

"Dr. Farouki is busy in a meeting, he invites you to be seated in the lounge and have something to drink with his compliments. Just tell the waitress to bring the bill to me." The little man was being condescending which was tantamount to racism, Robbie thought.

After about ten minutes a tall brown-skinned man wearing a well tailored suit entered the lounge. His eyes searched each table as he walked straight towards Robbie.

"Mr Molefe? I'm Jamal Farouki, how do you do?"

He extended a finely manicured hand as Robbie rose to greet him. Robbie couldn't help noticing the delicately refined features of the man and the articulated crispness of his voice.

"Dr Farouki, it's a pleasure to meet you even if I'm not sure what it is you want; your man didn't say."

"Please," the man paused with a self knowing smile "sit down and I will tell you. Some mutual trade union friends of ours gave me your name and on asking around, discovered that you approached our organisation last year, trying to meet our leaders."

Robert now knew who he was talking to; this man obviously represented the Islamic Hezbollah Movement, the crownpiece of Arab terrorist groups.

"We couldn't meet you then, but when your name came up again via the trade union movement, we decided to find out about you," he said almost apologetically.

Robbie knew that the spreading news of CCOE must have contributed to this meeting. When he had asked for a meeting before, he had been dismissed as a crank. Now, with the company behind him, doors were being opened and his financial muscle was making people sit up and take notice.

"Dr Farouki that was over a year ago, so why come to me now?" asked Robbie.

"Very simply, we only help our friends and we weren't sure of your credentials."

"I have already made the deal with someone else, I no longer need the items," said Robbie, calling the man's bluff.

The man's feet began to shuffle uneasily back and forth across the carpeted floor; he was in a state of mental panic and this was the time to pounce.

"Maybe, just maybe..." he paused "we could do something together, for the good of both of us."

The Arab visibly relaxed, having found a form of escape, he leaned forward eagerly as Robbie slowly milked the situation.

Farouki had come from Iran with specific orders to get Robert to join their cause because several Islamic leaders in South Africa had asked for help from the Iranian Ayatollah. Robbie was seen by Iran as the link to help them overturn the hated Christian whites in South Africa. Libya's Colonel Gadaffi had also mentioned this to them, as they kept their eye on him through trade union informers. The ANC mustered help from the Soviet Communists who were linked with most of the world's powerful trade union movements and had raised awareness of the black versus white situation.

They needed an organiser for the ANC and one of the men from Zambia had suggested Robert Molefe, as various trade unions had been watching him carefully for some time. His climb from obscurity to a shareholder in a powerful trading house in such a short time had given them confidence in his abilities. At a meeting in Iran, heads of the fundamental Arab groups had agreed to give Robbie their full authority because they were going to throw their full weight behind the ANC. He was to be their linchpin with South Africa and organise the Cape Malays, providing them with funds and supplies.

When Robbie declined his offer, Dr Farouki was astounded; he knew that if he failed, his own life would be in danger. This had been an order from the highest authority.

"We need two million pounds for our campaign, some of the money will be used for hardware, some for training and the rest for the trade unions to help recruit workers in South Africa," Robert said, testing the water.

The man was confused because he had been sent with an offer and now the scenario had changed completely. The young man was naming his terms; he had to handle this matter delicately.

"Robert you don't understand, we are prepared to help you on our terms and those put to us by our friends in South Africa," he stated guardedly.

"Dr Farouki you are obviously a very busy man. I am fighting for something I believe in. You know your fight and I know mine. Now, if we can't agree on this we shouldn't be talking."

Dr Farouki was on the hook and he knew the young man knew it.

"We will help you but on our terms; we will supply the goods because we have access to all types of arms."

For half an hour the two discussed their own requirements; the Arab forgot his initial scare as time passed as he now had the young man talking to him. His natural wheeling and dealing nature again took over.

Robbie knew that he had the upper hand and when absolutely sure that his point had been made, he stood up to leave. This caught Dr Farouki by surprise and he again began to shuffle his feet as he mentally imagined his own head being severed from his neck on the hot sands of Iran.

"Dr Farouki, it would seem that we have no common ground and I thank you for your offer. If we need any help we will contact your group again."

Robbie calmly played his ace card while savouring the man's obvious discomfort.

"Mr. Molefe, perhaps we can arrange something in line with your wishes; but I will have to get permission first."

"Exactly how?" asked Robbie.

"We can let you have half of the money in supplies and half in cash for your group to spend as you see fit. How does that sound?"

Robbie slowly lowered himself back into his chair.

"What do you require from us?"

"There are certain countries that will not deal with Iran and we need a source of supplies. Your company has expertise in shipping goods from South Africa under strict embargoes and all we ask is that you do the same for us. It takes the certain type of skill, which you possess, to obtain necessary certificates to overcome these embargoes."

"What sort of things are we talking about?"

"Food, medical supplies, chemicals and a few other things that are banned to us; your company will source and supply these things, without taking any brokers fees."

"We have a deal. If you draw up a proposal we will meet tomorrow at the same time and finalise the agreement."

As soon as he could Robbie contacted the spokesman for the IRA and requested a meeting with the old man once again. He was told to ring again within twenty minutes. He recognised the voice immediately and quickly outlined a revamped program.

"Mr. Molefe, we have a deal. We won't renege on our side. I do hope you will honour yours," the voice clearly conveyed its intended threat.

"Do you mean you are not prepared to give us less money than agreed, surely that's in your own interest?"

"No, we have already put everything in place and cannot change that. However, if you repay the full profit immediately as agreed then we accept your offer."

Robbie knew that he was caught in their trap. Even though he had now managed to find the required money he would still have to find one million pounds to repay the agreed profit. Robbie replaced the receiver. Earlier he'd been elated thinking that he'd put one over on the IRA. He could have had two million pounds worth of supplies, one from the Arabs and one through the IRA; but now he was still stuck with his agreement.

That night he tossed and turned all night as his brain raced frantically seeking a solution to this problem. By morning his tired body drew itself to the shower and he knew what he had to do. Joan had monitored the proceedings with fascination without knowing any details. It would work out one way or another she told him, she had faith in him to make it work. Robbie joined the others at breakfast and they left for the office.

Within days he would have to take positions that could end his young life or make him a champion of the people. Mike felt the uneasiness within his brother and later that morning called Robbie into his office and asked him what was troubling him. They took a taxi and then walked along the Embankment. Robbie didn't tell him the full facts but instead gave him a detailed sketch of what to expect and what repayments were to be made.

Mike put his arm around Robbie's shoulder "don't worry, between us we can meet the payments," he said, happy in the turn of events that made his lifelong friend confide in him.

CHAPTER TWENTY FIVE

'A stronger man of the hour, spoke a word of lethal power'

<u>Pretoria - South Africa</u>

Dirk had been kept busy with the increased activity of the ANC, forcing the security man to take drastic measures against black freedom fighters throughout the country. Scattered reports from mainly English language daily newspapers alleged varying degrees of brutal unprovoked police attacks and indiscriminate killings. Accusations of unusually great amounts of physical torture being committed on black detainees by police and security forces whilst being interrogated, became commonplace. Reporters insisted that the scale of detentions had started to take its toll against popular organisations and that thousands of people were being held in dreadful holding camps and centres. Under existing security law the police enjoyed immunity from prosecution and as each new wave of protesters were rounded up, the force used against these activists became increasingly unrestrained.

Law abiding people in the townships were suffering most, treated with little difference from the young blacks trying to force changes on the government. Controlling these young fighters were the leaders of the ANC military wing, who had instructed their most trustworthy and loyal men to inflict the most damage possible; Dirk and his Askaris were stretched to the limit in searching for them.

This civil war had reached a sudden turning point resulting in giving Dirk a free hand to do what he saw fit. Under the vaguest hint of suspicion anybody, involved in alleged rebellious activity, could find themselves arrested. Slowly to begin, then with gathering rapidity, he had located core after core of senior ANC leaders;

dispensing with any formality and delivering an attack and kill policy. This drove the enemy further underground, making it more difficult to locate their leaders. Populace attitudes were quickly changing and he wasn't sure how much longer he could continue this legalised slaughtering. One thing he was certain of though was that this war wasn't going to end quickly and he had to continue his relentless task of hunting and killing, while he the free hand to do so.

Each day brought fresh condemnation by the press regarding the large number of missing people and those being found dead for no apparent or provable reasons; naturally the finger was being pointed at the police.

Dirk knew that no matter how hard they tried to conceal, or keep the lid on, these stories world reaction would soon force them to stop their activities. Once that happened their fight with the ANC would blossom into a full scale street warfare; because hope would return to the activists and they would openly start attacking the system once more.

People were becoming increasingly embittered with the police; graffiti was being painted on walls with slogans such as 'Viva Umkhonto we Sizwe' meaning 'Long live the Spear of the Nation'. Scores of relatively unknown townships started appearing on a growing list of trouble spots, which stretched security resources even further. Something had to be done quickly in order to speed up matters; Dirk's men were instructed to cut down and destroy any known leaders as efficiently as possible. The increased scale of the killings and detentions meant that Dirk's band of Askari warriors also grew in size.

Heading this group was a gentle looking grey-haired old man and except for the initial five members of the band, none of the Askaris knew of Dirk's involvement. They suspected that the old man was acting on orders from his white masters but none of them knew who these unknown men were; all blame was simply laid at the feet of the police force.

The confrontation spread with ever increasing cases of hit and run tactics by the ANC; staying in one place meant certain discovery and death. Continuing condemnation of the police was causing consternation to both black and white citizens; meanwhile the political wing of the ANC turned this to their advantage.

The indifferent Afrikaner press didn't print the stories to the same extent as the English language press, whilst state-controlled radio and television remorselessly tried to pacify and brainwash the population.

The government also had to contend with the increasing power of the black trade unions, which started to mobilise workers for the very first time. The unions were instigated by communist trained ANC members, who had visited the eastern bloc for training in Marxist teachings. Although the government tried its best to place restrictive clamps, the unions were growing as forced membership on workers.

Those workers, who could think for themselves and wanted no part of the union movement, were harassed and attacked until they were 'persuaded' to join. This move gave the blacks further political strength, at the same time as adding substantial sums to the ANC's funds.

The whites were reeling under this onslaught for the first time in their history and to maintain their momentum the ANC filtered the trade union funds through to the outside world in order to create various international propaganda offices and to successfully gain worldwide publicity for their cause.

The police were given wider powers and they used them to beat the townships into sullen submission. Trouble spots died down almost as quickly as they flared up and once again the leaders just went underground; to quietly smoulder like a volcano waiting to erupt again.

Several daily newspapers and trade union organisations were closed and their workers and supporters arrested. Young people carried on their resistance struggle because they had now become almost impossible to discipline; the law of the land was being tested in all areas. Many of the older residents in the townships welcomed the police back in their midst, fearing that carnage would return if they left again; but the townships were in a flux of change, with many gangs of youngsters raping, pillaging and killing at random with the police powerless to stop them.

When things seemed to have quietened down, Dirk was again summoned to a meeting at the Union Buildings in Pretoria. He knew all of the men seated in the minister's plush office, each of equal special security rank to himself.

"Gentlemen, we have not had an easy time during the last few months; although we have contained some of the problem, we have not stopped it," the minister began.

They had all been made to report on a weekly basis and were fully aware that the situation was far from under control and that most of the ring-leaders had escaped.

"What we have to do now is hit back at the ANC while they are trying to gather their thoughts."

This was a new twist as they all knew that the leaders were fleeing to the surrounding African countries; which happened as soon as the police had started gaining the upper hand.

"We have decided to teach them a lesson that they will never forget! We are going to chase them into their hideouts in the frontline states."

He sat back gauging their individual reactions; army, air force and police were represented and generally they didn't like the idea one bit because they were already spread too thinly on the ground. Only one man had a thin hard smile spread across his face.

"We are going into Botswana, Zambia, Mozambique and Lesoto and need to synchronise all our information on known hideouts, offices and camps in these locations. The operation will be called 'Donder' and will take place on the last day of this month; giving you exactly three weeks to prepare."

Most of the high ranking officers were not happy with this instruction. It was fraught with danger and they knew if it went wrong their armed forces would become the scapegoats.

"What will the rest of the world say?" asked an army colonel sharply.

"At this moment we don't really care; our people's lives are in danger and the hue and cry will die down before long."

"How far do we go?" questioned an air force major.

"If necessary you go right through Africa and you don't take any prisoners because we must stamp them out once and for all."

The room fell silent: They had been trained for just such an occasion but now that it had arrived, they all had doubts.

"Gentlemen, you must use air attacks and then clean up with commandos on the ground. We must inflict as much damage as possible. Needless to say, it must be kept highly secret and you are all to co-ordinate your operations. The army will have total command for the ground attack and I will be responsible to you for anything that you require."

"Sir, could you please notify my head of staff about the operation?" asked the air force major.

"They don't need to know about the attack until it is under way, until then they have been instructed to give you full support."

Again the room fell silent as the minister watched these heads of security; they were the best he could find and he knew that they would carry out their orders to the letter.

"Right, that's all I have to say. Collect your full briefing documents from my secretary on your way out. Inside those files you will find a special telephone number to reach me at any time."

The meeting was abruptly adjourned when everybody stood up; he shook each of them by the hand and wished them luck with their operations. He expressly left Dirk until last and indicated for the security man to be seated again before walking the rest of his warlords to the door. The portly minister returned to Dirk, his face beaming from ear to ear.

"What do you think, hey?" he enquired in English, his heavily accented voice now filled with triumph.

Dirk replied to the question in his mother tongue because he hated using English; to his mind it was almost as bad as trying to speak one of the many African languages.

"It's about time, we've been working with our hands tied behind our backs for long enough."

"Well we've now got to commit ourselves and give one last final push to rid ourselves of these terrorists."

"I don't understand why I'm here; this attack has got nothing to do with internal security."

"Let me ask you a question; what do you think will happen to those that possibly slip through the attack, will they return here?" The smile broadened across the minister's face.

"No," replied Dirk "If they aren't safe here and they fear another attack on their bases, they would flee further into the bush."

"OK! So, if you wanted to protect your main leaders, where would you send them in order to regroup and lick their wounds?" enquired the minister.

"I would send them into the bush somewhere, possibly deeper into Africa" "Wouldn't you be worried that your hosts may possibly turn their backs on you when their own people start getting hurt? Would you take that risk?" The senior man was getting to the point slowly.

Dirk took more time to think. He could see the logic of the question, but he had to consider carefully all the possibilities.

"Wounded animals always head for their lair, but if he believes that the hunter is waiting for his return, he will find safety in hiding elsewhere. Possibly in another lair until the hunter has quit."

"Exactly, so where is this second lair?" The minister was determined to make his security man find the answer.

"The eastern bloc somewhere," Dirk said, shaking his head in realisation.

"Right and how do they get there?" said the minister nodding his smiling head forward and backwards.

"London!" Dirk said, moving his head in unison with his boss.

"Correct, get your men packed and ready. You are going to have to clean up the bastards that slip away into London." The minister's head was still bobbing back and forth.

Dirk heard what the man was saying and like the soldiers, he was being told to fight a war on foreign territory. Also, like the others, there would be no prisoners if they were found out and caught as there would be major repercussions worldwide. In his own country he could obtain anything that he needed at a moment's notice; London would be different. He knew that he would have to plan everything in advance, from his arrival to his departure, with absolute precision.

"Meneer, I will need all sorts of things while I'm there. How do you propose to help me get them?"

"Just make your plans and give me a complete list of your requirements; they'll be there for you when you arrive in London."

"One last question, do I work with the armed forces on this one?"

"Only if you want to, I would recommend that you join them and that way you will know some of the faces that you're going to be looking for. You can give them some advice who to seek when they attack."

"Do I tell them my role?"

"No! The less people that know, the more chance you have of survival."

Dirk suspected that this could be a suicide mission and if he were caught, his government would deny all knowledge of him; somehow he had to protect himself.

"Right, I will think of a plan and make sure you have my shopping list within the week."

The two shook hands warmly and after Dirk had collected his brief from the secretary, he made his way back down the marble stairway into the warm sunshine: If he botched this operation his career would be finished.

Johannesburg - South Africa

That afternoon at the small bungalow in Bryanston the five men met at the kitchen table. Dirk watched his four companions closely as they listened to him; he tapped the burnt out grey ash into the large ashtray, then extracted a leather pouch and refilled his pipe.

"I have come to trust and rely on your knowledge and now we have a mission to complete and this is one of the hardest assignments placed before us," he said in one breath before placing the pipe between his teeth.

The men at the table were used to being given instructions or being hauled across the coals but never before had their white employer even recognised their role in this battle.

"We have got to prepare ourselves to apprehend these fleeing ANC leaders who may arrive at certain known international venues together or individually and then wipe them out."

Like in a puzzle, they could see the pieces but couldn't make out the full picture yet; nobody said anything.

"I want you all to go home to your families tonight and I want you to think of a plan to get all of them together under one roof at the same time."

Dirk lit a match and placed it into the bowl of the pipe.

"Where are they going to be fleeing from and where do we expect them to be going to?" asked Shorty Majozi.

The smoke belched out in large clouds "I can only tell you that they will be arriving in a large city en-route to another destination and that we must catch them while they are in this city."

Dirk started to add careful adjustments to the plan laid on the table as the biggest problem was going to be how to get the explosives into a well guarded area without creating any undue suspicion. He knew where the attack would have to take place and had sketched a rough diagram of the building plan. They also needed to create diversions to take into account any unforeseen circumstances during their attack.

Slowly but surely their brainstorming session started achieving results, as his men thought like the unseen enemy. They decided to place the explosives at about four in the morning; giving less chance of their being seen. The deadly explosion would have to achieve its maximum impetus toward the centre of the building and that meant that several charges would have to be placed. Furthermore the timers would have to be set to go off within twenty four hours of the intended explosion as this would reduce the chance of the devices being located.

The last point was whether to set up a timed bombing or detonate the charge by means of a remote control; after much debate they decided that the latter was preferred to ensure maximum effect. That sorted, the group concentrated on an alternative plan just in case the activists intentionally staggered their arrival and departure times.

For all its cohesion the plan was vulnerable as there were too many unforeseen factors to consider; especially if the leaders arrived at irregular intervals. A big problem was how they were to capture and dispose of one leader, let alone several of them, without notifying or alerting the rest of the group.

Dirk told them that he needed a list of material that would be required for the mission by noon next day.

He returned to the Union Buildings at four o'clock the next afternoon with a substantial list of requirements ranging from train timetables to hand grenades. As planned, the minister was out when he handed his list to the secretary. Equally carefully, he got her to stamp and sign his duplicate copy; the minister's rubber stamp would be his only safeguard if he were caught by British police as the minister wouldn't be able to deny his government's involvement.

Dirk felt pleased with the way that he'd covered his tracks as he had seen what happened to fools who didn't cover themselves; they were dead or rotting in prison somewhere. Furthermore, this piece of paper would go into a special folder lodged with his bank and he would make another copy to leave with Annemarie as insurance against being betrayed. Feeling somewhat happier with his position, he steered the Ford out of the parking lot into the afternoon traffic, noticing that he was being followed by a red Nissan. Due force of habit, he kept an eye on it until it was overtaken by a builder's panel van and didn't reappear; he relaxed, feeling comfortable with his work that day.

CHAPTER TWENTY SIX

'Love bartered is gained and won, a traded life could be gone'

London - England

It was unusually hectic in the trading room that day as Mike and Robbie concentrated on the green flickering screens like two hawks. They had moved massive funds into coffee futures. There had been the standard rumours from the market that the International Coffee Organisation was close to agreement behind closed doors, where discussions had been taking place for three days now. Although most indicators pointed to a breakdown in the talks, which would send coffee futures through the floor, Mike had a strong hunch that world buyers would support growers for a few more years yet. While most traders covered their position, Mike had exposed his company to this high risk because he felt that the price indicator had fallen too sharply before their meeting and he banked on its price recovering.

For the last three days it had hardly moved two full points up or down and he knew that this slight fluctuation was simply nervousness in the marketplace. As prices bottomed out, Mike and Robbie carefully bought various lots at the lower price. They didn't acquire too many at one time, slowly buying as others sold.

They took on board some five hundred and eleven lots with each lot valued at thirty one thousand, eight hundred and seventy five pounds; this made their position worth more than sixteen million pounds sterling. This was a very nervous time for the two; they had not disclosed their position to anyone, not even Sharon because they both understood that they were gambling with their family's future.

Mike gambled that the parties would agree terms but, if they didn't, then they would lose more than two million pounds in one swoop. If Sharon heard about the gamble, Mike knew that she would pull them out immediately. Mike and Robbie were hoping to recoup most of the money to meet Robbie's repayment. For three days now they had almost chewed their fingernails to the quick and hadn't told anybody what they had been doing. Always hovering close by their screens in case of any breaking news, that would mean them having to react quickly, they could do nothing but watch in hope. Mike thought that they were going to win; if not, they wouldn't just lose a fortune but also the business. Robbie was running out of time for his first repayment to the IRA; having expected to have made at least a one third return on the loaned capital by this time he had barely squared the invested money. He hadn't been very successful on the commodity exchanges during the preceding months.

Mike watched the disturbing antics of his friend as payment day approached; Robbie's trading pattern became more erratic and like every gambler, he tried recouping losses by playing for bigger stakes. As each day passed Robbie's judgement became noticeably suspect and by the end of the week Mike couldn't bear to watch as his best friend became more and more depressed and moody. Mike asked Robbie to join him for lunch but, for the first time in his life, he declined; not standing for this snub, Mike ordered his friend to leave the trading room and join him.

They went to Savages Grill Room, hidden under the railway arches around the corner from Tower Bridge underground station. Down in the murky cellar they found a corner table out of the way as the usual lunchtime racket had already started.

"What the hell is going on?" demanded Mike.

"Why, what do you mean?" Robbie replied guardedly.

"You know full well what I mean, Robbie. You've suddenly gone mad. I've been keeping an eye on your trades, they're suicidal. You're playing the market like a punch-drunk idiot."

"No I'm not! My positions are almost square."

"Admittedly last week you were up, but not by much and then you bought gold on a downward sliding market and wiped out all the gains. Is that the trading of a sane man?"

This was the only man in the world that Robbie could trust but he knew that he couldn't tell him the full facts as it would certainly destroy their brotherly bond.

Sharon entered the office around mid-day and went downstairs to the trading room to find Mike and Robbie; but discovered that they had gone to lunch. This was unusual as they normally invited her along. She thought at first that they must be meeting a client and had forgotten to tell her; then one of the junior traders said that he had seen them together in Savages. She put on her coat and went to Savages in order to find out exactly what was going on; if the two of them were in some way keeping secrets from her she wanted to know about it.

When she reached the bottom of the wooden stairs she stood for a short while adjusting her eyes to the dimly lit cellar. She stopped twice briefly to speak to business associates before she saw the two in earnest conversation at a table in a dark corner. Instead of barging straight up to the table, in her usual manner, she ordered a drink and stood quietly observing the two men. Mike seemed to be lecturing Robbie. For some time she watched as the two argued; she couldn't make out what they were saying but, whatever it was, it looked serious. She quietly finished her drink and returned to the office.

"When you told me about the investments and the promised return, why the hell didn't you tell me about the payback conditions?" Mike demanded.

"I thought it would be easy to repay it through profits," Robbie's manner was defensive as he hadn't told Mike the full facts surrounding the deal or who his clients' were. He'd simply outlined details of the financial arrangements to him. If Mike knew who his clients' were he would somehow find a way to give them back their capital without knowing what the consequences would turn out to be. Eventually Mike calmed down and sat in silence for a while trying to get to grips with the problem. His mind was racing to find a way to help Robbie out of the hole he seemed to have dug for himself. He could see that the amount of money required could not be taken from other accounts, or even deducted from profits because it would be too obvious.

He looked Robbie directly in the eyes "as soon as we get back to the office I want you to close down on all the positions that you're holding and let's see what the deficit is, then we'll fathom out something."

"Maybe the market will move in our favour," insisted Robbie.

Mike couldn't believe that Robbie was still playing for time, "No way, you're still acting like a drunken gambler placing investments on rumours and losing. Let's do this thing properly or not at all."

They finished their lunch in comparative quietness and it wasn't until the waitress asked them whether they wanted coffee that Mike's face suddenly lit up "aren't the ICCO members meeting in London today?" he asked.

"Yes, but they will probably haggle for a week like they did in Switzerland last year," Robbie said dismissively.

"Great, this may be your loophole. C'mon drink up, we've got a lot of hard work to get through today."

Back at the office the two men quickly cleared Robbie's positions and then settled down to sort out what he had lost over the previous few days; it didn't look good.

Mike explained his plan to Robbie; they knew from past experience that when the market moved it was likely to be ten points either way. Both got busy talking to anyone and everyone worldwide who dealt in coffee; they spoke to traders, growers, shippers and users alike. All the answers were collated and carefully noted down; any extra details or hints, which slipped out, were meticulously recorded. They spent the time studying all the answers and conversations from London to Indonesia and by eleven that night, they had finished their research.

Robbie got busy on the computer. Everything positive was logged on one side of the screen based on a one to a hundred point system as each tiny scrap of information was logged. They told Sharon that they were working on an important coffee transaction for one of their investors and she went home by train that evening.

By one o'clock in the morning both men were absolutely exhausted as Robbie placed the final calculations into the computer; he could hardly bear to push the button to find out the result.

Mike pulled nervously at his tie as Robbie hit the return button. Up on the green screen flashed the answer in red, showing a consensus of opinion that the market would tumble and talks would break down.

When Mike arrived home that night Sharon was fast asleep as he slipped in beside her as quietly as he could. He didn't want to disturb her and he was exhausted.

She had heard the car enter through the gateway and the barking of their newly acquired Doberman pinscher bitch called Suki. Waiting until he relaxed beside her, she rolled over and gently ran her fingernails down the full length of his spine.

"Sorry, did we wake you?" he asked.

"No, but I was a little worried when I woke at twelve and found you hadn't arrived home. How did it go?"

"Not very well, all the indications are against my gut feeling because everybody thinks the talks will break up in chaos."

"So what makes you think that they won't?" she asked, her fingers gently continuing to stroke up and down his spine.

"Oh, it's just a hunch. All the growers come from third world countries and the first world will appear to have lost its conscience if it turns its back on the farmers right now."

"Mike, what's this really about? Don't try to bullshit me, I know something is wrong and I saw you two going hammer and tongs at each other today."

Sharon's question took Mike aback; if he lied she would know immediately and if he told the truth she would pounce on Robbie and stop his trading for the good of the firm.

"Robbie has had an extremely tough period and he needs to be taken in hand for awhile. One of his investors is threatening to sue us if he doesn't produce a profit."

Mike was thankful that she couldn't tell anything from his face in the dark.

"What are you going to do about it?" she persisted.

"I'm trying to help him. My trading positions are very strong at the moment and I'm going to take a gamble on coffee with him."

"Will we suffer badly if it goes wrong?"

"Let's just say that if we get it wrong, you and I will have to call in some large favours."

"Mike, just be sure you cover all the angles before you decide to gamble."

He breathed a silent sigh of relief as he felt her hand come to rest as she fell asleep once again. His brain was running at a million miles an hour. If he miscalculated it could end up costing their firm very dearly and he hardly slept that night as he went through everything that he had heard that day. Something wasn't right and then at five o'clock he suddenly realised what it was.

He fell asleep and was awoken again at six thirty by Sharon getting out of bed. After a quick swim he had breakfast and met the other two on his way to the triple garage. Walking past his black friend he grabbed Robbie's hand in the African double handshake and laughed.

"How's my black boy today?" he mimicked in African dialect so that Sharon wouldn't understand. Robbie winced at the patronising words and almost hit out at Mike before realising that he only played tricks like this when he was happy. The handshake promised that his true brotherly feeling towards him was unchecked; which was fully confirmed when Mike got in behind the steering wheel and winked at his brother.

At the office the two started the day slowly by contacting several floor traders and giving them very explicit orders to buy coffee in single lot amounts and most importantly, only when these became available. They didn't want the other traders to realise that there was a ready buyer in the market, because this would automatically force the present price upward. Each trader was told to keep quiet about their instructions, because if their strategy became common knowledge they would never deal with them again. Few traders were brave enough to risk the fury of this up-and-coming powerhouse, so they obeyed the instructions to the letter when the New York coffee exchange opened. The two watched prices blip up and down; they took each call to confirm the purchase.

Talks were still going on that evening when the exchange closed and to date they had about a quarter of the lots they required. That night the statement from the meeting in London suggested that the delegates were about to go home because Western buyers were becoming frustrated with the growers.

That scared several people and by the following day several large traders were dumping coffee futures onto the exchange in an attempt to redeem their losses. Everyone was suddenly sceptical that any agreement would be reached.

By six o' clock, Mike and Robbie ordered the traders to stop buying. They had spread their order across fourteen companies so that traders didn't realise that such a large block had been placed with one company. The market had moved down during the day and nobody was really interested in buying. Everybody was desperately trying to get out of the coffee market, the waiting started and after the meeting a communiqué was released that nothing further had been achieved during that day. Mike felt the tension heighten substantially, the delegates were still talking and that could be a good sign; but he wasn't sure. Market prices remained static.

Mike did not know he was gambling with Robbie's life and if agreement wasn't reached and the market fell, Robbie would have to sacrifice every penny of the Hezbollah fund simply to meet one IRA re-payment.

On the surface he remained calm and it was only when he got into bed at night and explained everything to Joan that he received the comfort he so desperately needed. How she regretted giving him those names now and she made up her mind that he wouldn't see the rest of them which she still had hidden away.

The following day a similar pattern developed as Mike and Robbie watched their green screens flickering but not yet moving anywhere on the coffee markets, every movement was downward as traders became more disillusioned. To break the monotony they went with Sharon to the Mincing Lane office, where they discussed routine business with some of the traders before having lunch at Savages.

Back at the main office nothing had changed, except that Alain had arrived back after an inspection tour of a new company, which had taken him away for several days. He was not aware of the unfolding drama and was ecstatic with the company's new acquisition. He gave Sharon a big hug to indicate that any animosity between them had disappeared completely.

Alain secretly carried a torch for his younger colleague and suspected Sharon had guessed this when she started acting the helpless female role. Like most men would have done, Alain immediately rushed in to help rather than let her make an idiot of herself. Sharon made it evident that she knew his judgement was good, though very staid and she got him involved by suggestion rather than force. Before he realised his position she had him busily involved in acquisitions. He, in his turn, had found his forte and enjoyed this new role. Searching for more and more companies and with two accounting experts, he would negotiate finances and go into the product and management practice of these new companies.

African Chess

When the ICCO meeting adjourned that evening one of the delegates, who had been interviewed separately, said there might be some hope for an agreement. However, most of the media experts listened to the main body of the delegates where nothing was being given away. Mike wondered if he were grasping at a straw as he cottoned onto this lone voice and what it was possibly suggesting. At ten o'clock the following morning a rumour filtered through that the meeting would break up by lunchtime, because several American and Western buyers had had enough of this haggling. The trader's rumour market was notching up by the minute and now it was going into overdrive. Robbie's heart sank at this news, but Mike wasn't prepared to listen to every rumour being spread by traders in the market.

He felt that this one positive voice had come from an impeccable source, by almost three o'clock and just before the New York exchanges opened, Mike and Robbie began to seriously contemplate selling their coffee futures because nothing was happening, time was running out and the strain was affecting them so much. They started working out what losses would be sustained by the company it was redeemable and when Mike was just about to give the order to sell when suddenly saw his screen go mad as a news item flashed across it. ICCO had managed to get all parties to agree and they were going to give the agreement a further two year trial period! Within seconds the world was buying coffee again whilst the two young men watched dumbstruck as the bidding rose almost twenty points in thirty seconds. Then their desk phones went mad with traders wanting their coffee lots back before prices went too high. In five minutes of brisk trading, every coffee future had been sold back to the market. By waiting a crucial two minutes they forced the price up by nearly thirty points.

Suddenly Alain wasn't the only happy man in the office; Robbie was off the hook as he watched the company making nearly three and a half million pounds. The news started to filter through the marketplace as traders realised that Mike and Robbie had captured almost every spare coffee lot available. Robbie's investors would make a handsome profit whilst others flocked to invest their money with the company. That night the four friends went out and had a meal at the most expensive restaurant in the area. Joan quietly said a little prayer for Robbie; things were back to normal again.

Mike told Sharon that he had noticed a lot of Arab funds coming in and they thought immediately of Mohammed; perhaps the young man's family was at work. Like a win on the races, everyone was watching the punter and backed the same horse, believing that there was inside information.

Only Mike and Robbie knew just how lucky the company had been. Even James McGregor had not been aware of the transaction until it had been finally concluded. He would have stopped them for sure, but Lady Luck had blessed them on this occasion.

CHAPTER TWENTY SEVEN

'Beneath the northern skies, the queen grabbed desirous prize'

<u>Pretoria - South Africa</u>

"Well that's that! The rest is in the lap of the gods because we've done everything humanly possible and he's strong and healthy," said the senior surgeon finishing off the last stitch.

"We'll probably know in the next twenty four hours whether or not he will pull through," replied the second man, looking straight towards Jay as he spoke.

A theatre sister assumed charge of the patient and was busily checking through the instruments as the two surgeons left the operating room. The anaesthetist removed the complicated array of pipes, leads and drips, while proceeding to make last minute checks of the man's pulse and breathing rate before bringing him round.

Jay leaned over Michael as he opened his eyes and even in his drugged state, he gave her a boyish grin before closing his eyes in sleep again. A sparkle had told her that he had recognised her and he now knew that she had kept her word and remained with him. Two orderlies wheeled a trolley through the swing doors and Michael was gently transferred from the operating table onto it. His chest was covered with a large patch where the surgeons had operated, his leg was now encased in a plaster cast and several areas of his body were covered with bandages.

Jay quickly changed back into her nursing uniform and hurried after the wheeled bed. By the time she reached the orthopaedic ward a staff nurse had already moved Mike into a bed and was busily fixing tension pulleys to his plastered leg as it was raised into the prescribed position by the correct weights which were added to the end of two trailing wires. Jay saw that the man's face was peacefully relaxed as she introduced herself to the staff nurse, who allowed her to stay with the patient, especially as Jay was a more senior nurse.

She then remembered his vital briefcase and hurried along the hall to the casualty receptionist. At the desk she found that their shift had changed and replacing the elderly lady, was a fresh-faced young man.

"I've come to collect a briefcase that I left here earlier today," she said into the speak hole. The man looked perplexed, he didn't know anything about her mysterious case as nobody had said anything to him; he casually turned around to see if he could see it in the room.

"I gave her specific instructions to keep it here until I returned for it," said Jay.

The young man went to the desk and searched behind it and then he tried the two cupboards, the only pieces of furniture in the room where things could be placed.

"Nothing here," he said.

"It's very important that I retrieve that case tonight, can you please call her and ask where it is?"

The man's eye caught Jay's angry glare so he picked up the telephone and after several minutes said "No answer, but if you like I'll try again in a few minutes."

She noticed that he had a nervous twitch as he pulled his mouth awkwardly to one side, "I'll call back in about an hour, make sure you locate it," she told him.

She went to sit at Michael's bedside and hadn't realised how tired she was, she thought back to the explosion and how long ago it now seemed. The constant work since then was beginning to take its toll, her charge slept peacefully and would probably sleep through to morning because his system was still filled with drugs and his natural body resistance would make him sleep while the repair process was taking place.

Jay was trying to decide what to do when a man and a woman entered the ward and spoke to the staff nurse who immediately pointed towards her. They made their way across the open floor to the bed.

"Hello, how is he?" asked an elegantly dressed woman.

"We'll just have to let nature take its course; everything that could be done has been done," Jay replied.

"We're his parents and have just driven up from the Drakensburg, we only heard about it some two hours after it happened," said the woman's companion.

He moved to the opposite side of the bed, not saying anything as his eyes travelled slowly from the sleeping face to the suspended leg.

"How much damage is there?" he quietly asked Jay.

"They had to open his chest as he has three broken ribs, a slightly punctured lung and the leg is shattered. Under those bandages are some nasty lacerations and burns to the body."

"What are his chances of survival?" asked the woman tearfully.

"He has youth and strength on his side it all depends how he overcomes the shock factor, otherwise everything will be OK."

"Good," mumbled the man.

His parents took several items from a large bag and placed them inside a cupboard beside the bed.

Jay drew a long breath as she saw the missing briefcase inside the locker! She decided not to do anything about getting it out until his parents had left. They remained with their unconscious son for about an hour before telling the staff nurse that they were leaving. When they had gone Jay quickly removed the briefcase and arranged for a taxi to collect her and to take her straight home. Before having a shower she hid the bag behind some old folded towels in her linen cupboard.

London - England

Sharon was seated at her desk steadily going through reams of computerised sheets before her. They contained numerous and intimate details of various small public companies as they were again on the buyout trail due to the company being awash with cash. Investors were pouring funds into Mike and Robbie's division; which was now earning vast sums of commission money for the firm and she had to do something positive and secure with this mountain of cash.

Until recently the firm had only acquired small private firms to spread their size and product base; but she now felt that they were ready to expand into larger and more adventurous acquisitions. James McGregor was seated opposite her as she had asked him to search their files for public companies with current trading problems. His bank had details of all public companies on file - the good, the bad and the indifferent – as they were always on the lookout for good investment possibilities and potential. He relaxed, as the young woman scanned the paperwork that he had brought for her, because he knew the companies he would choose but wanted to see which ones she would pick out from the lists.

For an hour Sharon carefully went through the pile and then looked up at James. "These three," she said, tearing off the top sheet of her pad and handing it to him.

He scanned the names carefully, noticing that only one of his choices was among them; he had been sure that she would have selected at least two of the five he had short-listed.

"I picked these, have a good look at them again," he said, extracting a sheet of paper from his jacket pocket. Sharon looked at the names then went back to her computerised printouts for a second look. She examined the various marked companies in depth then looked up again.

"Not enough assets," She shook her head firmly.

"What kind of firm are you looking for?"

"One with a large asset base as we want to convert their satellite companies to cash by selling them off immediately at a profit."

"Right, I'll get a list of all the shareholders and then arrange to get everything that we have on file for these three companies sent to you as quickly as possible."

"Thanks James, I appreciate your help."

As she got up she also appreciated that he was treating her less as a second father and more as an equal. She led the way downstairs into Mike's office, where he was busily tapping out something on his computer.

"Hi James, how's tricks?" he asked, looking up from the keyboard.

He stood up, took the other man's hand, indicating for him to be seated.

"What did you think of this month's results?"

"Pretty impressive, but don't you think you're going too fast?"

"Not really, the growth has all been out of trading profits."

"And we don't have any outstanding borrowings," Sharon interrupted quickly.

"I know you're not over-extended yet, but please keep an eye on things as you could overheat if you grow too quickly: I've seen too many other companies do that."

They had always respected the older man's opinion and so far he had been correct with his advice, always hovering in the background so that he didn't miss a trick.

"That little coffee trade for instance made a lot of money for you, but..." he paused, "It was a lucky gamble. Don't do that kind of thing too often or one day it will catch you out and burn you badly." He had let them know in his own discreet way that he was aware of their goings on.

"It won't happen again," Mike said half apologetically.

"James is right; if I had known what you two were doing I would have had your hides for breakfast. It wasn't very smart," Sharon interrupted quickly.

"Enough said, come-on you two the bank is treating us all to lunch; where's Robbie?" asked James, now knowing that he had an ally in Sharon who would keep the men in check.

"Right, it's decided then! We're going for a dawn raid on Fraktill Industries."

Mike was addressing the three seated around the boardroom table. They had spent all morning checking the documentation brought to the meeting by their banker. It was agreed that everything was ripe for a takeover, now that they had the bank's full support. During the session they calculated how many shares were controlled by shareholders outside the company's working directors – who only controlled a minor holding. If they could persuade the outside shareholders to sell their shares then they would control their first public company. They didn't have enough funds on their own but, like most geared takeovers, the bank would underwrite the amount required. As they intended asset stripping, the money this could have realised would then help to repay the loan. The shortfall amounted to slightly more than five million pounds which, with its record, the bank was happy to back CCOE with and get a large block of shares into the bargain. James McGregor suggested a reputable merchant banking company that might act for the South Africans in the takeover as they needed somebody with knowledge of these matters and who would acquire and handle the share transactions.

"How long will the whole transaction take to effect?" Robbie asked James.

"Lets see, by the time you have announced your higher bid for shares and had forms printed and sent out, it could take at least six weeks of hard preparation"

"What if they oppose us and make a counter bid; then how long?" Robbie pressed.

"How long can pigs fly?" James shrugged his shoulders.

"Give us a rough idea," said Robbie.

"Robbie! If they can arrange the extra finance required we would be mad to pursue the matter," Mike butted in.

"We've worked out a scheme that would make it impossible for them to match your offer, unless they were heavily backed," James continued.

Sharon interrupted him in full agreement

"If they did that, then it wouldn't be advisable to continue. We're offering a fair price for the shares. Any more and the company wouldn't be able to repay the bank."

Both young men were now happy with these answers and for another hour they all remained seated at the table discussing the proposed takeover; the directors of CCOE were a little more than excited by the prospect.

Four weeks to the day, the firm of Gray, Mouton & Faraday sent out the necessary proposal to all shareholders of Fraktill Industries. Their company had fired its first shot across the bow of the opposing team. By that same night the Evening Standard had received copies of this offer and had contacted George Mouton for a story; it made the late edition. It wasn't one of the great coups of the century but the speed and size at which their company had expanded made financial news columns worth reading.

By the next morning the chairman of the public company had clearly lodged his opposition with all the daily newspapers, radio and television. Both companies gathered at their respective boardroom tables, busily establishing tactics. The media, as usual, appointed their champion in advance; the youngsters got their vote. A battle slogan was dreamed up by reporters and the story was portrayed as the David verses Goliath saga. City whiz kids sat back and watched with some delight, even though this new young company within their ranks made them a touch nervous. Nobody liked fast growing winners and they were certain that the company had misjudged this attempted buyout. Pundits in the city had seen this all before: Fast growing companies rising quickly only to fall by the wayside; whereas the steadier climbers went on to become leaders of industry. Once a company started along the CCOE path it was difficult to stop them; they became a gobbling machine, buying anything that was half successful.

Sharon, Mike and Robbie were having more fun than they had had playing the futures markets. Every hour brought an interview or some new twist forcing them to change plans on the move. Everything was controlled by them and that's what they most enjoyed about the buyout; it wasn't in the hands of the weather or the whim of some far distant trader, as were the commodity markets. Secretly they all admitted that a sense of danger played a major role in their enjoyment. The coolest head was that of their banker, who had been through this hoop many times before and was used to all the backbiting and nastiness which was all part of vicious takeover bids.

The day before the closing date for acceptance of their offer a hammer blow was delivered by Fraktill Industries: They announced that they would be offering a higher price for their shares. In their East End office the small group were shattered by the news. The counter offer was far in excess of anything that they could offer and there was nothing left to do. They knew that they were beaten when an internal telephone rang and Mike was told that large investments were being recalled. They knew that somebody had focused on them because it had all happened within a matter of hours.

"Who have you made enemies with?" demanded James impatiently on the telephone.

None of them could think of anyone who would outbid them. They had made substantial profits for all of their investors, so why withdraw funds at such a crucial time?

"I can smell some form of collusion here. First of all your bid is overturned then investors start withdrawing funds so that you can't raise your bid. Something stinks to high heaven." The bank manager's tone was tinged with accusation.

Mike put down the telephone and immediately went to the trading room to find out more about the mysterious investor. He asked for the settlement sheets and within ten minutes he had the full force of the bank checking and double checking all the names of suspect investors. They had to find out who was behind the investments as much as McGregor did. It took four hours for them to come up with a name. All investments led through various companies forming a chain from England, to Switzerland, to the Cayman Isles and back to England.

The directors listed for the British investing company were Arabic and one name stuck out immediately from the rest. The three looked at the report in front of them.

"Bloody Mohammed!" seethed Sharon.

"A so-called friend," Mike told his banker on the open telephone line as the others listened in, "We spent nearly two weeks with him last summer."

"Well, you would be foolish to go up against them, there's big money there. Let's go for one of the others," advised James.

"Like hell!" spat Sharon "No matter how much money he has behind him, just give us twenty four hours. I want to speak to him first."

By that afternoon Mike and Sharon had arranged a meeting with

Mohammed's brother in London. He knew who they were immediately they called. He stuttered through the preamble, claiming that Mohammed was abroad. Robbie, listening on his extension, had the feeling that Mohammed was in the room, giving his brother instructions.

Mike and Sharon left their office early and paid a visit to their security vault before driving to St Georges Hill. In their gate-keepers cottage Mike searched through several video tapes and then copied three of them. Sharon went straight to her study where she settled in front of her computer and after several minutes located a file. She printed out the details from it and within half an hour, the two were driving quickly along the A3 to London. They parked in an underground garage in Park Lane then walked to the building where the meeting was to be held. They were shown into a plush office with gold carpeting and expensive gold and silver draped curtains. The top of the single desk was covered with finest leather. Neither spoke as they seated themselves in two Louis XIV chairs. They were kept waiting for twenty minutes and didn't say anything because they had already agreed that undoubtedly the place would be bugged. The door opened with a flurry and a young man entered. His features, except for the well trimmed moustache, did not hide the fact that he was related to Mohammed.

"Hi, I'm Ahmed. Mohammed has told me all about his Oxford friends and my home is your home. Please be seated Mike."

His voice carried a definite American twang. The two knew full well that he was here under instruction and Sharon attacked from the outset.

"You tell Mohammed that we want him to withdraw your company's support for Fraktill Industries and to stay out of our business," she commanded forcefully.

The young man shammed absolute surprise, feigning how hurt he was by denying any knowledge of this particular company.

"If Mohammed wants to play games with us then this report will be published in tomorrow's Evening Standard. So he'd better contact us immediately," demanded Sharon.

Knowing that he was not used to such a demanding performance from a woman, she played this to her advantage as she placed a photograph in front of him.

"You may have the money to play games with us but we have the strength to crucify anybody that crosses us."

The man was clearly alarmed by what he was reading and his initial smugness had totally disappeared as he brought the meeting to an abrupt end.

"Ahmed," Mike called over his shoulder, "tell Mohammed that if he hasn't called us by midday then we will have that picture printed in the national press within hours. Don't think this is idle threat, I think the Arab world would be very upset to see a picture of Mohammed being screwed witless by that particular Jewish army general gentleman. He will probably find his bacon being cooked by his own countrymen."

They left the office and recovered their car from the garage then headed back through the city to the East End. By the time they reached their office Mohammed had called asking for a meeting the following morning. Mike and Sharon had a secretary set up a meeting in the Hilton Hotel, because they didn't trust the bugs in his own office.

By midday Fraktill Industries announced that their sponsor had withdrawn their offer and now they were ready to negotiate terms with the CCOE. Mike and Sharon both knew that Mohammed wasn't going to forgive them for the way that they had overturned him and that he would attempt to get his revenge somehow and for however long it took; but as long as they had the pictures they felt reasonably safe.

James was surprised when the news came through that the buyout was now going ahead. He knew for certain that the Arabs hadn't capitulated through friendship. There was something deeper and more sinister involved and quietly decided to keep tabs on the youngsters' individual activities.

CHAPTER TWENTY EIGHT

'They feared the steady blade, when mortal souls would be repaid'

<u>London - England</u>

Shorty Majozi left the building and walked briskly under grey skies along the pavement towards Pentonville Road. He had been inside the London headquarters of the ANC and pretended not to see the men in the car in case he was being watched. At Angel underground station he crossed over the roundabout and continued down City Road, stopping continually to either look at items displayed in the windows or to tie his shoelaces. He was simply making sure that nobody was tailing him. Reaching Old Street Station he turned right past the post office accounts office and then left into Bunhill Row. It had taken him some twenty minutes so far and he figured that if he had walked at full pace he could complete this journey in less than ten minutes. Entering a block of council flats he went to number 101 and knocked on the door. It was opened by the grey-headed old man who Shorty greeted in their common African dialect; he then walked down a short hallway into a lounge where Dirk Lemmer was seated at a dining table.

Spread before him were maps, timetables and various building blueprints; briefly looking up, he indicated for the two men to be seated.

"Piece of cake, my black brothers welcomed me with open arms and now I'm almost an ANC leader," Shorty's high pitched laugh rose from deep within his stomach.

"What did you find out?" asked Dirk.

"Not much, except that I will meet several ANC members tonight as they generally congregate in the evenings."

"Good, now have a look here. These building plans were supplied by the security division at our embassy and give complete details of the place."

Shorty picked up the plan and carefully studied the details, memorising all aspects of the building before having to return there "If we can get them together on the first floor that will be the ideal place to hit them," he pointed to an area on one of the plans "I will check it out tonight if I can, to find out where there may be good hiding places."

Immediately upon arriving in London two days earlier, Shorty had been instructed to make contact with members of the ANC; while the others were placed on observation duty. During the flight sat apart from each other for security reasons and had met up again when they checked into 'The White Hotel' in Bayswater, overlooking Hyde Park. There were eight of them altogether, four blacks and four whites; Dirk now had twice as many men as he had on his first visit to London. This time they were of his own choosing, each one a handpicked trained killer. Six men were to have two hours on duty and four hours off just in case they were spotted. To prevent anyone becoming suspicious, they acquired three old panel vans and parked them at different locations within sight of the building. They also parked two cars close at hand just in case they needed to move quickly. They had various escape routes checked out, although these were few and far between because of the heavy traffic.

Dirk visited the South African Embassy for a meeting with the head of overseas security. The man had given him some of the items he had requested from his minister in Pretoria and they made arrangements to meet up several days later at a warehouse in North London where the rest of the equipment was housed. The man told him that he'd managed to acquire two flats as well; one in Bunhill Row and one overlooking the ANC headquarters, from which Dirk's men could observe all the comings and goings. Dirk was using the first flat as his headquarters, so that they could watch the place from ground level and from which they could be far more mobile.

By day three, a comprehensive routine had been set up and they could see that most of the visitors to ANC Headquarters were either members of the activist group already stationed in London, or were sympathetic acquaintances.

With only three days left before *'Operation Donder'* was to be carried out, there wasn't much time to establish an identification list or penetrate the headquarters for a full survey.

Just after midnight the doorbell rang and the old man eased himself off the couch to answer the call. It was Shorty Majozi returning from the ANC meeting, as he entered the lounge Dirk came in from the bedroom.

"It seems that most of these men are Ndbele from Soweto. They get together every night to plan how to recruit new helpers from London's West Indian community. "Whilst they were busy I slipped upstairs. On the first floor there's some kind of drawing office where they design posters, copy literature and photocopy leaflets," he sketched a plan that he passed across to the white man, Dirk studied it at length as Shorty continued.

"The second floor has two box rooms with four bunk-beds for overnight visitors; these are only used by anybody passing through London. Unfortunately they always seem to have two or three people using them every night."

"This could be the place where they house all the refugees," said Dirk, passing the drawing to his older companion.

"In the cupboard they must have at least twenty or thirty used mattress rolls," Shorty continued eagerly.

"If we could get them all into the top section we could take them out in a single strike," remarked the old man.

"Only one problem," observed Dirk. "If there are that many people in the building at the same time, we won't be able to enter and fix explosives without being seen," retorted Dirk.

Shorty Majozi had become the chief of security's eyes and ears within this den of slime. It wouldn't be long before they found a way to clean out this pit of vipers Dirk thought.

"We are going to have to direct the main blast onto the first floor; then everything from above will collapse and everyone on the ground floor will be engulfed by the falling debris," said the old man.

"Another thing," said Shorty. "Here is a list of names and addresses of all employees working there; I found it laying in the bottom of one the cabinets."

They knew that they wouldn't find an easy way into the building and that victims of *'Operation Donder'* would be starting to arrive in London by the middle of next week; time was running out for their final preparations.

The following morning Dirk and the old man drove to Woodford Green, to an Industrial Estate where they easily found the company that they were looking for. Inside the yard were rows of containers stacked three high; despite its appearance this was not a container depot but a small storage facility. Outside the main gate Dirk drew up in front of the red BMW that he had been told to watch out for. He got out and went to the driver's window; they spoke for a short while before the red car left. Dirk quickly swung his own car into the gate past a temporary looking wooden building and across the open parking area, down one of the lanes between the locked containers. All the boxes had consecutive numbers stencilled on their front doors. His eyes searched until he found a white container with the number he was looking for. Drawing to a halt in front of the steel box he turned to the old black man beside him

"Here we are; to look at that box you wouldn't think it contained anything other than tins of paint." The old man opened the back of their car, whilst Dirk fitted the keys given to him by the man in the BMW and both locks easily snapped open. Partially opening one of the two doors, to initially see inside the container, he saw that it was half filled with black carry bags - all zipped closed. Eventually he had selected ten bags and ordered his companion to place them at the front of the container. They hurriedly placed seven bags in the back of the car and the other three on the back seat. Dirk relocked the container, making sure that the locks were properly closed by tugging at them, before sliding in behind the wheel. They drove out of the industrial estate and headed back to Bunhill Row and London.

'Operation Donder' took place in the early hours of Friday morning, carried out with impressive military precision. Crack troops went into Lesotho, Mozambique, Botswana, Zimbabwe and Zambia at the same time, all their main targets were hit at exactly four in the morning. Whist special foot soldiers were airlifted by giant Hercules troop carriers and flown to their various drop zones; Mirage and Impala jet fighters began their strafing runs at exactly the same time. As people tried to scramble to safety they were cut down mercilessly by incoming troops. Soldiers continued flushing out rebels as they moved toward the hideout areas, killing them on the spot; dead bodies were left scattered everywhere.

In the tiny landlocked country of Lesotho, forty two people lay dead and dying. Their government ministry claimed that only twenty nine had actually belonged to the ANC, the rest were supposedly innocent civilians; the other countries suffered similar losses. The South African troops collected the necessary proof of ANC targets, together with propaganda material and anything else they could find. The world awoke to the scene of screaming presidents on television stations worldwide, avowing that the South African troops had attacked innocent civilians. In Pretoria the South African Government produced all their evidence showing the complicity of the African frontline states in attacks on the South African people. South African government ministers went on record to state that this was only the beginning of their fight against the ANC and that further reprisal attacks could be expected shortly.

The front line states switched their bleating from one of innocence to pleading for help from the civilised world, as they were unable to defend themselves from this mad super-power in their midst.

The ANC panicked, believing that this drive against them would probably round up the few remaining leaders not caught in the initial attack.

The Communist world immediately arranged for existing camps to be disbanded and all the ANC members were whisked away from any immediate danger to safety. Arrangements were made for their transfer to the Eastern bloc for regrouping and further training. A substantial amount of these leaders were to be flown via London to specialised training camps in East Germany and Russia.

As the rebels started drifting into London they were being housed at the ANC headquarters and the security spotters stationed in the vans reported new arrivals daily. Dirk and the old man kept a careful watch on the numbers; because they had to exactly time the assault on them before they were all whisked away again. Shorty Majozi obtained the names and ranks of the military members by digging into the files and copying any information that he could find. Dirk was pleased with the way things were panning out; from his central headquarters he knew exactly what was happening. He decided to make his move exactly one week after the initial operation, as this would allow time for any stragglers to arrive. Any they missed would have something to tell their grandchildren about.

They would have to place the explosives on Thursday night or Friday morning; but as he had foreseen, the problem was that the place was now continually occupied by fleeing activists and the only person with access to the building was Shorty.

During the week the old man busily prepared the charges and by Wednesday everything was ready. Dirk had no choice but to trust Shorty alone to place all the explosives in position. The old man gave Shorty daily lessons in the art of handling and setting explosives but the doubt in Dirk's mind was that Shorty had no practical experience of bombs or the like.

By Thursday the old man had devised a simple method of activating a series of bombs; each bomb had it a simple radio transmitter attached to it, so that they would all detonate together when triggered. All Shorty had to do was place the small packages around the building in areas where they wouldn't be located. At his final briefing session in the early hours of Thursday morning it was decided to move most of the redundant equipment back to the storage facility. Some of Dirk's men were told to occupy the second flat in the block overlooking the ANC building.

At seven o'clock that morning the required articles had been moved to the storage yard and their present headquarters thoroughly cleaned out so that it would appear that no one had stayed there for several months.

Mike, Sharon and Robbie travelled to the office on Friday morning in their new chauffeur driven car. The company was well on its way to becoming the largest animal feed business in Europe because, with their recent acquisition of Fraktill Industries, the company had the means to import, store and process vast amounts of feed for poultry, cattle and the pet trades.

Their commodity futures division was back on course and the investment sector of the city poured capital into the company. They had taken another trading floor in Mincing Lane, because their six initial traders had now increased to fifty two, another set of offices across the road had also been acquired. The whole of the original second floor was turned into a main boardroom and four plush directors offices; the three youngsters now had an office each and Alain occupied the fourth.

All three still travelled together from Surrey each morning when they held impromptu board meetings in the car. Major decisions were made and later ratified with Alain. This particular morning, when they had almost reached the Mile End turnoff, Robbie suddenly asked to be let out. Unbeknown to the others he sponsored a second office for his South African business; here too, his silent membership had grown at a fantastic rate over the last two years. Robbie made his way through Whitechapel Market looking totally out of place as a young black man wearing an expensive Bond Street suit was not the norm in this area. He moved in among the milling pedestrians up the market and then turned into one of the side streets leading off Whitechapel Road. The traffic noise started to fade as he walked towards his office. Entering the building in Wodeham Court, he suddenly felt it; a chill travelled down his spine and his mouth dried instantly, his senses were suddenly placed on high and full alert.

While Shorty was out shopping for provisions, Dirk and one of the other white men went back to the storage depot where they replaced items that were not going to be used again. The black killer had been instructed to do his shopping in Hackney Green, some distance away, to collect several carrier bags. These would then be used to smuggle the bombs and timers into the building. He took the tube from Angel to Whitechapel Underground Station where there was a street market stretching as far as the eye could see. He started along Whitechapel Road keeping his eyes open for fresh fruit, which he hadn't had since their arrival in England.

Dirk drove to the storage area and turned into the lane, driving slowly between the highly stacked boxes. He stopped the vehicle and then unlocked the container before storing the remaining black bags. This time they came away three new black bags which were packed with revolvers, knives, grenades and machine guns; just in case they had to suddenly change plans.

By midday everyone, except Shorty, had congregated in the new headquarters and Dirk gave them a last minute briefing. The attack was scheduled for two o'clock on Friday morning; the six explosives were set for that time.

The old man skilfully primed the detonators then tested the radio transmitter again. Twin lights on the black transmitter lit up and at the same time, an orange light appeared on each one of the deadly packages. He flicked a switch and little red lights blinked on and off; all he had to do was to push the red button and everyone in the building would be blown to smithereens. Quickly flicking the switch, so that all the lights went out, he placed the transmitter into the table drawer.

Shorty arrived back at the flat laden down with carrier bags containing food and drink for the team. He had to edge sideways through the door before taking everything to the kitchen.

"You were supposed to be back here at eleven, it's nearly one o'clock. Where the hell have you been?" demanded Dirk angrily.

"Sorry boss, I'd almost finished my shopping when I nearly bumped into an old friend of ours. So I followed him to his place of work," an evil smile crossed Shorty's face.

"Who is this friend that is so important that he can almost jeopardise our operation?"

"Robert Molefe, he's only two miles away," a triumphant grin creased Shorty's hard features. "This time he's dead," he knew he was voicing the feelings also sweeping through the white security man.

During the afternoon Shorty twice visited the ANC headquarters, each time he carried plastic carrier bags. The first filled to the brim with fruit, below which, hidden from prying eyes, were two packages that had been carefully wrapped in white cotton. He laughingly handed the guard at the door a large navel orange from the top of his bag and then quickly made his way to the first floor and unlocked one of the drawers in a desk. He placed one of the packages inside before locking the drawer again; as he was finishing his task he heard footsteps descending the wooden stairs from the top floor. He quickly sat himself in a tilting chair and placed his feet on the desk just as a young man appeared. He greeted Shorty and asked him whether he was going to join them on the ground floor; Shorty nodded and the young man continued on down the noisy stairway. Shorty efficiently placed the second packet in a hiding place he had made under a faulty board in one of the stairs and then slowly clomped on down to the ground floor; counting nine people in the room. He still carried the plastic bag which was now only half filled with fruit. In the kitchen Shorty encountered several women busily preparing sandwiches and coffee for the men in the main room. His face flashed a smile "Here, fresh fruit for our visitors. It will taste sweet to their parched tongues."

For almost an hour he mingled freely with the growing crowd, listening to their harrowing accounts of bravery and how they had escaped. He found the London head of the ANC and told him that he would only be gone for a short while because he wanted to collect an old friend he had bumped into earlier in the day.

Shorty returned to the flat after having walked towards Pentonville Road then doubled back on himself, making sure that he wasn't being followed. For some minutes Shorty described to the other members what he had done and how the group was building up in numbers. He also told them that two of the most senior members of the military wing were due to arrive today. However, Shorty was worried because one of these men had escaped from one of his South African killing parties knew who Shorty worked for. Then there was that white girl who knew about the 'Voice of the People'.

"What time are they expected?" asked Dirk.

"A car has just left to collect them from the airport; they'll be here within two hours."

"Well, we'll have to rush our program; what would they say if you took someone with you?"

"Don't worry, I'll get inside and place the next two immediately."

Shorty got up and collected other bags which, this time, were filled with sweet confectionery.

Back at the ANC door he again greeted the guard; this time handing him a jam doughnut from his bag. They both laughed and Shorty entered the building, steadily making his way to the stairs and the first floor. This time there were two women seated in the room, one white and the other black. For almost an hour the two sat and chatted with each other; they didn't want to stand around on the ground floor and were far more comfortable where they were, they said. Shorty paced around the building like a tiger looking for alternative places to hide his deadly consignment. Finally he decided to have a look at the top floor.

He noticed that some of the refugees had battered suitcases while some had haversacks which were scattered around the floors of the rooms next to makeshift beds. Shorty looked for the biggest and deepest suitcase; its contents consisted of clothing and dried food. He rolled open a heavy jumper, placing one of the packages at the bottom and then packed clothes over it and closed the suitcase. It was a cheap cardboard type and he easily found a key to fit it from his collection.

Moving to the bathroom Shorty found a hatch under the bath used for pipe work inspection. He quickly slipped the bomb inside and underneath the bath, before replacing the cover to its former position. He studied his handiwork and then used the toilet before descending the rickety stairs; his only fear was that the orange lights would somehow attract attention.

As he reached the ground floor Simon, the head of the ANC in London, called to him. He wanted Shorty to consider going with the others for specialised training in the Eastern bloc and wasn't going to take no for an answer. Shorty promised to be back at eight o'clock with his goods packed ready to take up the struggle; but he needed time to tell his family first. The man smiled and asked Shorty to wait until he had met the leaders; but Shorty convinced him that he couldn't wait if he wanted him to be back in time.

Shorty hadn't walked more than thirty metres down the road when two cars swung into it. He hid his face and hurried towards Pentonville Road, realising that he had made an escape by the skin of his teeth. Dirk was furious when Shorty returned; his blue eyes turned to ice as he screamed that they had not completed their objective as only four bombs had been planted.

The old man eventually calmed the situation by suggesting that they place these in front of the door or at the windows and with any luck, these would also help destroy the building.

By midnight the street had quietened to a murmur except for an occasional person strolling by. There were lights burning in the building across the way and they weren't all asleep yet. At almost two am, two of Dirk's men took a bomb each, the plan was to place them at the door and then make their way to the waiting panel vans and drive them to the far corner. His men now all wore gloves and balaclavas except for the two that needed to cross the road, they had cleaned the flat from top to bottom; any excess goods had been stowed in the vans in preparation for a hasty getaway.

Dirk, Shorty and the old man watched from the window above as the two black colleagues carefully approached the front door to place their deadly cargoes. Just as they reached the door, it opened and the guard and two others appeared. The three watched their two men trying to talk their way around the situation. Suddenly the guard pulled what looked like a gun out of his pocket and stood aside ordering the two into the building. One man turned to run, then suddenly dropped to his knees and forward onto the pavement. The guard pushed the second man into the hands of the others with him. He grabbed the prone man by the collar and dragged him backwards into the building before shutting the door. It all happened so quickly and the three watched their plan disintegrating before their eyes.

"We can't let them find the bombs, push the damned button now!" screamed Dirk at the grey-haired black man.

African Chess

Their building rocked as the six bombs exploded simultaneously. The security men raced downstairs into the street and saw that the building across the road was barely a shell. In a matter of minutes the place would be swarming with police and they had to leave immediately. However, their dead colleagues still had the keys to the vans on them, so they quickly hot-wired the vehicles and drove away form the scene. Dirk drove the car, ahead of the vans, toward Bayswater; where some embassy men would collect and dispose of these vehicles.

CHAPTER TWENTY NINE

'Some semblance would often seem, to carry a nightmare dream'

London - England

Robbie had not had a sensation like this for some time and he instinctively felt threatened. Turning, all he could see out of the ordinary was a crippled man inspecting the roadway. More quickly now, Robbie went on and into the building off Whitechapel Road.

For about five minutes Shorty stayed out of sight, until he was sure that nothing was amiss. Molefe had almost seen him so, keeping as close to the wall as possible, he reached the entrance that he was looking for. The sign at the entrance read 'Voice of the People', which he immediately recognised as an underground movement in South Africa, one that he had heard whispers about. Gently pushing the door open he slipped into the building and up towards the first floor. He arrived at a passageway leading to several offices and he carefully placed an ear against each door. In one room he could hear a man issuing orders when, suddenly, one of the doors behind him opened; his hand moved into his jacket, where he felt the reassuring handle of his knife. It was the young white girl he had seen in the ANC building earlier on, she didn't look towards him; instead she moved off and disappeared down the stairway. Shorty decided that he couldn't stay in here much longer, so he moved quietly down the stairs, after the young girl. He followed her towards the market and caught up with her before she reached the busy trading area. Stopping her, he told her that he had seen her come out of the building and wondered who the 'Voice of the People' was.

Joan immediately thought she may have another convert to their cause. The man was obviously not a London black and she detected a South African accent like Mike and Robbie's.

"Oh, well we are a South African group," she said hesitantly.

"I used to live there but because of the apartheid have been away for many years; I now live around the corner and wish I could return someday," replied Shorty.

"Maybe sooner than you think because that's what we are fighting for; it won't be long before your country has a democratic government," Joan insisted.

"Not in my lifetime," he said sadly. "How do you think you will succeed where others like the ANC have failed?"

Joan immediately rose to the bait, "let me tell you something for nothing, the ANC is a mixed up group of northern tribes but, tell me, which is the biggest tribe in South Africa? Which tribe banished all the other tribes from South Africa many years ago?" "The Zulu and the Xhosa," replied Shorty.

"Exactly, the time is coming when the white man will agree to letting the blacks share their rule, mainly because of the pressure from the ANC – but!" she wagged her finger at the man.

"But what?" Shorty was now fascinated.

"Do you think that the dominant Zulu, who control the Xhosa tribes and have nearly twelve million people, are going to let themselves be ruled by any other tribe in South Africa?"

"So what about Nelson Mandela?" Shorty quickly asked.

"Forget him! At the moment he is only used as the ANC prison mascot, I think he's someone to pin the flag to, but when the time comes the in-fighting will take place," she said confidently. What the white Englishwoman was telling him made sense because the Zulus and Xhosas were almost one nation. Except for a small division in the Xhosa tribe, where Mandela was a chief, the rest had kept a low profile all this time. Up until this moment he had been so wrapped up in his own war that he had never thought of the end game. Nobody saw them as any form of threat; but if the Zulu champions and Xhosa joined forces, they could annihilate the others very quickly. For the moment they were prepared to let the ANC and UDF take the main role in the struggle.

"Who is going to lead these tribes?" asked the man guardedly.

"That's what we are working towards; because our group has the support of over six million Zulus and Xhosas - almost half of all the people from those tribes."

"But who is leading this group?" Shorty asked again.

"When you join us and take our oath then you will find out, until then I can't tell you any more, I've already said too much," the young woman replied.

"Surely you don't expect me to believe this, do you?" Shorty was becoming more frustrated by the minute. He could see the truth in what she had said.

"You will have to be introduced to our group by someone who is already a member. But think of this; Nelson Mandela's own people will try to kill him when he has served his purpose."

"Why kill him if he's the black people's leader?" said Shorty.

"There's talk of him being released shortly, after a little while he won't carry the same idolatry for the people. The leaders of the UDF and the trade unions will also be looking for power and they will use his name to get their way and then disown and discard him. Just wait and see."

He thought deeply about Joan's statement and uncomfortably it made perfect sense to him; the Zulu and Xhosa were just biding their time and allowing others to take the lead until they were ready to put a younger man in control.

Joan continued. "In a few years from now the Zulus will take the mantle away from all the northern tribes, the Coloureds and especially the Asians. They will become the dominant force once again."

Shorty was staggered. This conclusion had been staring them all in the face and yet nobody in his arena had even dared whisper it; no wonder the Zulus had supported the whites. Together they were letting the extremist whites and blacks massacre each other, whilst they stood quietly by watching the squabbling tribes. He needed to think what the white woman had said; the enormity of her words shook him rigid.

Still stunned, Shorty glanced around the marketplace and then down the road towards the offices. He spotted Molefe walking towards them; he had been so engrossed that he hadn't seen the man leave the building. Hastily Shorty thanked Joan and slipped into the crowd. He had to get away fast in case the approaching figure recognised him.

"Who was that you were talking to?" Robbie asked Joan, as casually as his feeling of foreboding would let him.

"Just a man who had seen our offices and asked about us," Joan answered.

"Tell me exactly what you told him; word for word."

Robbie's tone made Joan stop dead in her tracks. His eyes had again taken on their hooded look and she now sensed the element of danger. Joan explained everything to him and when she had finished, Robbie asked several questions whilst guiding her to the brokerage offices.

Quickly moving away from the Whitechapel Market and across the road, then down one of the side streets, they tried to place some distance between themselves and this stranger. The whole time he checked and double checked the road behind him to see if they were being followed.

By the time they reached the city offices he knew in his heart that the assassins were back in London. The only way that they would be able to reach him was through Joan, so he had to get her out of the way because his and most likely her, life was under threat. They could have been following him for weeks without him being aware of their presence. He called the receptionist and asked for a car to be arranged for him immediately, emphasising that it should be a small non-descript model. He then walked through to Mike's office, sat down with him and explained everything; it was time to confide in his white brother.

When he had finished, Robbie was surprised to see Mike smiling; he thought that at the very least he would be ridiculed.

"You have done some stupid things my friend and I've helped you through some difficult times. I've known about your aims and your group for some years now," said Mike calmly.

"Robbie! You may think Sharon and I are stupid; but we are not idiots. We may not agree 100% with your politics, but you are part of us and if your life is in danger we will help all we can."

Mike didn't tell Robbie how he knew and neither had he told Sharon that he knew of Robbie's activities; for the moment his only concern was for his best and closest friend.

"Robbie, get away from here now! Sharon and I will look after the business. Just get your latest trading sheets up to date."

"What if it's the same crowd that tried to get us at the airport? They'll recognise you and Sharon," stated the black man.

"They're not after us, we aren't political animals, it's you they want," replied Mike knowingly.

Robbie returned to his office and quickly settled all his outstanding business; he told his clients that he was going on holiday and that Mike would handle their accounts in his absence. Robbie drove away from the office checking continually in his rear view mirror. On the way home he told Joan of his suspicions; he took various detours to make sure they weren't being followed back to Surrey.

Robbie had his secretary book two tickets to the Bahamas, telling her that it was a surprise New Year present for Joan. Nobody could sleep in the big house that night; every creak or blow of the wind made them jumpy. They were relieved when morning finally arrived and nothing had happened. When they assembled in the breakfast nook, Sharon turned on the television to see the news, as she did every morning. In silence they heard the full account of the overnight bombing in central London of the ANC Headquarters which had been blown to pieces. Robbie knew for sure that the South African security men were behind this outrage and somehow also felt that their next target would be any surviving members of the ANC.

They packed quickly so that they could leave the house immediately. Before going to the terminal they checked into the London Heathrow Hotel, as the flight was not until midday. From there they remained in contact with the office and at eleven o'clock they left the hotel, bound for Terminal Three; the whole time imagining that they were being followed.

Eventually Robbie and Joan got their cases weighed and quickly passed through Customs, not relaxing their guard until they were safely on board and winging their way to a sunshine paradise.

Mike and Sharon drove Robbie's car back to London, at the office, everything seemed normal there were no undue telephone calls. Feeling safe in the confines of this building, they started their work as usual.

Dirk made arrangements for some of his men to return to South Africa. The old man and Shorty Majozi were to remain with him in London as he wanted to have another go at Molefe.

On Monday morning the three took up their positions outside Wodeham Court and remained there all day; but Robert Molefe didn't turn up. The following morning Shorty Majozi entered the building and boldly walked up the stairs. At the top he opened the door from which Joan had appeared on Friday. Inside, four women and a man were seated at steel desks.

"Hello, can we help you?" asked one of the women.

"Yes, I want to speak to someone who works here; she's very short with black hair." Shorty explained.

"She's gone on holiday and won't be back for about two weeks. Can I help you?" the woman asked.

Shorty decided to take a wild chance. "Is Mr Molefe in then?" he enquired casually.

"No, he only comes in once a week, usually every Friday, to sign papers and our pay cheques."

Everybody in the room laughed, including Shorty.

"It's very important that I see him as it's to do with a security matter in South Africa," he gambled. Suddenly he had everyone's attention in the room as another woman lifted her telephone and quickly punched in a number; Shorty memorised the sequence as she tapped it out. The girl asked for Robbie and after several minutes replaced the receiver.

"He's not at work today; would you like to leave a message where he can contact you?"

"No, don't bother. I'll get a message to him," he made his thanks and left the room. Outside in the street he scribbled the number into a notebook and then he made his way back to the Bayswater.

With Dirk and Shorty at his elbow the old man dialled a number and asked for Mr Molefe. He was told that he wasn't in the office and when he stated that his call was urgent, the receptionist asked him to wait.

"Can I help you, this is Michael Roberts," came a voice from on the line.

"I need to speak to Mr Molefe urgently," replied the old man in almost impeccable English.

"Mr Molefe isn't here today, what is your business with him? "Replied Mike.

"I need to either speak to him or meet him; can you please give me a contact number or address?" But Mike had already heard the alarm signals sounding in his head as none of their clients' pronounced Molefe with the correct intonation on the last letter. Mike felt that the voice belonged to one of the South African security group.

"I'm sorry but Mr Molefe left this morning and he is away on holiday in the Far East for two months. I'm handling his clients while he is away. Perhaps I can help."

"Oh, this is a personal matter and I needed to contact him urgently," the old man retaliated.

"I may be able to leave a message at one of the hotels where he will be staying. Would you like to leave your name and contact number for him to call?" asked Mike.

"Don't worry, but thanks for your trouble." The receiver was replaced just as Dirk went berserk and smashed the glass he was holding against the hotel room wall, "three times I've missed that fucking kaffir! Three fucking times!" The following day the three men left on a South African Airways flight for South Africa. They had achieved their goal by killing sixty two activists in London. But adding one more to the list had become an obsession with the security man.

CHAPTER THIRTY

'A dark hour descends, a foundation quakes and life can bend'

<u>Pretoria - South Africa</u>

Jay strode across the ward and could see that Michael was awake and looking up towards the ceiling. As she drew nearer to his bed he looked at her and his face lit up with a painful smile.

"I just thought I would drop in and see how you are doing before going on to work," she said.

"I didn't have the opportunity to thank you for saving my life yesterday," he said simply." It was obvious to Jay that he was still suffering and was in great pain and discomfort.

"Well, how are you feeling today?" she asked quietly.

"Not too good, I'm still spitting blood but the doctor says that's normal. My chest feels as though a steam roller has driven across it and they say that's also normal; but they're not the ones who have to cough." She was pleased to see that he hadn't lost his spirit and humour and that his colour was returning. She knew that the pain would slowly lessen as he became stronger.

"It will be some time before you're up and about so let's take one step at a time, OK?"

"The surgeon told me that if you hadn't been at the Union Buildings when you were, then I wouldn't have made it. The Chinese believe that my life now belongs to you!"

"If you now belong to me then I order you to look after yourself for me; I like my possessions to be in good working order." They both

282

laughed and Mike held his chest as she watched the man going through his pain barrier, knowing that he was still very ill. At the same time his strength of body and will would carry him through this difficult period.

"I met your folks here last night and they're worried about you. Do you want me to call them and tell them you're OK and awake this morning?"

"If I know my parents they'll be here again soon and they'll already have a full medical report."

"Is there anything I can get for you?"

"Yes, did you find my briefcase?"

"It's safely hidden at my flat, so don't worry about it."

"You might have thought I was delirious but I meant what I said about recognising one of the killers; if anybody finds out that you have the briefcase your life could be in danger. Please don't tell anybody." His statement took Jay by surprise as all she had done was help this man and now he was suggesting a world of intrigue.

"I'm sorry to involve you this way but if the documents inside that case should ever fall into the wrong hands then both of us will never forgive ourselves. You are the only person I can trust at the moment."

"What about your parents, can't I give it to them?" asked the girl, now wanting to escape from this bizarre situation.

"No, if you can lock it away somewhere where it will be safe I would be forever indebted to you." The only two people who knew that she had the case were the two receptionists at the front desk. Jay made a mental note to talk to them.

"The people that would like to get their hands on it would have no compunction in killing for it."

"Don't tell me anymore," Jay ordered.

"Yes, you're right; the less you know the better. I would suggest that you don't visit me regularly because they could be watching us." She told him not to worry about her because anybody watching would automatically think that she worked at the hospital. She would keep her eyes open now that she knew of the danger. They talked for a while and then she said that she was leaving to go to work. Again he thanked her for saving his life as he kissed her hand and privately he still couldn't get over how closely she resembled his cousin.

Jay crossed the ward and spoke to the duty nurse and then went to the front desk where she asked the receptionist if she could talk to her alone. Once in her office, Jay asked her where the briefcase was and the woman explained that she had placed it in Mike's locker before going off duty. Jay told her that she had tried to reach her the previous evening because it was missing but not to worry about it because they would simply say that neither of them had seen it. The receptionist couldn't thank Jay enough for shielding her and would deny any knowledge of any case should anyone should ask about it. Jay left the hospital safe in the knowledge that nobody would be able to connect her with the important case and wondered if it was safe enough in her flat.

London - England

Mike was fed up because Sharon had been going on about Robbie's antics; her whole thinking was for and about the company and Mike felt his allegiance being torn between these two close friends. When he sided with Robbie's in this discussion she blamed him for their present situation and he felt their relationship was going through its first strained moment. Sharon had become so involved with the firm that nothing he said helped matters; she wanted to vote Robbie out of the company but Mike wouldn't accept this. This topic became so heated that now they couldn't talk civilly to each other any more.

He wasn't going to allow Sharon to dominate him as she obviously did with so many others before. In a moment of frustration, during one heated argument, Mike suggested that he would use Robbie's vote to oust her from the company instead. She immediately asked him to use one of the other rooms to sleep in and it caught her off balance when he had accommodated her request. She sulked for days and tried to force him to reconsider. Matters became worse when Sharon started going out for dinner, sometimes not arriving home until late. Then one night Mike was even more upset when she didn't come home at all and on the following day Mike noticed that she was wearing the same clothes as on the day before.

"Where the hell were you last night?"

"It's none of your business where I go or what I choose to do. You made your choice and so I don't have to answer to you."

Mike was so incensed that he stormed out of her office and vowed that they were finished; he went back to his office and fumed for some time.

When Sharon again left the house for her date that evening Mike decided to get his own back and called Diane Hicks-Brown to ask her out for dinner.

Mike drove to Virginia Water and found Diane standing at the doorway when he arrived.

"Where's Sharon?" she enquired.

"She's always at some darned meeting or other," he replied matter of factly.

Since their little affair Diane had regularly been in touch with him, they often met up when Sharon was away on business. They went into the drawing room where, seated in winged chairs, were Vicky and a couple which Mike took to be their parents. He saw that the man was a very young looking fifty something year old, while the woman was even more elegant than her daughters. For a short while small talk was exchanged. The father was used to young men paying attention to his girls; but when he realised who Mike was he changed tack as he considered his daughter in safe hands if she could make this catch! Vicky included herself in their dinner date as she considered the three of them to be intimate friends.

Diane, Vicky and Mike arrived at The Chukka Pub outside the gate of Great Windsor Park where Mike parked among the Bentleys and Range Rovers. Inside Mike recognised several people who he had previously met at the girls' house; Diane explained that it was a favourite haunt of the polo fraternity. She told him that even Prince Charles sometimes used this pub as a watering hole.

"Hello, Mike, what are you doing slumming it here?" came a voice from behind.

There was no mistaking that Scottish burr and he knew exactly who it was before turning to face him.

"James! I didn't know you came from this part of the world."

"Yes, I live just along the road and this is my local."

"Can I get you something to drink?"

"No thanks, I'm away home now; give my love to Sharon and I'll see you sometime next week," the banker said pointedly. Mike didn't miss the emphasis placed on his cousin's name.

They had something to eat and then returned to the bar where most of the conversation in the room centred on polo. Mike found himself becoming more interested in the sport as the night wore on. When the barman rang the brass bell for last orders he checked his watch and it was after eleven; he had not thought of Sharon all evening.

His two companions were more than delightfully playful as they made their way back to his vehicle. Once in the car the sisters tried to persuade Mike to drive it through a break in the picket fence and along a tractor track, where they wanted to show him their clubhouse. Had it been a four wheel drive then Mike would have agreed; but he didn't want his expensive car to run over any rough tracks just for fun. The sisters teased him for being a spoilsport, but he turned the car around and headed back towards Virginia Water.

"Turn here!" shouted Vicky suddenly.

The girls literally forced him to turn along a narrow track by grabbing at the steering wheel. There was a full moon in the cloudless sky and Mike could see the pale light of reflected water ahead. He drew to a halt and the sisters dragged him out for a moonlight stroll to the edge of a small lake.

"Let's go for a midnight swim," teased Vicky.

"Are you crazy, that water's freezing?" exclaimed Diane.

"You go if you want to, we'll watch you."

Mike knew that if he went for a swim then both the girls might be tempted to join him. He'd always enjoyed swimming in freezing rivers at night as a young boy back home. Both girls watched in dumb disbelief as he entered the water, seemed to send stinging ice bolts into him, yet, in some masochistic way, it was also vitally refreshing. No matter how hard he tried he just could not entice either of the sisters to join him. It was only when he emerged from the water that he realised what a foolhardy antic of bravado it had been as the cold night air started his teeth chattering and his body shivering uncontrollably.

"Quick, back to the car or you'll catch your death of cold," said Diane, helping to collect his clothing.

The three raced back to the car and once inside Mike started the engine and turned on the heater full blast. He felt his circulation returning whilst Vicky, who was wearing a cotton shirt, divested herself of the garment to use it to towel him down. Diane started rubbing his body to help his blood flow return and within minutes both girls had Mike stretched out along the reclined seats. Within minutes the windows misted up, the girls removed their clothing and both sisters now took their warming work far beyond the call of duty. The lonely vehicle hidden among the gigantic oaks, had its springs severely tested that night as it rocked and bumped in concert from the goings-on within it.

Mike reached Champagne Castle at about three in the morning and noticed that Sharon's car was in the garage. He made his way quietly up the carpeted stairs to his bedroom, undressed and dropped his damp clothing on the floor and slipped between the clean sheets, exhausted.

That same night Sharon had dinner with Alain and leaving the restaurant, she decided to teach Mike a lesson as she stumbled ever so slightly on the steps. She told Alain that she was in no fit state to drive back to Surrey. He linked his arm through hers as she mumbled something about probably staying over in a hotel for the night. Suddenly and without any warning, Alain turned her around towards him and planted a firm kiss on her mouth. At first she found herself responding and then she pulled back and looked long and hard at her colleague.

Sharon was calculating the risk because she didn't really fancy the man, he was good at his work but this was a different ball game. She was feeling sexually frustrated and had this been anyone else she would have had no compunction in using them for her own pleasure that evening.

"Let's not spoil a super evening," she said, leaning forward and kissing him gently on the forehead.

"You know I fancy you something terrible, don't you?" Alain said.

"You're married and we work together and that's the ideal recipe for a disaster. Let's keep on being best friends, hey?"

"Do you want me to drive you home?" he asked as she untangled herself from his hold.

"I'll be OK, just drop me off at the Grosvenor Hotel."

She continued with her plan to make Mike jealous by visiting friends until late that evening. When she returned home she made up her mind to talk to Mike. She went to his room and he wasn't in bed so she searched through the house and not finding him then went to the garage. His car was not there.

Sharon heard Mike arrive home in the very early hours, even though she'd been half asleep at the time. She waited until she heard the creak of his bed then slipped out of hers and padded through to his room. The first thing Mike knew was feeling her soft body against his back and her hand coming to rest on his penis, which slowly warmed to her gentle touch.

"Sorry I've been a bloody bitch, do you forgive me?" she whispered into his ear."

Mike turned over and slipped his arm under her head so that he could tickle her back.

"Nothing to forgive as we both over-reacted."

Sharon kissed him long and hard on the mouth, feeling him responding immediately. Then she started kissing his body from his head and working her way slowly to his feet. As she moved down his body she constantly caught the scent of a familiar scent, but not being quite certain and rather than get into another slinging match, she continued.

The two made sensational love and Mike, for the first time in their long relationship, took over the lead by working hard with touching, stroking and kissing her wanton body. She accepted his loving caresses with gratitude and he didn't penetrate until she was screaming with delight. Then he slowly fed her little, by excruciating little, with what she badly needed that night. They made love right through to the morning without sleeping.

He was awoken by Sharon at midday when she carried a tray into the room stacked high with warm croissants and a tumbler of fresh orange juice. Mike sat up and Sharon started feeding him, the love light sparkle back in her eyes. Sharon had taken his clothes to the laundry because they were damp. She wanted to ask him about that but thought better of it, deciding that whatever he had got up to, it was her fault.

They stayed in bed all day as Mike had suddenly taken on a new identity and was a different man. She consoled herself that whoever he'd been with had taught him well and she wasn't going to complain at that moment.

Things settled down between the couple and nothing more was said about Robbie. Sharon couldn't understand Mike's stubbornness and yet she admired his loyalty to his friend. Their life took on a new edge because Mike, like his father Ian, was subservient in some matters but when his metal was tested it was not found wanting.

CHAPTER THIRTY ONE

'Her tightening mood gave way, to mantling blood in ready play'

London - England

Sharon and Alain again went on the takeover trail. This time it was an American firm of grain producers and shippers and everybody knew that this wasn't going to be easy. The two were continually flitting back and forth like regular commuters to New York on Concord. Mike saw less of her that month than when she was having her argument with him.

James organised the finance through one of their subsidiary banks in New York. They were examining the possibilities of the proposed merger, unlike the previous coups; this one needed far more attention. Various governmental commissions had to be approached, different licenses had to be applied for before they were able to prepare their bid properly. The Americans were proud of their major companies and handing over control of one to a foreign source would be vehemently resisted. James and his banking colleagues tried, without success, to warn Sharon of the pitfalls, but she was determined to have a go. The banker felt that the time had come to consolidate their gains and appreciated that they had acquired a taste for takeovers, but he had seen too many companies come unstuck this way.

Sharon pointed out that it was nearly two years since their last major takeover and although the company had struggled for almost a year afterwards, it had eventually become the leader in its field. James countered that without the required Arab funds the company had battled to repay its debts on time. It was only due to good management that the company had grown after over a year of being almost stationary. When he realised that Sharon wouldn't take no for an answer, he decided to fight in her corner as he had promised the parents that he would keep an eye on their offspring.

Robbie only had one more payment to make to the IRA and would then be able to take possession of all the armaments and ship them to South Africa. Mike was still bothered by his friend's role; as both a political animal and a business tycoon, Mike believed the twin roles were totally incompatible. They had had several discussions about this, with Mike arguing that Robbie would far better serve his countrymen with his business acumen. Robbie didn't believe this, he felt that the real and meaningful power lay with the power of politics.

As soon as he freed himself from the umbilical business cord he would become a freedom fighter again, albeit not in the field. His business success had gained him respectability and strength in the UK, where he could compete with white men on his own terms, but in South Africa he would simply be a puppet of the white regime; with favours passed to him like crumbs to a dog.

He was determined to change all of that and wanted to be accepted for his own abilities and beliefs and not for his wealth. There were two ways in which to achieve this; the first – his preferred choice - by forcefully overturning the white politicians. The second was to become accepted by his people, black and white, in his mind this could take centuries to achieve. Mentally, he loved the hunt of big business but his heart ruled his head and Robbie therefore chose the first and more radical method, even if it meant his own demise; he had made up his mind about this all those years ago in a Pietermaritzburg Jail.

Robbie's group of shadowy supporters had grown and filtered into various key areas throughout the country; the sleeping Zulu lion was remaining dormant but aware of all the antics caused by the ANC's military wing. It didn't move, it wasn't hungry yet, it was content to let the ANC flies buzz around its head – waiting, there was time enough to their hunting!

The fame of Nelson Mandela - that legend in South Africa, the new messiah - was only because of his long incarceration. Robbie was aware that those originating clever old leaders of ANC would soon fade away when promises were not kept to the people of South Africa. Stupid, ambitious, greedy new leaders would take over the ANC and that's when the lion would once again stir.

Sharon arrived back at Champagne Castle, from one of her trips to New York, looking tired. The Americans were continually putting hurdles in front of her and to complicate matters, the FBI believed that they had found a suspected South African link which was stalling the takeover even more.

Only James and Sharon fully knew the true trading roots of their company, at a meeting with US government authorities they had for the moment managed to slip around the traps laid for them. They knew that if the Americans managed to unravel the complexity of the company and could show the direct link with South Africa, then their bid would be blocked. The FBI had stumbled upon a trading link with one of the large sugar producers in Natal; somebody had tipped them off about the connection, but, for now, they were unable to prove it.

Sharon and James were again re-called to New York and grilled like thieves for two days by eager Congressmen wanting to establish themselves in the media. They managed to survive the blistering verbal attacks and were able to produce evidence that the company was purely British; but the Americans weren't through yet.

Left behind in England, Mike felt sorry for Sharon being hauled through this baptism of fire; he knew that she was strong enough to survive but was worried as to how all this pressure would affect her later.

Robbie and Joan were always by going off to some meeting, or visiting friends and leaving Mike alone at home. At first he dutifully remained at home catching up with television, books and videos. This wasn't enough for him and although he began visiting friends he was still lonely. The magnificent parties continued, sometimes Sharon was with him but most of the time he would find himself hosting the parties alone. When she returned from America, Sharon couldn't get out of bed for two days; she and the rest of her team, was shattered.

Sharon decided to stay at home on the Monday. The two men went to work as usual and the day passed uneventfully, except for one call to Robbie asking whether he foresaw any problems with his final payment to the IRA.

Mike arrived home without Robbie and was met by Suki, the dog, but not Sharon. Normally she would answer with a whistle to indicate her whereabouts, unless she was playing a game with him. She would sometimes hide and it was his job to find her; but Sharon was nowhere to be found in the house, although he had seen her car in the garage. He walked through a heavily scented wood area then up and down the steeply tiered gardens taking in the beauty of the abundant multi-coloured flowers and shrubs in full bloom. There was only one place left, the cottage near the gate; where he found her lying on one of the beds. She didn't even turn towards him or acknowledge him as he entered the room. He walked over to the bed and leaned forward to kiss her when all hell broke loose. It took him totally by surprise as she struck him across the face with the flat palm of her hand; he reeled back in amazement. His face was still stinging from the fierceness of the blow as she left the bed, claws outstretched, to rip his face open. Mike desperately grabbed at her hands as her foot came up and caught him in the groin. As he dropped to the floor in pain she again lashed out at his face; she wanted to kill him.

She suddenly stopped the onslaught, went quite still and slowly walked over to the video and turned it on.

"You bastard, look at this! Yes, explain this to me right now and right here."

"It just happened, I don't know why, it just did," Mike tried to explain. Like a skulking dog he couldn't defend himself as it was all there for all to see.

Sharon ignored him and increased the volume whilst screaming." Look, I flew home early to be with you but as you weren't here when I awoke I decided to index and file some of our clips. I came here to the cottage and just sat watching some of our guest's antics at your party last Saturday. I picked out several useful bits and pieces and decided to put them onto one tape. On resetting the video machines before our next party, I found a tape I hadn't checked," she watched as his face turned bright red. "I wish I hadn't, I couldn't stop shaking; you and my best friend and her sister in full view in our pool having an orgy."

Sharon turned back to the flickering screen, watching Mike lovingly rubbing oil all over the sisters from head to toe and a few other places as well. Sharon winced as she watched them kissing his body and Vicky's expression as she took him into her mouth while he attacked Diane's breasts. For the first time in her life she felt disgusted by the scenes on the small screen.

"Please forgive me. I would never do anything to hurt you, it just sort of happened!" Mike pleaded.

Part of Sharon desperately wanted to take him in her arms and tell him that he was forgiven; but the other part refused to accept any form of forgiveness.

"Bullshit, these things don't simply happen! I was away and you fancied some other piece of skirt. Just answer one question; was it as good as it looks?"

"I must have been drunk, why else would I do such a stupid thing with cameras going on all around."

Neither of them said anything for a while, lost in their thoughts. They were both locked in mental turmoil; any questions and answers spoken now would be crucial to their future relationship.

"Mike, tell me something; do I please you in bed?" she asked simply.

"Of course you do!"

"Then why the hell did I have to witness that debacle. Why didn't you even have the common sense to erase it so that I wouldn't find it?"

"Doll, in a moment of madness I committed an unforgivable blunder. I thought that you and Alain were spending so much time in New York and I was being pushed into the background."

Like lightning she grasped onto what he had just said. All her energy over the last few months had been focused on the business, with Mike being placed in a secondary role. Why hadn't she realised?

"During this American fiasco," Mike went on "I've not made love to you once. You've either been exhausted when you get back or cooped up with Alain in so-called conferences. Tell me the truth; are you having an affair with him?"

Her defences were coming down and his best chance of success was to press the attack and hope that he succeeded.

"When I was presented with the opportunity, well... I didn't refuse. It was out of loneliness that it happened," he concluded.

That night they dined together. Sharon remained quiet and Mike didn't interrupt her thoughts. The jury was out and he could only await its decision. They went to bed, he couldn't bear the silence but he knew his cousin well enough to know that she had to think this one through by herself. If he said anything she would flare up again. Mike switched off the light pretending to fall asleep and heard a large sigh; the jury had made its mind up. Her arm stretched out making contact with his back and he rolled over and took her into his arms; she cried for the first time.

The next morning at the office Sharon called James and ordered him to withdraw their offer for the American company. He was relieved and a little more than pleased with her move and told her so. Alain, on the other hand, nearly went berserk having spent so much time preparing for this fight. They had almost won the race but were now withdrawing. He couldn't understand the reasoning and hadn't expected any change of mind, because on the plane back to England she had been fired up to take on the world.

The atmosphere remained tense all that day; Robbie noticed it even before Sharon told him of the change of plan. It appeared to all, that Mike and Sharon had privately discussed the New York takeover. She wasn't happy with the scrutiny being placed on the company from the British media as it could jeopardise any future high profile acquisitions. To lead them off the trail, Sharon decided to purchase a small company in the States to help finance their capital build up over there; no questions would be asked.

Mike and Sharon arrived home and had a quiet supper before retiring to the bedroom. Sitting in bed they tentatively discussed their relationship and how it could move forward. They openly discussed their innermost thoughts for the first time and Sharon admitted that she wanted to get married. Mike had carried this fear ever since they moved in together, he had always thought that as they were first cousins it would be impossible and someone would object; he explained this to her.

"Nobody will ever know because we'll be the only two to know," she replied.

"Where do you suggest that all this takes place then?" he asked.

"In Nevada, when I was in the States I saw these quickie marriage churches there. Nothing could be easier; all we have to do is go there."

"And our families; whose going to tell them about this?"

"We don't tell them and keep things as they are."

"If they ever find out, God help us!"

He wanted the relationship to continue but wasn't sure that he needed the strings of marriage under these circumstances to accompany it.

"Don't worry about it for now, you know my feelings. I've made up my mind to be true to our relationship and its time you did the same Michael Roberts."

Sharon seemed to be content with this and fell asleep. He tossed and turned all night.

Next morning Mike knew that if he didn't agree to marriage then the fantastically high regard that they held for each other would dissolve and die. She was as aware as him of the problems surrounding their marriage; but having exhaustively considered the pros and cons had decided the marriage would bring the business empire together under one roof. Presently she held the reins of power but not the majority vote; that still belonged to Mike and Robbie. By marrying her Mike would be forced to change his allegiance. Mike was vaguely aware of what Sharon could be after. Robbie might find himself out of the company and Sharon, being a Scorpio, didn't easily forgive and forget.

CHAPTER THIRTY TWO

'In gathered groups, soldiers wait, for their General, to create'

<u>London - England</u>

"The time has arrived and we must bury our differences if we're to move forward as a nation," said the man at the head of the long table. Seated around it in a plush conference room at the Grosvenor Hotel in London were the prime leadership of the ANC and the UDF. In recent months both factions had been pushing themselves forward in an attempt to become recognised by the world as the rightful heirs to the South African throne. The UDF had secured the backing of main trade unions, the Indian population and the people of mixed race. The ANC realised that they were becoming a threat to their struggle and the stronger the UDF became their power base, at root level, was eroded and challenged; they had to get the UDF back on their side.

Until now, the main bulk of the fighting had been carried out by the ANC with most of their support coming from disenchanted tribes in the north of the country. The ANC also managed to gain some headway from the Xhosa tribe through links with Nelson Mandela and others. The UDF had helped them in the past but were now becoming a force within their own right and beginning to challenge their authority. Neither party yet had the full support of the mighty Zulu nation.

Heading the UDF team was the head of the trade union movement in South Africa who had initially been sent to Russia for training by the ANC. The only ones to profit from their split would be the South African Government who would be able to divide and conquer their enemies if their split became public knowledge. They had agreed to meet secretly, away from the glare of publicity, in order to try to settle their differences.

They still had a common enemy to fight and to date, it was people like Desmond Tutu who had got most of the limelight; because of his religious status and Nobel Prize, the media had immediately homed in on him as the spokesman for all of Southern Africa's black population. The UDF wanted their champion and the Reverend Allan Boesak, was to be given more media coverage but, as had happened in Rhodesia before the country became Zimbabwe, the ignorant international media had then championed a pillar of the free speaking church and when the crunch came, Boesak had been swept aside never to be heard of again. Churchmen were used as a form of respectability by the ANC and the UDF; they used them to do their work and the media reported their words but, when the real battle for supremacy began, the churchmen would disappear from view. In most African countries the pattern had always been the same; the Christian Church, which helped the people initially gain the power, was soon replaced by Communist ideals.

Both these South African groups had similar views in that their country would become a one party state; one ruler, as in the African tradition. There would be harsh penalties for opposing factions and democracy would be unacceptable; all this based on the communist teachings they had undergone. Robert Mugabe had the charm but once in power stole everything that the thriving country had built up. African justice is the law of the jungle, there can only be one overall leader, anybody disputing this is soon killed off. It was purely a numbers game, whoever held power was going to be chief, but as both parties were of equal strength the lines had became drawn. It was now a battle for dominance and no longer a matter of equality; a war for power between these two parties. They argued about leadership and returned to their bases knowing that the other party wanted to have the upper hand in government; each knowing that when the time came, it would mean outright war between them.

At the 'Inn on the Park' in London, the Roberts family had arrived for their yearly meeting. This time both the brothers and wives had checked into the hotel as there was much to be discussed and many decisions to be made on behalf of the family group. Mike had sent the company's limousine to the airport to meet them and had arranged that the three of them would see them after work that evening.

They arrived at the hotel just after seven o'clock and after the initial greetings and hugs, settled down and the emphasis of discussion returned to South Africa; about what was happening, who was doing what and their friends. Nicole seated herself between Mike and Robbie; she was like a mother hen between her two boys. She held their hands in hers; their touch charged her batteries of love.

"How is my mother?" asked Robbie quietly.

Nicole had been waiting for this moment; the room suddenly went very quiet. They had all sensed Robbie's joy and sadness. The question had to be answered very delicately by Nicole as she put both of her hands in his.

"She is very well Robbie and has come to terms about you. It has taken all these years for her to forgive you and at last she realises your position."

Ian got up from his chair and walked through to their bedroom; Robbie thought he had looked decidedly uncomfortable.

"Now don't be upset, she has changed and wants to see you," continued Nicole.

His adopted mother had said the words that he had waited all these years to hear. Tears flooded into Robbie's eyes and droplets flowed freely down his black cheeks onto his smart suit. He leaned forward and hugged Nicole, all he wanted now was a reunion with his true mother.

As Ian reappeared everyone except Robbie saw him guiding a handsome black woman with striking plaited hair into the room. Robbie looked up and suddenly tensed as he saw her; trying to get his blurred eyes to focus properly. She had lost weight and gone a little grey but there was no mistaking who this lady was. She smiled gently at her boy and wanted to race across the room and hold him, but was hesitant.

"Mamie, is it really you?" Robbie asked.

"Robbie my boy, it's me," she replied holding her arms wide for him to come to.

Like a whiplash he shot out of his chair and across the room into the waiting arms of his mother. His first sensation was the softness of her body and her smell which had never left him.

"Mamie!, Mamie!, Mamie!, I'm so sorry," he cried.

He buried his head into the nape of her neck and let the floodgate open again. She held him to her and crooned a little Zulu chant and as she finished he picked her up and swung her around in his joy. Things happened fast from that moment which meant so much to all of them.

Robbie introduced Joan to a strangely wicked looking woman with a white beaded crown on her head and although the meeting was cordial enough, the two women were like bantam cocks weighing each other up for an impending battle. They both laid claim to

Robbie and Mike knew that Mabel was unaccustomed to her flesh being involved with a white woman. It was not the way of the Zulu, especially one bearing such high breeding; this would take time.

They had to show their proud parents around Champagne Castle before going to the Mincing Lane offices and then the premises of CCOE. Nicole contacted James McGregor and asked him to join them all for a meeting over lunch.

"How are you Mrs Roberts?" he warmly greeted Nicole first; she was still the main power in this group. Nicole took his hand and reciprocated his warm greeting before he made his way around the table to Ian and also Sharon's parents. Then he brought the family up-to-date with the company's trading record.

It was impressive with James's delivery straight and to the point. His bank's relationship with the dynasty had been a rewarding one and the London operation had now proved itself, despite his initial reservations. When James had completed his summary, Nicole thanked him and they then got down to business.

"We are all getting on in years, even Ian," joked Nicole "We have decided to retire gracefully as a unit."

Mike was handed some notes across the table by her husband; she hesitated a moment watching for reaction from the younger generation.

"C'mon, you folks are still spring chickens," laughed Sharon nervously.

She admired Nicole, who was two different people to her; a happy loving mother and the firm business woman. At present she seemed somewhat stern, yet her mouth revealed a slight hint of amusement at her niece's remark.

"Be that as it may, we've decided to let you three gradually take over the main business of our group in a way that we see fit. If you are as successful at running it as you've been here, then within two years we will pass on our shares to you."

This last bit had all three confused; she was giving them authority, but was not releasing the reins of power.

"There have been many changes in South Africa which have presented the group with many problems. This year we moved the bulk of our holdings out of the country," Nicole explained.

This came as a shock to the youngsters who hadn't even suspected that there had been any changes to the holding company.

"The main shareholding is now controlled from Switzerland and your company will be the flagship. We also need offices in America and we are currently negotiating a buyout there."

Sharon had been through the ropes on this and knew that it could be done and was secretly pleased with the announcement. Her little empire would grow with this type of backing.

"That means that we are going to have three main areas of operation. South Africa, Europe controlled by this office in London and America controlled from New York," said Nicole, removing her glasses slowly to survey any reaction.

It was Sharon who immediately grasped what this revelation was going to mean to them. At the top, in Switzerland, was the throne controlling three satellite corporations around the world. No matter how they spelt it out, the three youngsters had served their apprenticeships and were now to be split up to oversee the running of the business empire.

Mike's heart sank, he didn't say anything but looked across to

Sharon. Her mouth hung open; he could see what was going through her mind. Nobody said a word, as they watched Nicole replace her glasses. She studied the notes again, before looking up to continue.

"For nobody's ears but ours, James has agreed to join us as consultant head of the group until he retires, when one of you two will take over," Nicole said nodding at Mike and Sharon. "Robbie, you're to take over the running of the South African operation; we have arranged for you to come home without encountering any problems."

Fear crossed Robbie's face, he was happy at the thought of going home at last but there were people out there waiting to kill him. Michael put his hand on the man's arm; he was equally confused at why his parents were suddenly breaking up the group. Like drunken boxers their brains were reeling as they hadn't been expecting anything so drastic from this meeting. Nicole hardly gave them time to digest her words before bringing the meeting to a close for lunch.

That evening Sharon snuggled close to Mike, neither of them had said anything to the other about the proposed plans. They feared the worst but were too scared to say it out aloud.

"Mike, what are we going to do?" asked Sharon apprehensively. "James will be in Switzerland, Robbie in South Africa, one of us here and one in America. I just don't know. We're going to have to tell them that I'm not leaving you." Sharon whispered quietly.

"How do you tell your parents that we had a rush of blood to the head and got married last year? They'll go spare! I'm sure they know we live together, everybody else does, this is their way of splitting us apart," he rolled over to face her. "There's only one way to handle this," said Mike, seeing the anguish in his wife's face.

"What's that?" she asked, her curiosity aroused.

"If we want to save our marriage we tell them that if the business comes first then we will have to get a divorce," he was testing her, he had to know which came first in her mind.

She sat bolt upright in bed. It was an unthinkable contest. She glared at him.

"Right, we tell them as soon as we see them; in fact, I'm going to call them now. Let's get it out in the open," she leaned over him to reach the telephone.

"No wait, we do this slowly. Let's go into the meeting and hear what they have to propose first."

"What bloody difference will that make?"

"Calm down, we don't know what the full proposal is yet. When we have the full picture we make up our minds."

Sharon relaxed and the two consoled each other. Their relationship had had many trying moments which had been overcome; this unexpected turn of events was another challenge sent to test their metal.

At the office next morning, Nicole resumed where she had left off. The parents weren't looking as ragged and tired as they had the day before and everyone was alert to hear what was next.

"We reached the point where James is going to be temporary chairman. All of us were expecting at least one of you to disapprove; but it seems that you are not opposed to this suggestion?" She looked at them in turn.

Nobody agreed or disagreed and simply kept their eyes fixed on the elegant lady at the head of the table. She held sway, but they all wanted to know what the full package amounted to before committing themselves.

"Next, the American market, as you know well they don't like outsiders taking over."

She looked straight at Sharon, whose heart sank as all she could visualise at that moment was herself in New York and her husband here with the likes of Diane Hicks-Brown. Nicole looked at Mike as she paused; she had left the difficult part for last. "London is your baby Mike, you've nurtured it through sickness and health until it's become a fine adult; capable of standing on its own two feet."

She was stretching their agony. Mike looked at Sharon and knew, that if his mother didn't get her words out very soon, that Sharon would suddenly blurt out everything about their relationship and hang the consequences.

"The only way we can make it work properly is for you two to take over the company in America and leave Alain here to run this office."

She had said it now and straightened to await the expected barrage. It didn't come; instead there was a quiet relief. Robbie winked at Mike, he knew what must have been going through their minds; Sharon laughed openly and Mike just gave a loud sigh.

The parents waited; their youngsters were taking the news too calmly and the protests they had expected did not materialise. Their reaction was taken as one for the good of the company. Surprisingly, they weren't going to argue but instead, it seemed, they were going to accept their elders' decision as final.

"You three will still maintain your shares in this firm and you will also have equal shares in the new American company; so you still control the way it's run," concluded Ian, when they had run through all the details.

Later, back at the hotel, Nicole quietly told Mike and Sharon what James had revealed to her. She hadn't had the heart to tell anybody else at home. It would remain their secret.

CHAPTER THIRTY THREE

'Is such misery worth the fame, when a corpse seeks a new name'

Ulundi - South Africa

Events were moving very quickly, South Africa was in a flux of change, indiscriminate looting and burning of businesses, shops and transport were quickly becoming the accepted order of the day. From his office on the fifth floor of John Vorster Square, Commandant Roux pondered over several papers on his desk. Seated across the desk from him, was Sergeant Andrew Murray. The two men had been working on a case for some time and now they had the irrefutable proof that they had been seeking laid out upon the desk before them. It was now a matter for the chief justice to handle; the men had done their work. In a strange way both the men reacted differently to the situation; the sudden anti-climax had left them with the feeling of a somewhat hollow victory. Bennie Roux felt like tearing up the evidence before him, whilst Andrew now wished that he hadn't been assigned to this case in the first place. Trapping an unknown suspect was one thing, it generated great satisfaction, however, involving a colleague had left a nasty taste in his mouth.

The list of unsolved politically motivated killings were mounting day by day, yet nothing seemed to be done by the police to bring the offenders to trial, this was beginning to cause consternation among both whites and blacks alike. Behind the scenes Dirk Lemmer and his Askaris had been given a free hand to capture and interrogate political activists; but what the heads of government did not know, was that the clandestine law enforcers were taking the law into their own hands.

311

By now there were so many incidents that the group could not cope anymore. After a short period of torture the detained activists were promptly disposed of in order to short-circuit the formalities of prison, court and wasting time; all this just to make martyrs of them. They had instructions to kill the activists and to cover their tracks by making it look like internal killings; made easier by the tribal war taking place between Incatha and the joint UDF and A.N.C parties. The two sides were now freely killing each other in the nightly wars in Natal.

The Zulu people had taken to the streets and were hunting their enemy, Natal was quickly becoming a bloodbath. The security forces stood back and allowed the Zulu nation to have its revenge. In fact, on several occasions, they even assisted in helping to trace known UDF members.

Dirk was summoned to attend a meeting at police headquarters in Johannesburg and he had purposely left Pretoria before sunrise to miss the snarling traffic jams on the outskirts of Johannesburg. His first stop was at the house in Bryanston, where he silently listened to his team of Askaris making their individual reports. The only person missing from the kitchen table was Shorty Majozi. For several weeks now Shorty had not made an appearance and Dirk was becoming alarmed; it was unlike his black mercenary to simply disappear without letting him know his movements. The old man reported that they had seen him in Natal and that he seemed to be acting rather strangely; as if he was high on marijuana or African brew. Yet he hadn't staggered or slurred his words when they had spoken to him.

Dirk wanted him found and brought back to Johannesburg, he knew that any of his selected few could be his weak link, but had to proceed in the belief that the men surrounding him were professionals and wouldn't let him down. As each, in turn, reported their activities to him, Dirk handed them a new assignment. The whole meeting did not take more than an hour as he quickly summarised their reports and sent them out to do his bidding. He and the grey-haired old man sat across the bare pine table looking at each other until the others had left the room. Dirk slowly extracted the old pipe from his mouth once they were alone.

"Find Shorty, we must know what he's up to," he said venomously.

"You know as well as I do Mr Lemmer, if he doesn't want to be found then nobody will find him."

"You can find him. You're the only one who can think like him. So get out there and don't come back without him." The white man's voice cut through the room like a blade of ice.

Shorty Majozi arrived at his brother's house in Ulundi. He had travelled over four hundred miles that day from Johannesburg and was tired, he greeted his brother in the old African way. They joked and laughed and touched each other continually as they discussed local news. Then Shorty was ushered into the front room, where his aged mother sat in a large winged-back chair. He was her eldest and therefore, her favourite son. She rose in her frail manner to greet this boy whom she hadn't seen for almost twenty years; ever since he had left for the big city to make his fortune. The couple laughed and hugged each other, whilst outside jungle drums were passing the message around Ulundi that Shorty had returned home. In a matter of minutes, friends and family alike had gathered in and around the small house. They sang and danced until the whole street was filled with inquisitive neighbours. That night a street party was arranged, the women hurriedly prepared food and drink whilst the men all sat in the garden and drank gallons of homemade beer.

Shorty was a hero, nobody really knew what he did but he constantly sent money home for the family and everyone had heard how well he was doing in the big city. Scruffily dressed children stood around in awe of this man as he was obviously someone of stature and in turn, each one was brought before him for inspection.

Many of the children he had played with when he was a young boy were now grown up and married with children of their own. As the eldest, he had always been looked up to by his brothers and sisters and Shorty was enjoying his homecoming. He almost forgot the reason for his visit to Ulundi, he had been sent to expose several pockets of UDF agitators, supposedly Zulu brothers working amongst his people. The security forces had found out about them through some of the detained prisoners in Durban. Dirk knew that Shorty had originated in Ulundi and had instructed him to seek them out - to destroy the enemy. The party continued into the following morning; there were sleeping bodies everywhere, but the die-hards still drank as the morning glow appeared on the horizon. Nobody really stirred until the hot sun was high in the African sky. When Shorty finally arose from beneath the old tree at the back of the house, he saw the women, like a row of swallows on a telephone line, all seated on a long bench, preparing the noonday meal. He dragged himself to the latrine, then to the basin to splash the now tepid water across his cleanly shaven head and face to waken himself. His head thudded, it was rare for him not to be in full control, but this time he had an excuse and he had nothing to fear being in the bosom of his family.

He slowly made his way indoors; he wanted to check on the suitcase he had left in the lounge with his mother. The old lady, dressed in black, sat on her leather throne; she greeted her son as he entered the room and he fell on one knee by her side before he gently took her hand in his and started talking to her privately for the first time since he had arrived. Both of them had a lot of catching up to do; she scolded him for not being there to help bury his father, but she had found it in her heart to forgive him now that she had seen him again. Shorty guardedly told his mother of his life in Johannesburg, making sure not to let her know of his activities and the real reason for his return to Ulundi. The two fondly touched each other, somehow he had forgotten what real love was like; he was like a desert, dry and barren, trying to regain its former glory by soaking up the atmosphere surrounding him.

It did not take long to locate several members of the black police community; by now he knew where to look for help at the beginning of an assignment. What he quickly learnt did not please him as leading the group of agitators in Ulundi were the members of his own family. When he spoke to his unsuspecting brother about the matter, he was told almost everything. He even tried to get Shorty to join them in their quest to persuade the Zulu to join the UDF.

Shorty was horrified with what he heard and all around him were members of the UDF; the pockets of resistance that he was supposed to dispose of. He also knew that if other members of the security forces found out about their activities, then he would become suspect as well. The Natal police must already know of the family connection and above all, was that he knew his family would suffer horrible deaths at the hands of his security colleagues. His feelings and loyalties were being stretched to breaking point and somehow he had to deal with the problem before anybody else found out. By the weekend he had decided their fate as he placed small packages in each room in various inconspicuous hiding places.

He had decided that they should die quickly rather than be subjected to the horrible methods of torture devised by the security forces. The party resumed in his mother's house on the following Saturday evening and when almost everybody had entered the house, Shorty silently slipped away to his car. He lifted the radio transmitter from under the passenger seat and in a matter of seconds, the small house was a blazing inferno. Nobody within the house or in close proximity survived the massive blast and flying debris. As he drove away Shorty looked in his rear view mirror where, silhouetted against the bright orange glow, he saw a small boy standing at the front gate; his desperate screams for his parents were unanswered but they rang long and loud in Shorty's ears.

For several days Shorty remained at a safe house on the outskirts of Ulundi. The thought of his murderous deed haunted him and he couldn't forget the sight of the little boy; every time he closed his eyes the boy returned to him. Slowly his mind began to snap; the feeling of love that had been awakened in him now became a source of weakness. He didn't go out, couldn't sleep and didn't eat; he just lay on the narrow iron bed and slowly went mad, letting the true reality of what he had done to his family take its toll.

Within a week of the bombing, he changed from a vicious killer to a mumbling wreck. Had it not been for his training and his inner strength, he would have died. He blamed the white man for his misery yet, at the same time, he started to convince himself that what he had done was for the good of his people. One minute he was swearing revenge on a host of people, the next he was trying to pacify himself. His body was weak from lack of food and drink and there was nothing in the house except water. During the week he destroyed his identity documents, all papers and money associated with the security forces in an attempt to rid himself of his tremendous guilt. Late one night, needing to replenish his frail body, he drove aimlessly until he arrived at the nearby white town of Empangeni.

Slowly he cruised through the darkened tree-lined streets until he spotted a smallish white painted bungalow with an open window. He stopped the vehicle about a hundred yards along the road and took a claw hammer with him, in case he needed to prise something open.

Two children were fast asleep in their small beds, lit by the bright moonlight which glowed between the slightly billowing curtains. He desperately wanted to stroke the little girl lying there so peacefully, but knew that she might awaken to his touch. He went down the short passage until he found the parents room. Both were fast asleep and in the muggy heat, the man had kicked the blankets off of his body. Shorty made his way to the dressing table and expertly examined the contents before crossing the room to the man's bedside table; the luminous glow of his Omega watch told him what time it was. He found the man's wallet and as he lifted it, several coins fell to the floor.

The man sighed, rolled over and opened his eyes. Shorty waited to see if he would fall asleep again but he didn't; the young man realised immediately that there was a stranger in the room and moved to sit up. Shorty lifted the claw hammer above his head and brought it down with every ounce of strength remaining in his body.

The man was still dazed from his deep sleep and the last thing he saw was the figure at his bedside. His head split open like a ripe melon as he silently collapsed back onto the bed. The woman stirred but slept on. Shorty carefully made his way to the kitchen, opened the refrigerator, selected various items and sat at the kitchen table feasting. When he finished, he carefully placed several items into a plastic bag, replaced everything in its original position and quietly left the house.

Returning to the safe house he now had enough supplies for several days. He quickly washed his clothes, hung them in the kitchen to dry and then went to bed satisfied. He had avenged himself on a white man, who had been responsible for him having to annihilate his own family.

Several days later Shorty again drove to Empangeni as his food supplies were dwindling; he cursed himself continually because he didn't have any money with which to buy more food. As before, he selected a house in the white area with an open window. He entered silently and made his way to the bedroom. As he approached the bed and saw the sleeping white man, the ghost of his previous victim appeared to him inside his head. Shorty looked down at the motionless figure and saw the dead man's spirit, with its holed skull and glaring eyes, daring him into action again. The hammer fell four times, the white man never knew a thing; the only sound was that of crunching bone. It was very quick and silent, there was blood everywhere around the bed but Shorty couldn't see the apparition anymore. Again he exited the house from the kitchen, having sat down to a full meal at the table and taken supplies, making sure that everything was in its correct place. He had the man's wallet safely tucked into his hip pocket and the man's revolver inside his jacket. He drove towards Ulundi and back to his house of safety.

The police were baffled by the series of killings. They were causing deep concern to the local white population and the papers were playing it up for all their worth. The unknown assailant had been branded the Empangeni Hammer Killer.

Bennie Roux and Andrew Murray flew to Durban as they were asked to assist the local police in helping to trap the killer. They inspected both sites and discussed various aspects with forensic experts. There was no apparent reason for the killings which had been savage and demented attacks. Nothing bulky and valuable had been stolen and there seemed to be no political motive; so they concluded that it was the action of a madman. After three more attacks had taken place, Bennie sensed that the killer was a natural hunter. They laid several traps but the Hammer Killer avoided them with ease. Andrew was the first to have a break; he had been to visit an old friend from his training days, stationed at Melmouth, a little town between Ulundi and Empangeni. They were having supper when his colleague had received a call; someone in Ulundi reported to the local police that he had heard several shots coming from a house.

Shorty was seeing ghosts, the spirits of all the people he had killed. They were everywhere but, however desperately he tried, he could not persuade them to leave. He tried to kill them with his hammer; his room looked like a battle field as in his attempts to strike and eliminate the eerie figures, he all but smashed the walls of the house. One minute he was threatening the spirits, the next crying and apologising for his past actions.

They found the demented Shorty lying on the floor, pulling the trigger of the revolver constantly. He had long ago exhausted the bullets in the gun but was still shooting at the walls of the room. They took the demented man to Ulundi, he was placed in a cell, while Andrew took the gun back to Durban to check who its registered owner was. When he discovered the owner, Shorty was immediately transferred to a psychiatric police cell in Durban; they had the Empangeni Hammer Killer in custody. It was only when Bennie Roux saw Shorty that he realised who he was, this was one of Dirk Lemmer's killers; a man he had been seeking to convict for some years. Under relentless questioning Shorty slowly started revealing the role that he had played within the security forces. The two were horrified at his accounts of events. It was going to be difficult to prove his story. A team of psychiatric doctors testified that it was the ramblings of a madman. The only ring of truth was that all Shorty's alleged victims had been found dead, or had simply gone missing.

Shorty managed to implicate Dirk Lemmer, as well as revealing the names and parts played by the other Askaris. Bennie slowly gathered evidence, which he knew would have serious implications in South Africa and managed to build up a full case against the security team headed by Dirk Lemmer.

Bennie Roux had never really been aware of his younger colleague's full duties although he had always envied his position. Now he was more than pleased that he had been missed for the post of head of security. The two men concentrated their attentions on the security situation, the evidence was horrific but they didn't dare reveal the facts to anyone yet. Both were afraid that if they leaked their partial findings the matter would be hushed up, or the case would suddenly be stopped in its tracks by the security forces. They were aware that the orders hadn't been the responsibility of Dirk Lemmer alone and that instructions had come from higher up; being dedicated policemen they needed to know how high up this went. In the commandant's office they went over the evidence several times. There was enough material to prove their case and they would be able to prove several murders against Dirk Lemmer and his Askari team. What they couldn't prove just then, was that he was under orders from someone further up the hierarchy; for that they had to face him with all of the evidence and question him personally.

Bennie wanted to make the case public but Andrew advised against it as he knew they were playing with the big boys now. He also knew that they would have no compunction in destroying the two of them. Between them they decided to call in Dirk Lemmer and face him with the facts. If he didn't co-operate they would threaten to make the matter public by arresting him. Dirk arrived at John Vorster Square at the agreed time, he parked his car in the space reserved for him and then made his way to the fifth floor.

As the commandant took hold of Dirk's hand he made up his mind, then and there, that this man would never be allowed to kill again. The three men sat down and at first small talk filled the room, then Bennie slowly pushed a buff file across his desk towards Dirk Lemmer, who started reading about Shorty. The file contained a list of accusations but did not relate the circumstances in which they had been made, nor did it contain anything about the proof that they had managed to collect. Dirk silently read through the file and now knew why Shorty had not returned; he had to be silenced immediately. His own life and position was now on the line. When he finished reading he replaced the file on the desk. It had given him time to think, he looked straight at the Commandant and told him that it was a prefabricated pack of lies and that he wanted time to think about what to do. With that, he left the room and headed straight for Pretoria and the Union Buildings.

CHAPTER THIRTY FOUR

'One flash of instant surprise, came within the climber's eyes'

<u>London - England</u>

Robbie looked long and hard at Joan who, as usual, she was casually seated in the big chair in front of the fire, her feet tucked away beneath her kaftan and her thoughts miles away. The day she had dreaded most had eventually arrived; her man was about to return to his homeland and she could not feel anything but apprehension at their parting.

They had built up a comfortable life together in England, with nobody really thinking anything derogatory about their relationship; but she understood that Africa would be an entirely different proposition. Both races frowned upon mixed relationships however integrated society had become. Joan knew that she could not stop his return and to try would only entice his anger, but he had promised that as soon as possible, he would be back for her and in the meantime she was to continue his work from the London office until he returned. It took Robbie almost a full week to show Mike the positions of his trading clients, most of the accounts were related to his IRA and Hezbollah dealings. Both groups, together with several other freedom organisations, had decided to leave their vast investments within the company as they still needed to launder their funds. Mike understood the workings of these accounts and knew that he was the only one Robbie trusted enough to handle them for him; so they spent several days together making sure that the transactions were properly understood.

Robbie had managed to clear his outstanding accounts for the purchased hardware from both parties and now he was due to collect the items and ship them to South Africa. He was confident that they wouldn't object to Mike controlling their funds in his absence and anyway, Mike knew more about trading aspects of the commodity dealing than he did. With the handover completed, the company gave Robbie a good send-off on the Thursday. It was not often that Robbie drank to excess but he did and Mike had to drive him home.

Robbie had arranged for his deadly cargo to be shipped to Mozambique where he would collect it the following Friday. He had been informed that the ship 'M.V.Gulf Meranda' had left Benghazi in Libya with its full compliment. He had arranged with friends in Beira to tranship the load onto a smaller boat. 'Bazaruto'; was the intended meeting point, this island was once a Portuguese playboy centre before the civil war had taken its toll of Mozambique. It still contained remnants of old colonial splendour but now, with no visitors to the island, the jungle was slowly reclaiming everything. The group had notified him that they had acquired an old seaworthy dhow in Madagascar and that they were sailing it directly to Bazaruto to avoid unnecessary questioning from the authorities. Lack of funds had corrupted many government bureaucrats and the last thing Robbie needed was to be held to ransom by some petty officials. He planned to fly to Zimbabwe and then, with two associates, drive to Beira and on down to Vilanculas; a small fishing hamlet close to the island where he would meet the rest of the crew.

He was worried that once they left the Zimbabwean border they could be attacked by the remnants of warring Frelimo fighters, who were still defending jungle strongholds. Another alternative but yet not the best method because it would leave a paper trail was to hire a plane in Harare and fly the cargo to its transit destination; from there they could sail to the southern Mozambique border and trek across South Africa down into Natal. This trail was designed to cross jungle areas with little or no civilisation, helping to conceal them and their load from prying eyes. Whichever way he played it he knew that the going would be extremely tough once they landed.

Everybody at Champagne Castle, even Sharon, was very quiet that last night as they had reached the end of an era. The fun days of building all this up together had come to a sudden standstill. A large informal gathering of well wishers had arrived at the house, where a magnificent buffet was set out in the games room, to bid Robbie a fond farewell. Guests drifted in and out, some arriving straight from work whilst others turned up after having dined at home. Many of them had hoped and expected one of Sharon's well known lively parties; but were sorely disappointed when they found that this one was different.

At eight o'clock the telephone rang for Robbie, he recognised the unmistakeable Irish voice at the other end; the old man was livid. He told Robbie that he had just found out about his departure and that they had had a deal and now Robbie was leaving them in the lurch. He considered that Robbie had reneged on his end of the bargain. Rather than argue Robbie explained that he had been made to oversee the consignment and that, while he was away, he had organised with his white brother to continue the trading. The old man refused to accept the situation and ended the call with a stern warning about Robbie's future health if he crossed them.

The ship was already half way down the African coast and the IRA could not stop it now. Although the charter had not been carried out by the suppliers he felt strangely uneasy as these people didn't give anybody a second chance; nor did they try to understand a counter position.

Robbie returned to the party looking bothered but everyone, except Mike, thought it was because of his sudden departure. The party ended at about eleven o'clock, the last guests ushered to the door by Sharon who wanted Robbie's last night to be spent with the family and especially Joan. When they had all gathered around the large open fireplace Sharon organised coffee and liqueurs. Mike and Robbie moved out of earshot and Robbie quickly explained about the call and Mike, trying to allay his friend's fear, said he must trust him to handle the matter.

Robbie and Joan went to bed and made love all through the night, as if they both knew that this was the last time. Robbie regretted his decision not to take her with him; but his mission was going to be dangerous and he needed to prepare his people before she could come to join him.

In the morning they all travelled to the airport to see Robbie off and the one affected most by his departure was Mike. He seemed nonchalant up to the minute of separation, but when Robbie extended his hand Mike grabbed his lifelong friend in a tight embrace. The two men let their emotions take over at that moment. The girls stood back and left them alone, as they both understood.

At last Robbie embraced Sharon and thanked her for everything; he knew, for the first time, that she was really affected by his parting. Lastly, Robbie held his partner close. They had said everything the previous night, but he could feel her gentle sobbing as her body racked against his. Robbie had never really shown strong emotion yet now he felt his breath caught in his throat, he needed to get away as quickly as possible before his true feelings revealed themselves; he leaned forward and kissed Sharon very gently and whispered something softly in her ear. In a few short strides he disappeared behind the screen and Sharon took Joan's arm and led her towards the car park. Nobody said anything.

Harare - Zimbabwe

Robbie walked down the stairway from the Boeing707 that had carried him from England; he felt the African sun on his face once again and held back a great impulse to stoop and kiss the ground. His heart sang out as he was once again in the land of his forefathers. He quickly made his way through the customs hall to retrieve his baggage.

Nearly forty of his associates, all laughing and joking, were waiting to greet him as he exited. They had been waiting for nearly three hours and as soon as they saw him they shouted and began a peculiar dance. This was a common scene for Africans showing their joy, so nobody took much notice of the merry band. Robbie joined in as this felt so natural; during all those years in England he had never felt anything like this moment. This highly educated man could express his roots with his people; his joy was overflowing, the singing, dancing, laughing people moved away from the airport buildings across to the parking area. Most of them clambered into the back of beat-up panel vans and pick-up trucks. Robbie was ushered into the back of a Toyota Cressida and his Zimbabwean friend climbed in beside him. The little convoy left the airport and headed towards Harare.

His advisers were not happy with his plans to drive through Mozambique as vigilante activity in the area was rife and he was likely to be shot up before he reached Beira. Flying was almost as risky as the fighting groups on the ground tended to shoot at anything in the air. Several small planes had been shot down, because of their inability to reach great heights.

The following morning Robbie through his Zimbabwean friend managed to find a crop spraying dare devil white pilot prepared to fly him to Vilanculas for an exorbitant fee and no paperwork trail, the fee to be paid in American dollars before take off. Robbie agreed the terms, but held back any payment until he saw the plane ready to roll; he wasn't going to be ripped off by some white sky jock. The pilot told them later that he had acquired a battered Beechcraft from a friend and promised to meet Robbie at three the next morning as he wanted to land at first light and be back over the border by eight o'clock.

The two men then drove into the city centre as Robbie went on a shopping spree. The stores were bare of most items but his friend knowing the marketplace wheeled and dealed for Robbie to acquire the necessary clothing, lightweight tents, torches and various other items that he felt that he would need for the long overland trip. His friend woke him just after one o'clock. Everything had been packed into a panel van the previous day. They travelled south eastwards for an hour, the night sky pitch black and the beam of the van showing up the road for miles ahead. Then they swung left onto an old strip road and the journey continued for another twenty minutes as the driver skilfully kept the white van on the twin tarred strips the width of it's tyres. The vehicle slowed and turned into a large farm where it skirted the safety-fenced house; in the headlights Robbie could see the small Beechcraft, with its pilot sitting against the front wheel. They were spot on time.

Another white man climbed out of the aircraft and for a moment, Robbie thought it might be a trap; but the man was the farmer, the owner of the plane and he had been checking it over. Silently, the four men packed Robbie's items into the waiting aircraft and only then did Robbie extract the money from his back pocket. The pilot, after quick inspection, handed the wad of notes to the farmer for safe keeping.

Robbie bid farewell to his companions as he climbed into the small cabin and took the right hand seat as instructed. The little plane's engine roared into life then hurtled along the grass runway and up into the dark sky, neither man spoke until the pilot informed him that they had crossed the border with Mozambique. As a faint glow of daylight started to appear on the horizon the little plane began to descend; Robbie could just make out the line of the coast below them. They had timed the flight perfectly as, within minutes, they were passing over the little town of Vilanculas which lay in thickly wooded jungle and out to the left, they could see the island of Bazaruto.

The pilot banked left and Robbie couldn't see any sign of the dhow near the beach; he asked the pilot whether they had time to fly over Bazaruto. The man grudgingly banked the small plane toward the island. It took just eight minutes to reach the narrow strip of land, where they could see rows of once beautiful houses below them.

The pilot pointed towards a long strip of grass and explained that it was the old airfield runway and that he would be able to land there; it would be far safer than landing on the beach at Vilanculas. Robbie's eyes searched the coastline for any sign of the dhow while the pilot made two inspection passes over the old landing strip. Finally, having made up his mind, he came in as slowly as he possibly could with the engine almost brought to stalling speed. No sooner had they touched ground when Robbie realised what they faced; the undulating ground, which had seemed so flat and even from the air, turned out to be bumpy and full of solid clumps of grass. The little aircraft bounced and juddered all over its overgrown surface as Robbie tightly closed his eyes; he expected to be smashed to bits at any moment, but somehow the rugged aircraft came to a gradual stop. The pilot left the engine running and jumped out to inspect the undercarriage.

Robbie quickly started to unpack the items he had brought from the plane, as the pilot paced up and down the length of the disused runway, obviously looking for the best line of take off. When satisfied, he wished Robbie well, shook his hand and clambered back into the cockpit. With a wave, he turned the small aircraft into the wind and roared away across the track made on his landing. Robbie watched him rise into the orange sky and stood silently as the plane became a speck, heading along the coastline until it disappeared from sight.

The landing of the plane had not gone unnoticed on the island. Before Robbie knew it, a number of curious children, their ages ranging from three to something approaching sixteen, clambered up the hill to see the unfamiliar sight. Robbie beckoned to the eldest boy and asked if he had seen the dhow. The boy couldn't understand him as none of them spoke English, only Portuguese. After a frustrating few minutes, Robbie drew a picture on the ground between two tufts of grass. Realisation dawned and the boy pointed along the coast; Robbie, with the eager help of the children, collected up his belongings. With the boy in the lead, the merry band started down the hill toward the houses and the harbour. To Robbie's surprise, the only building of significance seemed to be the Old Portuguese fort and it was still in good condition. The boy led them into the fort's courtyard where he motioned to Robbie and the rest of the group to stay where they were and entered the building through its massive carved door. Before long he returned in tow with the strangest sight Robbie had ever seen; a man dressed in the full regalia of a Portuguese general, feathers in his hat and all! He explained in broken English that he had been the harbour master and asked Robbie what he wanted. He still considered himself the harbourmaster and the leader of the people of Bazaruto.

Robbie explained that he expected a dhow to be here waiting for him and then another ship within the next two days. The little old man's face beamed as he invited Robbie into his office and offered to help with the formalities. Then he instructed the children to place the gear in a room adjoining the office. Robbie had brought sweets with him, knowing that children made superb lookouts, he handed some out to each child. On Robbie's insistence they were severely told not to say anything to anybody by the harbourmaster.

Later in the day the children reported the sighting of a dhow to the harbourmaster. They all watched from the fort battlements, as it slowly made its way towards them. After what seemed an eternity it entered between the crumbling breakwaters into the tiny harbour. By this time the entire village had lined the walls to see the spectacle. The harbourmaster, in true form, went to the quayside to greet the newly arrived seafarers. They were all black and obviously exhausted after their long trip and back at the fort they greeted Robbie with tremendous enthusiasm.

Robbie took several hundred dollars from his wallet and asked his host whether it would cover their stay until the ship arrived in about two days time. The harbourmaster had not seen this amount of money in many years. It was worth twenty times its face value on the black market so he made sure that it was carefully deposited in an antique safe in his office. The men were shown to three rooms within the fort as the harbourmaster explained that they were used by him and his family; but that they would stay with friends and relatives until they left. They ate well on prawns and crayfish, supplemented with bananas, paw-paws and watermelons.

The ship didn't appear on the Friday as expected, when it hadn't made its appearance by Saturday morning, Robbie felt inevitable doubts creeping in. He could see that his friends were becoming agitated too, but there was nothing he could do about it; they all had to wait in the hope that there was a good reason for the delay. To add to their frustration, the only telephone on the island was in the harbourmaster's office and then it only connected them to the mainland. Robbie wasn't able find out if the ship had left Beira or not.

On Sunday morning they were awakened by the shouting of the children in the fort courtyard for there, now anchored some three hundred feet from the breakwater, was the most beautiful old rust bucket imaginable. Robbie shouted loudly, partly in happiness, but mainly for the others to come and see. They all danced and sang upon the parapet, ably assisted by the children. It didn't take long to carry their goods from the fort to the dhow. Robbie thanked everyone for their hospitality and they boarded the dhow which was to carry them along the coast back to Robbie's homeland.

During the morning the ship's crew, together with the small compliment of men on the dhow, transferred the lethal cargo across to the solid timbered dhow.

The ship's captain explained that he had been held up for repairs at Beira, which Robbie accepted without question; it was only later that he had cause to doubt it. By midday the dhow's skipper had steered them beyond the three mile limit and they had set sail south along the coastline. He anticipated reaching their landing point in South Africa by Tuesday morning; where Robbie had arranged for several four wheeled drive vehicles to meet them at a remote point between Black Rock and Lala Nek, to minimise their chances of their being caught out.

Everything went according to plan and they made the landing on. The only inhabitants of this area were the local game rangers; there were no other prying eyes to disturb them. From this point on they would have to take the utmost care as there were many police informers within the Zulu ranks and if anyone even suspected what consignment was being brought into the area, Robbie and his friends would pay the maximum penalty.

CHAPTER THIRTY FIVE

'Pledge of vows well believed, the ingrate and friend deceived'

<u>London - England</u>

They all felt a definite change in the house after Robbie left, at first Joan didn't know what to do with herself and somehow looked like a lost puppy moving about the place in aimless fashion. She went to work but the evenings were always the worst, as she stayed in the forlorn hope that he would telephone from South Africa. Michael and Sharon were so busy with their social life that the only people to left to talk with were the domestic staff. She started calling Robbie's friends associated with the ANC to supposedly discuss items of business, hoping that they would invite her around, but they never did. It felt to her as if she was being snubbed by them, or else they had been warned off by somebody; she had become so dependant upon her lover that she hadn't developed a life of her own.

Sharon also noticed a subtle change which started the day that Robbie departed for South Africa. Mike's eyes continually shifted from her to any doorway at hand, as if he expected his friend walk in at any minute; they had never been far apart from each other since birth. At work it was as if he had lost his right hand and she felt him slipping away and losing interest in the business. She needed his full support, now that she was preparing to hand over the London office into Alain's capable hands, so that they could get on with their American venture. At the weekend they were due to fly to New York to start negotiations with their lawyers to acquire a reasonable size company.

Mike asked her to postpone the meeting, under the pretext of not feeling too well, but she knew that he, like Joan, was awaiting word from Robbie. She explained that if he wasn't going to be there then she would have to go alone, because the meeting had taken months of negotiations to set up. By Saturday morning he still hadn't made up his mind and Sharon became frustrated with his negative answers, telling him that she was going to catch the flight that afternoon whether he was coming or not.

Mike felt he had had a portion of himself torn away with the departure of his friend. Every time he carried out a trade for the IRA or Hezbollah his thoughts dwelt on him. Now he battled to make proper decisions for his friend. In that first week he found himself unable to make money for Robbie's clients with his normal natural ease as a good trader. What he couldn't understand was that his own clients' trades were making money. This was brought home sharply to him on Thursday when he received a call from an Irishman.

"Mr Roberts, you assured us that you were a capable trader and we thought you were able to invest our funds for a profit. We took Mr Molefe's word for that," he said.

"Listen, I'm just getting to grips with it." Mike replied.

"We had an agreement with him. You are playing with our money, so the same rules apply to you as applied to him."

Michael felt a slight tingle run up his spine, the menacing voice made it quite clear that these people weren't prepared to lose under any circumstances, whether Robbie was here or not.

"I don't know what you're talking about, but don't worry we will soon have your position rectified," he said brusquely.

"You had better be right about that mister. We don't want any trouble."

Mike heard a distinct click as the line went dead, he cursed aloud, Robbie had placed him in a precarious position with these investors. They were untouchable threatening voices on the telephone, which only had banks as their addresses. He decided to remain in London and correct their investments; these were not people to play with and so he told Sharon that he definitely wouldn't be going to New York.

Sharon was livid; Mike always backed her in business and she couldn't understand his mentality now.

"You must be there," she urged.

"Please, put the meeting off for a week," Mike pleaded.

"Nonsense, you've been swinging the lead all week since Robert left. We've spent a long time putting this deal together and now you want to give up a golden opportunity."

She didn't want to part on bad terms with him; she knew that there must be a far more important reason for his not attending the meeting. Still, she was determined to have her own way and to open discussions in New York even if he wasn't there.

Mike and Joan spent the rest of the afternoon together, after Sharon had gone off to the airport. For the first time since meeting they were sharing a common hope that Robbie would call and tell them everything was all right. They settled in front of the television, sharing a warm rug for extra comfort. At the end of the programme, Mike teased Joan about their incriminating position if Sharon should walk in. To his amazement she burst into a flood of tears. Feeling very uncomfortable with this sudden outburst, Mike looked on helplessly. There had been times during the week that he had felt exactly the same way because his lifelong compatriot had left a massive void with his departure. She wasn't the only one needing to be comforted he thought, beneath the blanket he rolled over and took the weeping figure into his arms, pulling her towards him. For a while neither moved as they slowly drew strength from the comforting embrace as they lay under the blanket hugging each other tightly.

"Thank you Mike, I needed that." She looked deep into the young man's eyes and noticed that they were glistening. She hadn't realised how much he was hurting too and touched by the emotion she gently placed a full kiss on his mouth in gratitude.

Sharon waited in the cold outside the terminal for the service bus to take her back to her car in the long-term car-park. With all the chaos being caused by the weather the traffic had banked up come to a standstill. It was well below freezing and the ground staff was having trouble with ice that had formed on the planes' wings; American Airlines expected a four to five hour delay but couldn't be sure if they would be airborne at all that day, so she decided to give this trip a miss.

Champagne Castle was only a short drive down the motorway. The transit coach pulled into the long-term parking yard; she quickly found her car and pulled out into the snarling traffic, deciding not to use the motorway but to travel via backstreets that would get her home sooner.

"Mike will be surprised," she thought as she turned away from Weybridge town centre up the hill and went through the private gates onto the estate.

Neither Mike nor Joan had made a move except for this long and sustained kiss that had brought them very close in their loneliness. Both jumped as the telephone jangled.

"It'll probably be Sharon. I'd better answer it," he said.

"Hello."

It was his mother calling from South Africa.

"Mom, what a lovely surprise, how are you and dad?"

Just then Mike froze as he saw an unmistakeable figure silhouetted through the obscure glass pane in the front door. Cupping his hand over the mouthpiece he turned inside the doorway and hissed at Joan.

"It's Sharon, she's back"

Calmly he turned to face the door as she entered and smiled broadly. He quickly placed his arm on her shoulder and whispered into her ear.

"Its mom, here say hello," without giving her a moment to think he pushed the receiver into her hand. She chatted for a few minutes before hanging up.

When Sharon entered the room she surveyed the scene and snapped "I can't leave you on your own for an afternoon, without you getting up to some form of mischief."Then, turning on her heel, stalked out of the room.

"Do I look like an absolute idiot?" asked Sharon. They were sitting on their large double bed. Sharon carefully studied his reaction in her mirror as she pretended to rub night cream on her face. She noticed his slight fidget as he shut the book and placed it on the bedside table.

"Ever since that one slip, you've had this obsession that I try to get everything with a skirt into bed," retorted Mike.

"You know exactly what I mean. Did I say anything about you and her going to bed?"

"Not quite, but that's what you seemed to imply."

"That not what was meant Michael, but if the shoe fits then wear it." Her soft voice hardened noticeably.

"You go to New York tomorrow; I'm off to South Africa because I can't take this jealousy of yours any more," said Mike.

"What!" she snapped.

"You heard me, I'm sick of these petty accusations."

"When did you plan this?"

"About ten seconds ago when you started dishing up your own brand of persecution!"

Sharon was like a boxer, reeling from a hit by a glove loaded with a horseshoe.

"There's got to be a better way than having this continual bickering in our marriage." Mike continued.

"Mike, we're acting like spoilt children, let's talk this through?"

"What's there to talk about?"

The more he had thought about going home, the more he liked the idea.

"I realise that I may have antagonised you and for that I'm sorry. I also understand that you're worried about Robbie and that's why you don't want to come with me tomorrow; but running away isn't going to solve the problem."

This wasn't what he expected to hear, she had known all the time what he had been going through.

African Chess

"You don't understand, Robbie and I are like twins?"

"I know this only too well, but you and I also have a life to lead; he has chosen his path, you must choose yours."

CHAPTER THIRTY SIX

'He was loved as a son, when days of peace were known to come'

Ulundi - South Africa

Robbie and two others spent the whole day carefully digging out a large pit under a dry tree stump, making sure not to disturb the roots below the dead keeper. Carefully prying their way between the spreading mandrels, the men worked away like moles clearing an area large enough to house their deadly cargo. The parts had been meticulously oiled and greased before despatch to prevent rusting while at sea. Heavy canvas outer wrapping was placed around each item to prevent sweating and then covered by a sheet of black plastic so that no rotting or dampness reached it. Finally each piece in order of size was placed into the plastic lined hole, until they had everything securely hidden beneath the intricate rooting system of the old tree. Happy with their handiwork, Robbie wedged a series of heavy logs end to end into the earth above the roots then covered this with plastic and filled in the hole.

Carefully the men planted several tufts of grass and small bushes to blend in with the terrain over the spot. They levelled the remaining earth across the surrounding area and with old branches acting as besoms, swept away all tracks as they made their way back to the camp. Robbie knew that before sunrise they would have to be on their way across country to avoid bumping into ranger patrols within the game reserve. As the men tucked into their cooked meal they were all tired and happy with their days' work. The hum of the mosquitoes drowned the silence of the night as Robbie lay awake in his sleeping bag, waiting to move inland. For the first time since his arrival he was able to grasp that he really was back in South Africa after such a long time away. He could hear life all around him, night predators scavenging for food in the undergrowth, scurrying rodents leaving their young in holes while they embarked on quick trips and the incessant flying bugs. For many years he'd longed to hear these sounds again and now here he was drinking it all in with eyes, ears and smell; trying to capture everything in these few quiet remaining moments. The sudden sound of a snapped twig in the distance alerted him immediately. One of the others had heard the sound and also sat up.

"Let the others sleep, come!" Robbie whispered to the half awake man.

They made their way across to the vehicles, where they quickly found two loaded Uzi machine guns. Robert handed one to the man and indicated for him to hide himself within sight of the camp. From his position, behind some thick bush near the vehicles, he could also survey the whole camp area which was well lit up by the glow of their fire. His keen eyes searched, without success, to locate the other man who had blended in with the shadows.

Again that definite sound; but this time much closer to the camp. Suddenly, like two shadows separating from the dark, two black men moved cautiously into the ring of light. One, holding a large knife in his hand, made a slight hissing sound through his teeth as he pointed at the two empty sleeping bags. Robbie's companion stepped from his hiding place, the short machine gun pointing at the leading man.

"Ngabe ufuna?"

The two were in no position to argue with the menacing weapon aimed at them as they turned.

"Ugwayi," replied one.

Laughing quietly, Robbie moved from cover thinking that this was the most original answer that he had ever heard. Nobody could make up an answer like that on the spur of the moment. They were no more than common thieves looking to steal some tobacco; he ordered them to sit on the ground. After checking them carefully and finding nothing but the knife, he questioned them and discovered that they were villagers fleeing from war-torn Mozambique. Feeling sorry for the scavengers, Robbie gave them food, tobacco and some coffee before sending them on their way.

"You can have a good lie-in before leaving for Champagne Castle," said Peter.

Mike had managed to get a last minute seat to Johannesburg and Peter had collected him from the airport. Mike couldn't help noticing that the servant that had replaced Nellie was also Zulu. Walking to the bathroom of the guest flat over the garage, he looked into the room that Robbie had used when Shorty Majozi had visited them and imagined the whole scene again; it felt like it all took place a lifetime away.

Drakensburg Resort - South Africa
Later, making good time, he found himself passing the turn to the National Park by five o'clock that afternoon. Looking up at the last section of hill, he could now clearly see the farmhouse to the right and the thatched roofs of the hotel on the plateau above. Tales of the Vienna Woods played on the car radio and he was singing as loudly he could turning the car down the gravel track towards his parent's house.

Sitting with Ian and Nicole in the lounge overlooking his mountain range, was pure happiness to the man's aching heart, it felt as if he had never been away. Later, walking around greeting everybody, he was surprised to see both Phineas and Daniel were having their usual evening meal; out here time stood still he thought. He sat quietly chatting to his old friends in their mother tongue as the brilliant African sun dropped quickly behind the mountain.

Ulundi - South Africa

The men with him picked their way carefully through the dense tropical bush, fording endless streams at passable depths, as Robbie tried to figure out where they were headed. They certainly knew their way across the vast game reserve, staying clear of tracks and roads which could bring them into conflict with patrols. Just as sunrise started breaking, the two four wheel drive vehicles stopped and the driver in the lead got out and made his way back to them.

"The main gates are just ahead of us, we must wait until they are opened," he said.

"Why don't we simply cut the wires further down and drive through?" asked Robbie.

"That would not be wise. There are all sorts of alarms right along the perimeter fence since the ivory war was stepped up. We could be unlucky and draw attention to ourselves; it's better to wait."

These men were professionals Robbie thought; he was in their hands and would go along with their plans. The men drove the two vehicles into a river and started cleaning the thickly caked mud from them. At half past seven the leading driver pointed to his ear.

"Hear that, cars moving into the reserve; we will give it about twenty minutes then leave through the gate."

The two vehicles slowly made their way out of the bush and past the log cabin rest camp towards the main gate. Robbie saw four heavily armed patrol rangers inspecting each vehicle for unlawful souvenirs.

"What if they stop us and see all these arms, we won't get a mile down the road before the police arrive," said Robbie.

"Just relax and show no fear."

Two patrolmen stood either side of the gate, ready to shoot, while two more checked each vehicle. The only white patrolman sat in an office; their lead vehicle suddenly stopped about ten yards from the gate, blocking the way for all behind. Robbie's heart leapt into his mouth, as he heard it tick over several times. Then the driver got out and opened the bonnet. They could not reverse as a huge bus was right behind them, blocking any retreat.

"What the hell is going on?" whispered Robbie, as the driver got out.

"Stay there," he ordered Robbie.

All this way and then to get caught like this, he thought. The bus hooted as traffic started building up behind it trying to leave the reserve, Robbie noted that the patrolmen were becoming agitated. The lead driver shouted something at one of them and then closed the bonnet. The two drivers returned to their vehicles and his driver moved up gently against the lead vehicle, with a slight bump it started pushing it forward towards the gate; the black patrolmen seeing the two moving vehicles and not wanting any further disruption, waved them through the gate. Further down the road they stopped whilst the lead driver got out and replaced the HT lead he had pulled out earlier; two minutes later they were both heading down the road.

"What did you think of our plan," laughed the driver slapping Robbie's shoulder.

"Just like a military operation. What a bluff!"

They entered Ulundi just after midday and drove straight to an imposing house, set high on one of the hills overlooking the ramshackle town. After parking the vehicles in a large double garage, Robbie followed the lead driver up a narrow winding stairway into the large house. The front door led straight into a huge sitting room with enormous glazed windows at the far end. Scattered across the highly polished floor were wild animal skins and on the white walls hung various fighting implements of the Zulu nation.

The room was like a museum, it looked as if it was a shrine to the Zulu nation with its paintings of imposing warriors and events depicting great events for the tribe. They moved slowly towards a figure that was silhouetted against the bright glass background.

His mother had often spoken of this man when he was young; he was the unseen power behind the Zulu throne, his word was law and he was Robbie's father! Robbie had never met him because he considered that the boy's life would be in jeopardy if ever anyone found out that he was of royal blood.

"We finally meet my son, you have done well!" said the quiet voice.

The young man moved forward to meet his father for the first time, his heart beat with excitement as the old man came forward out of the glare of the bright light, so that his son could see him.

Robbie suddenly froze, the hairs on his skin strained at their ends as a tingling sensation filled his body he realised he had fallen into a trap.

"You!" he said. His hooded cobra eyes had suddenly become alert to danger as they focused on the figure of the old man walking towards him. It was the grey-haired old man that had been with the security man in London. The old man smiled gently at his son.

"If I had truly wanted to kill you in London then you would have died that day; but instead I protected you because you are not our enemy."

He placed his hands firmly on the younger mans' shoulders and looking straight into his eyes he said. "Welcome home at last my son, let my house be your house."

CHAPTER THIRTY SEVEN

When whirlwinds start wheeling, pillars of hope are set reeling'

Drakensburg Resort - South Africa

Lying stretched out on the sun baked black rock Mike couldn't help thinking back to the time of his initiation into manhood at this very spot. He was listening to the thunderous noise of the falling water, occasionally broken by shouts from one of the city dwellers that he had escorted to the spot. His mind was at peace for the first time in many years.

"Aren't you coming in?" said a young girl's voice.

Mike looked up at a young student hanging onto the edge of the rock.

"Later, I must at least get a suntan after all these years in England."

The student had gone out of her way to make conversation; Mike knew the signs and was keeping his distance.

"C'mon, it's lovely."

Sharon had said something similar all those years ago; which had led him into a lifelong situation. For the first time since their argument he found himself missing her. "Sorry no, go and find someone else."

Mike watched as the pretty student turned and swam in the direction of her college friends.

Why me? He thought; another time and place and he would have been flattered by her attention.

Nicole saw mixed feelings of happiness and sadness oozing from her son and decided to confront him with it at the first opportunity. When everybody was out of the house, the following morning, she called him into the sitting room, pretending to need his help to move the large sofa.

"What's the matter?" she asked.

"Nothing, I'm just so overawed at being back here after so long, I love this place mom."

"Michael!"

"Really mom, there's nothing wrong!"

"Then why didn't you bring Sharon with you? She is your wife or did you think that I didn't know?"

Michael flopped into a chair, he hadn't expected this.

"How... how did you find out?" Nobody knew because they had been so secretive about the wedding and here his own mother was telling him what he had been up to.

"You forget that I head a huge empire and you were seen in Nevada by someone who knew that you were my son."

"Nobody was supposed to find out," he said.

"When this friend called your hotel to try to arrange dinner he found out that there was a Mrs Roberts and thought you were simply having a dirty weekend and left you alone. When he described the pretty young blonde to me, I immediately knew that it was Sharon. So I had somebody check out the churches in the area and guess what!"

"So what's going to happen now?" he asked, relieved that the secret was now out.

"To start with, you're going to tell me why she didn't come with you."

"We've had an argument because I refused to go to a meeting in New York and came here instead."

"Not only wasn't I born yesterday, but I'm still your mother; that's not the full reason, so what else happened?"

He couldn't tell her that they'd had a flaming row over a quite ridiculous assumption on her part. Although it was based on his past behaviour, so it was quite understandable that she had blown a fuse.

"It's Robbie, he's involved with the ANC and now that he's back here it won't be long before the police cotton on to him, even though he may be a respected businessman for your company."

Nicole visibly relaxed; her son didn't know why she had brought Robbie back to South Africa.

"I'm going to get us some tea first and then I've got something to tell you that I should have told you a long time ago."

Mike listened in quiet disbelief as his mother related the story of her black son to him. So much was suddenly made clear as the story unfolded, his mother was like a magician, every time he thought he had come to grips with a trick she produced another rabbit from the hat. He tried to understand the full complexity of his and Robbie's intertwined lives which had been governed from birth by their parents.

"The main unexpected twist came when you and your cousin

foolishly decided to get married; but then that can't be helped if you love each other. In fact it will be an asset to the company."

"Bugger the company, you parents have played God with our lives." A sense of guilt made him explode at his mother; it seemed that everybody had played their part in this great plan except for him.

"Before you say anymore I want you to think about the thing as a whole and not just your misery because you and Sharon have had an argument," she said quietly.

Nicole got up and collected their empty cups, leaving the young man to absorb the entirety of her revelations to him. For a long while he sat looking out of the large window along the line of his favourite range of mountains. Far below the plateau he could see a thin dark line of horsemen steadily making their way down into the Sterkspruit Valley. He needed to get out into the open by himself and think about his future. He saddled his favourite horse and was soon setting off in the direction of the riders that he had seen; this would give him about two hours of thinking time before he caught up with them.

Ulundi - South Africa

Robbie stared at the grey-haired man in front of him and could see the tears streaming down his cheeks, flowing along the aged wrinkles like a network of drains. He relaxed for the first time since their meeting, as he watched a father's unabashed joy at meeting his son.

"Tell me everything about yourself," requested the man.

Robbie started at the Champagne Castle Hotel as far back as he could remember and told him everything leading up to today's meeting. The man took in every word with pride as he sat and shook his head in acknowledgement of this young man's achievements.

"And now you've come home to help your people."

"You are the last person I expected to meet," Robbie stated.

"Your purpose in life is only about to begin, now that you are back home," smiled his father.

Robbie was slightly perplexed, knew that his leadership qualities would one day be of use for his people; but this indicated that something far greater was to take place. "What is my purpose?" he asked tentatively.

"Like me, you have worked to destroy the Zulu collaborators within the ANC; the time is now right and you have to take your rightful place in helping our people into a new world."

Robbie had always known that he was a descendent of the Zulu royal family, but had always assumed that he was a bastard son with no say in tribal affairs.

"When I was much younger I fell in love with a woman and you were the result of that marriage. But to serve my people I had to become a servant of the white security forces."

He lifted a dried calabash to his lips and drank from it before offering it to his son.

"To protect my family from harm we sent your mother to my friend's hotel to work; I would sometimes visit her at Champagne Castle."

He took another sip at the container.

"We changed her name to Molefe, so that nobody would know

that she was of the royal family. I went to work as a security man finding out all about the ANC and killed their leaders where I could."

Like a gigantic jigsaw puzzle all the unanswered questions suddenly started falling into place for Robbie.

"All this time our people watched over you and your mother, until you left for England. By then you knew your destiny and worked inside the ANC headquarters sending reports back to us without anyone suspecting."

"What about my friend, George. Why did you kill him?" asked Robbie.

"We followed you and I let you slip away; but George stayed in the car and that white man found him. Everything would have been lost, so it was either him or you; I had no choice."

"Was it you that left the message that the security forces were in London that time I flew to the Bahamas?"

"You were very unlucky that time as one of our men saw and followed you; I knew that we would have to leave London after the bombing, so I left the message to warn you."

"And the attempt on my life in Johannesburg?"

"Again, there was nothing I could do to help you and luckily your friend's screaming scared Shorty, he was the white security's killer, who made his speedy escape. You two were very fortunate on that occasion, it could have ended badly."

"Did you have to kill Nellie, though?"

"Oh yes, we knew that she was an informer for the ANC. She realised the truth when she saw me that day and recognised me, she also hated your mother so much that she had to be killed before she could inform the ANC."

Robbie and his father sat alone and talked through their respective roles for the Zulu cause until late that night. Robbie hugged his father tightly and through his shirt could feel that the supposedly frail old man was all sinew and muscle and no flab. This man looked like any other elderly Zulu but, in the short time they had spent together, Robbie realised that his father was only old in years; his mind and body were as finely honed as a sharp razor. He had now decided to pass his knowledge on as he needed to join the other Zulu elders.

"Our nation thanks you for your gifts to them, we will use them well once we have managed to retrieve them from their hiding place below the tree," said his father.

Because of their close links with the Communist bloc, the ANC and UDF had superior weapons to use against the Zulus. Robbie's consignment would now redress this situation. Already word had got to the leadership that his son had arrived with enough sophisticated arms to rout the ANC in Natal. What had been a one sided fight would now turn full circle and the enemy was about to flee north again; just as they had done all those years before. The Zulu lion was beginning to rise and flex it muscles.

"I don't want thanks, it was my duty father," said Robbie. He realised that this was the first time that he had actually called the older man by his correct title, the word sounded strange to his lips.

"No, my son, it wasn't out of duty but much more importantly out of love for your people and your homeland; for that you sacrificed everything and one day will be a great leader."

"Tomorrow I must go to Champagne Castle to see my mother, why don't you come with me?"

"If only, but I must return to Pretoria and see what that white devil is doing and what news of the ANC."

Drakensburg Resort - South Africa

Robbie had made up his mind to spend the first week riding, walking and simply relaxing with old friends before starting his new job in Durban.

He arrived at the farmhouse just after four o'clock and went straight to his mother's cottage, only to find she wasn't there. "She must be up at the hotel. I'll surprise them all," he thought.

The two dogs were lying on a mat at the back door of the main house as he walked towards it. Suddenly the bitch rose, teeth bared as she made for him. Mike came out of the farmhouse to see Sheba attacking a black man, who was on the ground with his arm around her neck and Dodo was barking at both of them. He grabbed a broom and raced toward the flurry on the ground; Dodo saw him coming and playfully ran towards him, trying to seize the handle.

"Scat!" he screamed.

The man on the ground suddenly let go of the bitch and spun around to face Mike. The dogs had recognised Robbie just before attacking him when he had called out their names. Sheba had simply leaped up and knocked him off balance in her attempt to lick him in welcome. Mike dropped onto the ground beside his surprised friend.

"Why the hell didn't you warn us that you were arriving?"

"What makes you so important? Do I have to make a bloody appointment to come home?" They laughed heartily; they didn't have to explain why they were there - they both knew.

Mike still hadn't heard from Sharon when he and Robbie left the hotel heading for Johannesburg a week later. Peter had arranged for them to meet Commandant Bennie Roux to clear up some outstanding matters. Mike had called London several times to try to talk to her and nobody could tell him anything. The two had been out to enjoy the mountains of their boyhood together and discussed everything. Robbie related what had happened and his meeting with his father.

Johannesburg - South Africa

Peter was already in Johannesburg when they got there and together with the company lawyer, the two young men entered Bennie Roux's office at John Vorster Square to see Andrew Murray already seated beside his large desk.

"Mr Roberts, how nice to see you again," said the portly man standing up and offering his hand.

"Commandant, these are the two you wanted to meet and this is our legal representative, Bertie Cohen."

"Stay by all means Mr Cohen; but this is just a matter of clearing up a couple of details and doesn't need a lawyer to be present," said the policemen. They were all instructed to seat themselves in an arc around the huge desk.

"We know who tried to attack Mr Molefe and then killed your servant and many other people besides. What we don't know is why you were singled out, any ideas Mr Molefe?"

"No, none," replied Robbie.

"The man belonged to a crack hit squad involved with killing ANC activists. He is now in a mental home and will be unable to stand trial because he's completely insane."

"What do mean by a crack hit squad?" asked the lawyer.

Bennie and his sergeant knew that if they took the matter up with their superiors, it would simply disappear into a back room and never be heard of again. They decided that Peter had sufficient power and influence in the international business world to make waves big enough to ensure the matter wasn't swept under the carpet and trusted him to keep their names out of it.

"Gentlemen, what I'm about to tell you remains top secret and if it leaks out I will deny any knowledge of it; do you understand my position?"

Everyone knew exactly what the policemen meant as they listened to his hypothetical story of what he thought might have happened and who was involved. What worried Robbie, as they arrived back at the house in Melrose, was that his father could be linked with the rest of the security killers. Peter swore that he wasn't going to let the government get away with this atrocity and had more than enough clout to find out exactly where the truth lay.

Back at Peter's house, Robbie called the special number given to him by the old man in case of any emergencies. It was a shop in Soweto and Robbie gave the voice at the end his code name then left a message and a number where he could be contacted. That evening a call came through for Robbie and he took it in Peter's study. It was his father. He told him what he had learnt at John Vorster Square and what Peter intended doing about it.

"So that's where Shorty got to! Don't worry; I'll see to it that he won't be able to point a finger at anybody."

"Father, the damage is done. They know all about the organisation and surely as soon as one member is captured, he will reveal the names of the others?"

"Don't worry about me my son; your time for greatness has arrived. Use it well and thank you for your advice."

"You must be careful father, this story will soon break and they will be looking for someone like you to be their scapegoat."

"No matter what happens from now on you must listen to advice from your families, both black and white. Now, my boy, I must say goodbye for a while."

Robbie was surprised when he heard the distinct click as his father replaced the receiver; he was hurt at the way his father had cut him short.

He walked through to the lounge, where Peter and Mike were discussing what Peter intended doing the next day. Robbie listened and was disturbed by Peter's plan; he didn't like it, the hounds would be let loose and would seeking blood.

Peter had left the house by the time the two young men emerged for breakfast. According to Jane this was most unusual, because he normally only went to work at between eight thirty and nine. Peter had the bit between his teeth and had made arrangements for a working breakfast with the Minister of Law and Order, determined to flush things out into the open.

The minister listened to Peter's fantastic theory with a certain amount of scepticism, but promised to look into the matter. Peter was an old hand at negotiations and wasn't going to be fobbed off so easily; he threatened to produce names and dates if no immediate action was taken by the minister. Later that morning

Peter was summoned to an unscheduled meeting with the head of the South African Defence Force. Both ministers knew that if any news leaked out then one and maybe both, of them would be for the high jump.

The SADF man in charge of security quickly got busy trying to work out a plan to cover his tracks. He had the most to lose because ministers were changed every four years, whereas his job was on the line. Teams of officials quickly hid files and transferred accounts, closing anything that would point in their direction.

Peter waited a week before he received a call from the minister who assured him that they were looking into the matter. He suggested that there could be a small group of mercenaries involved. Never before had Peter dealt with such a slow procedure and told the minister that if the whole thing wasn't sorted out quickly then he would carry out his threat. The man on the other end said he appreciated that Peter wasn't playing around, but he needed time to shut all boltholes. Safe in the knowledge that this powerful government would be able to withstand the onrushing flood, he assured Peter of his absolute support. He only needed more time.

Mike and Robbie stood on the sidelines in Johannesburg for several days and then returned to their beloved Champagne Castle. Sharon was nowhere to be found in London or anywhere; either she was still playing games or something serious had happened. Mike was getting more worried as each day passed.

Robbie called Joan each night at eight promising that she would soon be able to join him because Nelson Mandela and others had been released and many laws were suddenly being relaxed so that black and whites could marry in South Africa. She refused to say anything about Sharon as she felt that she had caused enough trouble; however innocent it had been.

CHAPTER THIRTY EIGHT

'Mutual look of shame and fear, disguise arrived for all to share'

<u>Pretoria - South Africa</u>

Jay Jillions left Vortrekkerhoogte Hospital after completing her nightshift and walked to the bus stop across the road. She loved this time of early morning with the red dawn lying beyond the distant hills, the noise from the ever moving traffic not yet begun. All around her in the trees birds were busily calling out their mating tunes warning other feathered creatures to stay away from their domain. Jay listened to the morning waking around her as she waited for her usual five o'clock military bus to the centre of Pretoria. Two tired nurses and a female civilian were waiting for the same connection, she recognised the two nurses because they took the same bus every day; but it was strange to see a civilian on the base at this time of the morning. The woman was short and square with dark hair fixed back in a bun behind her head. Her old clothes looked as if they hadn't ever been ironed and she stood out from the others with their neat uniforms; Jay wondered what she was doing there at this time of the morning. She decided that she must be a wife of one of the injured servicemen in the hospital and had probably slept in a chair overnight, which would explain the state of her clothes. The green bus rounded the corner at the top of the road and trundled to a stop in front of them and Jay felt sorry for the woman, as she offered to let her onto the bus ahead of her. Jay noted the hard features and expressionless eyes as the stocky woman thanked her.

Tiny Lawson leaned back in his chair, in all his years as a reporter and editor he couldn't remember hearing such a fantastic story. Had the source not been so impeccable he would have dismissed it out of hand; but having a nose for a good story he had listened. Across his desk sat Peter Roberts, just finishing this unbelievable tale involving killings by government security forces; it sounded like something from a James Bond movie.

"Where did you get your information from Mr Roberts?" asked Tiny.

"If I told you the source, the story would be censored immediately; but I can say that if you start your enquiries at Sterkfontein Mental Home, you will find that the Empangeni Hammer killer is involved."

"So that's where he is now," said the editor.

The Sunday News was probably the most liberal newspaper in the country, continually in conflict with the government and Tiny Lawson as chief editor had been arrested twice for printing what he believed in.

"Over the years we've heard rumours of a killing squad and were never able to prove it. I think this time we'll take it carefully and get the full facts before going to press."

"These men have got to be stopped," insisted Peter.

"What is your interest in exposing them?"

"These bastards tried to kill a friend of the family in our own house and nobody, no matter how high the order comes from, is going to get away with that," replied Peter vehemently.

"I see, will you let us talk to this visitor?"

"No, I don't want my name, or that of my family and friends, brought into this matter. Do you understand?"

The editor scratched at his red hair then looked at his nails to see what they had unearthed.

"We're going to need more than just your hearsay," he said.

"I'm giving you a lead to possibly the biggest scoop you're likely to get in years. Either you take it on my conditions or I tell the other papers the same story and you lose the exclusivity," replied Peter calmly. The ruddy faced editor knew from Peter's record that he was a man of his word; a merciless trader who knew how to get his own way when he had to.

"All right, we get the exclusive for two weeks; if we come up with nothing then you make it a free for all."

Pretoria - South Africa

Dirk Lemmer walked into office 217 on the second floor of Pretoria's Union Buildings. For nearly two weeks he had been trying without success to make an appointment with the minister and now he was becoming desperate.

"Meneer Lemmer!" said the minister's surprised secretary.

"I've been trying to make an appointment with him and all the time he's busy; so now I've come in person."

"That's correct, he has a lot of meetings scheduled and won't be able to fit you in for at least a month," she fended.

"This is very important, if he doesn't see me the State is going to find itself in all sorts of trouble," insisted Dirk.

"What sort of trouble?"

"It's a matter of state security and for his ears only. I need about ten minutes of his time."

Two weeks previously the secretary had been given strict instructions from her boss not to make appointments with any of the security men; but this sounded important.

"Wait here, I'll have to find out whether he has ten minutes to spare today."

She walked into her inner office and closed the door. Dirk quickly slipped around the desk and opened the minister's diary to see just how busy he was really going to be. He had only three appointments written down; a meeting with the police chief, an opening of a fete and a meeting here with Roberts and Molefe.

"That bastard's back and coming to meet the government minister!"

Closing the book and replacing it, Dirk went and sat down in the brown corner settee, picking up a magazine. He needed to think about this betrayal by his own boss.

The door opened and the girl walked in again, "He can't make it today, but can you be here at eleven tomorrow morning?"

"Ja, I'll see him tomorrow."

He's scheduled a time only one hour later than that black ANC bastard he thought, as he descended the stairway; he suspected that he was somehow being set up. Right, they want to play rough do they, we'll see who wins, he fumed. In his mind's eye he saw the minister and Robbie Molefe as enemies of the country and such people had to die.

Johannesburg - South Africa

Rudy Norman drove towards the distant city of Johannesburg, he had just had his third meeting with Bertram Mark the doctor in charge of the Psychiatry Wing at Sterkfontein Mental Hospital. They had been at school together and Rudy had pumped his friend for information. At the second meeting Bertram had started telling Rudy of the outlandish allegations made by Shorty Majozi, the Empangeni Hammer Killer. Rudy had not asked about any prisoner in particular and had said he was doing a feature about stories made up by mental patients, separating fact from fiction and how it affected their thinking.

Bertram didn't want to make a circus of his patients and gave Rudy several stories which wouldn't hurt them. On Sunday Rudy wrote an extremely caring article, concentrating on the confusion aspect and what was needed in the way of care for some of this type of patient. The doctor was so impressed that he invited Rudy back to the hospital and then to his home, all the while feeding him with stories collected from his patients. He told Rudy of the case of the Hammer Killer, what he thought was truth and what was merely delusion in the man's deranged mind. Again Rudy wrote another sympathetic piece on what he had been told, not mentioning anything said by Shorty Majozi. Now that he had earned the doctor's gratitude and trust, he was allowed to go further he asked his friend to show him the file on the Empangeni Killer.

The doctor explained everything in detail about his schizophrenic patient and what he thought was the difference between fact and fiction. Rudy examined the files carefully, taking notes of names and places mentioned. Most of the material was disjointed but the reporter knew from experience that the information underlying this mysterious puzzle meant a scoop. As he drove home he listened to his tape again; he was sure that he had all the information he was going to get from the hospital. Somewhere in this fantastic mixture of disjointed information lay the biggest story of his life.

Back at the office he quickly checked with their library files, looking especially at all the dates, disappearances and deaths of the victims mentioned by Shorty Majozi. Their records showed only a few reported deaths, but checking through them the one fact that stood out, in Rudy's mind, was that everything coincided with his details. Later, in his editor's office, he and Tiny discussed whether there was really a worthwhile story for the newspaper.

"These dates and times are too accurate to be the hallucinations of a madman," said the reporter.

"Well, you're going to get nothing more from that source, so what do you want us to do now? We can't print this on the word of a mental patient because it just won't stand up."

"Boss, I want to pursue this and I'll need the help of one of our black reporters to interview the black families; I will personally meet the white families."

"You've got a week to convince me that there's a story, if not we pull it - understood?"

They had spent two weeks not getting very far, but the few facts they now had stood out and Tiny Lawson knew that what Peter had told him could possibly be proved. He called two of his top black reporters into his office and showed them the file, asking for their opinion; they both felt the same as Rudy.

Rudy was made the team leader and given a further three reporters, as the paper went into top gear to prove government involvement in these killings. Tiny knew that they had to move quickly as the team's probing questions would soon alert the opposition press and he wanted this story to be all theirs.

The search for proof took the reporters through the length and breadth of South Africa. Where known sightings, or strong suspicions of the killers were discovered the newspaper quickly rushed in artists to sketch anything still fresh in the witnesses' minds.

By the end of the week a definite pattern for these killers had been formed and three distinct faces began to emerge as the leaders of this unit of clandestine mercenaries.

Tiny Lawson examined the pictures and reports which were continuously coming in from his reporters all across the country. Then came the first big break; a letter setting out the names of special security force members, with a schedule of payments made from a special slush fund account, landed on his desk. There was no way of tracing who had sent the letter, but it checked out that the account was linked to a government special slush fund. Tiny immediately called Rudy into his office to show him the letter.

"Prove that this account belongs to any government body and get Sam to inspect Majozi's bank account as well as the accounts of the other names we now have. We need to prove that the government was the paymaster."

If he were able to tie all this together he could make the findings public, with the law firmly behind them.

"Rudy, also try to find out who the signatory to that account is as it will make interesting reading if it's a government minister."

By the following morning they knew that the South African Defence Force was the paymaster for the special bank account that financed the covert operation.

"At last!" shouted Tiny.

He now had all the proof he needed that the government was somehow involved in a shelter fund to finance the illegal killings of ANC and possibly other activists in the country.

"We've got them, get your minds on the job and give me your best front page report for Sunday's edition."

He dismissed the beaming reporters standing around his desk and then called Peter to ask for a meeting as soon as possible.

Peter arrived home beaming from ear to ear as he sat across the table from Robbie and Mike.

"You two have got some reading to do tonight," he laughed. He lifted his briefcase and extracted a bound manuscript which he set before them.

"This, gentlemen, is the complete story as told to us by Commandant Roux and what's more, it implicates the State."

There was no mistaking his pride in his achievement of assisting a newspaper to bring the killers to book.

"Can I use your telephone?" asked Robbie suddenly.

"Sure, you know where it is."

Robbie made his way to the study and called a number and gave his code before asking to be called back immediately.

"Look here Robbie, these are some of the assassins," said Mike holding the file out to him.

Robbie studied each of the drawings carefully, trying to memorise them as he flipped each page, then he saw a full blown-up picture of his father. Just then he received his expected call.

"I'm glad you called, because I want you to attend a meeting tonight," said the voice on the other end, "so be ready at eight and I'll collect you."

"They are going to print the story of your group on Sunday and your picture is there," Robbie said through gritted teeth.

"Don't worry about me, my son, I've been helping the papers and they won't be able to trace me as I've covered my tracks."

"I thought you'd better know at once," Robbie said, finding it difficult to conceal his despair.

"There will be many ruffled feathers before long; they are only excess baggage to a bird and can be shed without denuding it."

Robbie thought about this for a moment then grasped the meaning and smiled as the voice continued.

"Tomorrow is the start of your big adventure and I need you to play your part well, my son. I must go now, but I'll see you later." It was very disconcerting to Robbie to have the receiver put down so abruptly each time he tried to talk to his father. In the sitting room the other two were still busily looking at the file in front of them as he returned.

"This is the only complete file of events outside the Sunday News, so don't lose it!" said Peter.

After supper that night, Robbie and Mike retired to the flat and sat down to read through all the notes in the file.

"Mike, I'm worried," Robbie said.

"Why?"

"See this picture, don't you recognise him?"

Robbie opened the book at the picture of an old man.

"No, should I?"

"This is the old man that chased us around Heathrow Airport, it's my father," said Robbie quietly. Back at Champagne Castle, Robbie had told Mike about the meeting with his father at Ulundi, but no more.

"That call I made earlier was to tell him about the picture and he told me not to worry because his tracks are covered."

Mike understood the emotion his friend must be going through.

"He seems to know what he's doing and anyway, what can you do now? They're going to print it on Sunday," said Mike.

"I just wish that I could remove his picture from the rest of the files in the newspaper's office," Robbie looked at the picture with affection and then said again, "but I suppose he knows what he's doing."

"Talking about that, I wonder why that chap in the brown coat isn't shown here?" commented Mike idly.

They had been so busy with the file that both hadn't realised this significant point.

"Mike, you're absolutely right; if anyone should be there, it's him."

"I don't think I could describe him, except that he had a closely cropped haircut. I didn't get a good enough look at him as he was too far away for me to see him clearly." Robbie thought about what Mike had just said and replied that, if he were asked to describe the man, he wasn't sure that he would be able to either.

"I would be able to draw his eyes, but I'm not sure if I could get his face exactly right as he was too far away each time I also saw him," Robbie said. The two pondered over this for some time then returned to the file to see what other information might come to light.

"I'm meeting my father tonight so I've got to get ready as he'll be here soon," Robbie said.

That night, in the Sunday News Building, some of the cleaning staff quickly slipped through the offices where all the pictures and drawings were kept. Carefully searching through all the desks as they moved from office to office, they removed only a picture of an old man from the files. For two hours they carefully made sure that everything about the man was vague, including all the notes taken at the scene from an elderly witness.

That night, in Soweto, an old man slept silently on his steel-framed bed when the door was quietly opened and a young man entered and placed a pillow over his face. It all happened very quickly and was over just as quickly. The young man made sure that everything looked normal and nothing was out of place before he left the room as silently as he had entered.

The fire department was called to an accidental electrical fire in the news room of the Sunday News during the early hours of the morning. Jets of foam made a mess of much of the material, but a lot was salvaged and the vital documents about the banking details were still intact.

Tiny Lawson breathed a sigh of relief but was jittery because he wasn't too certain that this was an accident. He made sure that everything was immediately copied that next day, spare copies placed in their vaults overnight from then on and as an added precaution, handed one copy to their legal representatives for safekeeping.

Robbie met his father outside the gates to the Robert's grounds. They didn't say much as Robbie watched the man guide his car through the wealthy white suburb of Rivonia. The vehicle stopped at some large steel gates and the old man hooted twice. Robbie could see a security camera on the wall and knew that they were being surveyed by somebody inside the house before the large gates slid back and allowed the car to proceed towards the front door. When it opened, it revealed a thin-faced white woman who moved into the light and greeted them courteously; she asked them to follow her into the house. His father had not briefed Robbie, about this meeting, on their way to the house; he followed him dutifully into a room where five men were already gathered.

The minister of law and order rose to greet the men as they entered into the dining room.

"Welcome to my home," he said, putting out his hand to greet Robbie's father, "and you are Robert Molefe?"

Robbie took the man's outstretched hand and shook it warmly. The others all stood up as he was introduced to them individually. Shaking each one's hand in turn, he knew that he was being introduced to some of the most powerful men in the country. He sat down in the chair next to his father and looked at them in turn. Next to the white minister sat the head of the Bophutatswana people, to his left was the main political member of the Matabele tribe. Two white men sat opposite each other at the table and Robbie knew that the man to his right was the Minister of Bantu affairs and the black man sitting next to his father was the hereditary chief of the Xhosa people. He would never have believed that all of these men could covertly arrange a meeting together. They outwardly hated each other's tribal customs and they had been sworn enemies since time immemorial. The Minister of Bantu affairs started the proceedings by addressing each leader in his native tongue, thanking them for attending. Robbie noted that the man was a linguistic wizard as he spoke clearly and precisely to each person. He was glad that the group had agreed to conduct the meeting in the English language, which everybody at the table understood.

African Chess

Robbie was confused as to why he should be invited to such a high level conference, but it was plain from the outset that he had been expected by all the statesmen there. It would clearly only be a matter of time before his presence here would be explained to him.

CHAPTER THIRTY NINE

'Lurking man his shadow cast, earth nourished with hefty blast'

London - England

"What the hell is going on? These clients are losing everything!" Alain screamed.

He looked into the half dead faces of the young traders seated at the desks, like a row of dummies all kitted out by the same tailor. It was only midmorning as he looked at the screen again and tried to calculate what their clients' portfolio of investment had lost already this morning. As far as Alain could ascertain they were down by over seven million pounds and falling.

"Good God, this is disastrous."

"Can't any of you Muppets do something about this mess?"

"We were given specific instructions to maintain these financial positions," said a robotic face above a blue and white striped shirt.

"I'm giving you a direct instruction to get us out of the market."

"We've tried, but it's useless. These accounts are locked into a password and without it the floor will not sell the position."

"Somebody here must have the keyword," shouted Alain.

"The directors are the only ones with the power to unlock those accounts," came the sullen reply.

"Well find them, wherever they are and get the password; any further losses will be on our account and I don't know if we have enough funds to cover this loss."

African Chess

This stock market crash was proving to be more severe than Black Monday or the 1929 crash. Computerised dealing was forcing the markets downwards even more quickly and panic had now set in among traders, to the extent that they were refusing to take calls from clients in the hope that the market would recover once the American exchange entered the arena. Nobody had expected anything like this when prices turned down two days before and then accelerated its downward pattern yesterday. By today this had become every trading house's nightmare. Alain watched the dancing cursor of doom on the screen and reflected that they had been fortunate enough to get almost all of their clients' out of the market before too much damage had been suffered. Now, only two of their major investors were still locked into the falling markets, as he watched their losses compounding in front of his eyes. He was helpless to do anything but sit and stare at the green message being flashed around the world, pitching it into increasing alarm.

"Try to find Sharon in America, she may know the password."

For two hours they had been on the line to South Africa trying without success to locate either Mike or Robbie for their permission to extract the two investors from the market. Alain was pleased that he hadn't yet forwarded most of these funds to private banking accounts and there was still possibly enough money in trust to cover the massive losses being incurred.

Mike realised that Robbie had come in during the early hours of the morning when he heard a key turn in the door of their kitchenette. He knew it was his friend by the low soft whistle meant as a signal that all was well; so he fell fast asleep again. In the morning he woke Robbie by gently shaking him and then went through to the small bathroom and had a shower.

"Robbie, c'mon wake up. It's time to go to the meeting in Pretoria," he shouted at his friend, who had promptly fallen asleep again.

After several more minutes had passed, Robbie was finally persuaded to leave his bed and take a shower as well. Mike couldn't help thinking that he had never seen Robbie looking this exhausted before. He put it down to the man having had too much partying with his father, until Robbie reappeared from the bathroom and looked an absolute picture of health. It is amazing what an invigorating shower can achieve, thought Mike, as he finished getting dressed. A few minutes later the two went into the main house for breakfast to find Peter Roberts already seated at the long dining room table waiting for them.

"Now you're sure you know exactly where to go?" he asked them.

He had arranged for them to meet a government minister to explain about Robbie's attacker and his involvement with the government security forces. Peter was flying to Botswana that day because of some unrest at one of the diamond mines, so he couldn't attend the meeting. At the same time didn't want it put off, so he had asked them to go by themselves.

"Have you got everything you need?"

Mike lifted the brown briefcase from below the table, "It's all safely in here, don't worry, I won't lose it," he replied.

"You'd better not; it's now the only complete file in existence. They had a fire at the newspaper offices last night and are not sure what survived," answered Peter.

Outside the building Dirk Lemmer watched as two men, one with a briefcase, left their vehicle and walked towards the front of the sand-coloured building. Seated alongside him in the old van were Solly and Getieb who had been in jail for two years on suspected bombing plots. They had been found stealing explosive material from Rand Leases Gold Mining Company, but pleaded not guilty.

"Right go," he ordered.

They left the van and went to the car that had just been left by the two men. It took them only a few seconds to place a magnetic charge to the underside of the car, activated by a level balance spring when the vehicle moved away.

"Right, now let's get around to the front of the building and set the one for that government traitor," said the security man. The two older men carried buckets filled with explosive material and brooms to give the appearance of window cleaners as they made their way around to the front of the building. Dirk suddenly turned towards the two men and started shouting at them.

"Must I do everything myself! Why didn't you bring any cleaning rags with you?"

They were mystified with the sudden onslaught, then realised what was going on; the white man with the briefcase, who had just left the car, came back around the corner. He reached into the glove apartment for something and then hurried back to join his friend who was waiting at the main entrance. The two entered the huge building and disappeared from sight before the security man and his helpers moved forward towards the entrance.

"And there Mr Roberts you have the full story," said the minister.

Mike was so flabbergasted that he sat looking at the man with his mouth hanging open.

"I know it may possibly come as a shock to you but it's the truth, I can assure you."

"But when did this all take place?" demanded Mike.

"It's been in the pipeline for some time, but we couldn't do anything about it until now."

Its true then, thought Mike, politicians told their people one thing while planning the exact opposite.

"You must promise not to tell anyone what I've told you here today," said the minister. Mike felt sorry for the ordinary man in the street that had no chance against these professional liars.

"Yes I promise."

"Good, now I have to meet with several other top ranking officials and let them know what's been decided." He got up to indicate the end of the meeting.

Robbie had said nothing during the entire time, letting Mike do all the talking. Walking down the stairs Mike suddenly turned to his friend.

"Did you know anything about this when those men were trying to kill you?" he snapped.

"Really, Mike, I had no idea it was going on."

They reached the bottom stair and started towards the sunlight shining through the main entrance, when Mike suddenly realised something and stopped dead in his tracks.

"Jesus!"

"What's the matter?"

"I think he's here somewhere."

"Who?"

"Your white friend with the close cropped head. I think I saw him when I went to fetch my tape recorder."

Robbie had not felt any evil this time.

"I think you're mistaken Mike. I would have felt him if he was in the area," laughed Robbie.

"Don't joke; it's you he's after. Let me go and check outside, you wait here."

Before Robbie could argue, Mike turned and walked past the security desk and out of the door. Robbie watched his friend reach the end of the wide veranda and stand next to one of the large pillars, looking out for Dirk Lemmer.

The two coloured men started cleaning windows nearest the main entrance, while Dirk stood a little way off watching them. A security man from inside the building appeared and saw them. "Hey you, what are you doing here? You aren't supposed to be here until this evening."

Dirk immediately walked forward and flashed his identity card. "They are here on special assignment because they're working undercover."

"Sorry sir," said the guard, saluting at his superior. "But I have to do my job."

"Of course, but don't worry about them; we are expecting something here today and mustn't draw attention to ourselves, do you understand?"

The man winked knowingly at Dirk. "I'm just inside the door if you need me, OK."

"Another thing, even if they aren't here should you come out of the building, don't worry as well be watching from somewhere nearby."

Solly and Getieb started preparing the specialist explosion inside the four buckets placed either side of the main entrance, after the uniformed man had gone back inside. Once they were sure that everything was correctly primed, the two men gave Dirk the thumbs up sign to indicate everything was ready. His eyes searched across the long curving veranda. The ladders and buckets propped against the wall looked fairly harmless and he watched as several people moved about the place, without taking a second look at the items outside the main entrance.

Molefe, you're dead, even if you slip through the back door I'll get you today, thought Dirk.

Getieb came to hand him a little black box. "They're primed and ready to detonate. All you have to do is flick this switch and then press the red button, that's it."

"You two go home and I'll see you later," said Dirk.

Finding a comfortable spot near the far corner of the building, where he would remain undetected, Dirk sat down on the grass and waited for his quarry. He sat in the same spot for over an hour watching the main entrance and the car park from his vantage point. This spot was absolutely perfect because it gave him a clear view of their car at the back and a reasonable view along the line of pillars to the building's front entrance. If he'd had the choice he would have preferred a closer view of the front door but to get any closer would mean that he was unable to see if they left by the rear exit. The morning sun was rising high into the sky and a large number of people were already using the front door, sometimes obscuring his view completely. Most of them, he noted, were government officials going about their daily business; however, there were also several visitors and tourists mingling on the veranda in front of the building.

He looked towards the car again and saw a pretty young nurse heading along the side of the copper coloured building and towards him.

She can look after me anytime, he thought. Her tightly pulled belt exaggerated the movement of her hips under the crisp uniform. Nice bones, he whispered turning back to look along the front of the building.

"Christ!"

He saw Mike looking straight towards him and without thinking twice he flicked the switch and a red light appeared on the black box. Had the man seen him or not, he wasn't sure. Then he saw Mike turn towards the door again. He looked for the black man but couldn't see him because there were too many people milling around.

He's seen me and now they're going to go inside again to report it to that bloody traitor. Well, I'll show them he thought as he promptly pushed his thumb down hard on the red button. He saw the blinding flash before the thunderous roar reached him. Bits of masonry flew in all directions, tearing and smashing their way through everything in their path and jagged missiles hurtled outward through the air. Everything suddenly stopped as quickly as it had started. The roar passed and every bit of hurled stone had landed; a deafening silence replaced the noise. Nothing moved for what seemed like an eternity to Dirk, his attention was suddenly activated by a movement to his left and he saw the shapely young nurse start running towards the front of the building.

Got you at last, you bastard, he said quietly under his breath, watching a cloud of dust rise from the devastation! People, outside the blast area, stood by helplessly immobile. Only the nurse moved as she ran towards a screaming figure near the front entrance. The calmness suddenly ended when people started screaming and running around in panic. Figures were pouring out of the building onto the veranda to see what had happened. Amid the confusion and havoc, Dirk stood silently watching, in the smug knowledge that he had finally achieved what he had been trying to do for some years. Morbid fascination drew him towards the blast area, like a moth to a candle, to check that his handiwork had been accomplished to his satisfaction.

"No!" Robbie screamed to heaven, unable to move forward. He sank to his knees in the full knowledge that his lifelong friend had tried to protect him and had paid the ultimate price. He cried shamelessly as people raced past him to where the mighty explosion had taken place.

"Are you all right!" said a familiar voice in his ear.

"Your men have just killed my brother," Robbie replied, looking up at the minister standing in front of him.

"The same man that tried at Heathrow."

"C'mon!" said the minister, placing his hand under Robbie's armpit and lifting him up.

Robbie allowed himself to be led up to the office on the second floor and out of harms way. Together they looked out the window, down upon the confusion below them. All the support services were screaming in, sirens blaring. There was nothing to be done. Robbie suddenly froze solid and his hairs stiffened on his neck.

"There's the killer!"

"Dirk Lemmer!"

"I'll kill him!" shouted Robbie, turning toward the door.

"Don't! He's a trained killer and you won't stand a chance." The portly minister managed to restrain Robbie, then quickly lifted the telephone and called Bennie Roux.

Robbie could not take his eyes from Dirk, as he moved towards the crowd gathering around two of the unfortunate victims. They appeared beyond recognition. One man was standing and another was stretched out on his back with a young nurse busily working to try and save his life. The minister told Robbie to wait in his office because he was going down to see if he could help in any way. As he left, Robbie heard the key softly turn in the outer door. The shocking numbness meant he hardly cared seeing doctors appearing from nowhere and ambulance-men running with stretchers. He made sure that he kept Dirk Lemmer in sight as he tried to pick out Mike in the crowd of aghast onlookers. It was only when the ambulance-men moved to take the injured to hospital and the crowd parted to allow access to the waiting ambulance that he recognised the blackened body on a stretcher as Mike. To the other side of the stretcher, in amongst the crowd, he clearly saw Dirk Lemmer, also looking at Mike. What struck him most were the horribly distorted features etched on the man's face.

When the doors closed and the ambulance prepared to move off he saw Dirk turn and take a look among the debris. Then he set off at a brisk pace, heading towards the far corner of the building. Dirk reached the car park and got into his car. For three minutes he sat calmly tuning his police radio into various frequencies to find the one that the ambulance would be on.

"We're just turning into Struben Street and our ETA at the hospital is about six minutes. Please have a burns doctor standing by," crackled a voice.

Dirk started his vehicle and moved away from the car park, not even bothering to glance in his rear view mirror.

"I followed him through Pretoria and now he's at Pretoria General Hospital," the ministry guard said into a telephone receiver.

He could see the man he was following chatting eagerly to a woman on desk duty.

"He's enquiring about something in casualty, I think."

The guard listened to his fresh instructions and then quickly removed his jacket and tie. He moved to a bench in the long passageway, where he could keep an eye on Dirk. For five minutes Dirk seemed content to talk to the matronly figure behind the desk, then he moved along through a swing door at the end of the passage. The guard followed and noted that it led to the X-Ray department. Looking through the glass in the door, he saw the man look around, then enter one of the offices at the far end of the corridor. Not knowing what to do next, he waited near the swing doors, watching the doorway where the man had entered. The man with the close-cropped hair came out of the office and walked towards the swing doors, now wearing a doctor's white coat. He quickly returned to the bench and sat down, picking up a magazine to hide his face. The swing doors opened and the white-coated figure exited, making straight for the lift across the hall.

The guard didn't dare move until the doors had closed. He carefully monitored the lights to indicate which floor the lift was moving to. Four men in plain clothes entered the hospital just at that moment, their eyes searching keenly ahead of them.

CHAPTER FORTY

'Be wise and learn, matters of weight and deep concern'

<u>Pretoria - South Africa</u>

"Are you Pienaar?" asked one of the men.

"Yes Who are you?"

The man produced his police identification badge.

"Where is he now?"

"He's just taken the lift to the third floor which is a general ward," said Pienaar proudly. "C'mon, let's get up there before he gets away."

"No, you're going to stay down here. We have reinforcements arriving shortly and we need somebody down here who knows what he looks like to stop him," replied the detective.

He watched the three of them enter the waiting lift while the fourth went through the door and up the stairway. "If he gets past us don't forget he's a killer, so be careful."

The doors came together and then they were gone.

From his place on the middle step of the stairwell, Dirk immediately knew the men who filed out of the lift towards the general ward. He quickly pushed himself against the wall in case they turned and saw him. He knew that they were there for him so he moved up to the fourth floor and caught the lift back down to the first floor, in case they had a man on the ground floor watching for him. Slowly he crept down the stairs and carefully looked through the busy ground floor area for somebody stationed near the front door.

Stupid flatfeet, they've all gone charging up to look for me and leaving their backsides exposed, he smiled, as he moved towards the front door.

The guard looked up from his magazine and saw the white-coated 'doctor' moving past the lifts towards him. He waited until he was one pace past him before he moved towards the man's back, grabbing him around the throat whilst trying to get his arm into a lock behind his back. Dirk felt the arm on his windpipe and his arm being grabbed from behind; he dropped forward on his knee, using the assailant's forward weight to throw him over his head. The guard's only leverage was the arm which he held tightly onto, Dirk felt and heard the sharp snap in his shoulder, as his attacker landed on the floor in front of him. The winded man tried to rise but Dirk planted a kick that would have made any footballer proud, square on the guard's jaw, dropping him like a ninepin.

He didn't stop as he vaulted over the collapsing figure and ran to the car park, his left arm dangling loosely by his side. Battling to drive, he used his radio and placed a call to his office. He quickly gave his faithful assistant Annemarie instructions where to meet him and what documents to bring. This was the day he had always dreaded but for which he had made elaborate preparations. He saw Annemarie standing on the corner as instructed; she had two briefcases in her hands.

"I'm coming with you," she said, getting into the car.

With his limp arm she would be helpful to him, Dirk thought and he could dispose of her once he was clear of this mess.

"OK, did you arrange for the plane to be ready?"

Annemarie had always fancied the idea of staying in the Seychelles with him. She was the one who filtered his funds away and was the only person who could give him away.

"Don't worry Dirk; we'll get these bastards when we return."

"Well that's that, the hunter has become the hunted," said Mike, propped up in bed with his leg in traction. Sitting beside him were Nicole, Ian and Robbie.

"What about Jay, is she going to be all right?" Mike asked.

"Oh yes, she's a toughie that one, but she's going to have a bruise like a baseball on the back of her head," replied Ian.

"Poor kid; fancy, that woman on the bus racing up from behind and pushing her into her flat. Not funny being confronted by someone carrying a lead pipe in a carpet bag!" Nicole didn't try to hide her anger. When Jay had regained consciousness she discovered that the flat had been rifled and Mike's briefcase was missing.

"You'll be glad to know that the newspaper hasn't lost anything except one drawing, which is of little importance," said Robbie winking at Mike.

"Mom, could you please send her the biggest bouquet of flowers you can find? I owe my life to that girl," said Mike.

"Don't worry son, it's already been done and we've invited her to Champagne Castle, all expenses paid, to recuperate."

"That's nice," Mike said, feeling pleased that the family would be able to repay her for what she had done.

He thought of Sharon, who looked so much like Jay and found himself wishing that he'd taken her advice and gone with her to America. The hospital had moved him into a private room and he knew that when the family left he was going to find himself missing Jay – his personal guardian. Robbie stayed on with Mike after his parents had left.

"Why didn't you tell me about the government plan and how long have you known about it?" Mike asked.

"Honestly, Mike, the first time I knew anything at all was when I went to that meeting with my father the other night."

"Bullshit Robbie, this couldn't have been planned without your full knowledge and consent," Mike retaliated.

"OK, let me tell you exactly what took place that night with my father and then maybe you'll believe me," Robbie replied, smiling at his best friend.

"There were five men waiting for us, three black and two white and I couldn't believe my eyes when I saw who they all were. I still had no idea why I was there." He clearly pictured the clandestine meeting of a couple of nights before, as he continued.

"You all know why we're here, except for Robert, who doesn't know anything about our plans yet," said the Minister for Bantu Affairs.

The old man turned to Robbie and smiled gently. "My son, because of my past dealings, I am unable to be seen as a spokesman for our people. As you are my rightful heir, you have been chosen to speak for the Zulu people with my blessing and guidance."

Robbie stated he was mystified by the group seated at the table when the Minister for Law and Order looked straight him and spoke up on behalf of everyone seated at the table.

"As you know, the ANC has chosen to insist that they are the majority in this country and have successfully duped the world into thinking so. Then what happens to the eleven minority tribes, if the blacks as a whole nation join together and win this election?" the minister asked.

"Civil war among the tribes once again," replied Robbie, as the minister continued.

"Correct. If we joined together the Whites, Zulus, Xhosas, Tswanas and Matebele; these five 'tribes' control nearly eighty per cent of the country. So, in a vote terms we will win, do you agree?" Robbie nodded his head.

"For two years we have been negotiating and have now reached a suitable solution that will prevent any form of bloodshed in this land," he went on.

"And what's that?" asked Robbie, now gripped with curiosity.

"Proportional representation as agreed between ourselves," replied the minister.

"What do you mean by 'between us'?"

"All five tribes have exactly the same voting power in a secondary parliament which then attends to the day to day running of the country."

Robbie was still mystified by the word 'secondary'.

"We have divided the country into five cantons, or separate counties, controlled by each head seated at this table; but the country is managed as one single unit," he related.

Robbie could see the plan clearly in his mind; Zululand to the Zulus, Bophutatswana to the Tswana and so on but all governed by an equally shared government.

"You mean five chiefs controlling their own territory but the country will be run as in the United States or Switzerland?" he asked.

"Exactly right."

Robbie thought this made logical sense, because each sector was currently self-controlled anyway, even though at present a white government held it all together.

"And who controls the smaller tribes?" he asked.

The minister smiled and pointed directly at him.

"You do, you will be the people's choice," he replied.

Robbie felt his spine stiffen and his blood run cold. This wasn't what he expected.

"Me?"

"The Zulu, as a tribe have more voters than anybody else. You also have the credentials and educational background to be leader of the people."

Robbie's father placed his arm on the young man's shoulder. "If we let things continue as they are, then this fine country will end up being just another African dictatorship; with war and chaos ruling our lives."

"When is all this going to take place?" asked Robbie.

"We have drawn up a joint communiqué which is to be signed in public as soon as the time is right. In the meantime you will be introduced to the nation as the future political leader of our people - within two weeks," said his father.

Robbie sank back in his chair and whistled loudly; the Xhosa leader laughed loudly.

"If we Xhosa produced the second messiah in Mandela, then why can't you Zulu produce the third?"

Suddenly all tension was relaxed between the parties and they spent the rest of the night and well into the early hours of the morning, laying out what plans had been made before Robbie's entry into this political arena.

Two days later Mike's hospital door opened very slightly but nobody entered. He watched it rock back and forth, then a white handkerchief appeared. It moved up and down for a while before it was withdrawn to be followed by a large bunch of flowers, again being waved. These were then replaced with a large basket of fresh fruit and the fascinating ritual continued. Lastly a shapely leg appeared and the same routine was again performed. Mike recognised the leg immediately.

"Don't show it off, bring it here and let me stroke it," he laughed.

Sharon put her head around the door.

"Am I forgiven for deserting you?"

"Hello, my darling wife; there's nothing to forgive, we acted like two snotty nosed kids."

"I can't leave you and Robbie on your own for more than ten minutes and look at the mess you get into. I thought I'd better come and sort it out."

The two kissed long and hard to make up, both feeling as one again. Sharon slipped her hand under the sheet and touched him gently.

"We've made love in some funny places before now, but you can't fight back here. With all these wires and pulleys it should be fun."

They laughed as Mike grabbed his chest to avoid any splitting of his painful stitches.

Sharon explained that she had established their new company in America and had moved the head office from New York to Miami, so that they could enjoy the weather. She went on to tell Mike that Robbie's IRA and Hezbollah clients had lost all their invested funds. Robbie told her that he'd found out that the majority of the armaments had been doctored in Beira and that the IRA had sent experts in to remove parts so that they would not work properly. James had handed in his notice to the bank and would be taking up the chairmanship in three months. Until then they were going to take a well deserved second honeymoon.

Mike left hospital two weeks later and joined Sharon at her family home, she in the meantime had explained to her parents about their marriage and Peter, after his initial shock, had welcomed Mike as his son-in-law and nephew. Mike promised Robbie that he would be well enough to attend his inauguration speech at the Durban football stadium and he meant to keep that promise.

On the following day the couple flew to Durban and were met by Robbie at the newly named King Shaka International Airport and taken to the hotel where they and Robbie had a company suite. That afternoon Mike, seated in his wheelchair, was placed alongside the Zulu chief and Robbie was on his right side. His black brother wore Zulu traditional dress with leopard skin loincloth and the feathered headdress of a chief of the tribe. The loincloth was made by his true mother from a leopard skin given to her by the boys many years ago and he was presented his father's own headdress to continue carrying the family mantle. After going through the normal ceremonial dances one by one, the elders of the tribe declared their allegiance to their tribe and their new chief.

The overcrowded stadium rose with each speech saluting Robbie, until he quietened them down to give them good news.

"The Zulu have never been really political," he maintained. "We have stayed away from this form of conflict but now is the time to show the world the strength of our mighty nation as we fight the ANC on their own ground - and win. This will not happen for a while, it will take time because at first, there will be greed; there will be corruption; there will be bloodshed; before the majority of black people start to believe that as one, we move forward as a nation."

They could be heard throughout Durban as the stadium erupted; for too long the people had thought that the mighty Zulu had been scared to confront others in this political arena. Their time had come for the Zulu lion to rise and start hunting down and destroying those unscrupulousness and double dealing ANC members lining their own pockets, sorting the action or effect of making these people morally depraved.

"Umkozi! Umkozi! Umkozi!" the chant of "King! King! King!" rang out before Robbie was allowed to speak again. For twenty minutes he had them in the palm of his hand as he reminded them of former glories and how they had lived in harmony in Natal and how he would achieve this once again. Every Zulu, young and old, left the stadium with fire in his or her heart knowing that the Zulu people were about to lead their country again.

Throughout the land shivers ran through the nation when his speech was reported on television, newspaper, radio and good old fashioned word of mouth. The world press sat up and took notice of this new people's hero being presented by the blacks as a peace-loving man who would again lead South Africa. The ANC made immediate plans to dishonour this new upstart but when Government troops suddenly found a massive cache of arms in one of the ANC hideouts they immediately went on the defensive.

Day by day his stature grew as he made whirlwind tours to Europe and America, confirming that democracy was the way his country would go. Members of the new government sat up and took notice and made it clear that it wanted discussions with this man; he was seen talking to various tribal leaders throughout the country. Interest was flagging in the once highly popular ANC camp and they needed something to stop the forward roll of this man with his proper English accent.

Since the breakdown of socialism in so many countries the ANC had had to rely heavily on funds from outlawed terrorist groups; but then the IRA and the Arabic Hezbollah also suddenly withdrew their funding. No clear reason was ever given, but it was thought that they had lost large amounts of capital on the money markets. Most of the ANC support now stemmed from near-bankrupt African countries which hoped for handouts later on for their own struggles. They considered trying to kill the man, but the Zulu had him carefully guarded day and night.

The ANC's tarnished corrupted governmental look needed a boost as the young crocodiles looked to their leaders for guidance; they realised that there were none of substance left; they needed another hero such as Mandela. It later came out and world was not surprised to hear that several attempts were made on the life of Nelson Mandela before he passed on. These acts was put down to members of his own ANC in order to raise moral among its followers.

"This son of Africa has returned in glory to his homeland after being ostracized by whites and blacks alike," said South Africa's prime minister at a gathering of Parliament. I personally feel his proposed plan is the only workable idea put forward so far to save or country."

A murmur of approval filtered through the crowd at what he had suggested. Several hard line members, who had thought that the government was being too lenient with these black Marxists, were in favour of this plan because it meant that the whites retained a position of their country.

"Nobody wants bloodshed and this educated man has been brought up in a white environment and his thinking is not entirely one-sided for the black population," the premier continued.

Time had run out for the minority white government to struggle against world opinion and after the terrible ANC government debacle, this plan would give all sides what they wanted.

"Ladies and gentlemen, let's put this proposal to the vote."

They secretly voted on the future of South Africa in the large dining room, within the sacred wall of the Union Buildings. Half an hour later the result was read out to the gathering.

"Ninety four per cent have voted overwhelmingly to accept Mr Molefe's proposal," announced the speaker; a great cheer went up in the hall.

"He has proposed that the world press be invited to attend a meeting of all parties concerned next week at the Mandela Day Parade to announce the new formation of our great country – long live South Africa," declared the speaker, sitting down.

On Mandela Day, Robbie sat pensively staring out of his hotel window onto a serene garden filled with fully opened red flowers.

"Marry me!"

Joan nearly choked into the cup held to her lips at that moment, as she sat on the large double bed with him.

"What!"

"If I'm to help lead the country into a new era, then I can't have any skeletons hanging about in my cupboard," he said as he turned to face her.

She had arrived the day before and been whisked quietly to Peter's house by Sharon, before being ushered into his room under cover of darkness.

"This is South Africa my darling and if you aren't aware of it, I'm white and you're black and they'll crucify you if you do something like this," she said tearfully.

"That's just where you're wrong, because what would be more natural than to have a mixed married couple setting an example to the country to unite all races? Seretse and Ruth Khama did it years ago."

Watching him sitting against the background of the sunlit window reminded Joan of the wonderful times spent at her cottage when he was but a mere boy whom she loved dearly and now loved just as much.

"Come back to bed and I'll think about it," she teased, spreading her arms wide apart.

Robbie stood up flexing his naked body into a muscleman. "What you see is what you get," he said laughingly.

He raced across the room and dived onto the bed; taking her in his arms he rolled her over on top of him and looked deep into her eyes.

"You can be chief here and I'll be chief out there," he said softly nodding towards the window.

"All right, I accept your proposal my lord."

The prime minister was flanked on each side by the men who had attended the initial meeting when Robbie was told of his future. Seated behind this group on the podium was the entire cabinet, watching a full military parade through the streets of Pretoria. The press from around the world had been hearing conflicting reports of changes that were to be announced by the government and they were all gathered around so as not to miss anything. When the time arrived for the Prime Minister to make his usual Mandela Day speech, the press were given the story which the outside world had waited for so long to hear.

He announced that there were going to be democratic elections and that a combination of tribes had come together, as a political entity, to be led by Robert Molefe.

Cheering thundered through the streets from both black and white alike as the news was passed down to them. Everybody welcomed this new beginning, the ANC had failed the people but the sunshine nation was prepared to forgive and forget and start again. The noise drowned out Robbie's intended speech; instead, he took the leaders by the hand and led them forward to introduce them to the crowd.

Cameras clicked continuously as the four black men and two white ministers held hands and raised their arms aloft on the podium. When the noise had died down Robbie said one sentence which got them going again, each person knowing for sure that peace was a definite possibility.

"No matter what colour you are, let this country unite as we have united ourselves here today!" he shouted at the masses before him.

"Unite! Unite! Unite!" the crowd started shouting back, as everybody instinctively held hands aloft copying their leaders on the podium.

Proudly, Joan watched Robbie's face spread across her television screen. She had decided that she wanted to watch the event alone; this was his day and she did not want to intrude. Joan thought of a poem that she had heard somewhere as she spoke the words aloud.

"Time and Tide thus had its way

Changing like an African day.

Frowning Moon, for bright tomorrow,

Years of Joy, exchanged for sorrow."

Joan wondered if the words were made especially for them at this moment.

THE END

AFRICAN CHESS

By Frank Graves

ABOUT THE AUTHOR

His first published work in 1989 was a fictional political thriller named African Chess (Now revamped and updated).African Chess was loosely based on his South African upbringing and the then apartheid system in place before Nelson Mandel's release from prison.

His next major work published by Marshall Cavendish in 1992 was The Ancestral Trail and 'split' into two halves of 26 issues each, making a total of 52 issues in total, all contained consecutive page and issue numbers.

The first half, published throughout 1993, takes place within a mythological Ancestral World and describes a boy's struggle to restore good to the world. After the initial international run which sold over 30 million copies worldwide, the second half of that series was then created. The second half was published in 1994 and takes place in the totally different Cyber Dimension all about the same boy's attempt to find a way back to his own world.

The Culling is his third published work in 2014 and the details are that Western governments use scientific evidence that within a few years their world faces disaster from uncontrolled population explosion; especially by burgeoning third-world countries probably creating extra desert regions to ruin the industrialised world. No government would openly admit that it intends killing tens of millions of unwanted people worldwide. A number of major international conglomerates collectively called "The Affiliation" are enlisted to conceal this man-made earthquake programme without any awkward questions being raised... It is a survival war!